Nash

BY JAY CROWNOVER

Nash

Rome

Jet

Rule

Nash

A Marked Men Novel

JAY CROWNOVER

WM

WILLIAM MORROW

An Imprint of HarperCollinsPublishers

NASH. Copyright © 2014 by Jennifer M. Voorhees. All rights reserved. Printed in the United States of America. No part of this book may be used or reproduced in any manner whatsoever without written permission except in the case of brief quotations embodied in critical articles and reviews. For information address HarperCollins Publishers, 195 Broadway, New York, NY 10007.

HarperCollins books may be purchased for educational, business, or sales promotional use. For information please email the Special Markets Department at SPsales@harpercollins.com.

FIRST EDITION

Library of Congress Cataloging-in-Publication Data
Crownover, Jay.
    Nash : a Marked Men novel / Jay Crownover. — First edition.
        pages ; cm. — (Marked Man)
    ISBN 978-0-06-233303-2
    I. Title.
PS3603.R766N37 2014
813'.6—dc23

                                                                    2014006364

14 15 16 17 18 OV/RRD 10 9 8 7 6 5 4

Dedicated to any of you who might just need a little reminder
that you are awesome just the way you are!!!

I GREW UP IN a pretty small town here in the mountains in Colorado. It was a pretty place, but I stuck out like a sore thumb, which wasn't always the easiest thing to handle. I have always had my own style, marched to the beat of my own drum, wrote my own rule book, and pretty much forged my own path. I developed a thick skin and pretty rock-solid sense of who I was and what I was about early on. I had to, or I would've fallen victim to thinking what others said about me or thought about me held any water. That was years and years ago and still, that time, those feelings, stick with me.

I know this isn't the case for everyone, that some people have never been judged unfairly. But many have and they know that mean words and hateful actions are so much more far-reaching now with the world all being connected by a keyboard and a computer monitor. It gets tougher and tougher to brush off negativity and pessimism.

Trying to love yourself, to know your own value and worth, is something I think a lot of young girls struggle with and that can definitely flow into adulthood. We all have things that set us apart, make us special, make us who we are, and I would love to see those things celebrated and enjoyed across the board. Let that freak flag fly! (Or whatever equivalent you have.)

I think on the journey to finding the love we crave, the love we truly deserve, the first stop has to be the love we have for ourselves. That's a love that can never be lost and can only grow and get stronger the more it is fostered and developed. Appreciate who you are. Love what makes you different. Tell your story your way. Embrace the things that make you beautiful inside and out, and know that once you do, no one else can ignore those traits. Revel in the quirks that simply make you *you*, and do it with pride.

You can search throughout the entire universe for someone who is more deserving of your love and affection than you are yourself, and that person is not to be found anywhere. You yourself, as much as anybody in the entire universe, deserve your love and affection.

—Buddha

No one can make you feel inferior without your consent.

—Eleanor Roosevelt

Man often becomes what he believes himself to be. If I keep on saying to myself that I cannot do a certain thing, it is possible that I may end by really becoming incapable of doing it. On the contrary, if I have the belief that I can do it, I shall surely acquire the capacity to do it even if I may not have it at the beginning

—Mahatma Gandhi

The eyes of others our prisons; their thoughts our cages.

—Virginia Woolf

To love oneself is the beginning of a life-long romance.

—Oscar Wilde

I celebrate myself, and I sing myself.

—Walt Whitman

Love yourself first and everything else falls into line. You really have to love yourself to get anything done in this world.

—Lucille Ball

Saint

High School . . . Not the best years of my life

THERE'S A MOMENT IN every person's life, a point in time that will alter the course they are on, the path they are traveling, forever. The night of Ashley Maxwell's birthday party my senior year in high school was mine.

I wasn't the type of teenager that went to wild parties. I didn't drink and didn't mess around with drugs and boys, so really, there was no point in me going. I was also painfully shy, overweight, and awkward in my own skin, skin that tended toward ugly breakouts and flushed bright red whenever anyone tried to engage me in conversation. The halls of high school were torture for a girl like me, but I suffered through it mostly unscathed because I knew when to keep my head down and not to set my sights on friends or boys that were out of my league. At least I did until senior year, when my locker ended up right next to Nash Donovan's.

For the first few weeks of school, I kept to myself and ignored him, just like I did with all the popular kids and beautiful people. If I didn't engage, then he couldn't make fun of me or, even worse, look at me with pity shining out of the spectacular purple eyes that glowed out of his handsome face. It worked until the day I dropped a calculus book on his foot and he picked it up to hand it to me. I'll never forget the way I actually felt when my heart stopped and then started thundering in the next second when those spectacular eyes gleamed at me. I'd never experienced anything quite like it.

Nash smiled at me, quipped something sarcastic and offhand, making my poor, lonely heart turn over. He walked away with a wink . . . and I had a crush. A consuming, engulfing crush that built day after day, because after that embarrassing incident Nash went out of his way to say hello when we were by our lockers, and he always walked away with a smile or a nod. Each day I became more entranced, fell a little harder, and built the fantasy that we were meant to be something more than passing acquaintances into something grandiose and romantic.

I was a smart girl, so I knew my affection was onesided, but he seemed nice, charming, and it made me warm on the inside that he never teased me, or made me feel bad about my weight or looks, like so many of my peers did on a regular basis. Our simple interaction was good for my self-esteem, good for making me feel more like the rest of the teenage girls prowling the halls that swooned over him and his group of troublemaking friends. I had even worked up enough courage after a month or so to return his hellos without my fair skin bursting into flames. I didn't stammer or clam up when he spoke to me anymore and occasionally I even managed to eke out a return smile. I was pretty proud of myself, so when he asked me one Friday if I was planning on going to Ashley Maxwell's party, I had been equal parts stunned and thrilled. A shiver of anticipation shook me to the core and I couldn't stop myself from tumbling headfirst into a daydream where this was the start of something more than just an exchange of pleasantries in the hallway. It was all I could do to keep from twirling around in a circle of delight and clapping my hands like an overeager fanatic.

It was more than he typically said to me, and he was just so friendly and likable that I replied that I would try to be there. I didn't want to sound overeager. When he smiled at me and said that was awesome and we could hang out, I couldn't stop the feeling that attending a sloppy, unsupervised high school party seemed like the most important thing I had ever done in my short life.

My older sister, Faith, pretty and popular, fit in seamlessly to shark-infested waters that made up a teenage social circle. She questioned me endlessly about my sudden desire to mingle with my peer group, cautioned me that kids who were mean and unfriendly on a normal basis could be cruel and hateful when social status and alcohol were involved—but I decided not to listen. I figured the worst thing that could happen was that I would show up, not see Nash, or he wouldn't see me and I could just turn around and come back home and curl up with a book like I did most weekends. I was turning a blind eye to what I knew was the truth, but my desire for this particular boy to see me as something more than he did was all-consuming. It was making me ignore common sense and my own honed sense of self-protection.

I let Faith fuss over me for hours. She played with my fire-engine-red hair until it was curly and styled pretty and feminine. I let her pick an outfit that would never make me look like a size-four cheerleader but was fashionable and cute, and I even allowed her to slime a bunch of junk on my face that I knew would ultimately make my skin break out even worse. The end results were actually pretty nice. I looked more put together than I normally did. I thought I could just blend into the crowd, and really that was fine as long as those striking purple eyes found me. I felt more confident and secure than I could ever remember feeling before.

Faith told me not to arrive to the party until after eleven, so I waited anxiously, fiddled with my hair, and played through every scenario my overeager imagination could think of. Maybe he would ask me to dance. Maybe he would lead me outside and give me my first kiss. Maybe he would tell me he could see all the wonderful things that lurked beneath the surface and he wanted me to be his girlfriend. In hindsight, of course, none of that was going to happen and I really didn't *know* the kind of guy Nash really was, but still a crush is a crush, and it can run away from you pretty fast.

And so I showed up at Ashley Maxwell's blowout party, appropriately late, armed with Faith's mini-makeover and a racing heart filled with anticipation.

As I walked into the house I was hit with a blast of music, and the optimism I'd felt started to waver. A crowd of three guys I recognized from chem crowded past me as they joined the mayhem taking place in the living room. I couldn't find a safe place to rest my eyes; everywhere I looked, people seemed to be doing something that made me blush. I did my best to keep myself from gaping, but I felt the telltale heat creeping up my neck as I pushed my way through the sea of bodies. It was disturbing and I was beginning to think a new hairdo and some mascara would never be enough to make me fit in, in a place like this.

The kitchen looked a little less crowded, so I moved in that direction, keeping my eyes peeled for Nash. I was certain that if I could find him, this night would turn around. My stomach fluttered again as I thought about meeting that remarkable gaze across the room. I imagined his eyes glinting and crinkling at the sides like they did when he smiled, and I pictured myself suddenly at ease by his side as the rest of the chaos faded away. He would make all the discomfort creeping under my skin disappear.

As I rounded a corner someone bumped into me, spilling sticky, red liquid all down the front of my carefully selected shirt. I gasped in surprise and the jerk moved on without even apologizing. I was shaking and officially freaking out on the inside. It was all too clear that I didn't belong here, no matter how cute Nash Donovan was. My hands started to shake and it took every ounce of self-control I had to keep tears at bay.

Turned out, the kitchen was just as bad as the front of the party. Worse really, because the booze was apparently kept there and the crowd in that room seemed to be the drunkest of the drunk. It was like walking across a minefield of ugly remarks and dirty looks to get to the sink to try and clean up. I heard a few snickers, saw a few blurry looks cast my way, and it was enough. I planned to rinse off and go home. This place and these people were not for me, and I knew better.

"Who invited you?"

The question was slurred and followed with a heavy hand on my shoulder. The voice—and the hand—belonged to none other than the birthday girl herself, and she was drunk. Really drunk and out for blood. Ashley and I weren't friends, but she had never said or done anything overtly nasty to me in all the years we had gone to school together . . . I kind of felt like I was going to throw up.

"What?"

"Who invited you?" There was a sneer on her pretty lips, her big brown eyes glassy. "Why are *you* here?"

I wanted to say Nash had asked me to come, that he had told me we were going hang out tonight, but I couldn't get the words out . . . because just then he showed up.

He entered the kitchen followed by the Archer twins and Jet Keller. There was no mistaking it: these boys brought the party with them wherever they went. Nash had on his customarily sloppy look of torn jeans, skate shoes, and a band T-shirt. He also had a baseball hat pulled low over his forehead that did nothing to hide the high flush in his face or the unclear and foggy haze covering his eyes. It was obvious he was already wasted, or even high, and I felt the first threads of disappointment start to tie up my cracking heart. I saw his gaze skim over the kitchen, land on me, and keep moving. It made me suck in a painful breath and I had to bite the inside of my cheek —hard—to keep from really crying.

It was like he didn't even see me. He didn't smile, didn't wink, and didn't so much as incline his head in my direction. It was like I didn't even exist. I went numb. I felt like my blood had turned to ice and everything in the center of my chest ceased to work. I curled my shaking hands into fists and tried to frantically plan an escape route that would save me any further embarrassment or heartache.

Ashley apparently forgot all about my fatness and ugliness marring her party and bounded over to the new additions. If my heart filled with awful feelings at his flagrant dismissal, then it practically burst open when he scooped her up in his arms and let her inhale his face while he grabbed her ass. I wanted to choke on my embarrassment as I scrambled backward out of the kitchen. There was no more thought put to self-preservation, only to escape. I had a frantic, desperate need to put as much space between me and this party—but more so between me and Nash—as possible.

Mercifully, the tears didn't fall until I was safely at my car. In that moment, slumped in my driver's seat with black streaks on my face from the mascara I'd let Faith smear on, I knew the truth: the beautiful people stuck together and it didn't matter what was on the inside. Nash might be nice when it was just him and me at our lockers, but put him in a room full of people, give him a skinny and pretty girl willing to put out, and I was invisible. I'd been so stupid to think it was anything more.

So I did what was instinctive and resurrected the shield

around my heart. From then on, I ignored him every time he tried to tell me hello. I looked away from him when he smiled at me. I avoided my locker as much as I could when I knew he was going to be there and tried to focus on the fact that graduation was right around the corner and I would be leaving this small mountain town behind, along with this clueless boy who had hurt my feelings so deeply behind. I knew logically Nash didn't know how I felt, had no clue that I had thought he was different and special, but that didn't make the burn of his ignorance or my embarrassment any less hot.

In the warmth of early spring, with my college enrollment all lined up for fall and my insecurities carefully compartmentalized—the sting of my failed crush finally beginning to heal—I stumbled upon Nash and his friends outside smoking after school . . . My heart lurched, but none of them saw me and I scuttled by, hoping to hurry to my car and planning on ignoring him like I had been doing since the party, when his deep voice assaulted my ears.

"She's a mess. If she ever wants to get laid, she needs to look in the mirror and maybe do some work."

One of the other guys cackled at the nasty statement and I thought I was going to vaporize into a cloud of horrified smoke. He had to be talking about me and I couldn't move once I heard what he was saying.

I heard Nash snort as I tried to sneak by so they wouldn't notice me or my tears. I had never cried so much over any other person and it made me hate him a little—or a lot—as he kept talking.

"I mean, I'm not picky, I would take her to bed. I just might need to put a bag over her head first or something."

That sent the rest of the guys rolling in laughter as the ground beneath me fell away and a sob caught in my throat. How could I have been so incredibly wrong about someone? Any hope, any thought that he was different—that any pretty boy could be different—was annihilated with those hateful, harsh words. Words that forever changed the way I looked at the opposite sex.

Nash Donovan was a beautiful, wicked, and hot flame that burned me when I got too close. He was just the first stop in a journey dotted by disappointment, but somewhere along the way, I found my footing. My purpose. I just didn't know that as soon as I did, Nash would manage to turn my world upside down all over again, and only a fool gets burned twice by the same fire.

CHAPTER 1

Nash

Thanksgiving . . . Eight years later

MY FULLY RESTORED DODGE Charger was eating up the highway as I raced through the cold Colorado night. The massive engine was growling angrily in time with my thundering heart. Light flurries of snow were dotting the windshield, so I could blame the rapid blinking of my eyes on trying to see through the nasty road conditions and not the emotion threatening to overtake me. None of it registered, neither did the fact that I had to be pushing 120 and that terrified holiday traffic was undoubtedly scrambling to get out of my way. I was in such a fog, such a state of disbelief, that I felt numb and barely aware of what was going on around me. I had just found my uncle Phil, the one and only parental figure I had in my life, unconscious on the floor of his hunting cabin. He was cold and still. He looked like a skeleton, skin stretched over bones that appeared far too fragile. I was racing the "Flight for Life" the park rangers had called in to airlift him to the emergency room in Denver.

Just to add to the danger of the speeds I was traveling and the way my mind was on anything but the road in front of me, I put in a panicked call to Cora Lewis, my coworker and close friend. She was all kinds of take care of business and would rally the troops and get everyone else who mattered the information they needed without me having to worry about it. She would help take care of me; she always did.

I made it to the hospital in record time and surged into the emergency room on a tidal wave of anxiety and fear. I was more familiar with these institutional and sterile walls than I wanted to be. One of my closest friends, my surrogate big brother, Rome Archer, had tangled with a bunch of bikers and a bunch of bullets not too long ago, and I had spent hours upon hours nervously pacing these very halls waiting to see if he was going to pull through. But right now this visit felt like it might define the rest of my life. The security guard gave me a concerned look. I was used to it. When you had yellow, orange, and red fire tattooed along each side of your scalp and had ink from your collar to your wrist on each arm, people tended to think you weren't really a very nice guy. Funny thing was, I was typically a lot nicer than most of the guys I loved like brothers, but not right now, and if the nurse who sat behind the desk didn't tell me where my uncle was in the next second, I was going to straight up lose my shit.

I was just about to breathe fire way hotter than the kind inked all over me when I saw her walking toward me. She looked like an angel, even though her name was Saint. It fit her, Saint Ford, healer of the sick and hater of anything and everything having to do with Nash Donovan. She was beautiful, breathtaking, and she absolutely despised me. She made no secret about it. I had run into her more than once on my unfortunately frequent trips to this ER, where she seemed to be a permanent fixture as one of the attending nurses.

We had gone to high school together years ago, and while I was all for striking up a reunion of sorts, she was having none of it. She made a big production of avoiding me, or giving me nervous, sideways looks like she didn't trust me or was forced to endure my company. Only right now, in this moment, she was looking at me with equal parts compassion and seriousness in her soft, dove-gray eyes. It left no doubt whatsoever that things with Phil were really, really bad.

She put a hand on my shoulder and I felt like I was going to shatter under the gentle touch.

"Nash . . ." Her voice was light and I could hear the bad news in it. "Come over here and talk to me for just a minute."

I didn't want to. I didn't want to hear whatever horrible words she was going to have to say to me, but because she was so pretty, because she had the loveliest eyes I had ever seen, I just numbly did what she asked. There were worse people to take bad news from.

We took a few steps away from the nurses' desk, and I gazed down at her with trepidation. She was fairly tall for a girl, so we were eye to eye when she leveled it at me in a feather-soft voice speaking rock-hard words.

"Did you know Phil was so sick?"

I felt like she was asking me as a friend, or someone who actually cared about what was happening, and not as a medical professional. I knew logically she was just doing her job, but it made me feel better to pretend otherwise.

I didn't have any words that sounded or felt right to answer her, so I shook my head.

"I recognized the name on the intake paperwork and the two of you look an awful lot alike. I figured I might find you out here."

I gulped down my thundering heartbeat and nodded my head stiffly. "He's my only family." That wasn't entirely true, but he was the only family I had that really mattered to me.

She sighed and I tried not to flinch when she put a hand on my cheek. I knew she didn't like me, and for some reason that made the fact that she was being so considerate, so caring, hit home that whatever she was getting ready to lay out for me was way worse than I had imagined.

"He has lung cancer . . . the doctors are thinking stage four. He has an extensive medical chart. He's been receiving treatment for a while. We got him settled and gave him fluids. He might have pneumonia, so that's why he's struggling to breathe, and his oxygen levels are dangerously low. We aren't a hundred percent sure why he was unresponsive just yet, but we're trying to get him awake. The attending doctor called the oncologist listed in Phil's chart. It's a serious situation, Nash. I can't believe he didn't let you know how ill he was."

I let my head drop on my neck like it was suddenly just too heavy to hold up and her gentle fingers stroked along my cheek. It was startlingly soothing.

"He's been avoiding me." It sounded pathetic, even to my own ears.

She was going to say something else when a tiny, pregnant pixie and a hulking giant came thundering into the room where we were standing. I didn't recognize the older guy who entered with them, but he had an intent look on his face that was almost scary. He took one look around the empty waiting room and turned on his heel in a way that made it seem like he was on a hunt for information or someone who had answers. The cavalry had arrived. Saint went to pull away and I instinctively grabbed her wrist. I needed my friends, loved my crew of misfits and rebels, but right now I needed her more. I couldn't explain it. She gave me a wan grin and tugged her arm free.

"I'm gonna go check on him and see if we managed to get him awake so you can see him. Nash . . . you should consider quitting smoking."

The last of her words trailed away as I was steamrolled by a punk-rock pixie and engulfed in a hug I needed like no one's business. I let Cora do her magic and try and make me feel better. I also let the quiet strength and steady assuredness of the guy I considered my older brother try and ground me. Rome Archer was a rock and I needed that kind of stability as my world was shaking apart around me.

I was pulling it together, getting the emotions that were churning and rolling in check, getting my head around what was going on when *they* showed up. It was bad enough that my mom was there, but that she had the nerve to bring that asshole she married with her was just pushing the limits of my already tattered control.

She just had to go and call me Nashville . . . no one called me Nashville and lived to tell the tale . .

Cora. I think it was hearing my real name

mom's lips that had all the questions rolli

tumbling into place. I went from hoverir

calm to a volatile, molten core of fury that

this ER down in flood of hate and wrath.

Why was she here?

Phil made her his next of kin, his power of attorney . . . like she was somehow more important to him than I was.

Why?

She didn't answer.

Did she know he was sick, and for how long?

She did. Phil didn't want me to worry.

She tried to convince me it was all in my best interests and my top was about to blow with each biting question I fired at her, when my best friend, Rule, showed up with his fiancée. I had a moment of clarity and was starting to see through the haze of dread, anger, resentment, and every-thing else fueling my blood when Saint's copper-colored head popped back around the corner. Her words had already changed my life once tonight.

I had no idea that she wasn't even close to being done.

She cocked her head to the side, blinked those gray eyes at me like she wasn't just going to break apart the foundation of everything I thought I knew, and said, "He's awake and asking for you."

"He is?"

"Yeah, he said he wants to talk to his son . . . that has to be you, right? You guys look identical."

The world fell away. I stopped breathing, stopped feeling, and stopped living. I was just rooted on the spot, stuck in a moment where my beloved uncle Phil had somehow just morphed into my father. The lies, the secrets, the wasted time, the hollow feeling I had always carried around from being unwanted, not only by a superficial and uncaring mother, but also by a faceless, nameless father turned around and around, and I felt like I was going to pass out from the dizziness it caused.

"Holy shit!" Typical Rule, he brought me back to the white room with a clatter and blood rushing into my face and ears. I was going to lose it, but like she knew it, Cora was suddenly there, right in my face, always the voice of reason. Always taking care of her boys.

"Nash." Cora's tone was stern and no-nonsense. "Now isn't the time. We can work out all the details later. They don't matter. You have to appreciate that he's still here and focus on the now." Her bright eyes danced over to her man and then slid back to mine. "Plus you can't hit her and get away with it. I can." Her spiky blond head tilted in the direction where my mom was cowering next to her husband. I wouldn't put it past her to actually take a swing at my mom. It was why I loved her so much.

Cora moved to the side as Saint walked up to my side and put her hand on the crook of my elbow in a silent gesture to follow her.

"I got you, Nash." Her eyes were a thundercloud I wanted to stare at forever. That was a storm I would never complain about getting caught in.

"Do you?" I hoped against hope she was the only one who could hear my voice crack and that Cora really did lay my lying, conniving mother out on the ER waiting room floor.

"I do." She almost whispered it and I wanted to ask how long she had me for. Was she going to be there while I coped with putting my role model, the only person who'd given me their time, their love, who turned me into a man I was proud to be, in the ground? How about while I dealt with the fact that same man had lied to me my entire fucking life? I had no clue who Phil Donovan was, and as a result I was starting to wonder if I had a clue who Nash Donovan was. I couldn't explain it, I didn't know her. Barely remembered her from before, and really had no clue what kind of person she was beyond her personable and professional bedside manner, but I wanted her to be there, felt like I needed her to be there . . . it was too bad she fucking hated me.

It may have been Thanksgiving, but I was having a really hard time finding one single thing to be thankful for.

CHAPTER 2

Saint

One week later . . .

I ARGUED WITH MYSELF the entire way on the short trip from the hospital to his apartment. I knew better. I hadn't been a practicing nurse for very long, only three years, but I had been immersed in the medical field long enough to know that it was stupid to get involved, to make patients and what they were dealing with a personal matter. There should be no forming personal attachments, no taking one case more seriously than another, no treating any one person affected by a family member's illness or accident any differently than the next . . . but none of that logic or professional training mattered against the need to find out why Nash hadn't stopped by the hospital once since Thanksgiving to see his dad.

Phil Donovan had been moved almost immediately from the ER to the upper levels of the hospital where the oncology unit was located, so he wasn't even my patient anymore. That hadn't stopped me from stopping by at the end of my shift to check on him and see how he was doing. The older man who was the spitting image of his son was taking his prognosis surprisingly well, and I always enjoyed his easy demeanor. It didn't look good, he didn't look good. But I had noticed that he was never alone. There was always someone in the room with him when I stuck my head in. He seemed to have an endless parade of tattooed and pierced men and women who pushed aside the discomfort of visiting and spending time with someone so sick in order to keep him company and offer him support. Only it was glaringly obvious that his own flesh and blood hadn't been among them. It wasn't my place to question why his own kid hadn't made an appearance any of those times, and I wouldn't have been driven to do something so out of character had Phil not sounded so disappointed when he mentioned Nash's disappearing act.

It wasn't like I was overly anxious for another run-in with the brooding, tattooed hottie anyway, but tonight, when I popped my head in, Cora had been arguing with the older man. I knew her to be loud and up front from the time her boyfriend had been shot and nearly died in my ER. She was currently being very vocal in her opinion about Nash's current behavior. Phil was telling her to leave Nash alone, that he would work through things in his own time and that he didn't blame his son for not being by once since the holiday. She was really worked up, shouting that it wasn't right, that Nash was acting like a big baby and that he was going to regret wasting any of this time they had together considering Phil's prognosis wasn't good. She might look a little crazy and sound kind of abrasive, but I had to agree that she had a point.

I felt bad for eavesdropping and was going to duck out of the room and head home when her next statement sent a rebellious chill down my spine.

"He won't even talk to Rule. He won't answer the phone. He's missed work all week. Rome went to the apartment and knocked on the door until a neighbor came out and threatened to call the cops. I told him he should've just broken it down. I think he was tempted because he never got any kind of response. The idea of Nash sitting alone in that apartment hurting, trying to process this all on his own, is breaking my heart, Phil. I don't know what else to do."

Phil murmured an answer that was too soft for me to hear and I jumped as another nurse came around the corner. I saw her give me an odd look because this was totally not my floor, I rarely went anywhere in the hospital outside of the ER. Before I could talk myself out of it, I went back to my own floor, snuck a quick peek at the file we had on Phil Donovan that listed Nash's info as his emergency contact after some woman named Ruby Loften, and headed out on a mission to do I don't know what. I wasn't sure why I was so keyed up, so invested in either of the Donovan men, especially considering the bitter taste my history with Nash left in my mouth.

I loved my job. I'd wanted to be a nurse since forever. Fixing all my dolls' "owies" and making my big sister let me cover her in bandages and gauze when I was little had always been my favorite game, and I had worked hard and busted my tail off to be the best nurse and caregiver I could be. At twenty-five I was a certified ER nurse and I was thinking about going back to school and studying to get my master's in nursing so I could look at being a nurse practitioner. I graduated at the top of my class from California State University in L.A. and I chose emergency nursing for the challenge, the fast pace, and because I knew I wanted to help people when they needed me most. It was a different environment, different set of patients and problems every single day. I was extremely skilled at it, completely invested in giving it my all each and every day. So I knew that whatever weird pull this case and these people involved had on me wasn't something I had ever experienced with a patient or their loved ones before.

I should have known the instant those unmistakable purple eyes locked on to me, trying to place where they knew me from on the Fourth of July all those months ago, that Nash Donovan was once again going to set my well-ordered world on its side. Even after all the time that had passed, and even with the ages-old resentment and dislike I harbored for the darkly handsome young man—who, let's be honest, had only improved with age—there was still something about him that got to me. With just a look he made my blood heat and I had that deeply repressed feeling of longing and want whispering at me to remember. It seemed like I was always going to be stuck in a turbulent cycle of lust and hate where Nash was concerned, and I didn't like how extreme and out of control either of those things made me feel. In just a matter of a few short weeks, those feelings and the man who inspired them had me doing something totally out of character and against not only my professional rule book, but also against my own sense of self-preservation.

The traffic cutting across downtown was terrible. There wasn't any snow on the ground yet, but it was cold out and the hustle and bustle of Denver getting ready for Christmas was causing a nasty gridlock. Not to mention it was a Saturday night, so the rush of all the weekend warriors to get out and enjoy their freedom made a three-mile drive take almost half an hour.

Being around someone from my past, someone who remembered the former me, just brought all those insecurities I still struggled with to a lesser degree now right to the forefront of my mind. Especially when that someone was the adult version of the out-of-my-league teenage boy I'd had a painfully intense, supersecret crush on.

It had never been easy getting made fun of and hearing mean things said about myself. It hurt and tore down my already frayed self-esteem. I knew high school was fleeting, and that in a few years, none of those people would matter to me anymore, that Nash could be chalked up to a phase. But the way he made me feel when he ignored me, and even worse, the way it hurt me when I heard him saying awful things about me had taught me a valuable lesson, one I still held close today. People could only hurt you and disappoint you if you let them. They only had the power to hurt you if you thought they were special and above that. I didn't let anyone close enough, didn't let anyone touch my heart or emotions enough to risk that happening again . . . ever. I think that made dealing with my cheating boyfriend in college and handling the knowledge that my own father was a philanderer easier. Across the board, men in my life had disappointed me, and Nash was just the first in a long line.

Which made this need, this urgency to check on him, my nemesis, my teenage nightmare, even harder to process. Still, even though I was full of apprehension and doubt, I wheeled my new Jetta into a spot on the street in front of the Victorian, that had obviously been converted into some apartments, and got out. I gazed at the building for a second, trying to convince myself to mind my own business and just go home. I was still in scrubs, had my ugly work shoes on and my hair coiled into a tight, fire-colored braid that reached the middle of my back. I only had the barest hint of makeup left after a ten-hour shift, and I didn't know why I thought he would answer the door for me if he was ignoring his friends and the people closest to him.

I shivered because I hadn't grabbed a coat and decided I either needed to go home or just go in. My gaze slid over a sweet Charger that was parked in front of the building and I sighed. I dealt with death and horrific injury on a daily basis. I could handle a brief encounter with a ghost from my memories and survive the encounter. I was made of stronger stuff now. Besides, seeing Phil so sick and sad and the traumatic way Nash had responded to the news on Thanksgiving had me concerned for both of them. And despite knowing better, I knew that my concern wasn't going away.

I entered the lovely old building and looked around for the numbers on the door. It looked like the bottom floor had two apartments and Nash's was on the left. I was just getting ready to knock when the opposite door across the hall swung open and a girl stuck her head out. Her gaze skittered over me and then landed on my startled face.

"You his girlfriend?"

Her tone was friendly, almost overly so, and she looked like she should be on the cover a *Sports Illustrated* magazine. I wasn't overweight anymore, now I was just normal, healthy, but this girl had abs for days and boobs that deserved an award. Hell, if I was her I would be walking around in yoga pants and a sports bra in the freezing November weather, too.

"Uh . . . no."

"I just moved in. There's been someone pounding on that door every five minutes for the last week. It's driving me nuts. I saw the guy who lives there. He's a total babe. I keep waiting for a girl to show up and claim him. I thought it might be you. I'm Royal, by the way."

I nodded at her and cocked my head to the side. All single men should find themselves so lucky in the new-neighbor department. I bet Nash would just love her . . . well, once he got out of his funk.

"I'm just a friend. I thought I would check on him. I'm Saint."

She laughed a little and shook her head, sending her dark auburn hair sliding across her shoulder like only models in shampoo commercials did.

"Our parents were obviously smoking the same thing when they picked our names out." She inclined her head toward the closed door and her dark brown eyes flashed in amusement while I struggled to try and act like this scene didn't totally intimidate me. Really pretty girls like her always made it harder for me to act normal and unaffected. "Seems to be the theme of the week—checking on the sexy guy next door. That and superhot men. I swear all his friends are gorgeous. I wouldn't toss a single one of them I've seen out of bed. Even the really big guy with all the attitude and the scar. He was scary as hell but dead sexy."

I was getting uncomfortable. I did great with strangers when they were bleeding and needed my help, but this kind of interaction was out of my wheelhouse, even if I did agree with her on the hotness levels of Nash's crew of friends.

The guy with the scar was Nash's old roommate, Rome Archer. He was dead sexy in a warrior, take-care-of-business kind of way. I knew firsthand because he had been a patient of mine not too long ago. At the hospital the other night I caught a glimpse of Rule Archer, he was Nash's best friend and he was still gorgeous and dangerous-looking in his own unique way. Later on in the night, Jet Keller had shown up with a blond guy who looked like he had escaped from the 1950s and a another guy who was so undeniably handsome that it was necessary to look twice at him just to make sure your eyes weren't playing tricks on you. All three, hot and oozing sex appeal and trouble in different ways. I just didn't know this woman well enough to divulge any of those insights to her, not that I would be comfortable doing that even if she wasn't a stranger.

I knocked on the door more out of desperation to get away from her and her curious gaze than to see if Nash would answer.

Of course he didn't and I felt like an idiot. I shifted uneasily from foot to foot and tried to knock again.

"Good luck. He hasn't opened it for anyone else." She sounded amused and I flushed bright red. I would never get over feeling like I was always the butt of someone's joke. It made me feel kind of sick to my stomach, more so because she looked the way she did.

I was lifting my hand to knock one last time when the door suddenly yanked open and I was face to chest with a mostly naked, furiously scowling, obviously inebriated Nash Donovan. Those amazing eyes that were trapped somewhere between purple and blue blinked sluggishly at me and I let out a startled gasp as he grasped the hand I still had lifted up to knock and pulled me toward him.

"You must have the lucky touch, Saint. Good for you." The neighbor's laughing voice followed me into the apartment as Nash stumbled unsteadily backward, taking me with him.

He slammed the door closed behind me with a thud and tried to focus on me out of bloodshot eyes. He smelled like booze and cigarette smoke, and I couldn't help but wrinkle my nose up in distaste. I could physically handle myself. It was a job requirement in the ER, but at the moment, he looked kind of feral and I had to admit his glowering, grumbling presence was slightly menacing.

He was taller than average, but so was I, meaning he wasn't really looming so much as he was threatening, because he was so unfamiliar and unhinged in his current state. It would be a flat-out lie if I tried to pretend like I didn't notice that even in his disheveled and drunken state he was in good shape. He obviously took pretty good care of himself aside from pickling his liver and that awful habit of smoking. He had always been a darkly handsome guy, his midnight brows slashing and dramatic on a face that was full of character holding a hint of unknown ethnicity behind it. Those purplish eyes of his were out of this world and unforgettable. They were really too pretty and delicate-looking to be on such a masculine face.

I think it was the fact that all he had on was a pair of black boxer shorts revealing there wasn't an exposed part of his olive-toned skin that didn't have some kind of design inked on it that was making me a little bit overwhelmed. I liked tattoos, had a couple myself, but Nash's dedication to decorating his body was on an entirely different level. I mean, I wasn't surprised at the amount of artwork he was sporting, considering he had those brilliant flames tattooed on his head and a curved ring in the center of his nose. That was all designed to make a statement, to proclaim that he didn't have to live by anyone's rules but his own, which I guess was fine and worked for him, but it was a lot to take in for me when I already considered him a danger and kind of a douche bag.

I refused to admit I was openly checking him out. I couldn't help it. He was missing clothes, built and gorgeous, even if all that was under miles of ink.

"I ordered pizza."

I looked up at him and asked like a moron:

"What?"

"I thought you were the pizza guy, but you're not."

He stumbled back a few steps, grabbed the back of the couch, and sort of just slithered down until he was sitting on the floor across from me. He stuck his long legs out in front of him and rubbed his watery eyes with the knuckles of his hands. What in the hell was happening right now? It was like he had just folded in on himself right in front of my eyes. He was disappearing inside of himself.

"Are you okay, Nash? A lot of people are worried about you."

He gave a laugh that sounded so broken, so jagged, I felt it scrape across my skin, leaving goose bumps in its wake.

"No."

I wasn't following his slurred or broken side of the conversation, maybe because I was totally distracted by his naked torso. I had seen a few good-looking guys in their underwear in my time, some at work, some not. None of them in memory held a candle to Nash. Someone should tell him that what he did for a pair of black boxers could be considered a lethal weapon to a woman's sanity.

"No, what?" I had to make a real effort to try and follow his scattered additions to our choppy conversation.

He tilted his head back so he could look up at me. The flames over his ears were attached to more tattooed flames that curled up over his massive shoulders and onto the front of his chest. I guiltily wanted to see what they attached to on the backside of him. He also had what appeared to be some kind of intricately inked wings that draped all the way across his ribcage, down both sides of his corrugated abs, and disappeared into the front of his boxers on either side of his belly button. I couldn't even imagine how bad something like that had to hurt, but the tattoo work was impressive in its enormity and detail and so was the rock-hard body that it lived on.

"No, I'm not okay."

I blew out a breath and crouched down so I was more on his level. His gaze followed me as I lowered myself to my haunches. People told me all the time how pretty my eyes were and it made me blush and stammer. They were all right, gray and clear, and my patients seemed to find them soothing. But I thought, as I gazed somberly into the sad depths of his, that clearly no one who thought I had pretty eyes had ever looked into Nash's. I had never seen a more striking or unique color than the columbine blue of his. Sitting under those raven-black eyebrows, they were just magnetic.

"You need to talk to someone, family, your friends, or maybe a girlfriend. This isn't a good situation for anyone, Nash, and drinking and smoking a carton a day isn't going to make it any better. You need to be strong for your dad, but you also need to be strong for you. It seems like you have a lot of people you can lean on, they've been in and out of that hospital room all week. Trust me, this is not a fight you want to battle on your own."

He threw his head back until it thumped on the dark leather of the couch. He squeezed his eyes shut. He pulled his long legs up and clenched fists up on the top of each knee. He even had scrolling artwork inked on his skin from beneath the hem of his boxer shorts to his knee on one leg and to the top of his foot on the other. There was simply too much of it for me to pick apart all the separate images and designs. All I knew was that it was all bold, dynamic, and full of color and had obviously been put on him by someone with an incredible amount of skill.

"Until a few days ago, I thought my father had walked out on me when I was just a baby. My mom told me he was a deadbeat, that he didn't have any interest in being a husband or a father, so every time that asshole Loften talked shit to me, told me I was garbage, tried to put me under his thumb, I told myself it was cool because my mom deserved nice things, a guy to take care of her since my dad was an asshole. Only Loften is a judgmental, superficial prick and basically forced her to pick me or him. She picked him even though my dad was in the same fucking state all along and never walked out on anyone."

He gave that laugh that made me hurt for him again, and I couldn't stop myself from reaching out a hand and putting it on one of his balled-up fists. I could feel the tension and dissonance creeping all over him.

"Turns out the only adult I ever looked up to, that ever showed me I was worth anything just the way I was, fucking lied to me my entire fucking life. Phil took me in when my mom kicked me out. He pretty much raised me, taught me how to tattoo, gave me a future, and showed me how to be a man. I walked into that hospital room, took one look at him, and wondered how I had missed what was right in front of me all along."

He grunted and let his eyes drift shut again. I was following along as best I could with his story, but I was kind of lost. I felt like there was someone else he should be telling all of this to, but for whatever reason I was the one he had let in, both figuratively and literally. He hadn't known Phil was his father until the other night? That was huge and just as hard to work through as the fact that his loved one was terminally ill. No wonder he was a mess. I couldn't blame him.

"He looks like he's dying . . . so fucking sick, and he called me "son." For twenty-five years I called him Uncle Phil and now that he might not be around much longer, he has the nerve to call me son. I grew up thinking I wasn't good enough for anyone. Not my mom, not that shithead she married, not my dad who couldn't even be bothered to see what kind of kid I would turn out to be . . . only Phil made me feel like I was worth a damn, and now I don't even know what to do with any of this shit. Why didn't he just tell me? He was more my dad than my uncle all along anyway."

I sighed because he was spinning himself in circles and I could see the faster he turned the worse it was making him feel. I put my other hand on his and leaned forward.

"I don't know, Nash. What I do know is the only person who can answer those questions is sick and hurting just as badly as you are. And I know that the two of you obviously need each other right now. This is wasted time you will never get back. I see it every day and you will live to regret it if you don't move past it and go see him."

He was drunk, obviously distraught and not thinking clearly. I doubted he would remember much of this heart-to-heart when he sobered up, but there was just a nagging part of me that wanted to try and make this heartbreaking situation more manageable for him. I thought I still hated him, still held him responsible for all my shattered teenage dreams of love and romance, but right now I just felt sorry for him. It didn't matter how big and strong he was, or how much of a badass he appeared to be on the outside, not being able to fight back against something as devastating as cancer, especially when it was affecting someone he obviously loved, sucked. I knew it made him feel impotent and ineffectual, and right now it was obviously making him scared enough to think hiding from it was a viable option.

I gasped a little in shock when both of his wide hands suddenly seized my face on either side. His hands were a little rough but his touch was soft as his eyes suddenly flashed from periwinkle to a dark, intense indigo. His eyelids drooped down, and his erratic breathing suddenly slowed, making those flames dancing across his shoulders and pecs look like they were alive.

"You're really beautiful, Saint."

I narrowed my eyes at him and lifted my hands to wrap around his wrists. My fingers didn't reach all the way around and I didn't want to think about how sexy that was. It was on the tip of my tongue to remind him that he hadn't always thought that, in fact if my memory was correct he had said it would take an obscene amount of money and a bag over my head for him to be interested in spending any kind of intimate time in my offensive presence. I still felt the burn as the memory flashed behind my eyes.

"I just want to help."

"You are helping."

No I wasn't. I shouldn't have come here. He wasn't my problem. What he was struggling with and whatever complicated family dynamic he was working with had nothing to do with me, but it was like I was seventeen again and couldn't deny that there was just something about him that grabbed at me, pulled at my too-sensitive heartstrings.

I sighed and gave him a tight smile. "No I'm not. You need to let the people who love you, who care about you, in to help you out with this. That's a heavy load to try and balance alone. Especially on top of everything else with your parents. It'll be all right, Nash. You'll see."

His eyes got even darker, and it was like watching midnight fall over the sky. I was balanced on my toes, and he had a firm grip on my face, so when he suddenly pulled me forward I was both startled and off balance. I had to let go of his wrists to catch myself as I fell forward, and I swore the heat coming off his bare skin when my palms landed on the smoothness of his naked chest was enough to meld me to him forever.

I was going to ask him what in the hell he thought he was doing. I was going to tell him that I had stopped by more for his father's sake than his. I was going to snap at him that he was the last man on earth I would let put his hands on me after the lasting damage his unnecessarily cruel actions and thoughtless words a lifetime ago had done. I never got the chance.

One of his hands snatched up the end of my long braid

and wrapped it around his fingers like a rope. His other slid across the nape of my neck and unceremoniously jerked me forward until we were chest to chest, mouth to mouth, and I was plastered all along the very much undressed front of him. I pushed ineffectually at his rock-hard shoulders, tried to wiggle my way free, but he was too strong, had too good of a grip on my hair—and if I was going to be entirely honest, even drunk and sloppy he was one hell of a good kisser, so my effort to get away may have been halfhearted at best.

I had spent a good portion of my last year in high school wondering what it would be like to kiss Nash Donovan. Granted, in my fantasies it usually involved candles, soft music, and him being madly in love with me while I just laughed at him and told him there wasn't a chance in hell he ever had a shot at getting with me. Wouldn't it just be cruel fate to shove it in my face that even though I didn't particularly care for him, didn't think there would ever be a situation or set of circumstances in the whole wide world where I would let him put his hands on me . . . that as soon as I was tested in those beliefs I crumbled like the Berlin Wall coming down.

His lips were a little dry, his skin rough from too many days without a shave, and when he moved his head just a fraction to run his tongue along the seam of my lips, I refused to open, and I felt the slight brush of metal against my upper lip from that hoop in the center of his nose. I thought it would weird me out, but it made me shiver, and when he pulled my hair just hard enough to make me huff out a breath of pain, he got the entrance he wanted and I quickly slipped from indignant and annoyed to something squishy and foreign that made my heart rate pick up and my pulse flutter jerkily under my skin.

Man, could he kiss. He was intent on it, like whatever was happening between my mouth and his was somehow the only thing that mattered to him in the entire world right now. He used his tongue, his teeth, and somehow lured me even closer so I could feel the rapid rate his heart was pounding out against the flattened palm of my hand where it rested on the burning surface of one of his impressive pecs. I could taste all his vices as his talented tongue danced across my own and glanced against the sensitive curve of my upper lip. There was the tang of tequila, the acrid hint of cigarette smoke, a tinge of sorrow, and the unmistakable residue of injury caused by wounds self-inflicted by his stubbornness and fear.

One of us groaned and the other sighed heavily, and just as I was about to forget myself, forget why I was here and who this tattooed and inconsolable boy was to me and do something idiotic and unforgivable, there was a pounding knock at the door that had both of us jerking apart. His gaze was wild and hazy with a mixture of passion and confusion. I pulled back and jumped to my feet like that fire that was inked all over him was alive and could actually singe me.

I was breathing hard and felt like I wanted to maybe kick him or fall back on top of him and kiss him all over again. The banging on the door increased in intensity and I cleared my throat and shoved my now messy, tangled column of hair over my shoulder.

"Your pizza is here."

He just looked up at me like I had landed from another planet. He ran his tongue across the damp curve of his lower lip and lifted an eyebrow at me, like he was daring me to say something, like he was savoring the taste I had left on him.

I glowered down at him and turned on my heel to head toward the door. I should've listened to my instinct that had yelled at me as loudly as it could that I should just leave well enough alone. The past belonged buried in the Pandora's box of hurtful memories and savage misconceptions I left it in. Nash had no place in my here and now. No matter how gorgeous I thought he was, no matter that he was the best kisser ever or how desperately my libido was screeching at me that I needed to know exactly where those wings on his stomach and hips disappeared to . . . I knew there was more under the surface of him, and it wasn't very pretty.

"You taste like a bar floor that hasn't been scrubbed clean in a month."

I snagged the half-full carton of cigarettes he had sitting on the breakfast bar that divided the kitchen from the living room and waved the box at him over my shoulder.

"I told you that you needed to quit. Stop acting like a spoiled brat. Yes, people you love being dishonest with you sucks, but you're an adult now, so deal with it accordingly. You said your uncle took you in, believed in you, taught you a craft you clearly love, so focus on all he did do and not what he didn't do, because you don't know how much longer you might have with him. Man up, Nash. It's how we deal with the things that hurt us most that defines us."

I pulled the door open just at the pizza guy was getting

ready to pound again and slipped around him. I heard a shuffle of bodies, male voices muttering to each other, and I was almost out the security door when I heard the neighbor's sultry voice float across the hall.

"Honey, if you're gonna have this much traffic on a daily basis, you need to invest in a doorbell."

I paused just long enough to look over my shoulder. Both Nash and the pizza guy were staring at her in all her toned and glorious beauty. I rolled my eyes at the obvious display. Nash flicked his gaze in my direction and then back at the beauty queen.

"Who are you, exactly?" He sounded less discombobulated, less scattered.

"I'm your new neighbor."

I heard him chuckle and it made me grind my teeth together as I pushed through the door.

"Welcome to the neighborhood." I didn't need to see him to know he was grinning at her, and that she was probably spellbound by all that dusky skin and ink barely concealed by his boxers.

It shouldn't twist my guts up. It shouldn't make me want to pull all of her fabulous auburn hair from her head and knee Nash in the balls so hard his future grandchildren would walk with a limp, but it did and that was something I absolutely didn't want to think about. Not now, not ever.

CHAPTER 3

Nash

IT TOOK ME ANOTHER full day and a half to pull my head out of my ass and stop acting like a lunatic. I was a mess. Torn up about kissing Saint, mostly because I didn't regret it for a second but also because I knew better. In the haze of tequila and sorrow, I could still taste her, feel her pressed up against me, and it was the only good thing I could seem to recall in the last few weeks.

I would love to be able to say that Saint's surprise visit had smacked me across the face with some much-needed clarity, but that wasn't the case. After her hasty departure due to me mauling her like an uncouth jackass, I finished off the bottle of tequila I'd been steadily working my way through, before she'd interrupted me, and passed out on the living room floor. The next day was more of the same, only at some point I had made my way to the couch and had managed to doze off using the pizza box as a pillow. Oh yeah, I was totally behaving like a responsible adult.

I cracked open an eye when the front door to the apartment swung open and heavy footfalls made their way over to where I was straight up wallowing in my own piss-poor choices and inconsolability. The only person who still had a key to the apartment was Rule. Obviously he was done letting me have a pity party for one and was tired of me ignoring all his phone calls. My head felt like it was stuffed with cotton and it took more than a minute for my hazy gaze to clear enough to meet his angry, pale blue eyes.

Rule knew me better than anyone. We were best friends for a reason. There was no judgment, no censure, and no disappointment from either of us, even when the situation sometimes called for it. We were a team no matter what, and the role we played in each other's life was that of rock-solid support, and more often than not, official ass kicker of the other one when they needed it, which was clearly what he was thinking as he crossed his arms over his chest and lifted his pierced eyebrow at me.

"You look like crap."

"Well, that's accurate since I feel like crap."

"It's been a week. That's as long as I'm putting up with this shit from you. Take a shower, go brush your goddamn teeth, put some fucking pants on, and we're going to see Phil. Enough, dude. Yeah, that was a pretty nasty bomb you got dropped on you, but it doesn't change the fact we all owe Phil more than we're ever going to be able to repay in one lifetime. So get over yourself and let's go."

I grunted up at him and peeled myself up off the greasy cardboard. Yeah, I was a winner. I rubbed my hands over the shorn surface of my hair and waited for the room to stop tilting sideways. I didn't know what to say to the man who had raised me. I had walked into his hospital room that night, taken one look into eyes that were the exact same color as mine, listened to him call me son in a voice that had no strength behind it, and turned around and walked right back out. It was a cowardly move, not to mention insensitive and shallow, but my head was spinning all around and I couldn't find any solid ground to balance on. Phil did deserve more than that from me no matter who exactly he was in my life now; he had always been there for me, supported me when no one else would.

I shoved to my feet and promptly fell back on my ass. Rule reached out and put the hand that had the cobra head and his name inked across the knuckles on my shoulder to steady me. He shook his head, his spiky blue hair making it sort of hard to take his look of reproach seriously.

"Just give me twenty."

I would need that long to scrub the disgusting taste of stale booze and cigarette after cigarette out of my mouth.

Saint wasn't lying, I did taste like a barroom floor. That was an entirely different mess I needed to try and clean up. I knew she only stopped by out of some kind of professional obligation, because she was nice and kind, and obviously possessed a huge heart. I knew she wasn't particularly fond of me, but she had looked past her dislike and offered comfort and soft words when I needed them most, and in repayment I had acted like a jackass. I needed to apologize and see if I could minimize some of the damage. I wanted her to like me, wanted her to think I was an all right guy, and not just because I thought she was the most beautiful girl I had ever seen. It went beyond her awesome hair, rocking body, and soft gray eyes. I wanted her to like me because she had a way about her, a delicate kind of sweetness that I wanted to wrap myself all up in. It didn't make much sense, but nothing in my life right now did.

I had vague recollections of Saint from high school, still pretty but slightly heavier and painfully shy to the point of it being painful. She was smart and in all the accelerated programs Brookside High had offered, so our paths generally never crossed. There had been a point in time when I recalled our lockers being side by side and I had tried to engage her, made it a point to smile and say hi, but beyond that we moved in different circles and I don't think she wanted to slum with the likes of me. Still I remembered her hair and those eyes . . . even then the light gray was full of kindness and understanding. She wasn't the kind of chick my teenage self tried to get lucky with, mostly because she was out of my league intellectually, and even then radiated a class I didn't understand. Rule and I had spent most of our teenage years screwing anything that moved and partying in ways that the older versions of ourselves marveled at now. We were a couple of unscrupulous horn balls, and girls like Saint Ford, then and now, were not the kind of girls that wanted to get tangled up with guys like us.

Only to everyone's amazement Rule had settled down, was getting married in a few weeks to a bona fide society princess. She was just as smart, just as classy and beautiful as Saint, and she loved Rule with everything she had. Shaw

Landon was any guy's dream girl and Rule was the lucky bastard who'd landed her. Now he was going to make sure he got to keep her forever because he was putting a ring on her finger and changing her last name to his.

After a scalding-hot shower that made my skin red and woke me up enough to get my feet under me, I crawled into a pair of jeans and pulled a long-sleeved thermal over my head that had the logo of the tattoo shop where Rule and I worked on the front of it. Catching sight of myself in the mirror over my dresser, I had to wince. My face was covered in a week's worth of stubble and my normally clear eyes were lined with red veins. Despite my outward appearance, I was generally a pretty mellow guy. I had learned to go with the flow and take things as they came. I had to be the reasonable one with a guy like Rule as my partner in crime. He had enough attitude and a desire to stir shit up that I never needed to be "that guy"—the volatile, unpredictable type. Plus when you put bold and bright tattoos on the sides of your head, people took it at face value that you weren't someone they wanted to mess with. However, right now the reflection staring back at me was totally "that guy." I looked angry, confused, ready to throw down for no reason, and behind it all I looked sad . . . really really sad.

I sighed and pulled a plain black baseball hat on over my shaved head. I grabbed a hoodie and met Rule back in the living room. He had thrown the discarded pizza boxes and Chinese food containers away and tossed the empty bottles of Patrón I had lying around into the recycle bin. We had lived together for a long time before he had bought a house and moved in with Shaw. He knew where everything was and just gave me a "really" look when I shrugged.

"I was thirsty."

"Obviously. Between you and Ayden, I should buy stock in Patrón."

Ayden was Shaw's best friend and the wife of another one of our childhood buddies. She was model pretty, had legs that made men stupid, spoke with a light southern twang, and could drink most of us under the table. Jet Keller was another one of my friends who'd found the quintessential dream girl and decided to keep her until the end of time. It seemed to be happening to everyone around me lately.

Even Rome, Rule's older brother and someone else I looked up to because of the kind of man he was, had found his perfect match. I don't know that anyone would consider Cora Lewis a dream girl. She was too bossy, a little too mouthy, and a whole lot of stubborn packed into a small, colorful package, but Rome seemed to think she was great. They were two very different people, but together they worked, so much so that Cora was expecting their first baby sometime in March. Everyone I cared about was falling in love and settling down. It made me happy but also made me nervous because I had seen what happened in the name of love when someone made life-changing choices based on it. I was a child who had been cast aside by an uncaring mother in the name of love.

We walked out the front door and I turned around to lock it behind me. The door across the hall opened, and the goddess who lived there came strolling out with a gym bag in her hand. She was pretty, really pretty, in an overly exaggerated way. Had I not had so much on my mind and still felt like such a bastard for treating Saint like I did the night before, there was a good chance I would've been all over welcoming her to the building in a much more personal and hands-on way. As it was, all I could do was offer her a brief nod in greeting as her gaze slid over the top of Rule's crazy hair to the tips of his worn black boots.

"Nice."

Her tone was friendly and flirty and her dark eyes sparkled with humor.

"The building manager should put it in the ad that the view is across the hall, not facing the mountains. He could charge like a hundred dollars more a month in rent for it."

Rule lifted the eyebrow that had the rings pierced through it and looked at me sideways. I just shrugged and headed toward the front door. I held it open for her as she preceded us out.

"I'm Royal Hastings, by the way."

I shook her hand and Rule followed suit. I saw her gaze drift over Shaw's name that he had tattooed on the knuckles of his other hand. It was more effective than any wedding band could ever be. A ring came off, a tattoo never did.

"Nash, and this is Rule. Sorry about all the noise and chaos the last week. Normally it's a pretty quiet building and we all keep to ourselves."

She laughed and pulled the hood of her light jacket up around her dark red hair. Man, she really was a knockout and I should be all over her, but the desire just wasn't there and in the next sentence she brought up the reason why.

"It's been interesting for sure. You have an interesting group of friends, neighbor. The girl from last night was my favorite. The blonde with all the tattoos is loud, the brunette doesn't seem very friendly, and the other blonde was nice enough but she acted like I didn't have any right to ask what was going on. The redhead was super nice, kind of shy, even so she's been my favorite. If all those girls are attached to the sexy man parade that has been flooding in and out of the hallway, I have to say those are some lucky ladies."

I rolled my eyes and Rule laughed as we stopped on the sidewalk.

"The impatient blonde is mine. She's in the middle of planning a wedding and is pretty protective of her friends, so she's just a little fierce at the moment. The brunette is actually one of the nicest people you can ever meet, she's was just worried about this dumb-ass and the fact he's been AWOL all week. She married to the guy in the skintight jeans."

The hot neighbor nodded and continued to laugh.

"I see."

"The pregnant blonde with the ink is with my brother, the big dude that looks like he could rip the door off the hinges. The blond guy who kind of looks like Johnny Bravo and the other blond guy who is prettier than you are both unattached . . . just FYI." He cut his frost-tinted gaze in my direction. "I don't know who the redhead is."

This wasn't a conversation I wanted to have on the sidewalk in front of a stranger, or anywhere else for that matter, but they were both just staring at me, so I groaned and shoved my hands into the pockets of my hoodie.

"The ER nurse, Saint, she stopped by to check on me. I was pretty fucked up, drunk and out of it. She basically told me the same thing you guys have been trying to tell me all week. I need to get over my shit and go make peace with Phil before it's too late."

The neighbor shrugged and turned toward a new-looking 4Runner parked on the other side of the Charger.

"That was nice of her. Nurses are usually really impersonal and clinical, so it's sweet she reached out. You boys have a lovely day."

We watched as she drove away and Rule turned to me with a lifted eyebrow. I scowled and patted my pockets searching for a pack of smokes. I swore when I remembered Saint walking out the door with them.

"What?"

"New neighbor."

"So?"

"So?"

I walked to the passenger side of his gigantic pickup truck and waited until he popped the lock so I could climb in. Once I was in the seat, I slumped down and rested my head against the cool pane of glass and closed my eyes. I knew I had to go to the hospital, but I really didn't want to. What was I supposed to say to Phil?

Something like . . . *oh, so you're my long-lost dad . . . good to know, oh, by the way, thanks for waiting until you had cancer and might be dying to tell me . . . ?*

There just weren't words that made any sense.

"So a week ago I would have walked into that apartment and there isn't a chance in hell that you would've been alone.

That neighbor would have been with you and you both would've been naked."

I barked out a laugh and opened one eye to look at him.

"I've been too jacked up. I was so sauced the last week there isn't a chance in hell I could've got it up, let alone gotten it in."

But that wasn't entirely true. When I had pulled Saint against me, when she had finally opened up and let me into the warm, damp recesses of her mouth, I had gotten hard as a rock and there was nothing the river of tequila in my blood could do about it. Like he was reading my mind, Rule asked, "So what's the story with the nurse?"

"We went to school with her. She was like super smart, shy, kept to herself mostly. She didn't party or go out, so I don't think you would really remember her. I recognized her the night I picked Rome up from the ER after he got his head smashed in. My locker was next to hers senior year. She looks a little different now, lost some weight, I guess, and her hair is longer. She doesn't seem to care for me very much, but she was great the night Phil was rushed to the hospital and it was nice of her to check on me last night."

"But why would she do that if she doesn't like you?"

"I don't really know. I think she's just a really nice person."

Rule snorted. "She's hot."

I nodded. "She is."

"Sucks she doesn't dig you."

I blew out a breath. "I guess. It's not like I'm in the market for a girlfriend anyway."

"Why the hell not?"

It was a familiar argument we had now. Ever since he

had decided Shaw was it for him, he was on my case to settle down, to find the one girl that would make me think love actually stood a chance and that monogamy was worth trying out. While I was happy for him, for all my friends who had found "the one," I just didn't see that being the route for me. When my mom had tossed me aside for her idiot husband under the guise of love, I knew even at such a young age that was not something I was ever going to do. Love someone enough that they made me willing to sacrifice the rest of my life for them. I liked being single, liked having the opportunity to experience different women, different moments with different people whenever I wanted. I didn't need a girlfriend to be fulfilled, nor did I really want one.

"Dude, I just found out my uncle is really my dad, he has cancer, and my best friend is fucking getting married in less than a month. Not to mention my pseudo big brother is expecting his first child. You tell me where in any of that I have the time or the mental capacity to try and be some chick's boyfriend."

He grunted and pulled the truck into the parking lot of the hospital. I felt my heart rate start to pick up and a cold sweat start to trickle down the back of my neck. We climbed out of the truck and met at the front of it. Rule gave me a hard shove with his hand and grunted when I dug the point of my elbow into his ribs to retaliate.

"That's the thing, Nash, you aren't 'some girl's' boyfriend, you're '*the* girl's' boyfriend and when it's '*the* girl' you find the time for it, and you get your head around it really quick because the idea of being without her is about the worst thing you can imagine."

I didn't know what to say to that, so I just kept my mouth shut and followed him through the sliding glass doors and to the elevator. Unconsciously my gaze searched the long white hallways for a glimpse of fiery-red hair. I didn't see her and I couldn't decide if that made me feel relieved or irritated.

We got to the top floor of the hospital where the oncology unit was located and I had to follow Rule because I didn't know which room Phil was in. Man, I really did suck and I wanted a damn cigarette so bad it was making my skin hurt. The door was cracked just a little bit and Rule stepped to the side.

"Go in there and spend some time with the guy who raised you. He might have called you his nephew, Nash, but he always treated you—hell, all of us—like his sons. I'll give you a few minutes before I come in."

I nodded jerkily.

I took a deep breath and pushed the door open. The curtains were pulled slightly open and the winter light was casting eerie shadows across Phil's fragile form. He had always been a big, strapping guy, and now that I knew he was my father I could see all the similarities between him and me. It was so much more than our unusual eye color. He lifted his eyelids and looked at me. I wanted to shuffle my feet and clear my throat, but I didn't. I walked to the end of the bed so that we were just watching each other. He was so thin and his pallor looked awful.

I rubbed my thumb along the edge of my jaw and tried for a grin. "You scared the hell out of me, old man."

He grunted and lifted the hand that had some kind of monitor on it attached to miles of wires and tubes coming out of him.

"I was tired of all the poking and prodding. I wasn't going to spend Thanksgiving in a goddamn hospital. I just needed to get away. I didn't know I was sick, I thought it was just a cough."

"Just a cough?" I couldn't help the bitterness that crept into my tone. "I thought you were dead when I saw you lying on the floor of the cabin. Do you have any idea what that did to me?"

"I'm sorry, Nash. For all of it. I've made some bad decisions along the way, done some things I regret, but you, son . . . you were never one of them."

There it was. Son, something I had always wanted to be and never thought I would be. I rubbed my hand across the back of my neck.

"I don't even know what to do with that, Phil. I don't even know what to call you anymore."

"What you always did. I'm still just Phil, Nash. The things that happened between me and your mom, it was too long ago and had nothing to do with you. Who you are today is a man you should be proud of . . . a man I am proud of as a father, uncle, as a boss and anything in between. I thought I was protecting you, thought maybe getting sick was a sign. I thought it would just go away, honestly."

"Cancer? You thought cancer would just magically go away and that you could indefinitely hide from it? Hide from us?"

"Seems to be a family trait. Took you a full week to get your ass in here, didn't it?"

He had a point, so I just sighed and leaned against the edge of the bed. I wrapped my hands around the rail and stared at him. He was sick, it was obvious, but there also appeared to be a lightness in him that had never been there before. I wondered how hard it had been for him to pretend all this time, to listen to me bitch about my imaginary father and the blame I placed on him for the way things broke loose with my mom and her husband. Maybe it was true, and the truth really did set you free.

"I had to get my head around some stuff. I needed to do that alone." I knew it should be on the very tip of my tongue to ask why he hadn't disclosed that he was my father before now, why he had been keeping secrets from me my entire life, but I think I was kind of terrified of the answer. My mom had never made me feel like I was worthy of carrying her blood. I don't think I could handle it if Phil had any of that kind of reasoning behind his actions.

"Where you at with everything now?" His tone was hesitant and I felt like an asshole for making him uncertain of where he stood with me.

"I don't really know, but you've never let me down in my life, and I would never be able to live with myself if something happened to you and we left things the way they were. I owe you everything I have and everything that I am. I'm not going to let you fight this alone."

He cringed a little and looked away. The goatee that surrounded his mouth curled down on the sides and I felt my stomach dip.

"There isn't a fight anymore, Nash. The cancer has officially had a TKO on my system. It's metastasized, it's moved into my lymph nodes. Not much we can do but wait it out."

I gulped and felt moisture start to burn at the back of my eyes. I pulled the brim of my hat down lower over my forehead and blinked hard to keep the emotion in check.

"What about chemo, or radiation . . . hell, what about a voodoo ceremony? No options?"

He shook his head, and while I felt like he was giving me the worst news in the world, Phil looked like he had had plenty of time to come to terms with his fate and the lack of satisfying answers.

"I know this all new to you, and that you haven't had enough time to really come to terms with the lot of it, but I've been sick for a while and this isn't my first go-around. The time I had with you, with the rest of the crew, it was a blessing."

I felt anger start to coil back up in my gut and I had to concentrate on breathing in and out to stop from lashing out.

"You were sick before?"

He made a noise of affirmation and reached a shaky hand out for a glass of water. I walked around the side of the bed so I could hand it to him. Our matching gazes locked and I had to swallow back all the sour-tasting feelings this conversation was leaving in my mouth.

"Yeah. Same thing. Right before I bought the shop. It was a tumor in one lung and I had surgery to cut it out and then had to do treatment for a year afterward. It was one of the main reasons I was so eager to let you and Rule apprentice under me. There is a lot of crap work out there, people don't take the art, the work behind tattooing, seriously. I knew if I taught you boys the right way to do it, made you respect the skill and craft inside and out, if anything happened to me my legacy would be left in good hands. I beat it that time around, thought maybe I could beat it again."

"Why didn't you quit smoking?"

"Because quitting is hard. Because I thought I was invincible. I don't know, Nash. There isn't a good reason. I wish I had quit, and I hope you will. There is absolutely no reason for you to tempt fate."

I opened my mouth to say something else but got sidetracked when the door swung open and Rule walked in.

"All good in here?"

"Working on it, kiddo. Come in here really quick, I want to talk to both of you about something."

Rule shut the door and made his way to the opposite side of the hospital bed. Phil opened his mouth, and before he could start speaking broke off into an awful fit of coughing. It hurt me to watch the way the hacking cough moved his frail body. It took him a few minutes to catch his breath and Rule and I shared a concerned look over the bed.

"Damn, that hurt." He cleared his throat and shifted his gaze back and forth between the two of us. "I'm signing the shop over to you boys. We own the location outright, so the deed to the property is going in Nash's name. You two have been an unstoppable team since you were old enough to start giving me gray hair, you're also the best artists in this town. You both put the Marked on the map, gave it a style and a name that I never could. You made it yours and I think the two of you as business partners have a lot to offer this city."

Rule and I exchanged stunned looks and then looked at

Phil like he was speaking French and we didn't understand. We could tattoo, we could work with clients, but neither one of us had any clue how to manage or operate a business.

"I was looking for a new location, a second shop in LoDo. I wanted to expand, get our name and work to a different breed of clientele. I found the perfect spot. Signed a five-year lease on it, but now . . . well, now it's going to be up to you guys to get it up and running."

LoDo referred to the lower downtown portion of Denver. It was filled with bars, restaurants, and any kind of lease on a storefront down there had to be astronomical. Rule was the first to ask:

"Uh . . . you do realize we have no idea how to run a shop, right?"

Phil rolled his eyes and snorted at us.

"Of course I know that. I already talked to Cora. She's going to be your business manager. You really think once that baby gets here she's going to want to answer phones and schedule appointments for you boneheads all day? No way, that little spitfire was born to take care of someone, she'll wanna spend as much time with the baby as she can. Give her an office in the new building, she can handle the technical aspects for you, and if she still wants to pierce, she can schedule it on her own time. All you need to do is find a new shop manager and hire the staff for the new location. I have faith in you boys. You'll do me proud."

"You've planned this all out without bothering to ask either of us how we feel about it?" I couldn't keep some of the simmering anger I was feeling from bursting through.

"Nash . . ." Phil's voice dipped down an octave. "I don't

have enough time left to argue. I want my family taken care of, I want what I worked so hard to build to live on. This is the way to achieve both those things. Trust me."

I used to trust him without question . . . recent events made that a little bit harder to do.

"Where are we supposed to find a new shop manager? And how do you expect either of us to vet an entirely new staff of artists? Rule and I don't have any idea how to do that." I sounded a little bit petulant, even to my own ears.

"You'll figure it out. I have a few calls in to some people, some contacts I've made over the years. I'm not going to leave you high and dry."

Both of us had a million and one questions to ask, but Phil broke off in a fit of coughing that didn't seem to have an ending point. He was obviously uncomfortable and in an immeasurable amount of pain. Rule went and found a nurse, who gave Phil something that soon had his eyes drooping closed and his chest moving up and down in a steady rhythm. He faded out and Rule jerked his head toward the door, so I followed him into the hallway.

"Holy shit."

"Yeah, that about covers it." I took my hat off my head and then slammed it back on. "What the fuck are we going to do?"

"Figure it out, I guess. That's what we always do."

"This is insane, all of it."

"No doubt, but we'll just take it one step at a time. We got your back, Nash. Remember that next time you want to play ostrich and bury your head in a bottle of tequila for a week."

I did know it. "Thanks, Rule. Hey, give me just a minute. I wanna try and track down Saint and apologize."

"Apologize for what?"

"At this point I feel like I need to apologize to her for simply existing. Thanks for dragging me out of my stupor."

"Anytime. I'll meet you at the truck. I need to call Shaw. She still hasn't told her parents about the wedding. I don't care one way or the other if they're going to come or not, but I know Casper well enough to know she'll feel guilty if she doesn't at least give them the opportunity to prove they aren't horrible, even though we all know they are."

I snorted because he wasn't kidding and because it still made me laugh when he used his nickname for Shaw. Her super white-blond hair lent itself to the endearment. His words were also a harsh reminder that I wasn't the only one who had seriously screwed family dynamics. The building blocks that made me who I was as a person were chang-ing, being rearranged and placed in different places. I wasn't scared of change, one look at my body and anyone could see that . . . what I was terrified of was having to look back and see that my mom giving me up . . . letting me go, had nothing to do with a broken heart left from a deadbeat dad, but everything to do with me and the fact I wasn't what she wanted. It had to do with the fact that I just wasn't good enough, and even though I had long since made peace with never meeting her standards, it still left a mark.

CHAPTER 4

Saint

THE LITTLE BOY I was working on was just too cute. He was probably only five or six and the gash he had on his head was pretty nasty, but he seemed to be taking it in stride. The mom was a hysterical wreck, like they all tended to be when their babies got hurt, but a couple of stitches later and the advice to get some Tylenol and have the child wear a helmet when he was riding his bike and they were on their way. Of course I had to scrounge up a sucker to give the young patient. I couldn't stand seeing him leave without some kind of smile. Working on little kids was hard, but it always made my insides happy when I could fix them up and send them on their way with their tears dried up.

I snapped off my surgical gloves and nodded at the attending ER doctor as he moved on to the patient in the next room. It was flu season, so we were running at a fairly steady pace, not to mention the colder weather had the homeless population in and out dealing with a variety of weather-related injuries and symptoms. I always had to be on my toes, never knowing what was around the corner, which made my days move quickly and kept my job challenging and interesting. However, when I came around the corner and saw a familiar tall, dark figure leaning against the intake desk, I had to pause and decide if I wanted to turn around and run the other way before he caught sight of me. Nash wasn't a challenge I particularly felt up to dealing with today.

I was irritated at him for acting so selfish while someone close to him was suffering, but more than that, I was furious with myself for giving in and getting involved when I knew better. I was also peeved that even though he rubbed me all kinds of the wrong way, the kiss he had forced on me had had me tossing and turning in bed at night, and if I concentrated hard enough, I could still taste the imprint he had left on my mouth. Ugh . . . why did he have to be so memorable in every possible way?

I narrowed my eyes and straightened my shoulders as I headed toward him. The nurse behind the desk was gazing up at him with a look I could only describe as awed. She was probably a decade older than me, had four kids, and her husband was a cop, but that didn't stop her from falling into the charismatic snare that Nash seemed to so effortlessly weave around the opposite sex.

"What are you doing down here? Your dad is on the top floor." I saw him wince when I used the word *dad,* but I refused to feel bad about it. I had trouble with tripping over words and saying what I really meant with people, but for some reason, none of that was a problem when I spoke to him.

I tossed the paperwork I was holding to the admitting nurse and crossed my arms over my chest as he turned so that he was facing me. The baseball hat he was wearing cast the top part of his face in shadow, but I could see he had dark circles under each eye and that there were fine white lines of tension bracketing each side of his mouth. All in all he looked a lot better than the last time I had seen him. Well, better, minus the fact he was fully clothed, and even though I didn't want to, I could still picture him half naked in vivid detail. I really did want to know what the front part of that massive tattoo was attached to on the backside.

"Do you have a minute?" His voice was kind of gruff but he softened the question with a half grin that made my heart trip.

"Not really. We're pretty hectic today. The weather makes people go nuts, so we're extra busy."

He sighed and shifted so that he could shove his hands in the pockets of his hoodie. Out of the corner of my eye, I noticed the other nurses floating in and around the desk watching us with open curiosity.

"It'll just take a second, please, Saint."

I didn't really think big, tough, tattooed guys used words like *please,* not that it was going to sway me. He had an unwanted effect on me and I knew it was a good idea to keep my distance from him. Just as I was about to refuse, the other nurse behind the desk, the one who was clearly smitten with his handsome face, offered up, "I'll take the next room that just came in. You go ahead and take a breather for five minutes."

I wanted to shift my glare to her, but she was just trying to be helpful, so I bit my lip and tilted my head toward the waiting room. There were more private places in the hospital I could have led him to, but being alone with him made me nervous and anxious.

"Follow me over there."

He nodded and did as I asked. I felt the way his gaze burned into my back, and had to take several calming breaths and make sure I schooled my face into an impassive mask before I turned around to face him again. He sighed and used one broad shoulder to prop himself up against the coffee vending machine I had stopped by. We just stared at each other for a long moment. I was about to throw my hands up and walk away because the silence and his intense gaze gave me anxiety, when his quiet words surprised me.

"Phil's condition is really bad. He told me there isn't anything they can do. He's dying and he just seems to be rolling with it, I don't know how. I should have been here sooner."

His tone was somber and his eyes under the dark bill of his hat had lightened to the shade of lilac. I could see how glassy they were, how much emotion he was trying to swallow down, and it took every ounce of self-control I had not to reach out and touch him, to try and soothe him. He wasn't a wild animal that needed to be gentled . . . even if he kind of emanated that vibe.

"I'm sorry. Stage four is ugly and has a terrible prognosis no matter what kind of cancer it is."

He nodded jerkily and tossed his head back on his neck

so that he was peering down at me from under the brim of his ball cap.

"I'm sorry about the other night. I was really drunk, my shit was all over the place, and I swear I'm not usually that kind of guy. It was very nice of you to come over and check on me, and I acted like a dipshit. I just wanted to apologize, to tell you thanks."

I was dumbfounded. That wasn't what I was expecting from him, so I just stared up at him like a moron. He must have taken my silence as a rebuff because he pulled his hat off and scraped one his hands roughly over the top of his shaved head. His dark eyebrows dipped down low over those fabulous eyes and his nostrils flared out a little. With that piercing he had in the center of his nose, it kind of made him look like an angry bull.

"Cut me some slack here, Saint. My life went sideways and this shit has been hard to deal with. I know you don't like me, so it was extra nice of you to swing by. What I don't know is *why* you don't like me."

I jolted back and dropped my defensive stance. Sure, I had my reasons for being standoffish and keeping my distance from him, but I had never meant to make my discomfort and unease around him totally palpable to others, especially to him. The last thing I wanted was to relive that moment, either of them. There was no way I was ever going to tell him that his dismissal, his harsh words, had forever changed me, forever changed how I looked at the opposite sex. It was humiliating and obviously way more memorable to me than it was to anyone else. If he had no recollection of it, I wasn't going to remind him. He gave his head a shake and put his hat back on his head. He pushed off the vending machine and shrugged the wide expanse of his shoulders.

"All righty, then. I'll steer clear of the ER if I can avoid it because clearly I make you really uncomfortable. I just wanted you to know that I appreciated you reaching out when obviously you would rather poke your own eye out with a dull spoon. You're a really nice girl, Saint. I've always thought you were."

He pulled the hood of his sweatshirt up over his hat and turned around and walked away from me. Once he was out of sight, I had to put a hand over my pounding heart inside my chest and concentrate on not hyperventilating. He always thought I was nice? Then how could he have encouraged me, urged me to go out of my comfort zone, and then act as though I didn't exist? How could he kiss another girl right in front of me when I thought he was there for me? How could he say those hateful things that made me feel ugly and worthless to this day? Pretty boys shouldn't try to hurt nice girls . . . at least in a perfect world they shouldn't.

I didn't get any more time to dwell on it because one of the nurses came flying around the corner frantically looking for me.

"Crash on the interstate. Four cars involved, multiple injuries coming in. They need at least four rooms prepped, if not more. The ambulances are three minutes out, so it's all hands on deck."

I didn't have time to worry anymore about Nash or the past or how off balanced any time I was face-to-face with him made me. I shoved it all aside and settled firmly into the role I was most comfortable in. Here I had no questions, no doubts, I wasn't shy or hesitant, I was confident and secure. I just went to work and did what I did best . . . helped other people.

IT WAS A LONG and grueling shift. I had to stay late because after we had the accident victims taken care of, we had a fire, another accident, and not one, but two gunshot wounds. It was hectic and chaotic, and I appreciated that it gave me the chance to push aside all my emotions from my recent run-ins with Nash and categorize them as trivial and fleeting.

I was walking out, dragging my feet and unwinding my long hair from the tight bun on the top of my head, when I ran into the only person outside of my sister who I considered a friend here in Denver. Sunshine Parker was the assistant nursing director, my boss, and probably the most honest and forthright person I had ever met. She was just a tiny little thing, part Filipino, with jet-black hair and a smile that went on for days. She had made the transition to this emergency unit bearable considering all my weird social hang-ups that often made settling into a new environment challenging. She was a few years older than me, totally dedicated to her career and to helping people in need. I so wanted to follow in her footsteps. She was just like me, only she had no problems talking to people or interacting like a normal person. She also wasn't struck dumb by simple conversation.

"Hey you. Rough day?"

I was rubbing my fingers hard into my scalp where my hair had been trapped, and had to admit I was exhausted. Today I'd seen an excessive amount of blood and guts, even for an ER, and my short conversation with Nash had worn me out. I felt awful for him and what he was going through, but it also grated on my nerves that I cared at all one way or the other. I wanted to be immune to him. Only that didn't seem to be an option my hormones were allowing.

"I've had better. It was a busy one."

She tossed her blanket of shiny hair over her shoulder and cocked her head at me.

"You are an amazing nurse, Saint."

Those kind of compliments I could take. I grinned at her and pulled out my phone as it started to ring. The display showed my sister's face, so I silenced the call and shoved the phone in my pocket. I loved Faith, hard, but lately the only time she called me was when something was up with our parents, more specifically our mom, and the drama could wait for a second.

"Thanks, Sunny. That's always nice to hear, and coming from you it means a lot."

She grinned at me and put a hand on my shoulder, which had to look comical because she was so much shorter than me.

"Right. So believe me when I tell you that you need to find more in your life than this ER, or any ER. This is a job, a career, and yes, it's an important one, one that requires dedication and sacrifice, but it does not require that you lose yourself in it. You're a lovely, brilliant woman who has a bright future ahead of her. I see a lot of similarities between the two of us. Believe me when I say none of this means anything if you don't have anything else."

I made a confused face at her and shifted my weight so that she had to drop her hand off my shoulder.

"What brought that on, Sunny?"

She gave a little laugh and flipped her long hair over her shoulder again.

"I heard a rumor Dr. Bennet asked you out for drinks the other night, and you turned him down cold. Why would you do that? He's gorgeous, and you have work in common, so I know you would have things to talk about. Why didn't you even consider it? It just makes me worry about you. You've been here for almost two years, and you never socialize with us, never open up. I like you. I want you to be living the best life possible."

Dr. Bennet was the hospital's catch. He was twenty-eight, built like a fitness model, and had wavy black hair and dreamy green eyes that made most of the nurses and any other female whose path he crossed turn to mush. He was a total lothario, but a seemingly nice guy, and had been hinting around for the last six months that he would like to get to know me better outside of work. Generally, I brushed the attention off. I wasn't the type of girl doctors wanted to date, and there was no way I was in the market for an office hookup—not when I could hardly act normal as it was. But he had flat-out asked me on a date on Thanksgiving. Instead of responding, or trying to stumble my way through a mumbled excuse, I'd rushed off the moment the Flight for Life info had come in bearing Phil Donovan's name. I had seen the information on the chart, and I had the single-minded need to find Nash and see what was going on with him. I hadn't exactly turned the doctor down, but whatever draw Nash still had was just more powerful than getting to know the handsome doctor better.

"Come on, Sunny. I don't really think I'm Bennet's type and I don't go out because I don't really have time. I work, and you know how crazy things have been with my mom. I do live a good life."

"A good life is not the same thing as a fulfilled life, Saint. If the man is asking you out, then I would say you are most definitely his type. You need to buy a new mirror, one that accurately shows you what everyone else sees when they look at you. I'll never understand how you can't see that you're pretty much every man's type."

I wanted to tell her she was wrong, I did see what everyone else saw, but no amount of spectacular cleavage, a nice hourglass figure, and pretty hair could overcome the fact I had a hard time connecting with people, that trusting someone enough to let go and lighten up was nearly impossible for me, or the fact that trying to make small talk and just act like a typical girl was almost an insurmountable task for me. I was always so worried about saying or doing the wrong thing. I was saved from leveling more excuses, more justification at her, by my phone going off again. I could practically see my sister's frustrated face on the other end of the call.

"I have to take this, Sunny, but seriously, thank you for looking out for me."

"Sure thing, my friend. Someone has to . . . you're too busy caring for everyone else to care for yourself."

As if to prove her point, as soon as I cleared the sliding glass doors at the entrance of the hospital, Faith's voice rang shrill in my ear.

"Are you ignoring my calls?"

Faith and I were close. Since we were only a year apart, we had gone through school together until she graduated. Going away to college on the West Coast had been necessary for me, but it had also been hard to leave her behind. Now she was married to her college sweetheart. They had four kids under the age of seven and were expecting a fifth. She was the primary reason I had come back to Denver even though I loved the beach, missed the hospital and staff from my postgrad job in California, and had a really hard time returning to the town that reminded me of my younger self every day.

"No. I had to work late and got caught up talking to my boss on the way out. What's up?"

I heard her sigh as one of the kids screamed in the background.

"Did you talk to Mom this week?"

Considering my week had been crazy and spent alternately punishing and berating myself over Nash, no, my mom has not been on my radar.

"No. I was busy. Why, did something happen to her?"

My parents had been married for over thirty years, twenty-five of them happily. At some point, while I was gone and Faith was starting a family, my dad had decided that being home alone with my mother was no fun. Unbeknownst to any of us, he had started seeing his much-younger dental assistant who worked with him at his practice. The marriage had struggled on until my mom couldn't take the infidelity and insult anymore. As a result, a seriously contentious and ugly divorce started two years ago. It was drawn out, filled with hate and bickering, and had turned my parents not only against each other, but practically into strangers to Faith and me. That was the other reason I came home. I wanted my mom back.

My mom wanted us to have nothing to do with my dad. She was angry, irrational, and all her focus had been on Faith and the kids. It was driving my sister bananas, and after one too many teary and desperate phone calls, I had applied at Denver Health Medical Center and had come home to help out and try and minimize the damage. My mom was on the brink of a meltdown. I could see it coming like speeding lights at the other end of the tunnel, but there didn't seem to be anything I could do to prevent it. She was self-medicating, taking pills and drinking her weight in wine to try and deal with the hurt. It sucked for all of us, because even though my dad's actions hurt us all, it was impossible just to cut him entirely out of our lives, and that drove my mom crazy.

"Yes, something happened. One of the neighbors called me to let me know that the fire department was out at the house. Apparently, she went to the backyard and put all the old family photos in the barbecue and decided to burn them."

I groaned and made my way to the parking lot where my car was.

"Seriously?"

Faith exhaled and I could hear how tired she was. "Yeah.

The fire got out of control because of the wind and the amount of lighter fluid she used. It caught part of the back-yard on fire. I guess it wouldn't have been a huge deal if Mom had reacted, tried to put water on it or something, but the neighbor said she just stood there and watched it burn while laughing like a lunatic until the fire department arrived. She could have burned the entire neighborhood down. The homeowners' association isn't happy."

She hollered something at one of the kids and muttered something at her husband while I got in the car and turned on the engine.

"She's going off the deep end, Saint, and I don't know how to stop it. She's going to end up in a mental ward or in jail if we don't figure something out. She's gone from a hand-ful to a menace. What if she tries to hurt herself?"

I had to crank the radio off when a Band of Skulls song came blasting out as the car started. I turned up the heat and tapped my fingers on the steering wheel.

"I'm off on Thursday. I'll go and talk to her."

"Oh, Saint, don't. It just makes both of you upset. I just needed to vent to someone. I'm so tired of both of them."

"This is so sad, Faith. Someone needs to try and talk some sense into her. So she got dumped, it's not the end of the world. I know she took Dad's cheating really hard, and that she is having a hell of a time with the new girlfriend, but she really needs to stop it and move on. We did." I think it had been easier for me because I never really had any expec-tations of a man ever being able to be faithful to one woman.

Faith snorted and I heard the connection rustle as she shifted the phone from one shoulder to another.

"Says the girl who let one mean boy spoil her on love for the last eight years. Face it, Saint, the women in this family do not deal well with heartache."

I must have made an involuntary noise because her voice got sharp when she asked, "Did you see him again?"

I blew a breath out between my teeth and closed my eyes and let my head flop back on the seat. I never should have mentioned running into Nash when he came to pick up Rome after that bar fight a few months ago. All I wanted to do was go home, take a hot shower, and wash this day down the drain.

"He has a family member in the oncology unit at the hospital. I've run into him a couple times."

She made a growling noise in the back of her throat that had me chuckling at the protective gesture.

"Did you tell him to go to hell?"

Faith had long thought that I needed to tell Nash off, tell him how horrible his careless words had felt, and leave the damage he had done firmly at his door. She thought he was a thorn in my side that needed to just be yanked out quick and clean.

"No. I pretty much just turn into a mime around him. I just gape at him and stare at him awkwardly until he gets uncomfortable and goes away."

She laughed a little and I heard her husband ask her a question.

"It really is too bad he didn't gain a bunch of weight or come down with some weird flesh-eating disease that made him hideous to look at."

I drew a heart on the fog in the window with my index finger.

"No. He still looks really good, better than he did in high school, just a lot more tattooed . . . and you know, built." He was ridiculously handsome, and those eyes . . . God, those eyes were made to drop panties.

"That sucks and you shouldn't be noticing that. You should be telling him to eat shit and die. Stay away from him, Saint. For your own good. Look, I have to go. Justin needs me to watch the kids while he finishes dinner."

"I'll give you a ring after I talk to Mom."

"Ugh, all right. I still think that sounds like a disaster waiting to happen." Her confidence was overwhelming, but I needed to make sure my mother hadn't really gone too far over the edge in her heartbreak.

"Probably, but it has to be done. Kiss the kids for me."

"I will. Seriously, Saint, steer clear of Nash Donovan. I don't think your heart ever mended from the first time he stomped on it."

I told her good-bye and tossed the cell on the passenger seat next to me.

She was right. My heart had never been the same after everything he had put it through. Even if he hadn't known I had feelings for him, even if he had come across as a nice guy for a few fleeting encounters, the way he had blindly destroyed all that was just unforgivable, even now.

Once I had gone off to college and got out on my own, things had started to change for me. The healthy California lifestyle changed my physical appearance, and the fact that no one out there knew who I was, didn't know I was a nerd with no friends, made talking to people easier. It also made handling attention from boys not exactly easy, but manageable, and as such I started to date casually. Some of the guys I liked more than others, some I loosened up enough with to let them get past first base and even second, but it wasn't until I took my first job at a hospital in Los Angeles and met a male nurse named Derek that I was comfortable enough, trusted someone enough, to actually go to bed with him.

We had dated for three months, he was nice, had the same passion for the medical and health-related field and helping others that I did, and he was really, really cute. He seemed to like me, like a lot. He told me over and over that he thought I was funny, smart, pretty, and fun to be around, and he never pushed me. Things had progressed naturally . . . one thing led to another, and we ended up in bed together. That was where the one and only relationship I had ever attempted to have fell apart. The idea of being naked, stripped down and exposed to anyone, terrified me. The thought of being judged and found lacking had me breaking out in hives and into a cold sweat. There was nothing romantic or sexy about a girl struggling through sex, crying all over you, and bolting for the door as soon as it was over.

But Derek had seemed like a wonderful guy and wanted to stay with me, wanted to work on it, and eventually wore me down to the point that I had agreed to give the entire relationship another try. Only sex never worked the way I wanted it to, really never went the way he wanted it to, and it wasn't long before I found him in the arms of another one of the nurses on our rotation. Of course she wasn't crying and forcing her way through sex when I walked in on them at his apartment. The betrayal had stung and it had completely reinforced that I couldn't really trust a guy, that they would always pick a sure bet over a girl with hang-ups and insecurities any day. Besides, Derek had always been way more into me than I was into him, and frankly, having an excuse to walk away when he seemed so nice and caring was actually a relief. It was exhausting trying to force it, to try and pretend like sex was getting better and more enjoyable . . . I didn't blame him for wanting to take a girl that behaved normally to bed.

Moving forward, there had been a guy or two along the way who I had been interested enough in to try it out again with, thinking a one-night stand would be less pressure. I thought that if the guy didn't know me, didn't know how I worked, maybe I could keep the irrational fear of rejection and ugly judgment at bay. It never worked. I always felt sick and just wanted it to be over with, so after the second time I was called a frigid tease, I decided to stop trying to make something happen. I stopped thinking ordinary boy-girl stuff was in my future.

I didn't blame Nash and what he had done entirely for all of my hang-ups. A lot of them were bred into me by simply being me. I was the odd one, the one that didn't really fit. Faith was tall like I was, she also sported bright red hair, but hers was manageable and I don't think she ever had a zit in her life. She was cheerful and popular, played volleyball, and was on all kinds of committees and in clubs. She was the perfect mix of both my parents and somehow still managed to be a sweet and delightful girl. No one seemed to know what to do with me, even at home, where I knew I was loved unconditionally. Even with that, in an effort to help, my parents put me on diet after diet, dragged me to dermatologist after dermatologist, and enrolled me in activity after activity, all of which just proved to be waste of money. I knew their intentions were good, that they wanted me to come out of my shell and live a full life, but all they succeeded in doing was making me feel inferior and awkward in my own skin.

Of course none of my issues had been helped when right about the time Derek had proved to me that men were not to be trusted, my dad had decided that he was bored with my mom and that he wanted to trade her in for a newer model. It didn't matter that we were a loving, caring, rock-solid family unit that helped and supported each other. No, what mattered was a pair of perky boobs and a toothy smile that made him feel ten years younger. He didn't think twice about breaking our family apart, and I was left with a bone-deep understanding that men always picked the easy choice. If you put a pretty girl, someone that was obtainable and glossy in front of them, their penis was ultimately going to make a choice for them, and that sucked.

Even though I knew he wasn't for me, I had built an extravagant fantasy around who I thought Nash was back in the day. I liked that he was into art, thought the allure of him painting graffiti and being into tattoos and piercings was dangerous and cool. Most teenage girls did. I thought he was different, thought the way he interacted with me at our lockers made him above the way the rest of the typical teen-age boys in our school treated me. When I found out how wrong I was, it had shattered me and just dug the pit where my sense of self and all shattered pieces of confidence had fallen even deeper. It had taken becoming a nurse, finding a greater purpose, to enable me to go into that deep, dark hole and get all those fragments of myself out. I wasn't entirely whole, but I was a far sight better off than I had been as a teenager.

Faith was right. Ford women didn't deal well with heart-ache, and I was loath to admit that one drunken kiss from Nash had more of an effect on me, got more of a response out of me, than all three months of the gentle wooing Derek had offered me. I was shrewd enough to know that wasn't good, and I needed to take Faith's stern warning and steer clear of him. Nash Donovan wasn't good for my sense of self or good for keeping my life in the neat and orderly, straight-forward way it was running now.

CHAPTER 5

Nash

I WAS RUNNING ON empty and getting increasingly short-tempered. Instead of working noon to seven, I was having to go in at nine and stay until eight or later to make up for all the people I had screwed over by skipping their appointments in the midst of my mental breakdown the previous week. My appointment book was always pretty full, so trying to reschedule an entire week's worth of work wasn't just a nightmare for me, but also had Cora ready to choke me.

I was also trying to spend each lunch break visiting Phil, which meant there wasn't a moment of downtime in my entire day. He wasn't doing so great. His lungs had water in them and one of the pain medications they had him on wasn't agreeing with his stomach, so he was having a hard time keeping anything down. It was hard to see him like that, like he was just wasting away right before my eyes. Seeing him fading away from me had hundreds of questions rattling around in my mind. I really wanted to pin him down and get the story from him. The shock had worn off some, and now I wanted answers. I wasn't scared of his response anymore. There was no way Phil was ashamed or unhappy that I was of his blood.

I could've just hounded my mom until she gave the details up, but dealing with her was always a nightmare and I didn't know that she could be bothered to tell the truth. Cora mentioned that her dad seemed to be privy to the insider information and she was totally open to prying the story out of him if I wanted. Her dad and Phil had been enlisted in the Navy together years ago and had maintained a tight bond over the years.

I told her to hold off because I needed to give the people who'd been involved, who'd let me live a lie for so long, the right to explain their decisions. However, if Phil didn't decide to stop stonewalling me soon, I was going to take her up on the offer and not feel one ounce of guilt over it.

I was the only one in the shop. I had to finish a zombie Hello Kitty tattoo on a girl's leg. I was so over zombies. Every day it was zombie Elvis, zombie Marilyn, zombie Harry Potter . . . it was all zombies all the time. I mean I always made sure to give one hundred percent attention and dedication to every tattoo I put on a client. I owed them nothing less, considering they would be sporting my artwork forever, but really, I wondered if a lot of the younger clientele who ended up in my chair gave any thought to the passing trends. In five years zombie Elvis wasn't going to seem nearly as cool as it did now, so I had to make sure it was at least an awesomely done tattoo, even if the subject matter wouldn't always be relevant.

I was just finishing up and looking at the clock that sat on the front desk to see if I had time to go to the hospital, and was surprised when the front door to the shop swung open and Rowdy came strolling in. Rowdy St. James looked like a modern-day James Dean. He had a retro-cool vibe that was all his own and he was one of the funniest guys I had ever met. He made the atmosphere in the shop more lighthearted, since Rule could be such a dick and Cora liked to cause drama and be in everybody's business. I lifted an eyebrow at him and finished wrapping the girl and her zombie up.

"What's up, man?"

The client paid and told me how deliriously happy she was with her zombified kitty as I showed her out and locked the door behind her.

"You've been pulling some crazy hours lately, dude."

To make his point even more obvious I yawned and had to crack my neck.

"It's my own fault. I shouldn't have been acting like such a douche canoe last week."

"That was some heavy shit to deal with."

"Yeah, but I'm a grown-ass man. I was acting like a baby."

"No one blames you."

No they didn't, but they should have. It took Saint showing up and telling me to pull my head out of my ass to see beyond my own churning feelings and Rule strong-arming me into acting right.

"What are you doing here so late?" I asked as I started to straighten my station up.

"I was looking for you. I stopped at the hospital to see Phil and he mentioned the new shop. That's pretty cool."

"Yeah. I have no idea what I'm supposed to do about it, though."

He chuckled and leaned on the front desk while I wiped things down with strong antiseptic.

"Well, I don't know shit about hiring a new staff, and thinking you're going to find someone to replace Cora is a pipe dream. That mold didn't just break, it got shattered into a million pieces on the floor. The world couldn't handle more than one of her."

I laughed because he was right, and stood up so I could crack my back. I sounded like I was falling apart.

"True."

"I know a guy, he does custom renovations and stuff like that. He's a good dude, one of my clients actually. I just wanted to let you know I had a name when it comes to getting the place ready to be turned into a tattoo shop."

"Who is it?"

"Zeb Fuller."

I had heard the name before. Zeb was a fellow car guy. He had an old International that he took to the same mechanic I used whenever the beast had something wrong with it I couldn't handle on my own.

"Cool. I'll keep him in mind. I haven't even made it down there yet. Between trying to catch up here and spending time with Phil, I'm just running in circles."

Not to mention, even though I knew she wanted me to steer clear of her, I was still silently searching for Saint every time I stepped inside the hospital doors. So far I hadn't had any luck, but that didn't stop me from looking for her.

"Yeah, I've noticed that, and Rule is all in super-groom mode. Oh, how things have changed around this place in the last few years. I remember when we were all about a good time and a few cold ones."

"Hey, I still am." My argument was halfhearted at best. I was too tired for a good time.

He laughed at me and rolled his ocean-colored eyes.

"No way, Nash. Our entire crew is getting married and having babies, we're all growing up and settling down."

Rowdy was the youngest of our band of brothers, so it was funny hearing this coming from him. I hit the lights and pulled a black beanie on over my shaved head.

"Had to happen sometime, I guess, but marriage and babies . . ." I made a face. "Not for me."

"We'll see, brother. We'll see. Honestly, none of that was really why I tracked you down. I have an idea I want to run by you for the new shop."

Rowdy was an interesting guy. He was funny, the jokester of the group, but he also had a lot going on under the surface. I think that's why he and Jet were so tight, there was so much more going on there than most people took at face value. He was way more into the art of what we did for a living than the rest of us were. I think underneath his tremendous hair, perfectly groomed chops, and jovial persona lurked the soul of a truly artistic man. I appreciated it, and him, so if he had an idea, I was more than willing to give it a chance. Plus, it had to matter a lot to him if he was approaching me after everyone else had cleared out for the day.

"Shoot."

I was a little surprised to see he looked a bit nervous. There was a little flush of pink behind that big-ass tattoo of an anchor he rocked on the side of his neck.

"Cora mentioned there was an empty space on the top floor of the new space that had offices and stuff. I think you should turn it into a store. Keep the tattoo shop and the piercing stuff downstairs, but upstairs you should consider selling stuff . . . like our own brand. More than just T-shirts and shit like we do now. I also think it might be a profitable idea to showcase some original art by the artists. Like Rule did that mural in the man cave for those rich guys and the way you did the back of that restaurant in graffiti on Broadway. People would buy it, and in that location you guys could charge an arm and a leg for it."

I could only stare at him. He must have taken my stunned surprise the wrong way because he shrugged and lifted a tattooed hand to rub the back of his neck.

"Or not. It was just an idea."

I blinked and reached out to shove him in the center of his chest with my palm.

"A fucking brilliant idea. Goddamn, dude, Phil should have left you in charge of this new project. I had no idea you were so business savvy."

We walked out the front door and entered into the cold Colorado air. The chill sucked the breath out of my lungs and made me shiver inside my hoodie.

"I just watched what Rome and Asa did with that dive of a bar they ended up running and I thought we should try and up our game some as well. I love this place, love what we do, so why not take it to the next level?"

"That means whoever we hire to manage these shops in place of Cora is going to have to be a perfect fit. You don't happen to know anyone that can fill that role, do ya?"

I automatically patted the pocket of my hoodie looking for a smoke and almost threw a fit when I came up empty. Quitting sucked and I sucked at quitting, but I was trying hard, and every time I saw Phil in that bed, it made it a little bit easier.

Rowdy shook his blond head and pulled the collar of his quilted flannel up around his neck.

"Nope, but you'll find someone. You have great instincts about people and Rule is like the gatekeeper from hell, not to mention whoever you hire has to pass the Cora test. You need to give yourself some credit, Nash. This is Phil's life, his legacy . . . of course you're the only one he would trust with it. We're family, he wanted you to carry on the tradition and keep this place a home. You've got this, brother. Have some faith."

I just grunted and turned to walk to where the Charger was parked. Light flurries of snow were starting to blanket the ground.

I glanced at him when he asked, "Hey, I heard your new neighbor is a solid ten. What's up with that?"

I lifted a shoulder and let it fall. What was up with that was that her hair was the wrong color of red and her eyes were dark, not a lulling, gentle gray.

"Too busy, too jacked up over Phil . . . I dunno. Swing by for a beer and you can introduce yourself."

He didn't respond, just gave me a look. A look that clearly stated if I wasn't trying to actively get in the hot neighbor's pants, something else was going on. Luckily it was freezing, so neither one of us wanted to hang out on the sidewalk, and I got to cleanly escape without floundering around for a weak excuse as to my real reasons for not throwing all my considerable game at the hottie across the hall.

When I got to the hospital, it was almost nine. I tried to park close so I didn't have to trek to the front door and freeze my balls off on the way, but fate wasn't working for me and it took me five minutes to walk around the side of the complex to the front doors after finally finding a spot. I was muttering under my breath about needing a cigarette and rubbing my hands together to keep them warm when I came to a stumbling halt as I cleared the corner of the main building.

Saint was pacing back and forth on the sidewalk. The lights from the building were casting her in an ethereal and glinting light, like the heavens above were illuminating her with their glow, making each snowflake trapped in her amazing hair glimmer. She wasn't just *called* Saint . . . it was like some unknown force was trying to push me into seeing her as so much more. Her normally restrained hair was all over the place, rioting around her pale face like fire and copper. Snowflakes were gathering in the loose strands but she didn't seem to notice. She was dressed in her scrubs, no coat or gloves, and the cold didn't seem to have any effect on her as she meandered back and forth. She was moving frantically, her arms crossed tightly around her chest like she was trying to give herself a bear hug.

I knew she didn't want to have anything to do with me, that she wanted to pretend I didn't exist, but I couldn't just walk by her without asking her what was wrong, without seeing if she was okay. I wasn't that kind of person, and more importantly, it actually mattered to me why she was out here when she was obviously upset, and why she didn't have a coat or anything on when it was so cold out.

"Saint?"

I called her name softly and moved a little closer. When she turned around I could see the frozen tracks of tears on her cheeks and could practically feel the coiled tension coming off her body. I was surprised the snow that was landing on her face and clinging to her eyelashes didn't melt right off with all the heat and energy she was throwing off.

"Are you all right?"

She blinked at me like she didn't recognize me, and I thought maybe it was the hat covering my head. She opened her mouth and then let it snap close again like words just wouldn't come out. Her arms fell to her sides and she just stared at me, not saying anything or moving for a long moment. I was about to apologize for bothering her, yet again, when she suddenly moved toward me . . . she lurched like she had come untethered from the earth. I had no idea what she was doing, but the expression on her face was intent and focused, so I braced for her to smack me across the face or put a knee in my balls. With this girl I just never knew which way the tide was going to turn.

I wasn't prepared for her to throw herself against my chest. I was so startled I actually had to take a step back as I wrapped my arms around her waist. She put her hands up around my shoulders and curled her freezing-cold fingers under the collar of my hoodie and dug her fingers into the back of my neck. Her breasts smashed into my chest and her long hair coiled around my fingers where I was holding on to her lower back. It was silky and cool, like touching frost on a pane of glass. I was dumbfounded, trying to figure out what she was doing, when she slammed her mouth across mine. Good thing she was tall and didn't have to reach very far, because if I had been holding her up, there was a good chance I might have dropped her right back to the ground in surprise.

Her mouth was hot, frantic, wild, and desperate. She tasted like winter and some kind of tangy citrus. I knew this because she didn't hesitate to roll her tongue into my startled mouth. I had been kissed by a lot of girls, probably too many over the years, and not one of them sent me from comfortable to feeling like my boxers were ten sizes too small in a fraction of a second the way Saint did. It wasn't even that it was a great kiss. There was something behind it, something with more edge, more meaning than any other kiss I could remember. The way her soft lips felt pressed tightly against mine, the way she used her teeth with just enough bite, the way her short nails dug into the tendons on either side of my neck turned me inside out.

If we hadn't been standing outside getting snowed on, hadn't been standing in the middle of a sidewalk, I would have pushed her against a wall . . . hell, I would've found a soft spot on the ground and let her work out whatever was hounding her in the sexiest, nastiest way possible. If she needed a physical release to get her emotions out, I would be only too happy to volunteer my time and my body. I had a sinking suspicion if I was ever lucky enough to get her naked, I would never let her put on clothes around me again.

She slid her hands around to the front of my face and grabbed both of my cheeks. She started to shiver, and when she pulled back I was stuck in the rolling thunderstorm that was her gaze. I moved one hand up and wiped away a single, crystal tear that was stuck on her eyelash with my knuckle. She let out a shuddering sigh and closed her eyes.

"I'm sorry. I didn't mean to attack you with my mouth." She sounded embarrassed and sad at the same time.

I burst out laughing and took a step back as she let her hands fall. Some of her awareness must have come back because she started to shake. I sighed and pulled the zipper on my hoodie down so that I could hand it over to her. She looked at me silently for a second and then took it.

"Saint, you can attack me with any part of you at any given moment of any day. I will not complain . . . ever."

She laughed a little shakily.

"Thanks."

"Do you wanna talk about what has you out in the snow pacing back and forth?"

It was a long shot. She never seemed to really want to talk to me, but she still looked so haunted, I had to ask.

She shook her head and shoved her hands through her

hair. Some of the red strands floated up like a halo around her head.

"It's been busy all week. The weather makes things insane and it's flu season. I can typically handle everything that comes through the door. Sometimes it can get overwhelming and breaks my heart, but I do my job and can typically wait until I get home to process it all or fall apart."

I couldn't even imagine what she had to deal with on a day-to-day basis. Rule's twin brother, Remy, had been brought to this very ER when he had crashed his car on the interstate in a horrific accident. He hadn't made it, and it occurred to me that was something she had to see all the time.

"Today a teenage girl was rushed in. Her parents found her overdosed in the bathroom. She was just a baby, really, had her entire life in front of her, but she swallowed an entire bottle of pills because kids at her school were picking on her, bullying her. They were being mean to her, calling her awful names on the Internet, and she just couldn't take it anymore."

I saw her bottom lip quiver before she trapped it between her teeth. Her eyes lifted back up to mine and the gray had turned slate. I wondered if she was seeing her teenage self in that patient, and I felt a twinge of remorse that I hadn't paid more attention to her back then.

"I see death and tragedy all the time, and nothing makes it worse than when it's totally senseless. All she needed was some niceness, some basic human kindness, and she wouldn't be on her way to the morgue and her parents wouldn't be devastated. It's heartbreaking and so senseless."

She pulled her hands into the sleeves of my hoodie and looked up at me. "And I have to go talk to my mom tomorrow, which is the equivalent of getting a hundred root canals at one time. This day was vicious and I think I went a little off the rails for a second."

It was my turn to shiver.

"I'm sorry, Saint. That sounds awful."

She narrowed her eyes at me and tilted her head toward the front of building.

"How do you know? Have you ever had anyone make fun of you, been called awful names, had anyone made you feel like you didn't deserve to live just because you weren't the same as everyone else?"

I winced at her harsh tone and tried to put together how she could go from sweet to hostile toward me so quickly. Her train of thought moved liked a scared jackrabbit.

I reached out and grabbed her elbow and spun her around so that she was facing me.

"Look, I don't know what I did or said that makes you think I'm some kind of monster. I do know exactly what that's like, though, Saint. I lived with Phil for most of my childhood because my own mom didn't like me, didn't think I was good enough to keep around. I wasn't like her or her husband, so she didn't want me. She married a guy who loathed me before I was even old enough to question why. I heard it on repeat every day of my childhood, the names, the taunts, the derisions for simply being alive. So that's how I know. Granted, mine didn't come from my peers, but does that make a difference? Hateful actions suck no matter who is delivering them."

Something crossed her pretty face and I noticed that in

true redhead fashion she had a few tiny little freckles that dotted the bridge of her nose. She wrinkled the speckled feature and walked with me to the elevator. I could practically see her trying to pick apart my words as we moved together.

"Visiting hours are over but I'll sneak you in, considering I waylaid you outside."

"Thanks, so what's up with your mom? Why is going to visit her on par with the dentist?"

She made a noise in her throat and leaned against the other side of the elevator. I wanted to hit the panic button and trap us in here together for an hour or two so I could see if I could get her to put her mouth on mine again.

"She's always kind of been a difficult woman, even in the best of times, but now that she and my dad are getting a divorce, she's turned into something else and I long for the days of difficult."

This was the most she'd ever told me about herself.

"How long were they married for?"

"Long enough to decide that they didn't like each other very much anymore."

"That sucks, but isn't that how all marriages end?"

She lifted an eyebrow at me.

"Your mom is still married, and what about Rule? Didn't he propose to his girlfriend right here in the hospital? And Jet Keller got married, didn't he?"

"My mom is obsessed with Grant. She would fall apart if that relationship didn't work out, and that's not a marriage to me. Rule and Shaw are meant to be, and Jet totally married the right girl. I see those unions lasting the test of time, but who knows? People change, and stuff you thought you liked about a person can suddenly bug the crap out of you twenty years in."

It was probably the most honest I had ever been with any girl I was attracted to when it came to my thoughts on relationships and forever. I typically spent time with girls who didn't want to talk about long term or knew that if they did I was out the door.

"So you don't think you'll ever get married or have kids?" She sounded curious but also something more.

I shrugged and reached up to pull my hat off of my head and shove it into my back pocket.

"I doubt it."

She muttered something I didn't catch under her breath and walked with me to the desk. She talked to the night nurse, signed something, and came back over to where I was hovering off to the side.

"You're all set. You can only go in for a half hour, but that's better than nothing."

"I appreciate it."

She cocked her head to the side and blinked those cloudy eyes at me like she was trying to find something to say. I thought she was extra cute when she was all unsure like that.

She gave me a really sad smile and slipped my hoodie off to hand it back to me. I wanted to put it to my face and see if it smelled like oranges now instead of cigarette smoke.

"It's devastating when someone you think you can love ends up disappointing you in the end, so I understand where you are coming from. Thanks, for, well, everything tonight, I guess. I'm actually glad I ran into you."

She was walking away from me. I could never seem to

get a handle on this girl or really understand why I wanted to handle her in the first place. Maybe it was because we were talking about weddings, or maybe it was because I wanted to kiss her and a whole lot more, but I couldn't stop myself from blurting out, "Come to Rule's wedding with me."

She stopped and went absolutely still. She glanced at me over her shoulder and I could see her trying to say no without using the actual word. I lifted an eyebrow at her and gave her a grin.

"It's on Christmas Eve in a week. Don't say no, just think about it." I hooked a thumb at the closed door where Phil was at. "Come find me if you decide you want to give it a shot. It'll be fun . . . well, as fun as a wedding can be when the bride hasn't told her parents she's getting married and the groom is as unpredictable as Rule. Just think about it."

Before she could outright reject the notion, I slipped into Phil's dark room and closed the door behind me. I was surprised he was still awake, but those eyes that were so like mine were wide open and watching me with unmistakable humor.

"The redheaded nurse?"

I grunted and took a seat next to the bed.

"Yeah."

"She's very pretty and a total doll. She stopped by to check on me a few days ago, and when I told her I was bored out of my mind, she showed up with those. I coulda kissed her." He indicated a thick stack of magazines off to the side that had pictures of motorcycles and scantily clad women gracing the covers. Man, she really was sweet. She didn't have to do that for him.

"She's something else for sure. I've never met a chick

who runs so hot and cold. We went to school together when I was younger."

He lifted both his eyebrows and shifted his legs under the covers.

"You think it has something to do with when you were a pain-in-the-ass teenager? You used to run your mouth and not think about it all the time and you had a tendency to act like a little shit when the mood struck. You and Rule both. Maybe the man is paying for the sins of his younger self."

I pondered that and inclined my chin at him.

"You look a little better."

"Better is relative. The pneumonia is on the mend, and they tell me I might make it out of here by the end of the week. I'm going to have to look at hiring someone for home care, though, because the worst is yet to come, and I'm not staying in this hospital surrounded by machines, just waiting for the end to sweep in and take me."

I frowned and folded my hands together and rested my forearms on my knees.

"How can you sound so matter-of-fact about the fact you're dying? It rips my fucking guts out and you talk about it like we're discussing what to have for dinner."

"I've had longer to get used to the idea than you have, son. I'm sorry that I never could find the right words to talk to you about it before now. The first time around, you were just a little kid, and I thought I was invincible. This time, I know none of that holds any water."

That didn't make feel any better, but I guess nothing ever would.

"When are you going to tell me how all this happened? How did no one ever think I needed to know the truth about you and Mom?"

He sighed, which started a round of coughing that had his whole body contorting. I wanted to feel bad for asking but I needed to know.

"That's a long story for another place and time. Really I think you should ask your mother about it."

I threw my big frame back in the chair and glared at him.

"I want the truth, and I doubt she even knows what that looks like."

He clicked his tongue at me and shifted in the bed again. He just looked so frail and so unlike the man I had always wanted to emulate. It scared me.

"We are equally accountable for not telling you sooner. She made some bad choices, decided her future was going to look one way no matter what stood in her path—me, you, and anything else. I was grateful for the time I had with you, and the rest of the boys. Do I wish you had known that you were my kid sooner? Yes, but I also understand why your mother wanted to keep it a secret for as long as she did. I made some bad choices along the way as well, Nash."

"Why did you let her do this us? To me? My childhood was a nightmare until you got involved."

He gave me a look I recognized all too well. I saw it on Rule. I saw it on Jet. I saw it on Rome every time they looked at the women that had captured their hearts forever, so I answered for him.

"You loved her."

He closed his eyes and slumped down on the pillows piled up behind him.

"Love isn't something you can negotiate, Nash. When it happens, it becomes everything."

"Oh, trust me, I know. I've been on the losing end of love my entire life."

"You can't base love on the experience you had growing up. Loving someone you want to make your own has a different feeling, a different power than the love you have for family. It's different and the chains that bind it can be unbreakable." His voice cracked and his eyes slid closed.

He was fading fast, so I got to my feet and walked over so I could clap a hand on his shoulder. It took all my will not flinch when I felt how brittle he was under the black sweater he had on.

"I guess. I just don't know how anyone can love a guy whose own mom tossed him over. That doesn't bode well in my book. If Mom couldn't love me, how is anyone else going to for the long haul?"

He might have had an argument that would've made me feel better but he drifted off to sleep before he could give it to me.

I never considered forever with anyone. I didn't think it was for me, but when I thought about the way Saint's eyes shifted from light gray to pewter, and remembered the way she felt pressed up against me in both my desperation and her own, I was starting to wonder if I needed to reconsider my view on things.

CHAPTER 6

Saint

THE WEATHER HAD GONE from yucky to scary as I navigated the roads into the mountains and toward the upscale suburb of Brookside, where both my parents still lived. Mom kept the big house in the gated community. Dad had moved into a trendy condo closer to the main part of town with his girlfriend. There were miles separating them, but if you asked my mother, the distance between Denver and the moon wasn't enough space to get away from my father and his betrayal. I really did feel bad for her, but at some point she needed to start to heal or she was going to lose more than just her marriage and her sanity. Faith was hanging on by a thread, and me . . . I loved my mom, but I was over it. Men disappointed, it was just the way it was.

I wasn't exactly thrilled with the choices my dad had made. I didn't understand how he could so easily walk away from my mom and leave his family in the lurch, but blame only went so far. I could hate him forever for falling in love with someone else, throw him out of my life indefinitely because of the decisions he had made that had led to my mom acting like a lunatic, but it was more important to me to keep my family together. I just accepted that he was fallible. Faith and I would never welcome the new girlfriend into the fold with open arms, but I forced myself to tolerate her and worked on interacting with my dad in a nonresentful way every time I saw him. I think a little part of me expected nothing less from him just because he was a man and I had this belief that all men would ultimately gravitate toward the shiny, prettier, and his case younger option when it came to thinking with what was in their pants.

I had to go slowly and concentrate, which was harder than usual because I was so emotionally drained. I couldn't get the young girl, the horrible loss from yesterday, out of my mind. I also couldn't stop the endless replay of the way I had thrown myself at Nash from rolling over my eyes every time they drifted shut last night, which led to a sleepless night. Twice now we had shared a kiss in the midst of an emotional upheaval, both times it had made the situation more tolerable, more a shadow than a suffocating fog of bad feelings and hurt. I didn't want to name what that meant, but I couldn't deny that kissing him made me feel restored and set me back on solid ground. The fact he didn't push me away, didn't grill me endlessly about it, forced me to question all the memories I had that reminded me over and over again that I was supposed to think Nash was a heartless jerk.

I'd been seconds away from accepting his invitation to the wedding, even though the idea of spending time around him, around his friends and a bunch of strangers, made me want to hyperventilate. Thank God he had told me to think about it. There was some kind of current dragging and pulling between us that I didn't trust, didn't particularly like, but it was strong, and fighting its momentum was wearing me out, wearing me down. I actually *wanted* to spend time with him.

When he told me about his mom, how he used the words *I know how it feels, Saint* . . . it altered my entire perception of who I thought he was and who he really might be. Hearing that you were fat and ugly, that no one liked you, and that you would never have friends or get a boyfriend sucked coming from kids your own age, but kids could be mean and hopefully they would grow out of it. Being made to feel worthless and unwanted by a parent . . . that had to be devastating and nearly impossible to get over. I couldn't even get my head around it. I didn't want to examine too closely why that made a pang near my heart start to throb in pain or why the idea of him being against marriage and forever with one person made me a little queasy.

By the time I pulled into the driveway of my mom's house, the trip had taken an hour longer than it should have and a full-on snowstorm was working through the mountains. I jogged up to the front door and rang the bell. I did a double take when my mom pulled open the door. It was one in the afternoon, she still had her pajamas on, and she was holding a half-empty wineglass in her hand. As she swayed slightly and glared at me, I didn't believe for one second it was her first glass of the day, and that made my stomach drop.

"What are you doing here, Saint?"

There was no welcome in her tone, so I maneuvered past her and walked into the house. Before the split, she would have pulled me into her arms and hugged the life out of me whether I needed it or not. She would have asked me about work and my dating life. Now she looked irritated that I had crashed her pity party.

"Faith called me. She told me about the fire and I thought I should come and check on you. We're worried about you, Mom." I fought the urge to reach for her drink so I could dump it out.

She scoffed at me and slammed the door shut. I winced when some of the wine in her glass sloshed over her hand.

"You should be worrying about yourself, Saint."

We might not have the kind of mother-daughter relationship where we were the best of friends, but my mom had never purposely lashed out at me in anger before. I reached out and snatched the wineglass out of her hand and stomped to the kitchen, stung and annoyed by both her tone and her attitude.

"You shouldn't be drinking anything alcoholic while you're on so many different medications. This is ridiculous, Mom. You want to push me away by being purposefully nasty and by trying to force Faith to choose between you and Dad. You're making this situation harder on everybody. The stunt with the fire . . ." I shook my head at her. "Is that a desperate cry for attention? Who did you think was going to swoop in and save you if you got arrested for arson? Dad? Well, I hate to break the news to you, but he's moved on and so should you. Faith and I love you, Mom. That should be enough."

She ground her teeth together and glared at me. Her eyes were glassy and she was even more unsteady on her feet than I thought. It sucked to see her this way, but it strengthened the idea that opening yourself up to someone else just to have them hurt you in the end was such an awful idea.

"What do you know about anything, Saint? You've never had love ripped away from you, never even had a man of your own. I feel empty inside."

I sucked in a breath through my teeth and tried to remember that is was the wine and pills talking, but she was pushing the limits of what I was going to tolerate. I was going to tell her in no uncertain terms to knock it the hell off when she suddenly burst into tears and teetered over to the massive island in the center of the kitchen. She curled her hands around a stack of papers I didn't notice before and waved them around in the air between us. I saw a sheen of glossy tears coat her wild eyes.

"I got the final divorce papers in the mail last weekend, and on top of that, your sister let the kids spend the weekend with him and that . . . that woman. How could she do that to me? She knows how I feel about his new girlfriend being around my family. I just lost it. I literally went a little crazy."

She was breathing really hard and looked so jagged and frayed around the edges that I had to walk over and wrap my arm around her too-thin shoulders. I felt an additional pang of alarm. She was shaking really hard and I felt like I could actually touch her sadness. This is what loving someone unconditionally ended you up with. I never wanted to be here.

"That had to be really hard, Mom. And I understand

that you're hurting, but almost burning down the house isn't going to change any of it. There has to be a healthier way for you to deal with what you're feeling because I don't think claiming temporary insanity is going to keep you out of the hot seat for very long."

She peeked out between her fingers at me and I winced at the makeup smeared across her normally pretty face. She looked like a drunken and demented clown. I wanted my mom back, wanted my family to be like it was. Unfortunately, that was no longer an option.

"What should I do, Saint? Pretend like your father doesn't exist even though he lives in the same town and is flaunting his new, younger, prettier girlfriend in my face every chance he gets? You tell me, Ms. Smarty Pants, what should I do that's healthier than what I'm doing now?"

I let her shoulder go and moved back around to the other side of the island. Mostly I needed a little space to avoid wringing her neck. I hated that it was so easy for her to be mean now.

"I don't really know the answer to that, Mom. Maybe you just need some space away from it, away from them."

She snorted and tossed her head back to wipe her cheeks off with the back of her hand. All she succeeded in doing was making a bigger mess. She looked absurd and miserable.

"You ran away when it happened to you, Saint. You didn't come back for holidays or to visit, not for anything. All because you wanted to get away from a boy and hurt feelings. When college was done you took the first job you could find out there when all your family was here. Even when Faith started having all her babies, it wasn't enough to bring you home. Try and tell me all about the healthy ways of dealing with things, Saint, go right ahead."

I blew out a breath and curled my hands into fists on the marble top of the island. That was a low blow. She was on a roll and there was no getting through to her, and if I kept trying to reason with her while she was in this state, there was going to be irreversible damage done to our relationship, and as irritated as I was at her childish behavior, I didn't want that to happen. Part of the reason I was back in Colorado was to work on things with my mom, not to drive us further apart.

"Mom, the holidays are right around the corner. Try and pull it together or no one is going to want to spend time together as a family. I know this had been hard for you, that Dad disappointed you and broke your heart, but life goes on. It's going on two years, something has to give." I was used to my family being a safe zone not a war zone, and the change was horrible.

She groaned and gave me a hard look through her watery eyes. For the last couple of years we had done Christmas Eve with Dad and Christmas Day with her. It seemed to work all right, even if no one was comfortable with Dad's new girlfriend and Mom spent the entire next day lambasting us for spending time with *them*. I wasn't looking forward to a repeat and I doubted Faith was either. A nice family get together just wasn't in the cards, though.

"Try and remember that it should be about family and the kids this year. Look, the roads are bad. I wanted to see you and check in. I'm worried about you for real, Mom, that fire should have been a wake-up call. You need to really evaluate what you are doing to yourself and what that is doing to the rest of the family. I really don't want to have to bail you out of jail, or something even worse."

I gave her one last hug and headed back toward the front door. All I could hope for was that maybe somehow my words had penetrated, that the fact that Faith and I still loved her like crazy would make up for the fact my dad no longer did. Maybe instead of just telling her to get some space, I should try and make it happen. I had plenty of vacation time saved up: maybe I should try and drag her to the Hot Springs for a long weekend or something. I just felt like she needed some kind of clarity to get back to where she was before my dad had devastated her. I got back in the Jetta, which by now had a pretty thick layer of snow coating it, and started the motor to let it warm up. While I was waiting I found a Pixies song I liked on my iPod and called my sister.

It took a few rings for her to answer, and when she did she sounded harried and out of breath.

"How was she?"

I was rubbing my hands together to keep them warm and just grunted a response.

"That bad?"

I sighed heavily and turned on the windshield wipers to clear away the fluffy white blanket covering the windshield.

"She's a mess of pills and wine. She's being mean and hateful. She told me that I don't know anything because I'm a coward and left after high school and didn't home right after college." With Faith, I let the sarcasm get as thick as the snow. "She's lost her mind, but the final divorce papers came, so it's officially over. That's what inspired the bonfire. Honestly, I'm kind of worried about her, but I'm not sure what to do about it."

"Shit."

"Pretty much. Christmas should be fun this year."

There was a really long silence on the other end of the phone that made me frown.

"What's up, Faith?"

She muttered something again and let out a deep sigh. "I'm tired, Saint. I'm pregnant, I have a bunch of little kids that deserve an awesome Christmas for once, and a long-suffering husband that has finally reached his limit of my family drama. Justin and I are taking the kids to Aspen for Christmas. Mom and Dad are just going to have to deal with it. You're welcome to escape with us if you want, but we just rented a tiny cabin and you'll have to take a sleeping bag and bunk on the floor with Owen."

I curled my hands around the steering wheel and tried to settle myself. I couldn't say the news surprised me, but still it nipped at me. Faith was the one person I always relied on, who was always there for me even when I lived half a country away. She deserved a peaceful family holiday away from all the nonsense, but that meant I would be alone . . . because there was no way in hell I was tackling my parents and all their resentment and insanity on my own. No way.

"No, I'll be fine. You guys go and have fun. I'll drop the kids' presents off sometime this weekend so you can take them with you."

"Are you sure? You sound bummed out. You know we would love to have you."

I rubbed my fingers across my forehead and gave a sharp laugh that had no humor in it.

"I guess it just proves it's past time I get a life."

"Oh, Saint . . . come on."

"Seriously, Faith. I'm twenty-five, you're my only friend, the rest of my family is bonkers, and God forbid a guy talks to me, or even worse shows some kind of genuine interest in me. I turn into a mute. I need to get my shit together just as much as Mom does."

"Stop it. You're being too hard on yourself."

"Maybe. Hey, I'll see you this weekend, okay?"

"Are you sure you're all right?"

I wasn't, but that wasn't her problem. Suddenly the idea of being alone on Christmas, the thought of siting in my apartment sad and depressed, overran my usual hesitancy and sense of self-preservation. I was headed back to Denver with a plan, and I wasn't going to back out of it. Now I just needed to get back to the city in one piece because the driving conditions were terrible and the things running around my head had my concentration all over the place when it should be firmly on the road.

Traffic was moving at a snail's pace even with the snowplows out, and it seemed like there was an accident or car out of control every half mile. It took me almost three and a half hours to get back to the city and then another half an hour to get to the hospital because rush-hour traffic was at a standstill. When I finally reached the giant building on the cusp of downtown, I parked and ran inside. I felt kind of breathless, a little out of control, and I had to say it was exhilarating.

I hoped no one would notice that I was there on my day off, or notice that I was operating on a heady mix of panic and adrenaline. Of course I wasn't that lucky. Sunny was walking right across the entrance to the ER and stopped short when she saw me.

"Aren't you off today?"

I shrugged and shifted uneasily. I was a woman on a mission and didn't have time to stop and chitchat. I was worried that if I waited, all my nervous energy would fade and I would rationalize my way out of doing what I was about to do.

"Yeah."

"What are you doing here? Didn't I just tell you that you needed to get a life outside of this place? You're going to run yourself into the ground, Saint. I know you had a difficult time with that case yesterday, but you have to leave that here and not take it home with you."

I gave her a wan smile and tucked some of my long hair back behind my ears. When it was loose it curled and twisted all over the place and tended to be uncontrollable, so I just let it do whatever.

"I'm actually here looking for someone."

She lifted a black eyebrow at me and shifted the paperwork she had in her hands.

"Dr. Bennet? He was talking about you again this week."

I was opening my mouth to tell her no when the person I

was actually looking for came strolling through the door. He had that black wool hat on and dark pea coat over his always-present hoodie. His eyes flickered over me and he gave me a grin. There was just something about him that was so magnetic. He always seemed to be the only thing I could focus on when we were in the same room, and it wasn't just because he was so big and interesting to look at . . . it was something polarizing that came from deep inside of him.

"Hey."

Sunny made a noise in her throat and looked between me and Nash with big eyes.

I didn't give him a greeting back, didn't introduce the two of them, I just blurted out, "Yes, I'll go with you!" In a rush like the words couldn't get off my tongue fast enough.

I sounded like an idiot and I could feel a scalding blush burn up my neck and flood into my face. He lifted his dark eyebrows up but didn't say anything, or ask any questions that would have made me feel more awkward. He just dug his wallet out of his back pocket and handed me a business card. It was covered with bright ink and looked like the graffiti that covered the sides of trains and buildings in town. It was far more interesting and visually captivating than any other business card I had ever seen. It had his name on the front and the name of a tattoo shop. Of course he was a tattoo artist. What other job could he have that let him have yellow and orange flames inked on his scalp? It fit.

"The shop number is the one on the top. My cell is the bottom. Just hit me up and we'll figure it out as we go. They're getting married at the clock tower downtown on Arapahoe. I'm glad, Saint, really glad you decided to go with me."

He didn't draw it out, didn't make me scramble for an explanation or ask why I sounded like a crazy person with the way I accepted. He just gave me a little wink and continued on his way to the elevator. I watched him walk away and curled my hand around the card like it was a lifeline.

Sunny gave me a wide-eyed look and cocked her head to the side.

"So you have a handsome, successful doctor interested in taking you out and you are actively avoiding accepting his invitations out, but a guy that looks like a miscreant comes strolling in and you practically jump out of your skin in your eagerness to go out with him. Wanna explain that to me, Saint?"

I couldn't explain it to her. The desire to not be alone on Christmas outweighed any reservations I had about spending time with Nash. Plus she was my boss; I didn't think it was appropriate to tell her that kissing Nash made my brain turn to mush and being close to him melted the typically frozen barriers I had in place when it came to interacting with the opposite sex.

"He's a tattoo artist, not a miscreant. We went to high school together. Plus he doesn't make me nervous and anxious the way Dr. Bennet does." Oh no, Nash made me nervous and anxious in an entirely different way that had all my bits and pieces reminding me I was a girl and he was a boy.

She clicked her tongue at me. "I think it has more to do with the type of guy you think you can get. It ties back into that whole you not being Bennet's type. Well, you are his type and so much more than you give yourself credit for. You don't have to settle for a guy with a ring through his nose."

I wanted to argue that I liked the ring in his nose, it made his too-pretty face more masculine, but she kept going.

"Promise me, Saint. Promise that if Dr. Bennet asks you out, you'll accept and stop doubting yourself. Please, as your friend, I need you to agree to do it."

I didn't have the heart or the correct words to try and explain to her that Nash was a far larger obstacle to me getting to a place of confidence and self-worth than any gorgeous and successful doctor could ever be. But because I admired her, wanted to keep her favor, I numbly nodded.

"Fine, Sunny, I promise."

She squealed a little and gave me a one-armed hug.

"Great. The other guy looks like all kinds of trouble."

I shook my head and shoved the card Nash had handed me in the front pocket of my jeans. Now I only had the weekend and the first part of next week to not talk myself out of going with him.

"You have no idea."

He did look like trouble, but he also looked interesting and beautiful and I still wanted to know what the rest of that tattoo that covered so much of him looked like. I was telling her good-bye, wishing her luck with the rest of the shift because the roads were awful and cars were all over the place, when Dr. Bennet came around the corner. I saw Sunny's eyes light up and I wanted to kick myself for not leaving five seconds earlier. He walked over to us, all handsome and confident, and I felt a rock of dread settle in my stomach. If he asked me out right in front of Sunny, there was no way I was going to wiggle my way out of it. I had promised.

He really was good-looking. He could easily play the role of handsome physician on any prime-time TV show. I think the thing that took away from his appeal was that he totally knew he was good-looking and acted like that entitled him to things, and to people.

"Well, hello, ladies. Sunny, I need you in room 313B. Saint, are you just leaving?"

I opened my mouth and then closed it. I just blinked at him like an owl for a full minute before Sunny interjected, "It's her day off. I keep telling her that she needs a break from this place. Don't you agree?"

He chuckled and it was deep and pleasing, but it made me wince. What was wrong with me? I cleared my throat.

"I had a few errands to run and this was my last stop. It's nice to see you, Dr. Bennet."

Awesome. That sounded pretty normal and socially acceptable. He laughed again and flashed superstraight, superwhite teeth at me. Everything about him was just blindingly perfect, so why wasn't my heart tripping over itself the way it did when Nash's odd-colored eyes landed on me?

"Andrew, call me Andrew. I would be happy to keep you occupied on your next day off, Saint. When might that be?"

I wanted to groan and go find a gurney or a counter to crawl under. Sunny didn't let me waffle an excuse that I was always working, and it wasn't fair that she was the one that did my schedule so she could tell him with confidence:

"She's off on New Year's Eve since she's working Christmas Day. Right, Saint?"

I knew she was just trying to help, but I was going to strangle her.

"I am, but if you already have something planned, I'm sure we can work out something later on."

I balked when he reached out and put a hand on my shoulder. I almost flinched but just barely contained the reaction. I really didn't want this guy to put his hands on me. What was wrong with me?

"I would love to take you out on New Year's Eve. Some friends of my friends are having a party, and I would love it if you would be my date."

I was going to have an embolism. I barely had enough confidence that I was going to survive an evening with Nash and his friends, going to some swanky party on the arm of a doctor . . . I was going to have a nervous breakdown. I wanted to say no, wanted to tell him I wasn't interested, but Sunny was watching me with undisguised glee. I shoved my fingers through my hair and reluctantly nodded.

"Sure, Doctor . . . I mean Andrew. That sounds lovely." Only if *lovely* meant torturous and nightmarish.

His smile grew and he leaned over and gave me a kiss on the cheek. This time I couldn't help but cringe away. If he noticed, he didn't say anything. He just handed me his card, much like Nash did, and told me to give him a call. When he walked away I had no desire to stare after him and there was an unpleasant taste in my mouth. I let out an oof when Sunny's small frame slammed into mine as she gave me another one-armed hug.

"Sooooo happy for you. You're going to have the best time with him. I just know it."

I looked at the plain white card in my hand. It had the hospital logo on it, and Bennet's name and contact information. It was boring. It was basic. It was exactly the opposite of the card Nash had handed me a few minutes earlier. One was tucked safely away in my pocket, I could feel it there almost like it was calling to me. The other I wanted to chuck in the trash. Too bad Sunny would never forgive me if I set the plain white one sailing.

"We'll see." I didn't have high hopes for either venture, but I would force myself to go through with both of them. One out of fear of spending the holidays alone and something more I didn't want to delve into, the other just to keep my boss happy. Neither was a great reason to go on a date, but considering it was me, it would just have to suffice.

CHAPTER 7

Nash

ITHINK I WAS more nervous than Rule. Someone had brought a flask of Crown Royal to help him calm his nerves, but he kept waving it away and Rome wasn't really drinking much anymore, so that left me, Asa, Rowdy, and Jet to do the damage. Rome and I were the best men. The big guy was taking Cora down the aisle, obviously, which left me with Ayden. I was teasing Jet mercilessly about it because I had seen her in the pretty, pale blue gowns Shaw had picked out and there was no question she looked beyond good. It was fun but left me wide open for him to poke at the fact that I had rolled into the venue with Saint. I wasn't the type of guy who brought a date to an event like this, and considering the guest list for the wedding consisted of maybe fifty people at most, there was no missing her and the questioning looks coming from every direction.

The venue was dramatic and unique. It was set high over the city skyline, and you could see lights and the winter landscape of the Rocky Mountains for miles and miles.

Shaw wanted everything to look pale and cool; she said she wanted it to feel like being in the center of a blizzard. Anyone who knew the soon-to-be-married couple knew that the bride had a serious infatuation with Rule's superpale, icy-colored eyes. Clearly, it was what the entire wedding theme was built around. Rome and I had on matching black pants and button-up shirts, with ties that were the same color as Ayden and Cora's dresses. Rule had the same thing on, only he was wearing a black jacket over his with a pinstripe pattern running through it. We looked badass, way better than typical wedding finery, and I couldn't believe how steady my best friend seemed. I never thought he was going to settle down and now it seemed like the only thing in the world he wanted to do. I was a little envious, which surprised the hell out of me.

"So the nurse?" Jet gave me a look and handed me the flask. I grunted at him and took a swig of the burning, amber liquid.

"She doesn't like me very much. I'm trying to change her mind about it."

Rome was fidgeting with his tie and texting Cora back and forth. The closer she got to her due date, the more paranoid he got about her well-being. I think he would've kept her glued to his side or tied to a bed if the little spitfire would've allowed it.

"She showed up with you. She can't dislike you that much."

Yeah, she had showed up, but she kinda looked like she was going to be sick or like she was sucking on a lemon the entire ride over. Not that she hadn't looked gorgeous even with the unease clear on her pretty face. It was the first time I had seen her in anything other than her work wear, and man, could she rock a little black dress and sky-high heels like a pro. It was simple, understated, but with all that spectacular hair and flawless skin, she looked regal and elegant in a way a lot of young women couldn't pull off nowadays. She was a classic. Kind of like my car, and I had a feeling her ride would be just as nice if she ever let me get that far.

She wouldn't let me pick her up, had insisted on meeting me at my place. I had almost had to literally twist her arm to get her to agree to actually ride downtown with me, and after I'd won that argument, she had spoken maybe five words to me since. I deposited her with Phil, who had just looked at me knowingly and given her a smile. He was holding up pretty well, all things considered, and there was no way he was going to miss seeing Rule tie the knot.

Rule and Shaw were doing things really informal. There weren't going to be any sappy speeches, no first dance, just a quick ceremony, dinner with everyone they loved, and then Rule was taking her to New Orleans for a week for their honeymoon so they could spend New Year's Eve partying it up on Bourbon Street. That is, if they managed to leave the hotel room. Knowing my best friend, I doubted it. Personally I was stoked that they weren't dragging it out. They didn't need pomp and circumstance to make the love between them official.

"She showed up with me under duress." I grinned at him. "I don't really get her."

Asa chuckled and flicked his golden hair out of his eyes. "But you want to? Get her, I mean."

I grunted again. "Did you see her? Of course I want to, but she's throwing out some pretty strong 'hell no' signals, I'm not interested in pushing my luck." That wasn't entirely true. I wanted to push and push, not that I thought it would get me anywhere. I kind of dug the mystery to all of it. She always had me guessing.

I'm sure the conversation would have kept going, but Rule's dad stuck his head in the room where we were all gathered and gave his son a nod and a grin.

"The girls are ready to get this show on the road. I sure am proud of you boys."

Rule nodded and I saw his chest expand and release. The rest of the guys pounded him on the back, leaving just the three of us in the wedding party behind.

"You good?"

Rome clapped his brother on the shoulder.

"I'm fucking great."

We all chuckled and I gave him a fist bump.

"You are fucking great, and so is she, so this is gonna rule."

He lifted his pierced eyebrow at the pun and I grinned at him. We were tight for a reason.

"Let's do this. Let's get you married." I was surprised that there some pretty thick emotion working in my voice.

Rome fiddled with his tie some more. I guess when you had a neck like a fullback, ties weren't very comfortable.

He looked at Rule and asked, "Did Shaw's mom show?"

Rule shook his head. "Nope. I called her and told her

what I thought about the entire situation and promptly got told to go to hell. Shaw seems okay with it. Her dad is here with a chick that looks like she's maybe eighteen at the most. He wanted to walk Casper down the aisle, but she told him no. She's having Dad do it."

That made sense to me. The Archers had always been Shaw's real family. Like Rome had told Rule when he was thinking about proposing, giving her his last name was just a formality.

We lingered at the back of the room while Rule took his waiting mom's arm and made his way to where the ordained officiant waited. Fittingly enough, Brite Walker, Rome's mentor and an ex-Marine, was an ordained minister. He looked like a member of a biker gang, but was one of the most centered, thoughtful men any of us had ever met. He had played a big part in bringing Rome back to the land of the living, and neither Rule nor Shaw could think of a better person to guide them into a life as man and wife. Just like he had offered Rome a new start, their thinking was he was the best person to give them a new start on a life as a married couple.

The girls came out of the elevator and both Rome and I lost our breath. Cora looked like a fairy princess from a Disney cartoon—granted, with a full sleeve of tattoos and a round baby belly. Rome bent down and kissed her until it was almost awkward for the rest of us. Ayden was a knockout even on a bad day. The blue made her dark hair pop and the silly grin on her face made me smile back at her just as goofy.

"Jet is so jealous of me right now."

She scoffed at me and put her hand in the curve of my elbow.

"It's good for him. He was out of town all last week. That means he won't be able to resist me later."

"Does he ever? Resist you? Because if he does, maybe I need to tell him he's doing being married wrong."

She made a face at me and dug her nails into my forearm, which made me laugh. I knew that her and Jet couldn't keep their hands off each other, so I was only teasing her.

When my gaze landed on Shaw as she came out of the dressing room she had been in, I was surprised at the wealth of sentiment I felt at looking at her. She was beautiful. Like something out of a fantasy or anyone's vision of "this is the perfect bride." Her white-blond-and-black hair was twisted all up. Her dress was poufy and long, like a ballerina, and tied with a pale blue sash in the middle. She was holding on to the senior Archer's arm, and Dale looked like any proud papa should. Rome maneuvered around his dad and bent down and gave the beautiful bride to be a kiss on the cheek. It was a good day for all the Archers . . . and the rest of us as well.

I told her honestly, "You look perfect."

She blushed prettily and glanced at Rome.

He lifted the eyebrow under his scarred forehead and told her bluntly, "What he said. Rule is a lucky bastard for sure."

Shaw just giggled and looked impatient.

"Let's do this."

We all faced the front, the clock face behind Rule and Brite showing the beautiful Denver skyline and making the most memorable Christmas Eve ever. Jet and his band started to play "Silver Mountains" by the Deadstring Brothers and I don't think anyone in the room had dry eyes by the end of the song. Jet was in a metal band, could scream his ass off with the best of them, but when he used those pipes to really, really sing, it just did something magical to the people lucky enough to hear it.

We made our way down the aisle. I saw Ayden turn her head so she could watch Jet. He blew her a kiss that made her sigh, and I shifted my eyes around until I found the storm-colored gaze I was searching for. Saint was watching me. She had her full bottom lip clamped between her teeth, and she had her hands clasped tightly together on her lap. Her eyes were shiny and bright. She had pink in her pale cheeks, and even from this distance I could see her pulse fluttering in her throat. If I didn't know better, I would say she was looking at me with way Cora was looking at Rome, the way Ayden was looking at Jet. I couldn't get my head around it, around her, but man, did I want to. She was fascinating. I wondered if I'd ever really know what made the pretty redhead tick.

I didn't have any more time to ponder it because we reached the front of the aisle. I kissed Ayden on the cheek, did the same to Cora, which earned me a hard look from Rome. Rule and I shared a chuckle, and I took my place next to the Archer brothers. It was a proud place to be.

Jet and the band switched to "Everybody Needs Love,"

the Drive-By Truckers version, which was Shaw's favorite, and she and Dale appeared at the back of the elegantly decorated room. I heard a couple of gasps, saw some jaws drop, and out of the corner of my eye I saw Rule physically jolt.

"Damn."

The word was barely a breath of sound, and before either Rome or I could react, Rule was walking down the aisle in the direction of his future bride and his dad, who had stopped at his approach. Rome and I exchanged a knowing look and just shrugged when the girls looked at us questioningly.

Rule grabbed Shaw's face in both of his hands and kissed her like he was supposed to do at the end of the ceremony. Dale stepped out of the way and Margot, the Archer matriarch, called her son's name in frustration. It was totally a Rule thing to do. He was impulsive, a little wild, but there was nothing in the world that would keep him from that girl, so of course he was the one who walked her down the aisle and to their spot in front of Brite. I couldn't stop grinning like an idiot, and the one time I caught sight of Saint, I was happy to see she was smiling as well. That kind of love was hard not to appreciate.

Brite was grinning as well. His smile barely visible through his long, gray beard. Looking like a jolly, friendly Hell's Angel, Brite proceeded to marry my best friend to the girl of his dreams. It was awesome, touching, everything it was supposed to be, and so were their vows.

Shaw vowed to love Rule just as he was, to never ask him to be anything other than the man he was. She promised to wait out his bad temper and the hissy fits that he was prone to and to never question what color his hair was for the week. She vowed to love him like she had since the first time she had seen him, and vowed that he would always be her one and only. She told him that he was everything she had ever wanted. It was all true and it made me happy to hear her promise that for an eternity to my very difficult and complicated friend.

Rule was choked up, so it took him a minute to recite his vows, but when he did I knew the impact of his heartfelt words stunned all of us. He wasn't a dude that was good with emotion on the best day, even though Shaw had helped him with that, but today he was putting his heart out there for everyone to see.

He told her that he never thought anyone would be able to fill the void in his life that Remy had left when he died, but somehow she had gotten inside of him and there was no more room for anything else. She just filled his heart and his life so full there were no more empty spots and he knew that ultimately Remy would be thrilled for them. That, of course, had everyone misty-eyed and clearing their throats.

He promised to always take care of her, to make everyone treat her with the love and kindness she deserved. He told her he would love her even when she was a doctor and making three times the money he did, and vowed to do his best to give her anything and everything she ever wanted and needed from this point on. He whispered so that only those of us standing up at the front could hear, "You are everything to me, Casper."

A collective sigh went up from the group when Shaw smiled up at him through the tears running down her face and said simply, "All I want and need is you."

Brite called it good enough, they exchanged rings, we all cheered and offered hugs and high fives, and just like that, Rule and Shaw were man and wife.

We had all gathered in the back of the clock tower, took forty-five minutes for fussing, congratulations, and photos, when Phil slid up next to me and muttered in my ear, "You better work some magic or your date is going to bolt. She's a sweet little thing, but she's as skittish as a newborn filly."

I swore and maneuvered my way through the crowd, waved Rowdy off when he tried to stop me, and eventually had to ride the elevator twenty stories down to the lobby in order to find her. She had her cell phone in her hand and seemed like she was having an argument with herself.

"Saint?"

She jolted at looked up at me. There was no other way to describe the look on her face other than guilty. Like I had just caught her in the midst of doing something wrong.

She held her phone out like it was a shield between us.

"I'm just going to call a cab to take me back to my car. You go back to your friends." Her voice was high and breathy. I frowned because I didn't have a clue as to what was going on.

"If you want to go home, I'll take you back to your car." I hooked a finger in the knot of the tie at my throat and pulled it loose. I would give anything to read this girl's mind.

"No, no . . . you stay. It's fine. It was really lovely. Thank you for inviting me."

I was done arguing with her. She already had her coat on, so I just grabbed her wrist, the one she was holding out in front of her, and dragged her to the front door. Her high-heeled shoes clicked frantically as she scrambled to keep up with me.

"Come on."

She huffed out a protest and tried to pull free, but I didn't let her. I just marched her unwillingly to where the Charger was parked on the street. I was annoyed and I was frustrated, but more than that, I was confused why she had agreed to come with me if she didn't want to be here in the first place.

We didn't talk the entire way back to the apartment. She was breathing low and shallow, twisting her hands together, and staring straight out the window. When we got to the Victorian, we simultaneously climbed out of the car and I slammed the door shut harder than I needed to. I stared at her over the roof of the vehicle and she opened her mouth like she was going to say something, so I held up my hand to stop her. I couldn't figure out why one of us always seemed to be warding the other off.

"Just . . . have a good night, Saint."

I jogged up the sidewalk to the front of the building and didn't look back to see if she even got into her little car or not. That was pretty rude of me and I never did stuff like that, but this chick was messing with my head and I wasn't sure how to navigate that along with everything else in my life right now. I had the key in the door and was pushing it open when I felt small hands at my back. Before I could turn around and look to see what was going on, I was shoved forward into my apartment and the door was slammed shut behind me. I spun around to face Saint and she gazed up at me like a wild Valkyrie. Her red hair was curly and untamed all around her face, her steely eyes were open wide, and her chest was rising and falling in an erratic rhythm. A pretty awesome sight really, but I was still pissed off at her.

"This is so screwed up, Nash. I have no idea what I'm doing."

I didn't know what to say to that, couldn't say anything because all of a sudden she was right in front of me and her hands, shaking and nervous, were pulling on the buttons of my black shirt and stripping the tie from around my neck.

"What?" I sounded bewildered because I was, but there was no way I was going to stop her. Not when she was pulling the tails of my shirt out of my pants and her hands were brushing enticingly across my abs and lower back with a frantic haste.

"Everything that I know is logical tells me I'm so sure about things, and then my body sneaks up on me and screams at me and I feel like I don't know anything anymore. I can't tell if I'm coming or going. I saw you up there, you looked so handsome, so perfect, oh my God, I just wanted to jump you, and that so isn't me. And then I saw how happy everyone looked, so in love, and I almost had a panic attack, and I can't even explain why. I just had to get out of there. I'm sorry."

I put my hands on her shoulders to hold her away because this was insane. But she had her fingers under my belt buckle and my zipper was going down without a fight.

"Saint, stop. I would've just brought you home if you told me you were uncomfortable. Anyone might be in a room full of people that are emotional. And it was intense, because Rule and Shaw are intense. I would've understood, and no one could blame you for needing some space from it. Fuck, I was just happy you even agreed to go with me."

She stopped what she was doing, which was pulling my shirt off my shoulders and pushing me back until my ass was resting on the back of the couch. When there was nowhere else for me to go, she put her hand flat on the center of my chest and looked up at me with those thundercloud-colored eyes.

"I know, and that's what made me freak out."

"I don't understand." I was trying to be coherent and reasonable, but my dick was starting to pay way closer attention to what she was doing than my brain was.

"I don't know who you are, Nash."

"I don't really know who you are either, Saint, but if you gave this thing starting between us half a chance, we could change that."

She shook her head and leaned into me so that we were pressed so tightly together there was no end to her and no beginning of me.

"I don't know that you would like me once you got to know me, and the Nash I thought I knew . . ." She looked so lost all I wanted to do was give her a hug. "I hated him, but you . . . this Nash . . . all I do is want him."

It was convoluted and confusing. I probably should have had something brilliant to say to her, some kind of thoughtful insight to put this all in perspective. I maybe should have been able to read into the subtle subtext of her words and her tone, but she quickly sealed her mouth over mine. Then she shoved her hand down the front of my pants, and I lost not only any will to object but also my balance, and we toppled over onto the other side of the couch. It was more than just a free fall onto the cushions . . . it was a free fall into one another.

Her hair was everywhere. She tasted like oranges and fire. Her hand had a solid grip on my rock-hard cock, and I felt her pause for a second when her palm slid over the head and encountered the different pieces of metal that lived there. I had a Prince Albert through the tip and a little tiny barbell that lived just under curve of the head that they called a frenum piercing. Normally, I warned anyone I was going to get naked with that the piercings were there, but she never gave me the chance and she didn't seem like she had any intention of slowing the pace down.

The way we landed had her on top of me, her legs on either side of my waist. Her hands were all over me, the one inside my boxers making it impossible to have any kind of lucid thought. She was kissing my neck, returning to suck on my mouth, her hair felt like silken tentacles I was never going to escape from. Somehow, even though there was limited movement allowed and space was minimal, she got my pants down around my hips and moved my boxers out of the way so that I was standing up erect and proud. Her hand looked super pale next to the hard, red flesh, and when she used the tip of one finger to touch the piercing that lived right under the tip, my eyes rolled back in my head and I hissed out a breath through clenched teeth. Holy shit, no simple touch had ever had me ready to come like hers did.

"Of course you would be pierced." She sounded amused,

and I didn't know what to say to that, not when she bent down and ran her tongue over the flat of my nipple. I was practically pulsating her hand. She had me all turned around and lost. I was trying desperately to figure out what we were doing and where we were going, and I wasn't sure there was a map to show us how to get wherever it was she expected me to be at.

"Saintttt . . ." The word got garbled and lost when she lifted up off of me just enough so that she could wiggle around and get her black panties off under the hem of her little black dress. It struck me then that she was still fully clothed, even had her shoes on, and I was stripped and exposed while she did what she wanted, took what she needed from me.

Something about that didn't sit right, and I wanted to tell her so, when she bent down, kissed me again, and asked against my mouth, "Condom?"

All right, I was a decent guy, had a pretty sturdy set of standards and morals, but when a girl was this hot, made my head this fuzzy, had my heart beating so hard I was sure she could hear it, and she pretty much demanded I have sex with her, who was I to argue? I lifted my hips up and that made her gasp because now there was nothing between us where she was straddling me and I saw her eyes go from that oh-so-lovely gray to a slate color that hovered close to black. I handed her my wallet, told her to fish one out, wrapped my hand in her wealth of hair, and pulled her down so I could kiss her like I wanted to. I had to have some say in this after all, even if Saint calling the shots landed me under her, with all her damp heat pressed up close against me.

I kissed her with no lingering anger, no sadness, no desperation or bleakness hovering between us for the first time.
I just wanted to savor her tangy flavor, revel in the way she
rolled her tongue along mine, marvel at the way she sort of
swore and whispered my name at the same time. This was
how she should be kissed every time . . . by me and only me.

I felt her shift her weight and her hand that was sliding
up and down my shaft, trying to kill me with gentle pressure and a delicate touch. I couldn't see what she was doing
because the skirt of her dress was in the way. Hell, I couldn't
even tell if she had freckles across those awesome breasts,
because as close as we were right now, she was very obviously still keeping firm mental and physical boundaries in
place.

"Saint?"

I could feel the latex slide over me. Good thing she was a
nurse, she didn't have any trip up getting it around the metal
decorating my business.

"Nash?"

Her eyes were on mine as she sat up, put both her hands
right on the center of my chest, and seated herself down
on me, all the way to the hilt. She was tight, suffocatingly
so. She was hot and slick, and since she was on top, riding
me up and down in a torturous motion, all I wanted to do
was watch myself disappear inside of her. Everything about
this girl was bound to be shrouded in secrets, even what we
looked like when we were joined together. I loved it and
hated it at the same time. Kind of how I was starting to feel
about Saint Ford.

Whatever I had been about to say to her fled. It was odd. I'd never had sex where my partner was fully clothed while I was on display. I'd also never been intimate with anyone who seemed like they were desperately, furiously trying to get to the end, regardless of what I was or wasn't doing. Like she was using me to get to completion but wasn't even in the act with me. I put my hands on her, tried to get the strap of her dress down over her shoulder so I could get access to all that creamy, white skin, and scowled in concern when she flinched away from me.

Her head was tossed back, her hair was pooling in a fiery blanket across the top of my bare thighs, and her hands were curling into clawing talons on my chest. Her eyes were locked on mine, so I saw it brimming, saw the surprise, the wonder creep across the thunderclouds when she came apart. I also saw tears spring into her gaze and the way her chest started to rise and fall like she was going to hyperventilate as soon as the last shuddering crest of the orgasm wafted over her.

I mean I was pretty good in bed, or on the couch, as the case might be, but that was the fastest orgasm I had ever inspired in any woman, and as far as I was concerned, we hadn't even gotten to the good stuff yet. I was still painfully hard, still dying to get her naked and my mouth on any part of her that she would let me, but Saint had other plans.

She looked down at me like she just suddenly realized I was there, a living breathing person and not a vibrator. She jerked her hands off of my chest, scrambled off of me in a way that made my dick scream at both of us, and collected all that glorious hair into her shaking hands. The tears shimmering in her eyes started to fall, and before I could sit up and ask her what in the hell was going on, she was practically running for the door.

"I'm so sorry, Nash."

While getting left high and dry with a raging hard-on wasn't my favorite thing that had happened that day, I was more worried about the fact that she looked like she was going to shatter like an icicle hanging off the edge of a steep roof. She was shaking all over, her eyes were too big in her pale face, and her freckles were standing out in stark relief. The trails the tears were leaving made her look like something that was going to shatter.

"Saint, hold on a second." I had to struggle back into my pants, not easy when my dick was still ready and rearing to go, but she shook her head at me and dashed to the front door.

"No, no . . . I told you I didn't know how to do this with you. I have to go." The door slammed behind her in her haste to exit, and by the time I was semipresentable, tucked away, and had made it to the hallway with only a slight limp, she was long gone.

The other new redhead in my life, however, was coming in through the front door. She was all bundled up and slid her gaze over my rumpled and rough state and blew out a sharp whistle through her teeth.

"Bad date?"

I snorted and leaned against the open doorway, my arms up over my head. Royal had no problem checking out the show. Too bad none of it was for her.

"It started out a little rough, got bad, had a high point, and then ended with a whimper."

She let her gaze roam unabashedly over my naked chest, tattooed arms, and still-open pants. Why couldn't I be attracted to her? She was adorable, bold, and I liked her unabashed and unapologetic attitude, but there was no doubt about it, she wasn't going to be a substitute for Saint. The idea of it even took care of the uncomfortable problem in my pants.

"I gotta say, you are better than TV for pure entertainment value."

I snorted. "Glad you can find humor at the state of my dismal dating life."

She made her way to her own door and smiled at me over her shoulder.

"You're a babe, a little rough and dangerous, and she's shy and quiet. I saw her on my way in. You probably overwhelm her and she feels out of her depth. Give her a minute to realize you wouldn't be all up on her if you didn't think she was just as awesome as she clearly thinks you are. That is a pretty girl with a crush for sure. Boys need to be careful with pretty girls that have crushes."

I lifted my eyebrow at her.

"How do you know all that? You psychic or something?"

She pushed her own door open and laughed at me.

"Not even close. I have really good instincts about people. It serves me well in my line of work."

She looked like a yoga instructor or a high-end stripper,

and with a name like Royal, come on. I couldn't imagine what her job really was.

"What do you do?"

She lifted one of her own eyebrows back at me. "You wouldn't believe me if I told you. Don't give up on her, neighbor. She looks like she could use a guy like you, someone to shake her up, force her to have some fun. Have a good night."

She shut the door without giving me a real answer about her job, and I retreated into my own place. I needed a minute to clear my head and, more pressing than that, to work out my frustration in a hot shower. I'd never been so twisted up, so wound up about a girl before. Saint took effort, a gentle touch I wasn't a hundred percent sure I was equipped with. I mean, I was never the kind of guy who just barreled into a girl's life and turned it upside down. I never cared enough to do that. With Saint I was starting to want to not only turn everything upside down, but put it in a jar, or a box, and shake it all up and around until something completely different came out. A different Nash and Saint who could figure this shit out.

CHAPTER 8

Saint

I PACED AROUND MY apartment like a neurotic mess the rest of the night. I couldn't believe what I had done, or the way I had left him like that. I was mortified and stupefied at not only my actions, but that I had actually managed to get off with him. That had never happened to me before, and all the foreign goodness and startling knowledge that it was *him* that could get me there had me nearly blind with panic.

I spent all the next day cleaning and finding anything to keep my whirling mind busy until I had to go in for my shift. I barely pulled it together to go in for my rounds, but considering my phone was blowing up with an equal mix of angry text messages from my mom, and disappointed ones from my dad, I had to get out of my apartment. I called Faith to tell her and the rest of her brood family Merry Christmas, and even though I tried to keep it brief, I think she could tell I was upset and something was really wrong.

There was nothing she could do or say to stop me from feeling like I was a lunatic. I don't know what happened to me when I was around Nash, but something about him and me in the same room and I turned into an unpredictable mess.

Things had been all right. I didn't love not having my own car in case I wanted to escape the wedding and my own nerves, but his friends and all of the wedding party had been really nice, and his dad, or Phil, as the older man laughingly told me to call him, was delightful. Had I not known any different, I would have thought he was healthy as a horse. The nurse in me wasn't certain that being around so many people in his fragile state was a smart idea, but I could tell there was no way he would've missed the big event. This group was tighter than any band of friends I had ever encountered.

All of Nash's friends were gorgeous and covered in defining marks that made them an unforgettable group. It wasn't the tattoos or the fact that the groom was sporting a purple Mohawk that made me start to hyperventilate—it was the palpable love, the care, the respect and genuine admiration they all had for one another that made my skin feel too tight, made a longing I had never felt before start to stifle everything else inside of me.

The only person I had ever had that kind of bond with was Faith, and now that she had her own family and husband to take care of, I felt more and more on my own. Watching this mismatched group of men and women, seeing the bride and groom who were so clearly determined to overcome everything just to be together, made me feel out of sorts, achingly jealous, and as it throbbed in my blood, I felt like I needed to go. I couldn't take it anymore. And just like Nash said, I knew, had no doubt that he would have brought me home without complaint. I just couldn't get my head and my heart to line up on what they thought about that. On one hand, I wanted to take his nice-guy facade at face value, but I had been burned by my misconception of him before and I didn't think that was a risk I wanted to take again. I didn't know that I could handle being disappointed by him again now that I was just starting to get to a point where I wanted to think he was different than he had been all those years ago.

As I watched him walk down the aisle, so big and handsome, so colorful and distinct, there was no question that I wanted him. I felt desire, was unquestioningly aroused whenever he touched me, whenever he looked at me with those beautiful eyes. I wasn't used to that, and to all the heat and confusion that Nash had once again brought into my life. The buildup was coiled so tight inside of me that it was like a spring ready to snap . . . and *snap,* it had taken me right along with it.

If my colossal freak-out at the wedding wasn't bad enough, my confusing reaction only seconds after the only orgasm given to me by another person was enough to make me want to change my name and move to an island nobody had ever heard of before. Bursting into tears after sex was nothing new for me, even if these had been tears of gratitude rather than disappointment. But the way I lost it, the way I had run away like I had never run before, and maybe most shameful, the way I had callously left Nash with an unmistakably unsatisfied erection made me question my own sanity.

Obviously the other guys were wrong. There wasn't anything wrong with me sexually. I wasn't frigid or cold . . .

if Nash had gotten me any hotter last night, we would have melted together. Apparently I just needed the guy to be covered in ink, pierced in some unusual places, and tied to my past and the heart of my lack of confidence in the most devastating of ways in order to have an orgasm. He was beautiful, all dusky skin, corded slabs of hard muscle, and strong planes and valleys of sexy perfection. He was not a small guy, anywhere, and where I thought that would be intimidating, it just made me feel slight and exceedingly feminine next to him. It made me want him more.

On top of everything else I was kicking myself over, I still didn't get a look at the rest of that tattoo. I knew my thumb and forefinger barely fit around the circumference of his erection when he was aroused, that the metal he sported was blazing hot from being so close to his body, that he looked way better in white boxers than black because of his darker skin tone, that his eyes turned purple not just when he was mad, but also when he was turned on. That damn tattoo was still a mystery, though, and all the while I was lambasting myself, calling myself every foolish name in the book, I was still trying to piece together what it might look like.

I managed to get through the holiday shift with no incidents, and aside from Sunny asking me what was wrong every five minutes, it was preferable to listening to my mom scream and moan about her life and the way the holidays were playing out for the Fords this year. I was dodging Dr. Bennet left and right, because even though I promised to go out with him and I didn't want to disappoint Sunny, my instincts were screaming at me to cancel my date with him.

I was too unnerved, too off-kilter after what had happened with Nash, to think I could get through the date unscathed.

When it was time to go home I looked at my phone and winced when I saw I had a missed call from Nash. He didn't leave a voice mail, but there was also a text that simply said:

Merry Xmas Saint.

I owed him an explanation. I knew it, but I just didn't think I could do it. I had a difficult time expressing myself clearly when the subject wasn't embarrassing and undignified. How was I supposed to tell him that not only was he the first guy I had ever been with who made me feel that good, made me want to actually have sex? How was I supposed to explain that I didn't want him to be the guy who made sex fun, made me want it, because of the awful things he said a lifetime ago and the way they made me feel? How did I go about explaining that I didn't want to like him, didn't want to feel anything for him after the abysmal way his flagrant disregard for me in high school had left me feeling for a lifetime? Would he even understand that because of the younger him, because of those painful moments tied directly to his actions, I normally hated the idea of being naked around another person, loathed being exposed and vulnerable, so sex for me was always confusing and awful?

I couldn't explain it to him when I couldn't even get it to make sense to myself. When had all my dislike for him morphed into something that had me jumping him the first chance I got? And did that mean I was ready to forgive him for the sins of the past? I didn't have answers to those questions, and thinking about them made my head hurt.

I didn't text him back that day, or the next, when he asked if I was okay, or the next, when he asked if we could talk. I straight up ignored him. Phil had decided that if he was well enough to attend Rule and Shaw's wedding, he was well enough to try his luck moving his care home, so I didn't have to worry about running into Nash at the hospital anymore. That thought made me want to cheer and howl in frustration at the same time. But by the weekend he wasn't texting me anymore, and I resigned myself to the fact that whatever symphony of self-destruction I had created had played its last note. Since I was the composer, I had nowhere else to lay the blame.

Time flew and all of a sudden it was the beginning of the following week and my date with the good doctor had arrived. I wanted to go even less now than I had when he first asked me. I would have backed out, made some kind of excuse and played dead if only Sunny hadn't been hounding me about it every chance she got. I'd also made the mistake of telling Faith about it, more for her support than anything else, but she was tickled pink about the prospect of me dating anyone, so she was nudging as well. I was stuck and all I could do was power through it.

I had a similar argument with the doctor that I had with Nash about wanting to take my own car, only instead of being Nash and using gentle persuasion and unflappable logic to get me to ride with him, he looked at me disapprovingly and pointed out how odd it would appear to his friends if we didn't show up together. It wasn't an argument I wanted to rehash with someone so concerned about appearances, so I reluctantly agreed, and he told me he would pick me up at my apartment. I told him we should just leave from the hospital since the party was in Cherry Creek and it was closer, but again he gave me a look like I was silly and didn't know how dates worked.

So there I was at nine P.M. on New Year's Eve, it had been exactly seven days since my disastrous date with Nash, and instead of trying to make polite conversation, or figuring out how to make the most of my time with Dr. Bennet—Andrew—I found myself in the passenger seat of his very nice SUV pondering what Nash was up to. After all, it was New Year's and that meant kissing at midnight.

I sighed heavily and started when Andrew stopped the steady stream of conversation he was having with himself about himself. No doubt about it: the doctor was his own biggest fan.

"Everything all right?"

I forced a smile and fiddled with the ends of my hair, which I had left down and put into giant, loose curls.

"Sure. It's just been busy at work and with the holidays. I'm a little beat." And I'm obsessing over a guy I shouldn't be, but I didn't think he wanted to know that part of it.

"Did you always want to be a nurse?"

"Yep. I like nursing, like the rush of the ER, but mostly I wanted to help people."

"Ahh, you're one of those."

I lifted an eyebrow and looked at him out of the corner of my eye. We had stopped in front of an opulent townhouse in one the wealthiest suburbs of the city. My stomach dipped.

I could already tell this was going to be dreadful. We had been doing just fine when he didn't need me to join in on the chatter.

"One of what exactly?"

"Those people who went to nursing or medical school based on ideals and fuzzy feelings of giving back."

What? People went into these fields for reasons other than compassion and concern for the well-being of others? Since when? I was dumbfounded, so I had to ask, "Why did you go?"

He chuckled and made his way out of the car to open my door. He offered me his hand, which I begrudgingly took. I didn't like how soft, how perfectly manicured it felt next to mine. Those were hands that handed out plain white business cards all day long.

"I went because I wanted a good job, something that was secure, something that had status and prestige attached to it. Don't get me wrong; I love medicine, love healing, love being in the hospital all day, but honestly, if I could do the same thing and not have the same level of interaction with patients, I would. It gets old after a while, you know? Treating people who are often suffering from nothing more than their own dumb choices. My long-term plans involve going into private practice. I think that has to be the way to go so I can pick and choose the types of patients I want to treat. There won't be any more cheating husbands with vindictive wives or kids falling off of bikes for me."

That attitude was ridiculous, and if I was someone else, maybe I would have had the right words to tell him that.

Instead I waited until he turned around and rolled my eyes at the back of his perfectly styled head. It was a good thing he had his job and his looks going for him because it was pretty obvious to me this man was shallow as a rain puddle. He might be nice to look at on the outside, but I was starting to see his insides were pretty unappealing, which had me thinking of Nash yet again.

His looks were so dynamic, so in-your-face. Yes, he was good-looking, but it was in a really complicated way; you had to look past all the things on the outside that made him stand out from the norm to see how beautiful he truly was. His insides, though, I had long thought were devious and nasty, but what shined out of his periwinkle eyes was nothing but forthrightness and sincerity . . . that was the most beautiful thing about him. If anyone saw the two men I had agreed to dates with together, I knew instinctively most would look at Andrew and ask why I wasn't trying to snatch him up, but Nash . . . to me, he was the real prize . . . he was something unique and special in a way that I was having an impossible time letting go of, even twisted up about the past like I was.

"I hope it won't make you uncomfortable, but some of the young ladies attending this soirée are women I've had relationships with in the past. Typically, all the relationships ended well, but you never know what showing up with a beautiful new woman on my arm will inspire."

I wanted to kick him in the shin, or maybe mess up that ruthlessly gelled hair.

Seriously, not only was I going to have to spend the evening in a room full of strangers, but I was also going to be used as live bait for him to dangle in front of his exes. Oh boy, didn't that sound like fun?

"I'm pretty quiet. I don't exactly mingle well."

"Just smile and look pretty." He winked at me and I had to clamp my teeth down on my tongue to avoid telling him I thought he was superficial and all-around icky. He was making my skin crawl, and when I recalled the way Nash made it burn and quiver, I wanted to find the nearest exit and find my way back to the Victorian on Capitol Hill. I was such a mess.

It was apparent as soon as we walked in the door that my role for the evening was to be Bennet's show pony. He never once told people I was a nurse, never mentioned where I went to school or how we really knew each other. He just flashed me around and kept telling me to have a drink and smile. For the most part, everyone at the luxurious shindig seemed just as self-absorbed and fake as the good doctor was, so my only saving grace was that no one expected me to say very much. I just nodded and muttered noises that made it sound like I was interested and tried to remember it was just one date and it would be over soon. Sunny would be happy and I could move on with my life.

About an hour in, not only was I sick of spectacle and showboating, but I was completely bored out of my mind. I had had two glasses of champagne that I'm sure was expensive but tasted terrible and decided to go find a bathroom. No one seemed eager to point me in the right direction, so I went off wandering alone. The townhouse wasn't massive, but there were a lot of rooms, and as I was making my way down a hallway I heard high-pitched female laughter coming out of one of them. I was going to stick my head in and ask if I was getting close to my destination, when déjà vu kicked my ass right back to my high school days.

"What is up with that girl Andrew brought? I don't think she's said one word all night."

More laughter and I felt something lodge in my throat and my hands curl into fists at my sides.

"Maybe she's slow . . . you know, special. Clearly he only brought her because she's young and pretty. He wanted to make Heather jealous, I bet, since she got engaged and Tommy gave her that gigantic rock. I don't think Tommy knows Heather went to Aspen with Andrew a couple weekends ago."

"Like anyone would be jealous of her. She has the conversational skills and IQ level of a hedgehog. What was he thinking?"

A delicate female snort followed by, "She's probably easy, so he was thinking it's New Year's Eve and he wants to get laid. She's a sure thing, I bet."

I couldn't decide if I was more furious or offended. This wasn't how grown people were supposed to act. It was juvenile, it was way too akin to what had made me so quiet and reserved in the first place, and if my date had bothered to treat me as a person rather than an accessory, maybe these strangers wouldn't have any ammunition to lobby around like gossipy schoolgirls.

I had reached the end of my tolerance for nonsense. I kept walking down the hall and fished my cell out of my bra, where I had stashed it. Sure, a healthier, more mature response would have been to confront those women, to tell Andrew he was a conceited jackass, but I was just over it. I was not going to let strangers make me feel bad about myself. I did a bang-up job of that all on my own and at least I had real reasons for not cutting myself any slack. I made a call I should have made over a week ago.

The phone rang and rang and I remembered it was a big party holiday and he was probably out. Out with someone who wasn't me. I held my breath and was about to hang up and call a cab when his deep voice came over the line. He sounded like salvation and temptation all in one word.

"Saint?" He was obviously at a bar or some other place that was loud. There was noise and revelry in the background. Voices screaming, people partying, but the noise was fading as he moved away from it.

"I . . . I need a ride. Can you come get me?"

He was quiet on the other end of the line. Hell, if I was him I would say no to the crazy lady that had left me high and dry and then ignored me all week, but once again Nash was out to prove what I thought I knew and what was actuality were worlds apart.

"Where are you at?"

"I'm at some awful party filled with awful people in Cherry Creek. I'm sorry, I wouldn't ask, but I didn't drive and I'm sort of stuck. I have to get out of here . . . please."

He sighed and I could almost see him running his hands over his supershort hair like he did when he was aggravated. His eyes would also be dancing between purple and lilac. I sighed involuntarily at the mental image.

"Text me the address and I'll be there in fifteen."

I let out a relieved breath and pushed my hair off of my face.

"Thank you."

He muttered a dirty word that made me wince and then he sighed again.

"Anything, Saint. Anytime."

The line went dead and I shot him the address. I fully intended to hide in the bathroom until my rescuer showed up, only my none too brilliant plan was thwarted by a knock on the door and my lackluster date calling my name questioningly through the barrier.

"Saint? Are you in there?"

I guess I had been gone long enough for him to notice, or maybe everyone else had grown tired of his monotonous discourse on how amazing he was and he needed me around to feign interest. What a weasel.

"Uh, yeah, give me a second." I washed my hands and gave myself a quick once-over in the mirror. I was paler than normal, but there was no missing that my eyes were glittering back at me with anticipation. Shit. I wanted to see Nash. Wanted to be near him, wanted to touch him, and he hadn't even questioned why I needed him, so I also wanted to hug him out of pure appreciation.

I pulled the door open and met Andrew's questioning look.

"Everything okay?"

I cleared my throat. "Actually no. I don't feel so hot. I think I need to go home and get into bed." Preferably with a darkly hot guy who had eyes the color of the state flower and abs that should be on a billboard for men's underwear right alongside Beckham.

"What? No way. It's not even close to midnight yet. We can't leave."

I gritted my back teeth.

"You don't have to leave, Andrew, but I'm not staying."

His eyes narrowed at me and his demeanor switched from annoyed to slightly threatening.

"What do you expect me to tell my friends? Do you know what that's going to look like, you leaving and me staying? And what about midnight? These are all couples, Saint. Who am I supposed to kiss at midnight?"

What in the holy hell? I stiffened up and narrowed my eyes back at him. I didn't like confrontation, hated trying to express what was going on inside my head to another person, but this moron and his elitist friends had shaken something loose. I wasn't a teenager anymore. I was smart. I was successful and I was entitled to be treated as an equal no matter the situation.

"It'll look like exactly what it is. I don't want to be here anymore. I don't like you. I don't like your friends, and frankly, I don't care what you tell them. It's not like they'll listen anyway. Everyone here is too busy going on and on about how great they are . . . no one can get a word in edgewise. As for kissing me . . ." I moved past him and shook his hand off when he tried to grab my wrist. "No way in hell. Not at midnight, not under the mistletoe . . . not anywhere, ever. Good-bye, Andrew."

He called my name then swore at me in a really ugly way.

"When the rest of the nursing staff hears about this at work, you'll never live it down. Do you know how badly most of them wanted to be you tonight?"

That was the last thing I wanted, to be gossiped about, to be talked about behind my back, but that versus spending one more second with him seemed like the lesser of two evils.

I shrugged my shoulders and headed in the direction of the front door.

"I'm used to it." I grabbed my coat from the hook by the door and gave him a final look. "By the way, tell your friends my IQ is closer to Hawking than hedgehog. I was summa cum laude at Cal State Los Angeles. Maybe if you had taken three seconds and stopped trying to tell me how awesome you were, you would have known that."

The door clicked closed behind me and I shivered inside my coat as much from adrenaline as from the freezing Colorado air. I had on a knee-length skirt and a pair of knee-high boots that went great with my sparkly tank top. It was appropriate, cute, and not in any way suggestive, but it wasn't made for pacing up and down the end of the driveway waiting for my getaway ride in the middle of winter.

I heard the car long before I saw it come around the corner. It was loud, distinctive, made my ears ring, and there was no missing the black-and-chrome monster, much like there was no missing the car's owner. I barely waited until he rolled to a stop before hopping in the passenger seat. My fingers were numb and my cheeks were freezing cold, but the interior of the car was nice and warm and smelled like a mixture of Nash's cologne, Armor All, and cigarette smoke. I put my fingers in front of the heater vent on the top of the dash as he wheeled around and headed out of the affluent subdivision.

"Thank you. I hope I didn't pull you away from anything."

He cast me a look out of the corner of his eye and tapped his fingers on the steering wheel. He had the Dropkick Murphys playing low on the radio and I thought it seemed like a fitting musical choice for him.

"Nope. I was just at a friend's bar. Rule's out of town and Jet took Ayden to New York with him for a show he was playing. Rome is expecting a baby, so he's all about acting like a respectable adult, and Rowdy is my only single friend left, so we just hit the bar. Asa—he runs Rome's bar for him—is the only other unattached member of our little gang and he and Rowdy both set their sights on the same cute little brunette. You called right when they were trying to outhandsome each other. It was getting ridiculous, so I probably would've bounced early and headed home anyway."

He glanced over at me and I saw his gaze skim over my legs where the hem of the skirt had ridden up and my skin was bare between it and the top of my boots.

"You look really nice."

"You didn't always think that . . . I looked nice, I mean." I hated that my voice cracked and broke. He jerked his head to look at me and the lights from the dash made the dime-sized discs in his earlobes glint at me. I muttered my address when he stopped at a red light while he was still staring at me.

"Seriously? What the fuck are you talking about?"

I looked out the window and used my finger to trace a little stick figure on the condensation on the pane. I gave him a top hat and a bow tie.

"In high school you said 'someone would need to put a bag over her head if she wants to get laid.'" I turned to face him and he looked astonished and incredulous. "You and a group of guys you hung out with were smoking when I came around the corner and I heard you. I heard stuff like that all the time because I was fat and had awful skin, but it hurt coming from you because I thought you were different. You said I was a mess and needed to look in a mirror and do some work."

I closed my eyes and replayed that moment over in my mind. Even now it made my chest hurt and old insecurity rise up.

"And before that . . . before that, I thought you were so nice. Every time you smiled at me, every time you said hi to me, I thought it made you different. I went to Ashley Maxwell's birthday party because you asked me if I was going." I saw it all as clear as if it was happening right in front of me, and if I had bothered to look over at him, I would have seen the stunned confusion on his handsome face as he was trying to pull the puzzle pieces of our history out of his memory.

"It was so stupid of me. I felt like an idiot. You looked right past me and then kissed Ashley like she was something special. You didn't even know I was alive, and then you had to go and say those awful things about me. I went from thinking you were wonderful to hating you. The way you made me feel . . ." My voice dropped low and I could hear the old hurt, the old disappointment, in my tone. "It stayed with me for a long time, Nash."

It was quiet save for the guitars and bagpipes on the stereo and I thought maybe he felt guilty or embarrassed, but when we got to the front of my apartment building and I was turning to tell him thanks for the ride, I was startled when he turned fully in his seat and yelled at me like he was the one who'd been wronged for so long.

"Jesus Christ, woman, you're out of your ever-loving mind!"

I pulled back a little and frowned at him, alarmed at the vehemence in his tone. "What?"

"I never said anything like that about you. No way in hell, and if I ignored you at some stupid party, it wasn't on purpose. I was a fucking idiot when I was a teenager, Saint. My priorities were locked firmly in my pants. If a girl was a sure thing back then, you think any eighteen-year-old guy was going to turn her down?"

I gave him a sad smile and reached for the door. "But I heard you that next week, Nash. I saw you with my own eyes. It was a long time ago, but my memory is clear, and even if it was just a case of boys being boys, it still really, really hurt."

He shook his head and threw his hands up as far as the interior of the car would allow.

"Bullshit. I never even thought that about you, Saint, so there is no way I would've said it. I thought you were shy . . . and yeah, maybe pretty awkward and a little too studious for my taste, but I always thought you were pretty. Why do you think I said hi to you every day, tried to get you to talk to me? I thought your smile was beautiful, and when you finally loosened up enough to give it to me on a regular basis, I was stoked. Your hair is awesome and wild, I love that shit . . . and your eyes. Fuck me, but your eyes could inspire men to go to war, to paint works of art, to rip their god-damn heart out of their chest and offer it to you without a second thought . . . then and now. None of that has changed over the years, so there is no way I would have said that stuff about you . . . no fucking way. You heard me say, 'Saint Ford needs a bag over her head to get laid'? I don't think so."

He was really, really mad. I could feel it burning off of him and I didn't know how to react. For so long I had been the one feeling victimized, had used that turn of events to justify the way I acted with other people, but now that he mentioned it, as clear as that memory was, I had never heard him say my name.

"I—"

I jumped in the seat when the side of his fist slammed down on the dashboard in front of him.

"You what? Want an excuse not to like me because you know I'm attracted to you and you can't handle it? I heard negative shit about myself every day of my childhood, Saint. I wasn't smart enough, clean enough, polite enough, and Lord only knows my skin color and my eye color were all fucking wrong. You really think I would do that to someone else? Yeah, I might be guilty of not seeing you real clearly when you were right in front of me back then, and I may have inadvertently hurt your feelings by acting like a hor-monal idiot at that party, but if you had said something to me, told me you were going to be there to see me, I can guarantee that wouldn't have happened. I might have been running my mouth and talking shit, but I wasn't talking about you."

His eyes were almost black. I had no idea what to do. For my entire life I thought I knew, was so sure, and now I felt like I didn't know anything.

I shoved my hair back behind my shoulders and looked at him.

"If not me, then who, Nash? Who else would you have been talking about? I know you said it. I heard you and I saw you. Even if it wasn't about me, using hurtful words like that isn't right."

He slammed his hands on the steering wheel and growled at me, actually growled.

"Who knows? A teacher I didn't like, a girl I hooked up with, a girl who turned me down . . . I don't remember because I was a teenage guy full of stupid shit and a lot of anger back then. We all said stupid stuff on the regular, but I never picked on anyone because I knew exactly how crappy that felt. Back then, all I wanted to do was get laid, party with my friends, and forget that my mom was a ruthless bitch. My life sucked, I had a lot of moments where *I* sucked. I was barely hanging in there most days. I'm not going to deny I was acting like a moron because I more than likely was, but I know there is no way I was verbally attacking you like that."

"But—"

"But nothing. I wouldn't have said anything like that about you because I didn't think it. I thought you were pretty then, I think you're unbelievably gorgeous now, and all along I've known girls like you don't get into guys like me. Girls like Ashley Maxwell do."

I reached out and put my hand on his that was curled so tightly on the steering wheel. I had always been into a guy like him, that's why those awful words still haunted me.

"Nash . . ." The way I wanted to believe him, trust in him, was overwhelming and I had to admit he might have a point about telling him I was going to that party to specifically see him. Mostly I was caving and thinking there might be more to what happened back then because it made me feel less confused about the way I wanted him, the way he just lit me up with a mere look.

He looked at my hand and then into my eyes.

"Even if some jerk did say that about you, you should know that it was just kids being dumb and none of it was true. And I swear I never would have thrown away an opportunity to hang out with you if I knew you were offering it up. Back then, a party like that meant one thing—getting laid. I had a one-track mind. Words like that, others' opinions of you, shouldn't have that kind of power, Saint."

But they did and therein lay the problem. I was always guilty of letting other people's words and actions hurt me and dictate how I felt about myself, and it was costing me more than I ever thought. I wanted who he was with me now to be the real Nash, not the Nash that still haunted my memories with indifference and careless words.

He reached into his pocket and pulled out a pack of cigarettes. He shook one out and stuck it in his mouth. I gasped at him and reached over to yank it out of his mouth, which had him glaring at me even harder.

"No! I thought you quit?"

"I did, until last week."

He didn't need to say anything else. I knew what happened last week that would have made him start up again. I was to blame for that, but I could rectify it now if he let me.

I shoved the door open and turned to look at him. "Come inside with me, Nash."

He threw his head back against the headrest and shook his head in the negative.

"That didn't work out so great for me last time, Saint."

No, it hadn't, but I was tired from holding on to who I'd thought Nash had been, when the Nash from now was all gorgeous and accommodating in front of me. He had dropped everything and come to pick me up without question. I threw his unlit cigarette on the ground next to me and lifted both of my eyebrows at him. It was time to make new memories to replace the old ones that haunted me.

"I've never wanted to have sex with any guy like that before. I couldn't stop myself, didn't want to stop. I want you, want to touch you, feel you, and it was amazing for me. No guy, ever, has gotten me off before, Nash. Not that there have been a lot, but you are the only one. I can't promise you that I'm not going to freak out again. There's a good chance I might start to cry because I don't really have a handle on all the things you make me feel, good and bad, but I want you to come inside. I don't want the past between us right now." I didn't want anything to stand between us anymore.

He looked like he was going to tell me no. I don't know how I would have handled that, actual, undeniable, in-my-face rejection, but luckily I didn't have to find out because he threw open his door and climbed out of the car and looked at me over the roof. He wasn't going to disappointment me. That made my heart flutter and my tummy go all squishy and warm.

"Let's give it ten minutes. Ten minutes, and if it isn't going to work for both of us, let's cut our losses and no one gets hurt or"—one of his black eyebrows shot up and a self-deprecating grin pulled at his mouth—"left hanging."

"Ten minutes?" It didn't sound like nearly enough time to touch all that smooth, burnished skin.

"Ten minutes."

I could handle ten minutes without freaking out. Heck, when he kissed me the first time, it had lasted longer than ten minutes. I could do this, wanted to do this, but that didn't mean my hands stopped shaking or the idea of getting naked with him didn't have my stomach dipping and second thoughts trying to shove their way up from the depths. I talked a good game about letting sleeping dogs lie, but really I could feel they were always there, tugging hard on the leash.

On the plus side, getting naked with him again meant I was finally going to see the rest of that tattoo.

CHAPTER 9

Nash

TEN MINUTES. NO BIG deal, but something told me they were going to be the ten most important minutes of my life. Especially after what she had just revealed about the past and why she ran so hot and cold with me. That was some heavy stuff, made the way I needed kid gloves with her so much more understandable. She was into me, but she sort of hated me as well. That wasn't a spot I had ever been in before.

I even remembered both those moments in question. It was all kind of hazy and foggy with time, but I recalled the main parts of it. That party had been one of many. I'm pretty sure I had already been drunk before showing up. Ashley Maxwell and I had an easy thing going where if I showed up without a chick, I usually ended the night in her bed. I can't even remember what she looked like and I sure as hell don't remember asking Saint if she was going to be there. Parties like that were below her and I knew it. Hearing her take on the situation made me feel like an asshole and it made why she had suddenly started treating me like a leper back then understandable.

The day she had caught me running my mouth was less clear. I didn't remember what I had been talking about, or the words I had used, but I do remember seeing her come around the corner looking like she was going to be sick all over the place and crying big, fat tears. At the time I thought if we were actually friends, or if she wasn't so shy, I would have asked her what was wrong. She was too pretty to look that heartbroken.

I wasn't a saint. I was an angry teenager cast aside and trying to figure out what kind of young man I was ultimately going to become. That had been a rocky road for a while and I said dumb shit, used hurtful words when I was shooting off my mouth, but I had never been and would never be a gossip or a bully. Yes, whatever she had overheard me say was inappropriate and taken out of whatever context I was using it in, and probably made me sound and appear to be the biggest dickhead on the planet.

However, what bothered me most wasn't that Saint had stumbled across me acting like an idiot and held it against me all this time, but that she had just automatically thought whoever I was bitching about had been her. That spoke to self-esteem issues and self-doubt that I wasn't sure I was equipped to handle. Not to mention, I didn't really know how to show her the guy I was now versus the pissed-off kid I had been then.

I shadowed her into her apartment and followed suit as she tossed her coat on the back of her couch. I didn't even look around the place. When she turned to face me I stepped immediately into her space. I wasn't going to give her the option of running again. She was almost as tall as I was with those wicked boots on. I grabbed her hair in one hand and wrapped the curls around my fist and used my other to grab on to her chin. She was caught.

"We can do a lot in ten minutes, Saint. Where is the bedroom?"

She looked a little unsure and tilted her head in the direction of a doorway past the little galley kitchen. Since I was working on a clock, I didn't have a lot of time to waste. I kissed her and simultaneously moved her backward in the direction of the door. She moved with me, which made me sigh in appreciation against her lips. She got her hands under the hem of my thermal and started to tug it up over my back and ribs.

No way was that happening again. I hit the door and pinned her against it, which made her gasp a little and had her eyes widening in surprise. I had to say I liked how well we lined up. It would be super easy to tangle her all around me and get down to business . . . maybe after these ten minutes were up I would show her that ten more would be a great idea . . . and ten more after that. I gently untangled her fingers from the fabric of my shirt and lightly put my hands on her narrow waist under the hem of her sparkly tank top.

"My turn."

I think she was stunned, but she stuck her bottom lip out a little bit at me and I couldn't resist the desire to catch it between my teeth.

"But I want to see your tattoo." Her voice was breathy and had a catch to it that made my dick all kinds of happy.

I lifted an eyebrow and watched her carefully as I got her top off up over her head. She was breathing shallow and obviously she was anxious, but so far so good, and I still had time on the clock. I turned the doorknob behind her and the door opened easily with her weight leaned against it. As I continued to dance her backward I found the tiny little zipper on the back of her skirt and started to pull it down.

I kissed her again to distract her from the fact that I was steadily heading her toward the bed in the center of the room and told her in a husky voice, "Later. It's not going anywhere."

I wanted to turn the lights on so I could see all that pretty white skin I was uncovering and the way all her red-and-copper-colored hair looked all over it, and the bed, and me when we got there. I didn't think she was there with me yet, though. She was kissing me back, had her arms wrapped around my neck, but she was still stiff and she didn't seem like she was in any hurry to let me get down to business as I wiggled the skirt over her hips and down over those pirate boots.

"Nash . . ." There was hesitancy in her voice and I felt like I was running out of time.

I got down so that I was on my knees in front of where she was hovering on the edge of the bed. She looked like she wanted to bolt but she took a deep breath and looked down at me. Her eyes were swirling like a hurricane. In that gaze was an equal mix of desire, trepidation, and question. The way her breasts rose and fell was captivating. She put one of her hands on either side of my head so she was holding on to the fire that marked my skin.

"You okay?" I stuck the tip of my tongue in her belly button and she whimpered a little.

"No. But I don't want you to stop."

I looked up at her from under my eyelashes.

"Good, because I'm not going to."

I could see she had no idea what I was talking about and I figured surprise was in my favor. The boots were going to have to stay; it would take too long to get them off, but the cute, black underwear had to go. I sent out a silent hope that they weren't a favorite pair and snapped the elastic on either side, leaving her very much naked and exposed, right in front of my face. She was obviously turned on, but the way her stomach quivered let me know she was equally nervous.

She called my name in a panicked tone, and I felt her fingernails curl into my scalp, so I knew I had to distract her. No problem. She was shaking so bad and the heels on those boots were so high it only took a little nudge to get her to topple back on the bed. She started to wiggle away across the mattress, but I was bigger, and I think more determined to prove to her we should be doing this than her fear was. I trailed my fingers up the inside of her thigh and lifted it up over my shoulder. I was listening, because if she told me no, told me to stop, I wasn't going to push her, but all I heard was a breathy panting and my name said like a curse on repeat.

God, was she sweet in spirit and flavor. I don't think I had ever had my lips and tongue on anything that tasted as good as her. I don't know how much trembling and spasming was happening because she was freaked out, or how much was because I put my mouth on her. I caught her clit between my teeth and sucked—hard—which made her jolt so much that her hips lifted off the bed. I used her sudden arch to slide my hands up under her and hold her to my face.

"What are you doing to me?"

It wasn't a question, it was more a plea, so I just hummed lightly against her trapped flesh until I felt the rest of her body start to respond. Her thighs trembled, her channel got damp and oh so welcoming, and I took that as an invitation to add my hands to the mix. I let go with one hand and trailed it around so I could stroke her, pet her, lick at her until she was tossing her head from side to side and I could see her hands curling into the sheets on the bed. It was the most beautifully unrestrained thing I had ever seen in my life. She tasted wild, she tasted special and slightly illicit, and I knew it was the best ten minutes any other person had ever given to me. Even if we didn't make it to the end this time, at least I got to see her like this, feel what I was doing to her and how much she liked it.

I felt the crest of her orgasm roll over my tongue, felt her inner walls squeeze around my stroking fingers, and felt the tense muscles in her thighs go lax as she made a high-pitched sound in her throat and just sort of vibrated all around me. I gave her little nub one last hard flick with the tip of my tongue and rose up to my feet in one fluid motion.

I put my hands on either side of her hips and looked down at her replete form. Her stomach was fluttering with aftershocks, her pale skin glowed with a nice, rosy flush that I could see even in the dark, and her eyes were open, dazed and staring right at me. Yes, there were glossy tears in them, but they weren't falling and she didn't look half as shell-shocked as the last time we had tried to do this. She looked awed and slightly dumbfounded. My ego was thrilled with the results.

"Time's up, Saint. It's your call what happens from here."

She blinked slowly at me.

"It's not you getting me off that worried me in the first place, Nash. You already proved you could with very little effort. It's the other way around that makes me want to hyperventilate and run for the hills."

Her voice was barely a whisper and it squeezed something in my chest. She was so honeyed, so pretty, I didn't understand how she didn't just *know* any guy would bend over backward to get the opportunity to worship her. Saint naked wasn't something any decent man would ever pass on the opportunity to appreciate with his hands, his mouth— with everything he had and then some.

"I don't know how to make you understand that isn't a possibility. Nothing about you could ever disappoint any man, Saint."

She sat up on the bed and quaked a little. She was looking me dead in the eye when she reached behind her and unclipped the bra she still had on. She was perfect. I mean really perfect, all full breasts, smooth skin, and perky pink nipples. She was just about my favorite thing I think I had ever managed to lay eyes on, and I didn't have a clue what to goddamn do with her.

She scooted to the edge of the bed so her legs were on either side of mine and she was face level with my stomach. She put her hands on my abs and started pushing my shirt up. I grabbed it by the collar and ripped it off one-handed over my head. While I did that she tangled with my belt buckle. She glanced up at me and I could see her fingers were shaking again.

"Do you have anything? I don't keep protection on hand, because . . . well, you can probably figure out why."

I wanted to laugh, but she was really close to my dick and I was having a hard time keeping my thoughts in order.

I pulled out my wallet and tossed it on the bed next to her.

"In there." I felt like if I let her take the lead, this had less of a chance in ending with me having blue balls and a lonely shower again.

She muttered something I didn't catch and trailed the tips of her fingers along the tips of the wings tattooed all along my sides and down across my front. The very tip of each wing ended right next to my crotch and had probably been the most miserable tattooing experience of my life. I thought she was going to stop when she reached the top of my boxers, but she didn't. She pulled them down, setting my cock free, and traced the wings all the way down to where they stopped.

"Had to hurt." I didn't really want to talk, but if it set her at ease, I was going to force myself to do it.

"Like a bitch."

She put a finger on the PA where it decorated the tip of my erection and looked up at me.

"This, too?"

I snorted out a laugh. "The tattoo was worse."

"Ohhhhh . . ." She trailed off and tentatively reached for the wallet so she could find the condom. I was waiting for her to call the whole thing off, anticipating it, when she surprised me yet again.

"You're gorgeous, and really fun to look at. I think it gets even better when you start to lose your clothes."

I wasn't sure what to say to that, and then I couldn't say anything because she wrapped her fist around the base of my straining dick and gave it a firm squeeze. I swore and she looked up at me. I just shrugged and she did it again, which made a drop of pre-cum pearl up at the tip. I didn't know how long my self-control was going to hold out while she was exploring everything I was working with. I wanted to tell her to just let go, that if she let me I could use it all to make her feel really good, but it was her show for now, so I just clicked my teeth shut on the inside of my cheek and let her brush the metal with her fingers and roll the barbell around. It was the most torturous show-and-tell I had ever endured.

I muttered her name, threaded my fingers in her endless miles of hair, and gripped her head hard enough that I could tilt her face up so she was looking at me and not at my straining cock.

"Happy New Year, Saint."

Both her fiery eyebrows shot up and she looked at the digital clock that did indeed read midnight. She gave a little sigh and picked the condom up.

"Happy New Year, Nash."

She got the latex on just as efficiently as she had the last time and scooted back on the bed so I could crawl up and over her. She wrapped her legs, still clad in those boots, up around my waist and I lifted up her hips so I could slide inside her in one long, smooth stroke. I wasn't wasting any more time. I felt like I had been waiting for this girl, this moment, forever.

I kept my eyes on her face and she did the same on mine. Her eyelids fluttered and her chest started to rise and fall where it was pressed tightly against mine, but she curled her hands around my biceps and lifted herself up a little higher, which made me groan. I bracketed my arms around her head when we finally got into a rhythm that worked for both of us and dropped down so I could kiss her slightly open mouth.

I was rocking into her fast and hard, partly because I didn't want to give her the opportunity to change her mind, but mostly I had been dreaming about this for a week since she left me on Christmas and I couldn't stop. She was hot, she was tight, she pulsated and burned along me in a way that made pleasure coil and snap along my spine. I was desperate for her and I could feel the pleasure and want building back up inside of her. I was using my tongue in her mouth to mimic what I was doing to her with my body and her hands were getting tighter, the noises she was making in the back of her throat were getting more frantic, and I could feel her inner walls drag and pull against my dick with greedy and needy movements.

I wanted to pry loose so I could get my mouth on those perfectly shaped breasts, but there wasn't time. She gasped, moved her long legs up even higher along my sides, and I felt her break apart, felt something that defined this moment as something greater than anything else I had ever felt move across both of us, and I grunted, pulled her closer, and released everything that was consuming about her back into her. Maybe that would be the only way I could ever really show her that she was so much better than any self-doubt she might have. I'd never had an orgasm that hollowed me out before, never come, and right on the heels of the warm fuzzies that followed felt like it somehow mattered more than anything that had ever existed before.

I chanced a look at her face and her eyes were closed, but she had a soft smile on her lips. Even though there were indeed twin tracks of moisture trailing over her cheeks, she didn't look devastated or horrified like last time. Honestly, there was enough emotion pushing at my chest I wasn't sure that my eyes weren't glassy and glazed over as well.

I felt compelled to ask, "All good?"

I levered up off of her, and when I pulled out, the drag of sensitized flesh against swollen folds made both of us groan a little.

She pried her eyes open and sat up. She wiped her cheeks with the back of her hand and pulled one leg up to start working on those boots. Good Lord, she was going to kill me. All naked white skin, fire-colored hair, and sexy-as-hell black boots. I could die a happy man if that was the last image I got to take with me to the grave.

"Maybe next time we can try it without so many accessories in the way."

I chuckled because I was still mostly dressed from the waist down, had been both times, but really I wanted to shout in victory at the fact she was even joking about there being a next time and not showing me the door.

"Sounds like a plan."

She climbed off the other side of the bed and grabbed a robe that was hanging on the back of her closet door and flicked on the light. I blinked to get my eyes to adjust while she settled herself cross-legged in the center of the bed. She fiddled with the lapels and I remembered she mentioned not really liking to be naked. It was a shame, looking the way she did, she should never wear clothes.

"I wanna see the tattoo."

I brushed my hands over my head.

"I gotta take care of this first, and well . . ." I sort of tossed my hands up. "It's huge, and if you want to see it all, I have to get all the way naked."

Now I could see her really blush.

"Bathroom's that way." She pointed in the direction we had stumbled in from. "I think my curiosity is greater than my embarrassment might be at this point. I really do wanna see it."

I shrugged. "All right. I'll be right back."

I wasn't shy. I would've stripped for her right then and there, but as much as I needed a minute to figure out why I felt like my entire world was suddenly rotating on another axis entirely, I figured she could use the little breather as well.

I took care of the condom, ran some ice-cold water over the top of my head, and splashed my face. I looked the same when I gazed at myself in the mirror . . . same eyes, same face, same piercings, same ink . . . but something felt different.

I dropped the rest of my clothes in a pile on the bathroom floor after I shucked off my Vans. I picked it all up and trucked back to the bedroom. She was where I left her, sitting in the center of the bed playing with the ends of her hair. Jesus, she was going to kill me. She had also plugged her phone into the dock on her nightstand and the Kills were filling the room with moody rock and roll.

"It's a dragon."

I forgot I didn't have a shirt on when I had walked into the bathroom. I turned around so my back was to her and she could see the entire thing. I heard her quick intake of breath and the covers rustle as she moved across the bed.

"It is. Phil did it for me. We started the day I turned eighteen and finished it the day I turned twenty-one. It took over six hundred hours in the chair."

A lot of people had dragon tattoos. No one had a dragon tattoo like mine. It was done in a traditional Japanese style. The colors were all screaming hues of bold reds, greens, yellows, and golds all over my skin. The tail started on the top of my foot, it wound all the way around my calf, covered my thigh, took up one entire butt cheek, the body twisted and turned across my spine until it reached my shoulder, where the fierce head was always watching me, the wings flared out, completely covered my sides, ran all along my ribs, and ended right next to my dick, the talons were gripping each shoulder in fierce, clutching hands, and the fire it was breathing rolled over my collarbone on each side and danced up the back of my neck until it forked off and marked each side of my head over my ears.

It was massive, had enough detail that it looked like it was going to fly away with me in its sharp claws at any second, and I knew enough about my chosen career field, the skill level involved in the piece, that the reason it was so spectacular was because Phil cared about me. I was more than his protégé, more than his kid, I was his walking, talking legacy of an art form he had simply loved and honed over the years. My dragon was his *Mona Lisa*.

"It's so beautiful." Her hands lightly stroked over my spine, and up along the ridges of my shoulders. "It's so much more than just a tattoo."

Something lodged in my throat at the fact she understood that without being in the industry or me having to explain it to her.

"I was pretty messed up when I was younger. I didn't know what to do with it, so I did a bunch of dumb shit. Got arrested spray-painting a bridge, got into a brawl at one of Jet's shows and sent some kid to the ICU, tattooed a bunch of dumb, pointless crap all over my body. Phil saw I was spiraling, tried to get me to stop it. He called me out and told me straight up I was acting like a toddler looking for attention from his mommy, which is exactly what I was doing."

I sighed as her hands trailed over the wings and skated lower across my ass. She was petting the dragon, but it felt like she was trying to soothe me as well.

"He told me he would teach me how to do what he did. Tattooing always seemed like a cool thing to me, and when he offered to show me and Rule what art was really about and how to put all our feelings of being cast out to creative use, it was what stopped my free fall."

I shook my head at the memory and gave a wan grin. I

had to grit my teeth because her soft hands had found their way to the front of me and there was only one place they could stop.

"One bargain I had to make with him in order to apprentice was no more shitty tattoo work. Phil wouldn't tolerate it if I was going to represent him and his shop. He told me I had to agree to let him and only him tattoo me until the apprenticeship was up. I agreed, and he started the back part of the dragon that day. Of course as we went along he let Rule get his licks in on my skin as he got better, but pretty much only Phil got to pound on me with a needle for years. This was the result. He said I needed something strong, something that reminded me that people always had my back and would protect me from those that wanted to hurt me. He knew I had a rough time with my mom, so he was trying to make me feel less alone."

My voice trailed off as her hands moved up my chest, across my collarbone, and to my head.

Her voice was quiet when she asked, "Why up here?"

"I was never going to be a cubicle kind of guy or a kindergarten teacher. I wanted something that really solidified the idea that I was doing my own thing and that my mom's approval or lack thereof wasn't something I needed to work on getting anymore. When you tattoo your head, or your face, even your neck and hands, it makes a statement. It clearly defines that this is a choice not a fashion accessory. I was pretty used to getting looked down on, getting torn up at home, so having strangers and the general public gape at my ink never bothered me. Plus it's a great conversation starter. I get asked everywhere I go about it, so I just hand them a business card and tell them to swing by the shop. I can't count how many new clients it's gotten me. If I grow my hair out you can't even tell it's there, which is why the fire the dragon is breathing goes over my shoulders as well."

"It's amazing. Really beautiful."

I turned around and put my arms around her. She was on her knees on the bed, so we were almost on the same level. I kissed her stunned mouth. She tasted like sex and mystery.

"So are you."

She didn't say anything and I saw her flush. She never said anything when I told her how attractive she was. Most chicks ate it up with a spoon, tried to play coy, but Saint just ignored it like I never spoke. I wasn't sure what to do with that. I wasn't trying to flatter her, to lure her to bed. I was just telling her the truth.

I brushed my thumb over the owl tattoo she had on her collarbone. She had another one on her hip where her underwear normally covered it, a small cross, and on her back right between her shoulder blades was a traditional Catholic saint depicted in all its detailed grandeur.

"These are all well done, and I can guess they have a lot of personal meaning behind them. I can always tell."

She lifted an eyebrow and put her arms around my neck as I leaned over and took her back to the bed with me stretched out on top of her.

"How can you tell?"

"They're in places no one can see but you. They aren't flash designs off the wall, and even though they are all pretty tiny they have a lot of detail." A tiny smile flirted with her mouth. "The owl is for wisdom, I bet; the saint, your name?"

She shook her head, and the way we pressed against each other I could feel her body start to soften and melt into the pressure of my much bigger frame. I liked the way my dark skin contrasted so vividly against her much paler skin tone.

"Saint Agnes, patron saint of nurses. My sister is Faith, so that's the cross, and the owl . . ." She ran her finger over the tip of my nose. "You got it. They don't have anything on the stuff you've got, but I've always been happy with them."

I worked a hand between the two of us and started to untie the knot at her waist. The lights were still on, so I wasn't sure how far she was going to let me go before getting shy on me again. Hell, I was counting my blessings she hadn't kicked me out the front door after the first ten minutes were up.

"Body art isn't a contest. The only person that has to like it is the person stuck with it for the rest of their life. As long as you love it when you see it, that's all that matters."

I rubbed my thumb over the cross when her robe slid open.

"I had a girl artist do it. She was nice and made me feel really comfortable. You are the only other person who has ever seen it."

I was kissing her on the side of the neck, drawing a lazy pattern on her hip with the tips of my fingers, but her words made me still. She told me I was the only guy to ever get her off, but I didn't really think about that translating into the fact that she hadn't been with very many men. It made the world tilt back on that parallel axis again. I loved the idea of being the only guy who got to see her special markings, the only guy who got to make her feel special and good in a way only great sex could.

"Thank you. That matters, Saint, I hope you know that."

I ran my tongue along her collarbone and down the center of her chest. I was surprised she hadn't asked me to stop or at least hit the lights. But she was rolling with it and I had another condom somewhere in my wallet, so why not see how far she would let me go? She was so soft and lush, not at all stick-figure skinny but a handful of curves and warm flesh. She did indeed have a very light dusting of freckles that crossed the top of both breasts, and I wasn't surprised at all when I pulled her turgid nipple into my mouth that she tasted like velvet and candy on my tongue. I rolled one and then the other pink tip across my tongue, leaving them both shiny and pointy while her eyes had gotten darker and heavy-lidded.

"Whaddaya say, Saint? Wanna give me another ten minutes?"

She gazed up at me like she was trying to figure something out. There was confusion, but more than that, her face and eyes had darkened to a cool shade of slate.

"Who are you, Nash Donovan?"

I gave her the most honest answer I could to that question. "Sometimes I don't know, but most of the time what you see is what you get, Saint. I know you think I was once someone else, but I'm telling you I was never that guy. I'm not saying I was great or even likable back then, but I wasn't whatever it is you think I was."

She didn't say anything for a long minute and we just watched each other. I thought she was going to ask me to get dressed and leave, but to my surprise, she wrapped her legs up around me and whispered in my ear.

"Ten minutes was your idea, Nash, I'm willing to give you all night."

Well, with permission like that, I was going to see exactly what I could cook up before she either passed out from exhaustion or asked me to go.

I had never looked forward to a challenge more and I refused to wonder if one night or any number of minutes would be enough with this girl. She was something different. It radiated out of her, and I wasn't sure I was anything special or a guy lucky enough to be the one to grab on to it.

CHAPTER 10

Saint

IDIDN'T HAVE TIME to get weirded out that Nash spent the night, or to sit back and evaluate all the things I let him do to me, or all things I had been bold enough to do to him. I don't know where any of those typical fears and uncertainties that normally strangled me when it came to sex had gone, but when my phone went off before six in the morning on New Year's Day, I was still very much naked and very much wrapped deliciously around a very large and naked man. There was no time to freak out, because the hospital was the number calling, and when it came to work, that was my first priority, and not all the tattooed and toned skin that stretched across Nash's back, even as tempting and alluring as it might be.

Sunny was upset. Two different staff members had called off, and not only did she have to go in and cover one of the shifts but she needed me to go in as well. I was scheduled to work that night, so it meant being at the hospital all day, which sounded awful considering Nash had kept me up well into the early hours of the morning, but it offered me an easy way out of dealing with the day-after awkwardness, so I readily agreed.

When I got off the phone he lumbered sleepily to his feet, got dressed without giving me any kind of guilt trip or hassle, gave me a quick kiss on the mouth, and told me to give him a call when I got a chance. He left without any kind of interrogation, any kind of uncomfortable dance around the topic of are-we-or-are-we-not-doing-this-again. He left the ball firmly in my court and made it clear that it was entirely up to me if I wanted to keep it in play or not. He put me in charge, which wasn't something I was used to outside of my career, and I had to admit the power of it, the choice being mine, made the entire situation with him easier to get my head around. It also made the fact that I was well on my way to admitting I had to forgive him for past sins the only option if I was going to move forward with whatever it was we were now doing with each other.

When I got to work it was chaos. Injured partyers from the night before abounded. There was a horrific home-construction accident involving a chain saw and a missing hand; a cop rushed in who had been involved in a domestic dispute with a couple and got a knife in the gut for his effort; a toddler had gotten into the bathroom cleaner under the sink; and two women in labor: one was breech the other was having premature contractions. I didn't have time to think about anything else or worry about the curious looks Sunny was giving me whenever we were in the same room or passed each other in the hall. I was dragging majorly by the time my actual shift in the late afternoon started and was in the break room guzzling coffee like it was lifeblood when my tiny little boss finally cornered me.

"Soooo?"

I jolted and sloshed the hot liquid over my fingers. I gave her a dirty look and found a paper towel to clean up the mess.

"So what?"

She rolled her eyes at me and poked me in the arm. "So how was the date with the doctor? You sounded exhausted this morning when I called, so I assume it went well. I bet you made a beautiful pair."

I tried to keep my face impassive but I couldn't keep looking her in the eye. Not when I had ditched the awful doctor and spent the rest of the night being thoroughly debauched by Nash.

"I ended the date early."

Her eyes got big and she wrinkled her nose up at me. "You had him take you home early?"

I sighed and tossed my paper cup of now-lukewarm coffee into the trash.

"He was a jerk and so full of himself. His friends were appalling and the party was really just a group of people standing around trying to outdo each other. I was uncomfortable and bored, so I called a friend and left early. Dr. Bennet and I are really not compatible."

She gave me a considering look.

"The guy with the nose ring?"

"What about him?"

"Is that the friend you called?"

I refused to feel bad about it or ashamed. There was nothing wrong with Nash. In fact, there was so much right with him I was having a hard time remembering why I needed to watch my tender heart and fragile feeling around him in the first place.

"Yes."

She made a noise and followed me out of the room. One of the medical assistants handed me a new file and told me there was a patient waiting in one of the rooms for me.

"I know based on first glance you wouldn't think he was a really nice guy, but he is."

She shrugged and started walking the other direction from me. "What I think really doesn't matter, I guess. Do you even realize that you've been grinning all day? I've never seen you do that. You always look so serious and intent, but today"—she took her index fingers and tugged up the corners of her own mouth—"you are just one big ball of cheer. That makes me happy for you. I don't care who put the smile there, Saint, I just care that it stays."

I was smiling, I hadn't really thought about it. I was also sore and tired, had a hickey on my collarbone, and my favorite pair of black underwear was in the trash. I would also never be able to rock my knee-high boots again without having X-rated recollections of last night. I still wasn't a hundred percent sold on the fact I could get involved with a guy who had disappointed me so much in the past, that I could trust all these things he was making me feel about him and about myself, but there was no denying I felt lighter, more normal than I ever had with a guy before.

He was the only one I had managed to have a normal, sexy, and sensual time with and I wanted that, wanted more than that really, if he was willing to offer it up. Not only did I desire this Nash, I think I actually liked him and had to admit that I cared about him. We were so entangled in this entire thorny mess, I wasn't sure how either one of us could get out of it without drawing some kind of blood and suffering pricks of irritation.

I didn't have the luxury of turning it over in my head to the point of exhaustion. My second shift was just as busy as my first, and by the time I crawled home, I was too tired to function, let alone contemplate what I was going to do about Nash or about us. I worked the next two days in a row, and though I wanted to text Nash or give him a call to let him know I was at least thinking about him, I couldn't seem to find the right words. On the third day I decided to do something out of the box. I sent him flowers at the tattoo shop, a pretty bouquet of roses in red, yellow, and orange that matched the fire tattooed all over him. The colors were fitting in another way as well. Red meant romance and maybe even love, yellow was kindness and friendship, and the orange passion and enthusiasm . . . we had those last two covered for sure. I did it partly because the idea of sending a big, tattooed brute of a guy flowers made me laugh, and partly because I wanted to *show* him that he was on my mind.

I didn't stop to think if he would think it was dumb, didn't get insecure or worry about how he would take it. I just did it and sent along a card that simply said: *Thanks.* I was thankful for the ride, thankful for the night in my bed, and mostly thankful for him just being him. I hoped he would understand all of it.

By the end of the day, I got a picture text message of the giant bouquet sitting in the center of the desk in the very masculine shop. No one was in the picture, but several pairs of tattooed hands were in the background throwing up the devil horns in approval. It made me laugh. Nash's response was short and sweet:

Never got flowers before . . . They are as pretty as you are. Thank you.

I didn't know what to say to that, but it made me feel like everything I thought I knew about myself was wrong. I sent him back a smiley face and went back to work. Work was always my go-to when I had things in my life that I couldn't seem to get a handle on.

When I got home that night I was going to call him finally but was waylaid by an emergency phone call from Faith. Apparently my mom had run into Dad's new girlfriend at the grocery store and an ugly scene had ensued. Things had been broken, property had been damaged, and my mom ended up with assault charges leveled at her. Faith had begged Dad to convince his girlfriend not to press charges, knowing Mom would pay for the things in the store she had destroyed, but he was zero help. He wanted Mom to get help, to get over it, and I couldn't say I totally disagreed with him. The whole situation sounded ridiculous and completely out of control. My mom had gone too far, and my words about not wanting to bail her out of jail were coming back to haunt me.

It was either have Faith load all the kids up in the car and drive her pregnant self to Brookside in order to bail Mom out, or bite the bullet and do it myself. Of course that was the only option, even though it was something I absolutely didn't want to do. So I left work, drove up to the mountain, and went and bailed my mother out of the slammer. It was ludicrous and like something off a cheesy reality-TV show, and it made me really wish I had managed to find the time to touch base with Nash, because for some reason, talking to him always made me feel better.

My mother was less than thrilled to see me. Maybe because she was embarrassed. Maybe because she was covered in some kind of unidentified sticky substance and was sporting smudged makeup and an unmistakable black eye. Or maybe it was because she was led into the waiting room of the tiny precinct by a police officer younger than me still wearing handcuffs and looking pitiful. Or maybe it was because he was calmly telling her not to miss her court date and that she might want to consider starting anger management classes because the judge was sure to require them for her.

She caught sight of me and her head dropped a little. I took her arm and guided her out the front door and into my car. She didn't say a word to me, but I could see that she was crying silently. I was torn between the urge to hug her and the urge to throttle her, but my frustration at her, the situation, and the state of the family had reached its breaking point.

I huffed out a sigh and looked at her out of the corner of my eye.

"Okay, Mom. I need to know what the plan here is. Are you just going to keep chasing every kind of pill you can get prescribed to you with a gallon of wine every day and use that as an excuse for all your behavior? Are you going to cross the line and actually hurt someone, maybe even yourself? Are you so lost in hurt and anger that you're going to miss being a part of your daughter's pregnancy because she is scared of what you might do? I hate to break the news to you, Mom, but no one . . . I mean NO ONE . . . is going to be willing to ride to your rescue anymore if you keep this up. At some point, accountability needs to come into play."

She didn't respond, just continued to sit quietly crying in the passenger seat while ignoring me. I didn't know what else to say to her. This had gotten so far out of hand too long ago and I wasn't sure how to pull it all back in. When we got to her house I pulled into the driveway and turned to look at her. She sniffled a little and looked at me out of red-rimmed eyes.

"Your dad was my high school sweetheart. We dated all through college and I sacrificed everything so he could go to dental school. I gave him a beautiful family, and I thought we were happy. It hurts so much worse when I think about the idea that he just fell out of love with me than the fact that he moved on. How can someone's feelings for another person just go away, Saint? After everything?"

My heart twisted for her.

"I don't know, Mom, and I can't pretend to understand how badly Dad hurt you, but I do know what you're doing isn't making you or anyone else feel better about it. Dad might have fallen out of love, but you still have two daughters who love you and grandkids who miss having a happy and healthy grandma to spend time with. We matter, too, Mom, and all of us hate to see what you're doing to yourself."

"I just want him to hurt as badly as he made me hurt."

"Well, that isn't going to happen."

"It isn't fair."

I shook my head. "No, it really isn't, but trust me, getting divorced and having to start over is the least in life that isn't fair. I had to watch the parents of a way too young girl realize that their daughter died for no other reason than people can't figure out how to be nice to each other. It isn't that hard, just be nice and people might not have to suffer needlessly, but that isn't the world we live in, so young girls die. That isn't fair, Mom. People falling out of love is vicious and it sucks, but there are far worse things you could be going through. I know that sounds harsh but it's very true."

Something moved across her gaze and she looked away from me.

"I forget what a remarkable life you've made for yourself, Saint. The strength you have to have to do what you do is admirable and I very well may have lost sight of that in all of this. I hope you know that beyond everything else, I am very proud of you."

Wow. I hadn't been expecting that.

"Thanks, Mom."

"Now put some makeup on and maybe a push-up bra and land one of those doctors you work with and I'll be over the moon."

And there she was . . . that sounded more like my mom.

"Stay out of trouble, Mom, and maybe quit the pills." I tried to keep it light but I made sure she could see the concern I had for her in my gaze. I wanted better for her but realized she was going to have to take some steps herself in order to get it.

She shut the door and headed up to the front door. I waited until she went inside and pulled out my phone. I didn't think about it, I just found his name in my phone book and pushed the button to call him. He answered on the second ring.

"Hey."

"Hey." My voice dropped a little huskier against my will.

"What's up?"

"Are you busy?"

"Yeah, right now I have a client and one more after. Why, what's going on?"

I chewed on my bottom lip and tapped my fingers nervously on my knee.

"Nothing really. I just had a really weird day and thought maybe hanging out with you would make it a little better."

He was quiet for a long minute and I thought he was going to tell me I had missed my window or that maybe if I had bothered to call him sooner we could've made plans. This is why I sucked so bad at the boy-girl thing. It was rude to just assume he would drop everything and make time for me. I knew his life was busy and he had a lot of friends and people clamoring for his attention and time. Who was I to ask him to be available for me when I finally forced myself to make the time for something other than my job?

"Yeah, we can hang out. Do you care if it's later? I want to swing by Phil's. He wasn't looking very good yesterday when I checked in on him, and I won't be out of here until after eight, so like around ten or so?"

I was off tomorrow, so he could show up at midnight for all I cared, just as long as he showed up.

"That's fine. Do you want me to feed you?"

He chuckled and I heard him say something to someone in the background.

"No. Let's go do something fun. Wear something you don't mind getting dirty."

That was intriguing and had me curious, which was bizarre because I hated surprises.

"What does your idea of fun look like, Nash?"

"You'll have to wait and see. Later, Saint."

He hung up and I was left staring at my phone in wonderment. I didn't know what I was doing, didn't know what he was doing to me, but there was no doubt he made my day better by simply being. I shuffled through my music and landed on the Vines and headed back to the city.

I called Faith and filled her in on the situation with our mom. She sounded so stressed out and so sad, I felt bad for her, but Mom was an adult and had to make her own choices and suffer her own consequences. There wasn't much we could do. We talked for most of the drive home. She couldn't believe I had bailed out on the doctor. I hadn't exactly told her who my rescuer had been. I knew she wouldn't like it. Not after the way my younger self had broken at the hands of Nash's thoughtless actions and words, directed at me or not.

I still didn't fully believe that he hadn't been talking about me, that he was just running his mouth. The vehemence in his tone, the anger in his eyes, made me want to believe him, but I just didn't know. Frankly, even if he was talking about someone else back then, the words were still cruel and awful. If I let go of that memory, admitted that there was a distinct possibility that my own shattered sense of self, my own broken self-confidence, had fabricated what I wanted to hear, what I just expected to hear about myself back then, then it followed that I had to admit that everything I had done, all the roadblocks I faced in my interpersonal relationships up to this point, fell on me. That was a tough pill to swallow.

I cleaned up the apartment a little, took a shower, and braided my long hair, made myself a bowl of cereal for dinner because my stomach was turning up and down, and dug around in my closet for something that was okay to get dirty but didn't make me look like a bag lady. I settled on a pair of yoga pants and a button-up flannel shirt over a tank top. It wasn't going to win me any prizes on *Project Runway,* but I doubted it would send Nash running for the hills. It took me a second to recognize that I wasn't freaking out at him seeing me like this. Maybe because he had seen me so often in my scrubs at the hospital and sans makeup while I was working. Or maybe it was because there wasn't a part of me he hadn't had his hands or his mouth on and he didn't seem to have any complaints. Had I been anyone else, I think his nonverbal appreciation of my naked form would have been a huge stroke to my ego, but being as I was a weirdo, I was just glad he kept his actual thoughts on the subject—good or bad—to himself.

He showed up a few minutes after ten, gave me a quick once-over, pulled me into a kiss that had me panting and winded, and hauled me outside to the car. He was dressed in what I assumed he wore to work and I could see that he had dark shadows under each eye and a scruff on his normally clean-shaven chin. He looked drawn and worn out. I struggled a little with feeling guilty for asking him to give me some of his time.

I asked him shyly, "Long week?"

He opened the door for me and ushered me into the car. The interior was still warm and he had the Tossers playing on the radio. Every time I was in this monster of a car, Celtic punk rock was coming out of the speakers.

When he got back behind the wheel, he looked over at me and gave me a lopsided grin.

"Well, hearing from you was a highlight of it for sure . . . and the flowers. You had the shop rolling. I'm never going to hear the end of it. But Phil isn't doing so great and I keep asking him about how I managed to go my whole life without knowing that he was really my dad and he keeps telling me to talk to my mom. I would rather eat glass. Plus now that Rule is back from his honeymoon, we have to start figuring out what we want to do about the new shop. It's all just kind of piling up."

"I'm sorry about Phil and I can totally relate to the mom thing. I had to go get mine out of jail today."

He barked out a laugh and looked at me. "You're joking?"

"Nope." I proceeded to tell him all about it, which meant I was the one carrying on the conversation for a full fifteen minutes as he wound back across the city to the warehouse district out past Coors Field.

He asked questions along the way, but never interrupted, and I couldn't believe how seamlessly I was engaging with him. That never happened to me. He stopped in front of a huge garage and poked the code in a big metal gate and drove through. I had no idea what we were doing in this part of the city or at this location, so I looked at him questioningly.

"How is car repair fun?"

He tsked at me and pulled the Charger up to one of the closed bay doors.

"I rebuilt this entire beast from the ground up. It was my saving grace back in the day. This car and Phil were pretty much the only things that kept me out of jail. It was how I figured out there were more productive ways to spend my time than getting in trouble and trying to get a reaction out of my mom. Phil told me that I needed a classic, something that would last the test of time. He told me if I took care of it, babied it, loved it, that it would do the same for me. I realize now he was trying to teach me about more than cars. He helped me pull it out of a junkyard and we spent years making it into the beast it is now."

He got out of the car and punched in another code on another electric keypad, and the big, bay door started to roll up. The garage was dark and intimidating at first glance, but as he pulled the car in, the headlights danced across a bunch of old cars in various stages of repair. It clearly wasn't just a garage but a custom car shop.

"My buddy Wheeler owns this place. He helps me out with the Charger when I need him to and we trade out work. He lets me use the paint shop occasionally."

I couldn't help but lift an eyebrow. "A car guy named Wheeler? Really?"

He laughed and got out of the car. He reached behind

the seat and pulled out a black bag and a roll of something I hadn't noticed earlier.

"His first name is Hudsen, and who are you to talk? You're a nurse named Saint."

He handed me the rolled-up bundle and I noticed that it was paper. I had no idea what we were doing and told him as much.

He just took my other hand and we navigated the cars and toolboxes to the back of the shop, where there was a sealed-off room. He turned on more lights and smirked at me. His eyes were glittering with violet threads of merriment. I bit back a sigh. Really I could just stare at him all day and be happy.

"Back in the day I used to take a bunch of spray paint out and go tag a bunch of stuff to blow off steam. I thought it was cool to break the law, to leave my mark all over the city, until I got busted and Phil had to pay a huge-ass fine to keep me out of jail. That was how I got into art, into design. Really, I think I wanted to get busted doing something illegal so my mom would have to deal with me, but that's neither here nor there anymore, and it's still fun to paint with cans."

We went into the room that was all white, had a crazy ventilation system, and had ventilators for breathing hanging on the wall and a bunch of stuff that was obviously used to paint cars in it. Nash tossed the bag on the floor and now I could hear the cans of paint inside it roll around together. He took the paper out of my hands and walked over to one of the walls that had a wire hanging from it and a bunch of metal clips.

"I can't go out and paint walls, buildings, or trains any-more, at least not unless I'm getting paid to do it, but graf-fiti is fun. It's bright and wild, there are no rules, and after tattooing stuff for other people all day, sometimes I need a change of pace. It's nice just to get out and do my own thing, remember my own style. Wheeler lets me set up in here. No mess, no vandalism charges, and it's always pretty fun."

I watched as he hung up two pieces of paper that were almost as tall as me and about as wide as a door. He crouched down to start taking the multitude of paint cans in all the colors in the rainbow out of the bag. I had never had some-one let me in on one of their own little rituals before, never was close enough to anyone for that. There was the pull he had on me acting up again.

"I can't even draw a stick figure, Nash." He was a profes-sional artist, for goodness' sake, how was I supposed to be comfortable even playing around with that kind of skill level and talent judging me?

He grumbled something under his breath and crammed a black baseball hat that was in the bag on his head back-ward. It was a good look for him.

"Saint, not everything is win or lose. We aren't in com-petition with each other, we're here to have fun and spend some time together without a bunch of noise and the outside bugging us. Just relax and let go."

I took his word for it. I didn't have a choice. I had missed him this week and wanted this time with him. I felt like he was giving me a peek inside the inner workings of his head. We stood side by side and considered the giant canvases. He started on his first, and before I even picked up one can of paint he had the entire background filled with swirling, primary colors that were bold and eye-catching. I couldn't tell what he was doing, but it was fascinating and mesmerizing to watch.

I bit the tip of my tongue and started Bob Ross–ing some happy little trees and clouds. Before I knew it, I forgot all about Nash, forgot I was in an auto body shop, and just started actually having fun. I added a rainbow, and then I needed a pot of gold. Of course, since I had a lopsided and runny pot of gold, I needed a leprechaun to go with it. By the time I was done, I was laughing so hard I had to hold my sides, but the paper was covered in a sloppy, drippy mess that no one would want, but it was hysterical to me, and when Nash looked over my shoulder at it and just tilted his head and squinted his eyes to try and make it out, it only made me laugh harder. This is why people kept telling me I needed to get out more. I couldn't ever remember giggling so hard and unrestrained.

I stepped around him to look at the creation he had been working on and my laughter got trapped in my lungs. My jaw dropped open and I turned to him with gigantic eyes.

"Is that me?" I sounded like I was being strangled.

"Really? You have to ask?" His tone was humorous, but there was something else underlying it.

The picture he had created was a cartoon character, exaggerated and outrageous. The colors seemed to pop off the paper. It was a nurse in an outrageously sexy outfit, the kind girls wore for Halloween when they were on the prowl. She had wild red hair and was holding a cartoon syringe in one hand and a heart in the other. Despite the exaggerated proportions and obvious enhancements to make her shockingly sexy, she was me. The hair, the eyes, the face . . . all of it was me. How on earth had he done that in the twenty minutes we had been screwing around?

"It's amazing."

"I keep telling you that so are you. You just aren't listening." He moved to take the painting down and I reached out to stop him.

"Can I have it?"

He lifted an eyebrow. "Of course."

It was huge, I had no idea what I was going to do with it, but the idea that that was how he saw me . . . sexy, beautiful, and in control . . . I didn't want to let it go.

"Nash, let's go somewhere."

"What do you mean? I was just gonna come back to your place with you if that was cool."

I took the painting he offered me and hugged it to my chest.

"I never went on dates in high school, never had a guy try anything funny or get handsy so I could tell him to stop. I didn't kiss my first boy until I was almost twenty years old. I want you to take me somewhere kids go to fool around. This was fun, and I haven't really ever been the type to just let my hair down and have fun. I think parking with you in a car sounds like a blast." It also sounded hot and sexy and would fulfill every teenage fantasy I had ever concocted that involved him.

"Saint, it's cold out, we both have empty apartments, we're both tall, and I'm not anywhere near as small as I was in high school. It might sound fun, but the reality is going to be cold and cramped." He was grinning lightly when he said this, though, and I knew he just needed to be persuaded.

I put one of my hands on the center of his chest, felt his heartbeat steady and sound under my fingertips, and looked up at him with pleading eyes.

"Please, Nash."

He sighed and put a hand under my braid at the back of my neck.

"As long as you realize I probably won't stop at second base and that means your ass is the one that's going to be naked and cold, then I'm in."

I giggled, actually giggled, which I don't think I had ever done before tonight, and kissed him on his scruffy chin.

"Deal."

He put the stuff from our painting party in the trunk, hopefully because he wanted the backseat free . . . goody . . . and we started to head out of the city kind of toward Brookside.

"Where are we going?"

"Lookout Mountain."

It was just outside Golden and where Buffalo Bill Cody's grave was located. I had heard about it but had never actually seen it. You were supposed to be able to see the entire city from up there.

"Is that where you used to take girls?"

"Uh, no. By the time I knew girls had more going for them than the fact that they smelled good and would do my homework for me if I told them they were pretty, I was pretty much living with Phil full-time. Dude is a player, way worse than Rule or I ever was. I had the house to myself pretty much every night, so when I got the opportunity I just took them home."

"What do you mean 'got the opportunity'?" I remembered girls hanging all over him in high school. It didn't look like he had to work too hard at finding a willing bed partner.

"I hung out with a dude in a band, every chick's idea of the perfect rebel, and the captain of the football team. I was just some guy with a bad attitude that was constantly getting told what a mistake I was at home. I didn't know how to talk to girls that mattered. I had girls floating around that were easy and would put out . . . they didn't really care who the guy was. That means they could've been into Rule for the night, or Jet. Opportunity definitely had to play into it."

That was so odd. My perception and the reality of everything back then just seemed so different. I wanted to ask him more about it, but we got to an outcropping of rock that was flat and just long enough and wide enough for him to park the car. He killed the headlights and threw an arm over the back of the seat and looked at me in the now-dim interior of the front seat.

"We can go back to the city. You say the word."

I didn't answer him. I lifted up and wiggled over the back of the seat instead. I pulled off my flannel shirt along the way. He left the car running, but it was still January in Colorado and we were high up in the foothills, so it was brisk in the car and the windows were already fogging up. He watched me for a second and then got out of the car. There was no way he was fitting over the seat like I did, and he pulled his wallet out on the way. He handed me the square foil packet and climbed in, pulling the door shut behind him. He stripped off his hoodie and hat and we sat facing each other.

I thought he would grab me and pull me to him, but a ghost of a smile teased around his mouth and he pushed back his broad shoulders so that he was lounged across the leather seat.

"This is your game, Saint. How do you want to play?"

He was always putting me in the driver's seat, pushing my limits, making me say what I wanted from him. Maybe that was why I never froze up with him, why I never had to question what was happening between us, because everything that was happening was what I was asking for. There was no room for rejection or judgment that way.

I shivered, and not at all from the cold.

"I want you to kiss me."

He reached out and caught my braid in his hand and used it to reel me in. When our mouths touched, it was so much more than a simple kiss. He tasted like the past and like the future, the then and the now. He felt so strong and solid, but his lips were soft and searching. His skin was rougher than normal, but when he pulled me closer and our noses bumped, the glide of that little piece of metal he wore was smooth. He twirled his tongue with mine, and used his teeth on the plush curve of the inside of my lip. I gasped into the kiss and felt him chuckle. Before, I would have automatically assumed he was laughing *at* me. Now I knew he was just amused because it felt that good and he knew it.

My hands were on his chest and I used them to start pulling his shirt up across his flat stomach. He helped by lifting his arms up as much as he could. Considering the confined space and how broad across he was, it took a little finesse to get the fabric out of my way. Goose bumps danced across his golden skin and I bent my head to trace the ones across his collarbone with the tip of my tongue, which made him grunt.

"Now I want to kiss you."

He was still holding my hair like a rope, so he had to loosen his hold when I ran the flat of my tongue over one of his nipples and then the other.

He swore and muttered, "Headed in the wrong direction for that, pretty lady."

I traced the ridges of his defined abs with my fingers and watched in delight as the muscles tensed and flexed along with the caress. It made it look like the wings along his abs were fluttering in the night air.

"No I'm not. I'm a little worried about working around all that metal down there, but I'm definitely headed in the right direction."

He swore again and I started working on his belt buckle. It wasn't something I had done more than once and Nash was working with some heavy-duty equipment, but I was fascinated by it all and wanted to make him feel as good as he always made me feel.

"Just act like it isn't there."

"Why? It might be my favorite part."

He laughed again, but it turned into a groan when he fell out hot and hard into my waiting hands. He was throbbing, thick and anxious, as I hovered over him. I rubbed my thumb over the ring in the tip, and his entire body jerked in response. I let out a breath I wasn't aware I was holding and he muttered my name softly as the moist air caressed his ready flesh.

I dropped my head and pulled the pierced head into my mouth. It was a texture and sensation overload, must have been for him, too, because he bowed up and his hand jerked on my hair hard enough that it hurt a little bit.

"Jesus." No, not quite, just Saint, but I would take it as a sign he liked it.

I rolled the hoop across my tongue, skated down over that hidden barbell and farther down the shaft until I felt like I couldn't take any more. I slid back up and repeated the exact same motion again, only this time I added a hand around the base that I squeezed with my bobbing motion because he was just too much to take in. He said my name again, I felt the legs I was using to brace on tense and his stomach go rock-hard, but right as I was starting to taste the slippery, salty release that would let me know it was a job well done, he pulled at my hair so hard it actually hurt for real, and yanked me up and off of him.

He was breathing hard and his eyes were indigo. "If you do that much longer, one of us is gonna end up cold and horny. Hint: it won't be me."

He started pulling on my stretchy yoga pants. I was super glad I had worn something that was easy to wiggle and twist out of with very little room and big, impatient hands getting in my way. He abandoned the bottom half of my outfit and went to work manhandling my tank top off over my head. I had to admit it was gratifying that I could actually feel how ready, how needy, he was for me. That was a powerful mood enhancer, and as soon as I got my panties off over the toe of my sneaker and he had himself covered, he pulled me down over him and we both made a noise that could only be described as animalistic. It was guttural, deep, and we both felt it as we joined together.

I leaned forward a little and he took advantage of my new position by pulling my nipple into his mouth. I felt the tug and pull all the way at my core, just like I felt the way that metal he was wearing pressed insistently against my G-spot. I moved up and down, set a quick and hurried pace because it was cold and because I knew he was already close. It felt amazing; he always knew what do to build the pleasure up, to take me out of myself and just feel, but given the tight quarters, the limited mobility either of us had, I could tell he was holding back, could see the tendons in his neck straining while he waited for me to catch up.

"Nash . . ."

"Shit, Saint, you're gonna have to help me out here. Give me a hand." Both his hands were occupied helping me maintain the sexy ride up and down without hitting my head on the roof of the car. I glanced down at him and his meaning was clear. Sure, he could have finagled it, let go with one hand, but he was doing it again, pushing the boundaries I thought I knew were clear.

I didn't even like to admit I touched myself to myself, and he wanted me to do it not only in front of him, but while I was on top of him, joined to him. It was a clear challenge, one I should be pissed he was throwing down right in the middle of sex that was supposed to be nostalgic and fun, but I wanted to come, wanted him to let go because I could feel it pulsating in him. I loved how rigid and hard he was where he was buried inside me and he was holding on by a thread, forcing me to take one more step out of my comfort zone, trying to obliterate what I thought I knew.

I didn't think, just let the hand that wasn't holding on to the back of the front seat for balance dip between our undulating bodies, between my slick and spread folds, until I was touching that little heart of pleasure that was already sensitized and tight.

"Oh my." It was barely a whisper that was drowned out by his roar of completion, just by watching me do what he asked.

It didn't take much, just a feathery pet, a light stroke of a fingertip and I was shoved right over the edge right behind him. I was a lot quicker about it, but he pulled me across his heaving chest and sealed out mouths together in a kiss that tasted like satisfaction and always.

"That was probably the hottest, most beautiful thing I have ever seen." He sounded gruff and a little winded.

I didn't know what to say to that, never did, so I put my cheek on the hard curve of his pec and told him, "We're getting really good at having sex while you're still wearing your pants."

He laughed drily and ran his hands softly up and down my spine. He didn't call me on it, but I knew it bothered him that I never responded to his compliments. I wasn't sure I was ever going to know how, that we were ever going to see the same person he saw when he looked at me.

CHAPTER 11

Nash

"WOW, DUDE, THIS PLACE . . . it's epic."

Rule let out a low whistle as we walked through the empty space that was going to be the home of the new shop. Time just kept rolling on, and before I knew, months had come and gone and I still hadn't been to the place. Now I felt like a loser because it *was* epic and it was sandwiched between two of the busiest restaurants in LoDo, across the street from a popular sports bar, right around the corner from all the coffee shops and boutiques that drew people to LoDo in the first place. It was right in the heart of the thriving city and way more stylish and trendy than the Marked was. I felt seriously out of my depth here.

I rubbed the back of my neck and looked at Rule out of the corner of my eye. We didn't exactly fit in here, and I had no idea how he and I, two beer and chicken-wings dudes, were supposed to make a place that looked like mimosas and caviar a moneymaking business. I felt like we were scaring the locals just by being here, and there was so much work to be done. All of it was overwhelming.

Before Phil had tied us into the place, it had been some kind of exotic tea and coffee shop. It wasn't in any way set up to be a tattoo parlor, which is why Rule and I had taken the afternoon off to get the lay of the land and meet Rowdy's friend so he could look the place over and tell us what he thought about it all. I thought it seemed like a long shot, but Rule was intrigued by it and he was totally on board with Rowdy's idea about expanding what we did and turning the upstairs into a retail store. Besides, I owed Phil nothing less than making his dream a reality.

"We are going to turn this into such a badass shop." Rule sounded so sure of that.

I wish I had his enthusiasm, and admittedly some of my hesitation came from the fact that Phil's health was steadily declining. I was watching the disease wither him away, and there was nothing I could do about it. So investing in this shop, getting excited about it the way Rule was, seemed to me like I wasn't even waiting until Phil was gone to act on his wishes. Plus he was still pushing me to ask my mom for answers to all the questions I had, and I didn't want to waste any of the time we had left arguing about it with him.

"I feel like we're going to need to offer our clients infused water and hot towels, as swanky as this location is."

Rule laughed and walked to the glass door at the front to let in the guy who'd knocked. They shook hands, and now that I could put a name to the face, I knew I had seen him in Rowdy's chair more than once. Zeb Fuller was a big dude with dark hair and a serious, unsmiling face. This wasn't a guy who looked like he had ever lived life easy and carefree. He had Rowdy's signature old-school style of tattooing scrolled all along both sides of his neck and peeking out of the sleeves of his long-sleeved shirt.

He walked over and shook my hand as well and let his gaze search the mostly empty space. He totally looked like the kind of guy that could tear the place apart with his bare hands and then build it back up. I could see why Rowdy recommended him.

"Swanky digs."

I chuckled at hearing my thoughts spoken aloud.

"Yeah."

"So you want it gutted and made to look like the other shop? What exactly is the idea?"

Rule and I shared a blank look and then I shrugged.

"I have no idea. It needs to be a functional shop. It has to have room for at least six artists to work and a piercing room that's closed off from the rest of the space. We need a front desk and a waiting area and upstairs is offices, but we were thinking about turning it more into a store."

He didn't say anything, just kept his eyes moving around the space. I looked at Rule, who looked back at me and shook his head. I snorted out a laugh.

"Is it obvious we have no idea what we're really doing?" I felt like I had to ask.

Zeb cracked a grin, which made him look less intimidating. "Well, with a cherry location like this, you don't really have to do much. People will come in and check it out just because of where it's at, and if you add shopping to the mix . . ." He whistled through his teeth. "You're gonna make bank."

We walked with him through the rest of the space, and I was blown away by how much of it there was. The Marked was a pretty big shop. I mean, none of us ever tripped over the others and the waiting area comfortably held up to ten people at a time, but this place doubled that. I had no idea how I was supposed to manage something like that, let alone remodel and staff it. I felt a slow burn work up the back of my neck.

At the end of the tour, we ended back on the main level of the shop, and Zeb was writing things down on a pad of paper he had produced from out of nowhere. Rule was asking him questions and I was just standing there feeling useless and panicked. Zeb looked up and took in my expression.

"I'll draw some stuff up, put together a couple quotes. What's the time frame?"

I sighed. "Well, Cora's gonna have to be in on the hiring and the actual business setup, and she's due fairly soon, so like maybe May?" I didn't even know when I needed to have the place open by. I sucked at being a business owner. "That gives her time to be at home with the baby while remodeling is going on."

Rule nodded. "Yeah, I would think May would be good, we would be open for a lot of the summer tourist business then."

Zeb made a couple more notes and muttered something under his breath. He gave a quick nod then stuck the pen he was using behind his ear.

"It's gonna be some work, not gonna shit you, but this is a great space and I think with minimal effort, I can give you something that reflects what you guys are about but also fits in with what the downtown crowd looks for as well."

"Sounds perfect." Rule and I agreed.

"I'll touch base after I get some ideas on paper, and we can talk firmer time lines and budgets. I know Rowdy threw my name in the ring, but I appreciate the shot."

Rule lifted the eyebrow that had the studs in it and ran his tongue over his lip ring.

"Any friend of Rowdy's . . ."

Zeb barked out a laugh that had no humor in it. "Yeah, Rowdy's a good dude and I appreciate he doesn't hold my past against me. Neither does Wheeler." He dropped the mechanic's name as I tilted my head a little to consider the common connection we shared.

"The past?" I had to ask.

He sighed and that massive chest that looked like he regularly did bench presses with a Buick rose and fell.

"I shouldn't say anything because it's cost me more than one job, but if we're gonna work together, you might as well know that I served time. I got out over two years ago, but I have a record."

"Served time for what?" Rule's tone was sharp, but we both knew Rowdy wouldn't send us anyone that was a danger to the business or anyone's safety.

"Assault. I made some bad choices, and I paid for them."

Well, that wasn't awesome, but none of us were strangers with the other side of the law. Hell, less than a year ago Jet had gotten locked up for a day for beating the crap out of his dad. Granted, the old bastard deserved it and way worse, so the lot of us tended not to pass judgment when it came to past mistakes.

I told him simply, "As long as you can do the job and the price is fair, I don't care about what happened in the past. Our working relationship is all about what's going on in the here and now."

He seemed to take my words at face value and we all exchanged business cards. He left, and Rule and I walked out to the front of the building so I could lock the door.

"What do you think?" Rule's tone was curious.

"I think I want a cigarette."

He cut me a dirty look and followed me to where the Charger and his truck were parked on the street.

"Seriously?"

"I think that I don't know what I'm doing. I look at that space and can't even imagine tattooing there or the kind of clients we might have. I think I have no idea how to run a business, or how to get Phil to tell me the truth, and I think I'm falling for a girl who can't seem to trust me fully, and as a result won't let me get nearly as close as I want to. Do you know how much that sucks? I never wanted to get this close to any girl, ever."

"Whoa . . ."

He laughed at me a little and reached out and clamped a hand on my shoulder.

"Chill out, brother."

I swore and propped a hip on the fender of the Charger and crossed my tattooed arms over my chest.

"Seriously, Rule. I feel like I'm losing control of everything. The ride can stop anytime and let me off. Being dizzy sucks."

Both his eyebrows shot up and he took up a spot next to me, his pose almost identical to mine. "Listen, Nash, you need to breathe. You have a lot going on right now, and trying to deal with it all at one time is going to make you flip the fuck out. Phil won't tell you what you want to know, so go talk to your mom. Seriously, that's the easy solution, and if Ruby the Great won't tell you what you need to hear wait until Cora's dad gets here for the birth of the baby and ask him."

It made sense. I just wished I could do it without the talking-to-my-mother part.

"As for the shop and being a business owner, you are not in this alone. I'm here, Cora is here, Rowdy has your back, and we still have Phil. The success or failure of this shop will not be solely on you, Nash. We all want it to succeed, we all want to make Phil proud whether we do it in time for him to see it or not."

He was right . . . more than my future was at stake here and I needed to remember that.

"As for the girl . . ." He bumped me in the arm with his fist. "There is no falling. You fell. She's got you and there is no getting loose from that. So she's guarded, so she's hard to figure out . . . did you stop and think maybe the reason you like her, that she matters, is because she isn't easy like all the rest? Easy is very forgettable, my friend, complicated and difficult stays with you forever. Believe me, I married it."

I looked at him and tried to think of something to say that could refute what he said. There wasn't anything.

"We were all a bunch of pricks back then; it took finding the right person to make me not want to be that guy anymore. You, well, you were always the nice one, but even the nice guy can have a bad day. Eventually she'll get over her hang-ups over the past, and if she doesn't, you move on because that means she's not into the guy you are now."

I huffed out a breath and watched it turn into vapor in the cold in front of me.

"When did you turn into the relationship sensei?"

"All my friends and family are falling in love around me, I'm just trying to keep them from making the same mistakes I made with Shaw. I wouldn't waste any of the time I did getting to her if I could do it all over again."

I would've made fun of him for being sappy and sentimental, but I had been there for the journey he took to get to his girl. It wasn't always pretty and they had both hurt more than they needed to along the way, so discounting his words of wisdom didn't seem very smart.

"All right. I guess I'm gonna cruise up the mountain and try and see if I can have a conversation with my mom without strangling her or trying to choke myself out."

"Good luck with that. Hey, you still bringing the nurse to the Bar this weekend?"

It had taken a week of persuasion with both words and sexual lures to get Saint to agree to come out and meet my friends. Ayden and Shaw were champing at the bit to get to actually meet her outside of the hospital setting.

"If she doesn't back out on me. She's really shy and timid around new people."

"You better tell her if she plans on sticking around, she needs to get over that, or else Cora is going to put together an ambush and the girls will end up on her doorstep without you there as a buffer."

That was exactly what would happen, so I made a mental reminder to push Saint a little harder the next time we hung out. I didn't mind pushing her, usually the results ended up with us naked and wrapped around each other, but I was still leery of pushing too far because I just didn't know where her breaking point was. And frankly, I didn't know where mine was either. I liked her, really liked her, in bed and out of it, but there was always something unknown about her that kept me on the edge. She was a strong girl, had to be in order to do her job and be as good at it as she obviously was, but outside of her work and away from the hospital, there was a veil of vulnerability and unease that surrounded her. I could practically see the struggle she was having within herself when we were together. She wanted to be with me, wanted to spend time together, but the gears in her head would start turning and I could see her trying to figure out how much of herself she could give to me and still feel safe.

I was also doing my best to show her a good time. Ever since the incident in the backseat of my car, I kept it in the forefront of my mind that she essentially had missed out on all the teenage nonsense that went along with boys figuring out how to get into a girl's pants. So I took her to the movies and tried to get my hands in her shirt. I took her out for pizza and made out with her on her doorstep when I dropped her off. I tried to get her to go on a double date with Rule and

Shaw, but she had balked at the idea, not ready to be that fully ingrained in my life yet, which led to the question of what exactly we were doing together.

I had never spent more than one night or one weekend with the same girl, so to me we were doing something that looked like starting a relationship. To her, though, I just didn't know. She texted me, called me when she had free time, but never stayed the night at my place when she came over and never asked me to stay when I was at hers. Granted, she never asked me to leave either, but there was just a lot of gray area happening, and I felt like I was navigating all of it blindly since I had never even been interested in starting something with anyone before. I knew she was special. I just didn't know how to show her that beyond what I was already doing.

The drive to Brookside went quick, mostly because my mind was running over everything and didn't give me a minute of peace. I pulled into the driveway and breathed out a grateful sigh that at least my idiot stepfather Grant's SUV wasn't anywhere to be seen, unless it was in the garage. That was highly unlikely because what good did it do in the garage where the neighbors couldn't see it, marvel at its awesomeness, and be eaten alive with envy at Grant Loften's obvious wealth and prestige? Fucker. I would never hate anyone as much as I hated that guy and God willing there would come a time that my fist and his face had a meeting.

My entire childhood had been spent under his disapproving eyes. I could never do anything right, was always treated like a burden by him. One of my clearest memories of his sheer shitheadedness had been when I couldn't have been more than four or five. I had just discovered crayons. I loved the colors, loved to swirl designs on anything and everything I could get my little, unruly hands on, including the walls. It was just crayon and what little kid didn't draw on the wall? But to Grant it had been a crime akin to murder. To this day I can see him snapping every single one of the crayons and making me watch. I remembered the acrid smell of bleach as he made me scrub not just my bedroom wall where my art lived, but all the walls in the house. I was just a little kid, but to him that didn't matter. Just like now, he never thought I did anything right.

What made it worse was the fact that he obviously loved my mom, treated her like she was a queen, and gave her whatever she wanted. He just had no time or use for me. And I would never, ever forgive him for making her choose between the two of us. Of course my mother should have picked me, I was her child, it was her job to love me unconditionally, but she hadn't, and it was Grant who had made her have to make that call.

He was a man who had always been about appearances, a man all about prestige and perception, so the fact that I looked the way I did, acted how I wanted, had never made my time under his roof pleasant. As an adult . . . every single time he looked down his nose at me, every time he puckered his lips in disdain at what I was wearing or what I was saying . . . it took every ounce of self-control I possessed not to knock all his perfectly veneered teeth down his throat.

I jogged up the walkway that still had a light dusting of

snow on it and knocked on the door. How sad was it that I was a stranger in the place that was supposed to be where my family lived? I saw my mom's dark head peek through the window and then it took a solid four minutes for her to decide to open the door. We faced each other through the glass of the storm door and there was no mistaking the look of disappointment that flashed across her eyes when she took in my black hoodie, baseball hat, and jeans. I looked like I looked every other day of the year, and it was always lacking in her eyes. It shouldn't still sting. I was an adult, had been on my own for way longer than she had ever pretended to raise me, but still there was always a tiny part of me that wanted her to see worth in me, even though it always ended up with me feeling like she had drop-kicked my heart.

"What are you doing here? You didn't call, Nashville."

God, with the full name. I think she used it mostly because she knew how much it irked me.

"No I didn't, but I want to talk to you for a minute, and I figured I could catch you at home."

She played with the ruby necklace at her throat and put a hand on the door. My mom was a fairly tiny woman. I got my dark skin tone and hair from somewhere in her lineage. I could only assume everything else that made me who I was I got from Phil. Thank goodness for small favors.

"Grant will be home shortly. He won't like that you dropped by unannounced."

And just like it had always been, what Grant liked always won out over what was right and decent.

"It won't take too long, Mom. Seriously, just give me five minutes."

"You drove for two hours just to talk for five minutes, Nashville? That makes no sense." Always with the censure and disapproval. It was a miracle I had managed to turn out as normal I as I had.

"Mom . . ." I sighed and narrowed my eyes at her. "Phil is getting sicker and sicker. He has around-the-clock help at home, but he's hardly eating and he sleeps all the time. I see him every day and I ask him every time to explain to me what in the hell happened. Someone needs to give me answers, Mom, and I'm not going anywhere until I get them. If you want me gone before Grant comes home, then you best start talking, otherwise I will hang out in the driveway and gladly have it out with him. No one wants that, I'm sure. What would the neighbors think?"

She looked like she was considering her options, and when one of the neighbors pulled out of their garage and looked over to see what was going on, I snorted at the irony as she finally relented and opened the door to let me in.

I followed her into the kitchen, where she begrudgingly offered me a drink. I turned her down and leaned against the counter while she poured herself a cup of coffee.

"I want to know why you never told me who Phil was. I want to know why you let me think my dad was just some deadbeat who took off on us. I spent my entire childhood thinking you couldn't deal with me, didn't love me because I reminded you of a stranger that disappointed you." I glared at her for all the years of blame and guilt she had needlessly let me carry on my too-young shoulders.

"Phil was here, he took care of me, and he obviously cared for you and would have been in both our lives. I think I deserve to know what happened and why it took him facing death for the truth to come out."

Her hands curled around the mug and I saw her pale a little under her makeup.

"What difference does any of that make now, Nashville? What purpose does rehashing any of it serve?"

"Stop calling me that. Nash, just Nash, and you know it. The purpose it serves is I want to know why I wasn't ever good enough, why you still look at me like I'm a disappointment. Phil doesn't get to pass on, get to die without me understanding why it mattered so much for him to keep your secrets."

She heaved a sigh like I was annoying her more than anything else and looked at me over the rim of her mug.

"I met Phil when he was on leave from the Navy. I was in New York on vacation the same time he was there for Fleet Week. He was good-looking, a handsome and dangerous young man in a uniform. I figured no one would get hurt if we indulged in a harmless fling. I thought it was just temporary, just a young girl sowing her oats, but it turned into something more. I came back home, back here, and when Phil's service was up he moved out here to be with me. He was always very dedicated and chivalrous, he just wasn't what I was looking for in a long-term partner."

She cleared her throat and set the mug down on the counter. She wouldn't look me in the eye.

"I liked Phil, he was a lot of fun, and for a while the relationship was a great time, but when it came time to settle down, I wanted a life that didn't fit with a guy who rides a motorcycle and thinks tattooing is a viable career—that was not in my long-term plans. I broke it off with Phil when I met Grant. Grant is the kind of man who could provide a future, could provide the kind of home I always wanted. I knew what the right choice for me was between the two men without a question."

I scowled at her because hearing her talk about Phil's life and choices was hearing her belittle my life all over again. Her hands went back to the necklace at her throat and she twisted the ruby around and around.

"I didn't know I was pregnant when Grant and I started seeing each other. When I figured it out I just assumed the baby was his."

I choked a little. "Jesus, Mom, you were sleeping with both of them?" That was more than I needed to know for sure.

She narrowed her eyes at me. "I was young and figuring life out, Nashville. Anyway, Grant and I got engaged and married before you were born. We were both excited with the prospect of having a little boy, and Phil had opened the shop and started his own kind of life. Everything was going to be perfect."

She walked to the other side of the kitchen and I realized she had moved as far away from me as she could without leaving the room.

"It was pretty clear the second you were born that you were Phil's and not Grant's. You were all brown like me, but the hair was Phil's and those eyes . . . even as a baby they were too bright and too unmistakable. They were Donovan eyes. Grant was furious, accused me of having an affair, and told me it was him or my bastard baby. He couldn't face everyone in Brookside knowing the baby wasn't his. I thought he was going to leave me for sure."

I already hated the guy, but now I wanted to pull all his teeth out with rusty pliers.

"I didn't want to lose him, so I explained about Phil, about the relationship. Grant eventually realized that no one would judge him for taking care of a child that was left by his father. He refused to be on the birth certificate or give you his last name, though." I could literally feel the temperature of my blood drop.

My hands clenched into fists at my sides. "But Phil didn't go anywhere. He just didn't know I existed."

"No, he didn't, and, in a perfect world, it would have stayed that way. Grant took care of us, provided for us, and we told you that your dad had abandoned us. But as time went on you just looked more and more like Phil. One of his friends saw you with me at Cherry Creek Mall when you were about four and told Phil. He was furious, threatened to take me to court, to fight for custody. Grant didn't want that kind of mess, didn't want the whole sordid tale out in the public, and we didn't need child support, so we made a deal. I begged Phil, pleaded with him to keep his real identity and relation to you a secret, to keep it quiet until you were older. He very reluctantly agreed, but only as long as he got to be in your life and only as long as I agreed to let you have his last name. I never put a father on the birth certificate, so making you a Donovan officially was the easiest thing in the world."

She twisted her hands together and had the nerve to look at me like this was somehow my fault.

"When you got older, you were too much. Too wild, too loud, too hard to handle. You didn't want to dress nice or play with the right kind of kids, Grant was already resentful that he was raising Phil's kid, but the way you were, how much you looked like Phil, it was his breaking point. It was just easier to let Phil handle you, try and put you on some kind of path, because where you were going wasn't any kind of place Grant or I wanted any part of. You were always so much more Phil's son than mine."

My back teeth snapped together, and I felt my temper start to surge in an angry torrent under my skin.

"I was a kid. Maybe if you hadn't constantly been on me about shit I couldn't change, like my eye color, I would have picked a more acceptable path to you. You never gave me the chance. You were always too busy trying to make Grant happy to worry about what all that vitriol was doing to your kid."

"You were always too much like your father, even though you didn't know who he was."

"He loved you, still does."

Her mouth tightened and turned white at the corners.

"He loved the idea of me. He never really knew the real me."

"Why didn't you tell me when I was older, when I went to live with him permanently?"

"He didn't want to."

"Bullshit."

"Fine, he wanted me to be the one to tell you and I refused. I didn't think Grant or I needed to deal with the fallout. You had moved on, Phil was a better parent to you than I ever could have been. It was all said and done."

I wanted to throw something heavy at her. I wanted to break every stupid piece of Williams-Sonoma cookware in her fancy kitchen. My fingers curled into fists at my sides.

"But I'm still here, Mom. Still trying to live my life, and now the only father I'm ever going to have is dying and there is nothing I can do about it. You robbed me of that relationship because you didn't want to deal with the fallout, because you didn't want to inconvenience that dipshit husband of yours? How does any of that sound right to you?"

"What's right for me has never been what's right for you, Nashville. You don't even use the name I gave you."

"Because it's ridiculous . . . all of it. What's right for me isn't what's right for you because I'm an actual human being with feelings and emotions, and you, Mom . . . you're a goddamn monster."

I had always longed for her attention, thirsted for her love and approval, but now looking at her, seeing the absolute lack of remorse or regret in her eyes, I was thankful she had simply let me go. If I had tried any harder, worked any more to make her love me, who knew what kind of miserable, unfeeling robot I would have become at her hands. As an adult, I was still pissed at her, still resentful she had such an easy time letting me go, but I was also overwhelmingly grateful that I wasn't anything like her and her people.

"I'm not a monster, Nash." Finally, my name. "I'm just

not the mother you wanted or needed, and frankly you were never the son I wanted or needed. Having you made it pretty clear I was never cut out to be someone's mother. Why do you think Grant and I never had any more kids? We wanted it to just be us."

"Thank God for that."

I pushed off the counter and headed toward the door. I knew once I walked out, I had no reason to ever come back. This solidified it for me, it was why Phil had pushed and pushed me to make her be the one and tell me the entire sordid tale. I was finally free of any chains to the past that she might have held. I didn't need her approval. I was a good man, had a good life, had the best friends in the entire world, and I was working really hard on figuring out how to have a good woman on a permanent basis. There was no need for my mother to be proud of me or find worth in what I was doing, because I was proud of myself, and Phil had given me that.

It didn't matter that I had no idea what to do with the new shop, or that Saint had me spinning in circles. I would figure it all out, and there was no way I was going to let him or anyone else down while doing it. Not because I needed validation or appreciation, but because that was just the kind of guy I was. The kind of guy my father had raised me to be.

CHAPTER 12

Saint

IKNEW HIS VISIT with his mom was going to have him in a dark mood. He didn't talk much about her, or why he had been raised mostly by Phil, and the fact he was quiet about it spoke to me more than I think words could. He'd mentioned more than once that the reason he was so quick to anger, so quick to run his mouth when he was younger, was because of how unhappy he was with his mom, that he acted out for attention and to rile her up, so I knew his visit was going to have him feeling raw and out of sorts. I wanted to do something to make him feel better.

He had gone out of his way to show me a good time, to take me out and keep things between us fun and playful, but always keeping a sexy edge to it all so that I knew he wanted me. I felt like it was time I returned the favor.

He showed up at my apartment sulking, thunderous, and in a full-on bad mood. His eyes were all dark and swirly, and no matter how much I tried to get him to talk about it, he just grunted one-syllable answers at me and scowled at nothing and no one in particular. I couldn't really shake him out of it, and when I suggested we get out of the apartment, he just looked at me like I had lost my mind. Really, he wasn't fit to be around other people, but I couldn't stand to see him so unhappy, so I was going to drag him into a better mood kicking and screaming if I had to.

It was a testament as to how much he wanted to please me, wanted me to have a good time, that he agreed to leave the apartment with me in the first place when clearly he would have been content to sit and wallow in his awful mood for the rest of the night. I could have kissed him all over his shaved head for that alone. When we got into the Jetta and he didn't ask any questions as I drove downtown, I could only hope my plan didn't backfire and end up with him in an even more sour state of mind.

I had to find a place to park and he gave me a questioning look as I took his hand and guided him toward the ice-skating rink that was located right in the heart of Denver's downtown at Skyline Park. It was only open a few months out of year, in the winter, and you could skate for free if you brought your own skates. It had always been one of my favorite parts of growing up in a cold-weather state. There was nothing like gliding around the ice in the dark while white lights twinkled over your head. There was something so fun about doing something so quaint right in the middle of such a metropolitan area . . . I hoped Nash felt the same way.

He looked at me and lifted one of his midnight-dark eyebrows.

"Seriously?"

I shrugged and bit my lip.

"What? It'll be fun."

"If by 'fun' you mean me spending the entire time on my ass, then yeah, fun."

I bumped him with my shoulder and he wrapped an arm around my shoulders.

"You used to skateboard. I'm sure you can keep your balance long enough to make it around a couple times without falling."

I remembered him rolling around back in high school, so I was sure he would be fine despite the pensive look on his face.

"That was a long time ago, Saint."

I made him let me pay the guy to rent us skates and was secretly thrilled inside when we sat down to put them on and he got on his knees in front of me and helped me lace mine up. I couldn't resist the urge to bend forward and kiss him on the top of his head. I liked the way the scruff of his supershort hair tickled my lips. I looked up when I heard giggles coming from a group of young girls watching us.

"You can concentrate on not falling, and it'll take your mind off of today."

He grunted at me again and rose to his feet in a graceful move that had my belly tightening and the girls next to us sighing. He begrudgingly put on his own skates and towered over me as we trudged out to the ice.

It was rough going for the first ten minutes. Nash was a big guy, and while he typically moved with a lot of grace and ease, perch him on a razor-fine blade on top of frozen water and he just sort of turned into an out-of-control freight train. I wanted to be sympathetic, wanted to help him out, but I wasn't strong enough to keep him upright and his dirty mouth and hostile expression had me folded over in fits of laughter that was making it hard for me to stay upright myself.

Little kids buzzed around us. Teenage girls twirled and flittered by, obviously trying to catch his attention. Dudes on hockey skates blazed past in a bid to impress, but Nash was focused on trying to stay up and on me. He finally found his balance enough to make it around the rink once and I reached out to grab his hand. He snickered at me and squeezed my cold fingers.

"I've never been ice skating with a girl before."

That made goose bumps run up and down my arms. He had been the first for me in so many ways, I never really thought I could return that for him.

"Good."

I glided next to him and watched him out of the corner of my eye. Some of the tension that had been around his mouth and some of the darkness in his gaze had lightened.

"You know you can talk to me about it, right? About what went down with your mom today?"

I was doing a pretty good job at keeping him and this thing between us within boundaries I was comfortable with, but I didn't want him to think that if he needed me to listen I wasn't willing to do that. Sure, we had some killer sexual chemistry and a really intimate draw that pulled us together, but we also needed to like each other enough to share things with one another if we were going to keep hanging out.

His thumb traced over the back of my hand and I stumbled a little, almost taking us both down to the hard surface of the ice. He was just so good at being distracting.

"Nothing to talk about. She's just as unpleasant as she always was, which makes me feel awful every time I talk to her. I left today knowing pretty much that I'm done with her. She's not my family, she never was."

I sucked in a breath and due to the cold air, it made my teeth hurt.

"That's really sad."

"I guess. It's just the way it is."

I had a fair amount of resentment built up at my dad, considering the way he had acted and the way he had chosen to leave my mom. But even though I didn't approve, didn't appreciate the drama and heartache he had caused, I couldn't imagine just walking away from him forever. Couldn't see myself ever just declaring that he was no longer a part of my life or my family. My insides twisted at the fact Nash had to make that kind of call on top of dealing with his father being so ill.

I squealed in surprise as the big body next to mine suddenly pitched forward and went down in a spectacular splay of strong arms and legs. Nash managed to turn before he hit the ice and I ended up hitting his chest with a thump that knocked the wind out of the both of us. He wrapped his arms around my waist and shook with silent laughter.

"Okay, Saint, you win. This is ridiculous. I can't stay pissed off when my ass is broken."

I rubbed my cold nose along the edge of his jaw.

"Well, I *am* a nurse. When we get home I can take care of all your boo-boos in the best way possible."

I heard him sigh.

"Can you do it naked?"

I laughed because he was such a guy, and when I told him of course I could do it naked, that meant our time on the ice was over. It was nice, made me feel good about myself and about the way I was with him, that not only had I shaken off his dour mood, but I managed to make him laugh and take his mind somewhere else. I wanted to think that not anyone would've been able to achieve that, and when we got to the apartment and he proceeded to get us both very naked and very much into the best mood possible, I had to wonder if being with me like that was as special and different for him as being with him was for me. It sure felt that way.

The next morning I was standing in the little kitchen in my apartment making coffee and finger-combing my still-shower-wet hair. I was feeling pretty mellow, pretty languid and satisfied, because I hadn't been in the shower alone and was still basking in the after-orgasm glow when the front door swung open and my sister came flying in unannounced. She looked harassed and stressed out, tired and so very pregnant. She didn't have any of the kids with her and there was a high flush in her cheeks.

"Mom just called me." She stomped across the living room and I shot a nervous gaze to the back room, where I had left Nash getting dressed with the promise of having coffee waiting for him when he was done. I didn't want Faith to see him here, didn't want to try and figure out how to explain what I was doing with him, because I didn't really know and words had never been my strong suit.

"Okay. Is something wrong?"

She huffed out an aggravated breath and plopped her round form in one of the chairs at my little dining table.

"She's moving."

I adjusted my robe and kept an eye on the hallway.

"Okay." I should've been asking where Mom was going, but I was too concerned about Nash popping around the corner in all his naked and tattooed glory to focus properly on what my sister was saying.

Faith shot me a dirty look and shoved her hands through the front of her hair. "What do you mean, 'okay'? She's leaving Colorado. Is that still okay?"

"I mean she's an adult and has been acting like a lunatic for two years. Maybe getting away from Brookside, away from where she can run into dad and any reminders that he moved on, is what's best for her."

"But we're here. The kids are here. She shouldn't have to pick up and move her entire life to another state . . . Dad should. He's the one who messed up."

She was right. Dad *had* messed up, the blame for the way our family was divided did fall squarely on his shoulders. Mom would've never gone so bonkers, acted so drastically, if he hadn't sent her into a tailspin. But in all honesty, I was proud of Mom for taking a stand, for taking the reins back in her life and doing something for herself. Blaming Dad for being a jerk, not getting over the fact he had a wandering eye, wasn't going to put Mom back to sorts, but I really thought a change of scenery and some room to breathe might. It had done wonders for me when I needed it most after high school. Faith was right that Mom shouldn't have to move, but the fact that she was willing to finally be accountable for some her actions made me happy inside. This was just the way our family looked now, and both of us were going to have to live with it. And trying to tell Faith that she would feel the same way about Dad moving, that he also would miss out on spending time with us, with her kids, was just going to have to wait because I heard movement from the bedroom.

I sighed . . . more because Nash had finally emerged from the bedroom than because of what Faith was saying. He was on his way to meet Rome at the gym, so all he had on was a black tank top and a pair of black-and-white nylon track pants. His head was covered in that ever-present black hat he liked to rock, and I had to really try not to let out a dreamy sigh. He was hot, like stupid hot, there was no missing that fact. He was pulling on his black hoodie and texting on his phone, so I don't think he even saw Faith when he walked right up to me and put an arm around my waist. He pulled me to that massive chest and dropped a hard kiss on my mouth. He smelled clean and slightly flowery from my body wash, which would have made me grin had I not seen Faith glaring at me over his shoulder.

"Don't forget to show around nine tonight. The Bar, it's kind of a dive and there isn't really a sign, but it's off Broadway and the Charger will be in the lot, so it's hard to miss." One of his midnight-colored brows shot up. "If you bail, I won't be held responsible for what the girls do in order to get to know you better."

His friends wanted to meet me, like for real meet me, not just passing by in the hospital halls, and I was panicked at the very thought. It made what we were doing seem more important than I wanted it to be, but I couldn't figure out a way to slip out of it gracefully, and honestly, I could tell it mattered to him and I didn't want to disappoint him.

I cleared my throat and put a hand lightly on his stomach. It was rock-hard and I wanted to pet it.

"Nash . . ." His other eyebrow shot up. "This is my sister, Faith. I don't know if you remember her or not. She was a year ahead of us in school." The implication was there: she knew all about the scars he had left on me when we were younger.

My sister was looking at him like she wanted to stab him in the heart, but Nash just gave her a lopsided grin and made his way toward the front door.

"Hey, Faith. Nice to officially meet you. Seriously, Saint." His voice dropped a little. "If you don't show, it's gonna bum me out."

I sighed again and put my hands flat on the counter in front of me. "I'll be there. Promise."

He smiled at me for real and vanished out the door, leaving me and my seething sister alone.

I held up a hand when she opened her mouth. "Don't even start."

She hefted herself up from the table and marched so that she was poised across the counter from me.

"Are you out of your ever-loving mind?" It would have been better if she screamed it at me, but the fact that it was almost a whisper twisted my heart.

"Probably." I picked up my coffee, more to have something to do with my hands than anything else. "He's different, and I just don't mean from how he was in high school. He's nice, funny, and gorgeous, plus he makes me feel good . . . like really good. I like being around him and he's having a really hard time right now with his dad, so I want to make it easier for him. I think he kind of needs me right now."

"This is the same guy that made you run to the West Coast, Saint. He hurt you bad enough that you hid from everyone, ran away from every relationship your whole life. This is a terrible idea."

I raised a shoulder and let it fall. "I know. I'm trying hard to let it go—the past, I mean. He says it was a misunderstanding. That he wasn't talking about me, and I really want to believe him, and the thing with the party . . ." I shrugged. "Maybe I read more into that than I should have. Teenage boys are just horn balls. I don't think he would've ignored me had he known I was going there just for him. He doesn't even remember seeing me there."

She screwed her face up in an ugly scowl. "Of course he said that! How else was he going to get in your pants if he didn't tell you that! Use your damn head, Saint. He is not the guy for you. It's time to get over that idiotic crush on the 'bad boy,' or whatever. Grow up."

"He's not like that, Faith. He's a really nice guy. He cares about his friends, he works almost as hard as I do, and he's been really, really great the last few months or so about all the weird hang-ups I have. He doesn't care that I get awkward and can't make words work, he doesn't cling when I freak out and bail on him, and he . . ." I made her look me in the eye so she could see how important this part was. "He makes me feel normal in bed and out of it."

"You can do so much better, Saint."

That made me angry, so I set the mug down and crossed my arms over my chest. "Better by whose standards? He's the first guy I ever liked, ever. He's also the first guy that I want to believe when he tells me I'm pretty. He's the first guy I have ever been around that I want to strip naked and tie to a bed. I've never had any of that with anyone else, Faith."

She snorted and glared at me. "Of course he thinks you're pretty, you're goddamn beautiful and anyone with eyes can see it. But what about before? What about when he didn't think you were so stunning? Do you really want to be with a person that shallow? And this sudden about-face . . . the niceness . . . what if it's all a calculated act to get you to fall for him because he does need you right now? What about when he doesn't need to lean on you anymore, Saint? What then?"

I bit my lip because that was the heart of my fear where Nash was concerned. I knew she was just trying to protect me from more heartache, but her harsh words hit home some serious reservations I had about this thing Nash and I had growing between us. "He told me he always thought I was pretty. That I was too smart and too shy for him to think twice about, but that he always thought I was pretty."

"Whatever, Saint. Even if he didn't say that nasty stuff

about you, he said it about someone, and that still makes him a royal asshole."

That was what I struggled with. On the rare night I found myself at his place, that was what prevented me from staying the night, kept me from openly asking him to stay with me, and really it was what kept me from fully being able to trust him. I still didn't feel like I knew who he really was. The Nash I was sleeping with, the one with the sad purple eyes every time he came from his Dad's house, the one who made me stretch what I thought I wanted and was comfortable with in bed, I was well on my way to falling back in love with. But there was this nagging doubt, these poking questions that jabbed under my skin, that there was still the part of him that could be hatful and cruel, and I just didn't trust it. I had the unwavering knowledge that men, even men that I thought could do no wrong like my father, could forsake a relationship, no matter how great it was, for something they perceived as better. With that floating around in the back of my mind, I couldn't allow myself to completely trust him, mostly because I was positive that if he disappointed me again, let me down, I would never get over it. The first time, when he was just a fantasy, had been hard enough; now that he was reality, it would kill me if he turned out to be someone I couldn't appreciate or respect.

"I don't know what to tell you, Faith. I'm trying to be careful, I'm not going to take any risk that puts my heart on the line, but I enjoy being with him. Can we change the subject back to Mom, so I don't have to fight with you?"

She didn't look like she wanted to let it go, but ultimately

I was twenty-five, not seventeen, and I had to live and die by my choices, not anyone else's.

"She's putting the house on the market and has already rented a condo in Phoenix. She has a friend down there who is also recently divorced. I asked her to consider waiting until the baby got here, but she already has a Realtor and movers hired. The house will sell fast."

"I really think it'll be for the best." I honestly did. Being in that house, that town, she couldn't escape the memories of Dad and her failed marriage and shattered heart. Maybe in Phoenix she could get a little bit of herself back.

"You moved all the way back here to help her out, to be closer to her and us. She's not even thinking about that, and now, looking at what is happening, I almost wish you had stayed in California."

She pouted a little and I rolled my eyes at how dramatic she was being.

"You're still here. The kids are here. I love my job and I love my boss. If I want to go back for my master's, I have a bunch of different schools to choose from. I don't regret coming back to Denver. I'm happy with my life, Faith."

I was. I really was, and now with the addition of Nash and the new and exciting way he tended to force me outside of my comfort zone, I was even starting to appreciate all the new things in it.

"Would you have said that a few months ago? Before him?"

That was a tricky question. I never had any complaints about my life. I was doing what I was meant to do, what I had always wanted to do, so I was fulfilled, but I don't know that I was exactly *happy*.

"I'm not sure," It was as honest as I could be.

"Well, I have to go save Justin from the kids. He has to work tonight." She sounded put out and disgruntled.

I walked around the counter and put my arms around her in a hug she stiffly returned.

"Don't worry about me or Mom. We'll all be fine."

She gave me a sad smile and headed toward the door. "I wish I could believe that. I've seen what broken hearts do to the women in this family, and it never ends well."

She had a point, so I just stared at the door after it shut behind her.

I had the day off and didn't really know what to do with myself. Lately, when I wasn't working I was with Nash. Before, when I had a day off I would spend it reading, or just puttering around the house, or with Faith and the kids. How boring was that? I had no social circle, no place to be, or anyone missing me. Maybe Sunny was right and I was just starting to see what living life fully meant.

I got dressed and decided instead of staying at my apartment and brooding, I was going to go shopping and find something cute and sassy to wear to the bar tonight so that when I met all of Nash's crew I would feel confident and as comfortable as I could be. I wasn't going to let my insecurity and nervousness ruin what could be an enjoyable night out, even though I knew I was going to be on the spot. His friends wanted to meet me because we were spending so much time together lately, and I knew that it was unusual for him to be interested in the same girl for so long. I just hoped their reaction was different from Faith's. I didn't want them to tell him he could do better, because a secret part of me wanted to be the best thing that ever happened to him.

"IT DOESN'T BOTHER YOU?" I was a little drunk, possibly sloppy, and talking way more than I normally did. Someone was passing around tequila shots, and to calm my nerves I may have had more than I meant to.

Shaw was really sweet and really pretty. She had made a beautiful bride, but up close and personal, the softness and sweetness that shined out of her was hard not to just melt into. She was also pre-med and really close to getting her undergrad, so she had about a million and one questions about what it was like working in an ER, which meant I got to talk about my favorite thing, my job. I could do that with or without the tequila.

She shook her head and gave a sardonic little grin. "If I got mad every time a girl hit on him—or tried to pick him up—or gave him sex eyes, I wouldn't have time to feel anything else. It just comes with being with a guy like him."

Rule and Nash had gone off to play a game of pool at the back of the bar with my other tablemate's husband, the rocker, as well as a blond guy with really big hair and a big tattoo of an anchor on the side of his neck. Ayden was probably the most beautiful woman I had ever seen up close and personal. Her eyes were spectacular, and even though I found her intimidating and slightly cool, her drawl was charming and her sharp wit was infectious, so despite my inherent hesitation and irritation that Nash had left me alone on purpose to get grilled by the girls, I was doing all right carrying on a conversation with both of them.

"But they are being so obvious."

I was talking about the group of college-aged girls that had gathered in a loose huddle around where the guys were playing the game. A collective sigh went up when Jet, Ayden's husband, bent over the table to take a shot. I mean there wasn't much he could hide in those tight pants he had on, but still, if that was my other half, my skin would be crawling. It already was and I didn't even know what Nash was to me. I mean I was starting to figure it out, but I wasn't brave enough or secure enough in myself or him to give it a name.

Ayden laughed a little and licked the salt off the back of her hand that had been left over from the last round of shots.

"They always are. You just have to know that even though the girls are looking, the guys never look back. You can't be with someone and not trust them completely. It will never work out."

Considering Jet was not only gorgeous but also in a band and on the road a lot, I guess that meant she really, really trusted him.

I made a face and blurted out with tequila-scented courage, "But I remember all of them in high school. They slept with everything that moved. How can you know that they are any different now?"

I blinked in shock because that wasn't appropriate or something I would normally ever say. I felt a flush fill my face, but Shaw reached out a small hand and put it on my arm. I wanted to crawl under the table and hide.

"I was a few years behind you in school, Saint, so I know. I know what Rule was like, I remember very clearly how bad they all were. People change. Time makes us grow. Life happens, good and bad, and it's the person you love, the man inside you can't live without, not the sum of what he did or didn't do when he was younger and still figuring things out."

Ayden picked up her beer and nodded solemnly. "I spent years and years trying to bury a past that is really ugly, that I thought in turn made me really ugly. Who I am now is not that person, but I wouldn't exist without those experiences."

I bit my bottom lip. It was tangy from lime and booze. A tight breath shuddered out of my lungs and I let my gaze dance from one of them to the other. They were lovely young women. Strong enough to deal with the attention their men garnered, kind enough to welcome me into the fold with no judgment because they wanted Nash to be happy. I just didn't know that I could ever be as clear on the past versus the present as they seemed to be.

I propped my elbow on the table and put my chin on my hand.

"I was fat."

The both blinked at me and then shared a look. Ayden's light twang asked, "So?"

"It made me shy and awkward, something I never out-grew. I got picked on a lot in school. People were mean, it hurt, and now even though I'm not that girl on the outside, I am still totally her on the inside, and it makes me act like a weirdo."

Shaw pushed her long hair back over her shoulder and looked at me questioningly. "What does that have to do with Nash?"

I waved a hand sloppily in the air in front of me. "You trust Rule, Ayden trusts Jet . . . but to me, why should I trust anyone when there are girls like that throwing themselves at him? Boys like pretty girls that are no work." I said it like I was an authority on the matter.

They shared another look and Shaw told me point-blank, "Nash isn't like that. First of all, he is the least judgmental guy in the world, and second, he has never, and I mean *never*, spent as much time with any single girl as he has with you."

Ayden made a noise and patted me on the knee. "I hate to tell you this, honey, but those boys have the pick of the ladies they want to spend time with: skinny, chubby, blond, brunette . . . you name it and they can have it. The point I think you might be missing is that clearly our boy has picked you to spend time with and he has made that choice over and over again." She pushed some of her dark hair out of her face and lifted a dark eyebrow at me. "And believe me, none of them are scared of doing a little work."

I was listening to their words, but at the same time one of the college girls broke from the pack and waltzed up to the table. Nash was leaning on the pool cue, and even though she was clearly headed in his direction, his gaze was locked directly on me. He was watching me closely and all I could do was stare back. I couldn't ever imagine trusting someone, loving someone so unquestioningly that you just *knew* that you were the only person they were thinking about, the only person they wanted. That seemed like a fantasy to me. That couldn't exist in real life . . . could it?

"I don't know if that makes me feel better or worse."

They both started to talk at the same time, trying to reassure me that Nash was loyal, that he was a great guy, that he was the nice one in the group, that he was typically the voice of reason because Rule was such a hothead and Jet tended to be moody and emotional. I listened to it all with half an ear while I watched the coed put her hand on Nash's chest and smile coyly up at him. I don't know what bothered me more, that she was openly flirting with him, or that it bothered me so much. It made me very uneasy to watch it happen.

Nash shook his tattooed head, took a step back, and handed his pool cue to Rowdy so he could wind his way through the throng of ladies. His eyes stayed locked on mine. I think he could tell I was upset, and not by anything the girls said, but by the overt attention he was drawing. He wasn't mine, at least not in any kind of spoken, official capacity, so it shouldn't matter, but it did.

He dropped his hands on my shoulders and I felt him drop a light kiss on the crown of my head. It was that, those simple little gestures that tried to untie all the things I thought I had knots fastened securely around.

"Everything okay?"

Shaw and Ayden nodded and I gasped as he turned my chair around so I was facing him. He put a hand on either side of the chair so I was caged in and forced to look up at him.

"Seriously, are you all right? We can go if you need to."

I felt like I couldn't breathe. It would be the second time he had left his friends early because of me, because I just couldn't get my head together. I opened my mouth to respond, to tell him it was fine. His friends were actually really wonderful. I had a nice enough buzz going that I could fake my way through another hour or so, but I didn't get the chance to speak because Rule suddenly appeared at the table, his light-colored eyes wide in his handsome face.

"Rome just called me. Cora's in labor."

Everyone was suddenly in a flurry of activity. Jet and Ayden, Rule and Shaw, all flew out of the bar without bothering to pay the bill. I looked at Nash in surprise as he waved the outrageously good-looking bartender over with a flick of his fingers.

"Why is everyone freaking out?" I didn't understand the sudden rush and hasty departures.

Rowdy materialized and pulled a bunch of bills out of his wallet that was attached to his pocket with a chain and handed it to the bartender.

Nash put a hand on my wrist and helped me to my feet. I was a little bit wobbly, so I put an arm around his waist.

"She's early, the baby. Cora wasn't supposed to be due until closer to the end of the month. Man, she's gonna be bummed out her dad isn't here."

He pulled out his phone and started firing off text messages.

"How many weeks is she?" I slipped easily into a role that I was comfortable with. Jealous, slightly drunk, not-quite girlfriend made my skin hurt.

He looked at me like I was speaking another language.

"She's probably fine. She's just petite and the baby is probably pretty big considering the size of her dad. If your friend is at least thirty-seven weeks, that's considered full term, and she and the baby will be fine."

He hustled me out of the bar and I balked when he stopped by the Charger and not the Jetta.

"You were doing shots with Ayden, so I know you had to be drinking more than you're used to. I don't want you driving, so I'll take you home and we can get your car to-morrow."

He put the key in the door and I looked up at him in a mixture of appreciation and fear. I really wished he didn't make it so easy to like him . . . more than like him, really.

"I know you're worried about your friends. I can call a cab." His eyes got dark like they did when he was feeling something strongly.

"Saint . . ." His voice was scratchy and gruff. He ran his thumb over the curve of my chin, which made me quake. "I worry about you just as much. I'm not sure when that hap-pened, but it did. I'll get you home and then go to the hospital."

I gulped and silently nodded. He helped me into the car and we took off into the night. He was tense; I could feel it, and while I could rattle off a bunch of medical reasons why things would probably be fine, I knew that wasn't what would make him feel better. He already had one person he loved slipping away from him; the thought of losing another was probably torture. I reached out a shaky hand and put it on his arm where it was resting on the stick shift. The muscles were rock-hard and had a fine tremor in them.

"Nash." He looked over at me and I could see the fine lines of worry bracketing his mouth. "Do you, uh, want me to go to the hospital with you?"

They were all a family, all loved each other, leaned on one another. I was an outsider. True, the hospital was my home away from home, I was way more in my element there than I was in this car trying to offer this brooding man comfort. But it was the right thing for me to do. I could see it when his eyes shifted back to periwinkle, and his arm where I was touching him softened a fraction.

"Yeah. I really do."

"All right. Let's go then."

The wheels under the powerful car squealed, and I got tossed to the side as he wheeled it around in the middle of the street and headed across town toward the hospital. This was a surefire way to have me sobering up way more quickly than I would have if I just went home to sleep it off.

He parked and I had to practically run to keep up with him as he headed for the front doors. It was a good thing I was tall or else I got the feeling he would have just dragged me along behind him. His hand was hard on mine and I could feel nervous moisture coating his palm. He was headed for emergency, so I had to dig my heels in and yank him to a grinding halt.

"Labor and delivery is this way. They probably moved her over there already."

He grunted and begrudgingly let me take the lead. I didn't miss the questioning looks I got from the night staff as I skated by holding his hand. He was the kind of guy who attracted attention anyway, and given the fact they were still all gossiping about my disastrous date with Dr. Bennet, this didn't bode well for me not being the topic of conversation anymore.

The crew was all gathered in the waiting room, minus Rule. Nash nodded at the guys, who were pacing back and forth, but went to the girls for the info.

"What's happening?"

Shaw was twisting her hair around her finger and her green eyes were huge in her face.

"She's early, but not too bad. Thirty-six weeks. Rome was freaking everyone out. I think he's having a little episode, so his mom came and got Rule to keep him in line. The doctor was scared of him."

Nash snorted and I had no problem imagining the scene between Rome and the doctor, considering I knew exactly how intimidating the big ex-soldier could be.

"Anyone call Joe?" He looked at me and clarified: "Cora's dad."

Shaw nodded. "Rome did on the way in. You might want to call Phil."

Nash went tense next to me and his eyes flashed back to dark. I knew his dad was like a fill-in parent to all these guys. The tattoo shop he had created had become their home. The idea of a new life coming into the world while he was on his way out had to gall and burn. I squeezed Nash's hand and he looked down at me.

"I'm gonna go talk to the staff and see if I can get any insider info. Okay?"

He gulped a little and his mouth turned down.

"I'm gonna make a call."

He looked so sad, so torn, it pulled at my heart way harder than watching some girl throw herself at him had. I reached up a hand and put it on his cheek. There was a tick there that had more than my nurse's instincts firing up, wanting to take care of him. That wasn't good. I wanted to be insulated, wanted to have enough space that there was no chance that this man could hurt me again, and I felt that safeguard slipping further and further away.

I went and inquired about the patient and the baby. I used my employee status to get more info than they would give the motley crew gathered in the waiting room. By the time I met back up with Nash, everyone looked solemn and stressed out. Babies took a long time to come into the world and it was going to be a long night for all of them.

"She's doing great. She still has a ways to go before she is really in the thick of labor. The baby's vitals are strong, so I think everything is going to be just fine. I would say everyone just needs to settle in and wait. The baby clearly has her own agenda and doesn't know there are rules she should be following."

"Sounds like her uncle; she's already showing her Archer roots."

Shaw's dry comment broke the rest of the tension, and grateful eyes as well as relieved smiles met my little debriefing. I gasped a little when Nash wrapped me up in his arms and pulled me against his chest so that he could hold me while he propped himself up against the wall.

He put his lips to my temple, and I felt his chest expand and retract. "I'm so glad you're here. I'm so over being at the hospital, but at least you make it bearable."

I didn't know what to say to that, so I wrapped my arms around his lean waist and let him hold on to me. I needed to figure out fast how deep in I was willing to go with him. The reality that he wanted *me* here, not because I knew how to navigate the ins and outs of the hospital, but because he wanted *me*, was something I felt I needed to really get my head around.

I didn't want to get hurt, but I had never considered that by handling this wrong, I could very well end up hurting him. I didn't like that idea at all.

CHAPTER 13

Nash

"CORA BROUGHT THE BABY by. I can't believe how tiny she is."

I nodded and handed Phil a glass of water. He looked awful. It pained me to see him like this, wasting away, the bedroom in his condo was basically converted into a hospital room. The more time went on, the skinnier he got, the worse his pallor looked, and I could hear how gasping and sucking each breath he took in and out sounded. I bent my head down and stared at the carpet between the toes of my Vans. I didn't want him to see how hard these visits were getting for me.

"She looks like a little doll when Rome holds her. She almost fits in the palm of one of his big bear paws. She's too tiny to know it yet but she has all the men in her life wrapped around her finger." I joked about it but it was true.

Remy Josephine Archer was a fuzzy, blond-haired, perfect miniature replica of her mom. Her eyes were still infant dark, but at the center there was no mistaking the crisp, clear Archer blue. She was going to have Rule's eyes, Remy's eyes. She was going to do her namesake proud, and Cora's dad was already so in love with his granddaughter, he was talking about moving from Brooklyn to Denver. Little R.J. was the first baby for any of our patchworked family and there was no doubt she was going to be horrendously over-protected and ridiculously loved. She deserved nothing less.

"How are you guys doing at the shop without Cora?"

Phil started coughing, and I looked up at him under my brows. He sounded so awful, it made my heart squeeze so hard it stalled for a beat.

"It could be better. I can't take as many clients, there was so much she handled. The first half of my day is messing with new clients, doing shit on the Internet, and paying bills. It sucks. The construction at the new shop started, so when I'm not trying to handle business at the Marked, I'm down there. Rule and Rowdy found a couple good artists we're going to bring in to pick up the slack and see if they'll work out at the new place, but for someone to run the desk and sit up front." I just shook my head.

He coughed again and it made his entire thin frame shake and quake. "You aren't going to find another Cora. She's one of a kind, and once she's ready, she'll be back. I want you to call this girl I met the last time I was in Vegas. I was doing a convention there and she was one of the pinup models there for the guys to take pictures with."

I snorted out a laugh. "I need a business major, not a model."

"You need someone who can handle all the bad attitude you guys throw around and that fits in with the rest of the shop. Someone with heart and a certain badassness. She was smart, she was beautiful. I took her info for a reason. Call her and see if she would be interested in coming out for an interview."

I just wanted to make him happy, so I agreed. "If you say so."

"I do. I might be sick, but I still know what makes that shop run. Plus I think she might be more inclined to come help you guys out and make the shop a success than anyone else you're going to just happen upon."

"Why do you think that?"

"Because the past ties us all together, Nash. None of us would be where we are now without the things that happened to us back then. Her name is Salem Cruz. Tell her I gave you her info and maybe mention she should look up the shop's website so she can check out the artists' page."

He was being cryptic and evasive, but that was pretty typical Phil-speak, so I didn't question it. Besides, he changed the subject.

"How's your pretty nurse?"

That was a good question. I didn't have the first clue how she was. Ever since she spent the night at the hospital with me while we all waited on Cora and the baby, she had been slightly evasive. We were still spending time together, still spent the night together as often as either of us could swing it with our busy schedules, but there was something there now, some kind of distance, some kind of shield she had up, and even though I didn't want to admit it to myself because I was in deep now, it felt like she was drifting away from me.

I wanted to ask her, wanted to make her admit we were into each other, that this thing between us was serious, and after almost three months she had to see that I was committed to being with her and no one else. But instead of being closer, she seemed to want more space between us. She hadn't even let me do anything for her on Valentine's Day. It was a difficult situation, and while I had no problem pushing her into bed, making her see and feel how perfect I thought she was, out of bed I was seriously worried that if I tried to make her put a label on, tried to force her to admit she cared about me beyond what I could make her feel in the dark, she would leave.

I got that she wanted to be careful, that she wasn't fully convinced she could trust me . . . trust any guy, really. I couldn't blame her. She had told me about her dad and his girlfriend and about some guy she had been involved with while she was in college, and how both cases of infidelity had left lasting marks on her already distrustful soul. I wanted to shake some sense into her. I had worked so hard to get close to her, there was no way I was going to screw it up by sticking my dick in the first willing female that came along, but I just couldn't seem to get her to believe that.

She sort of glossed over the situation with the guy in college, but when she talked about her father, about the way her family had been so close, about the way her mom had gone off the deep end in the wake of his betrayal, I could hear in her voice how hard that had been for her. His unfaithfulness had cut not just her mother but all of the women in the Ford household deeply enough to leave lasting scars. She talked a good game about tolerating him and the choices he made, about turning the other cheek to keep the peace and to keep him in her life, but the resentment was there underneath every word she spoke. I couldn't say that I faulted her for that, because even from the outside looking in, I could see her dad had done a shitty thing and left the family in the lurch. I just didn't know how Saint was ever going to get to a place where she could let it all go, put her faith in the fact that I wasn't like that . . . if she didn't come to terms with the fact people could be fallible, even people we had looked up to for our entire lives. The resentment she held on to was justified, but if she couldn't figure out what to do with it, I didn't know what that meant for us going forward.

Her father had disappointed her, solidified that foundation of mistrust I had broken ground on years ago, and I wasn't sure how to make her see that I would do anything within my power to keep from letting her down like that again. I was not her dad, nor would I ever want to be the kind of man who threw his loving family over for a quick piece.

"She's difficult."

He laughed, an actual laugh, and it made me smile down at the floor. I felt him reach out and he put one of his thin hands on the crown of my bent head. I closed my eyes and felt my breath shudder in my chest.

"That's the catchphrase of your life at the moment, Nash. 'Difficult.' You are a strong man, a good man, and you can handle anything life throws at you, no matter how difficult it may be. I want you to know, this man—the man you are now—he is a man you can be proud of. You are the greatest thing I ever created. Don't doubt it."

Well, shit, if that didn't just make me want to bawl all over the place. I had to clench my hands hard into fists to keep all the emotion down.

"All I ever wanted was for my mom to tell me that. Now I know hearing it from you—the person that got me here—is a million times more valuable. Thanks, Phil."

I was still having some difficulty thinking of him as my "dad." His fingers patted my shaved head.

"I should have been braver. Shouldn't have been so concerned that you would hate me for not telling you. I wanted your mother to be accountable, but once you came to stay with me permanently . . . I should have told you the truth."

"Well, I wish I had known sooner, wish I could have time to appreciate one parent being proud of me. The choices she made make it really easy for me to come to terms with the fact she might have given birth to me, but she was never really my mother."

"I was proud of you long before you had any idea you were my son, Nash. Your mom is a complicated woman, she always had a pretty clear-cut idea of the way her life should look. Neither you nor I fit in that vision."

He moved his hand and I finally looked up at him. If I was swallowing it all down—the feelings, the time lost—the history was glassy and bright in his eyes.

"She should have just let you take me from the get-go. It would have saved everyone a lot of heartache."

"We can't go back in time, son, all we can do is move

forward smarter and far more carefully." He broke off in a coughing fit that didn't look like it was going to end, and ended up needing his oxygen and some pain medicine. I helped him with both and realized I was going to have to cut the visit short.

I got him settled and tried not to worry that every single time I saw him it felt like it was going to be the last time.

"Call Salem. She's just what you guys need, and I think you guys will love her."

"Why do I feel like there is more to that story than you're telling me?"

He gave me a weak grin and his eyes drifted shut. "You know me; I always like to offer a helping hand when I can: you, Rule, Jet, Rowdy, Cora. I made my own little family out of lost souls. I'm hoping as time goes on, you guys will extend the tradition. I taught you well in everything I thought you needed to learn to have a good life, son."

He really had. Every life lesson he felt I needed to know, he had used his own unique way to teach me. I got in the Charger and cranked on the radio so I could listen to the music loud. Flatfoot 56 blasted through the speakers and I thought maybe if I drowned out all my other senses, I couldn't feel the pain that seeing Phil disappear in front of my very eyes caused. I sent Saint a text because really she was the only thing that was going to make me feel better.

Sure, I could go get drunk with Asa at the Bar, I could call Rome and go throw weights around at the gym, Rule would drop everything and come by and listen to me gripe, Rowdy would pull himself away from whoever he was into for the night and come entertain me and Jet . . . well, Jet was always out of town anymore, but I knew I could call him and bitch. I had friends, people who loved me, were suffering the loss right alongside me, and yet she was the only one who dulled the burn, the ripping feeling that was left after that kind of visit.

Gonna order pizza. Wanna come over after work?

Her: *Won't be off until late.*

Doesn't matter . . . you could actually stay the night this time.

That was a low blow and was wussy and passive-aggressive. But I felt like crap, so I tried to man up a little more with my next message.

I had a rough visit with Phil. He is barely hanging on, it looks like. I would like to see you, and I would like for you to stay with me.

There wasn't a response back for a while, so I had to start the car and head toward home. My insides were all twisted up and there was a sour taste running all along my tongue. I wanted to hit something or let something hit me.

I was pulling up in front of the Victorian when she finally sent me a message back. It galled. I had never waited around to hear from a chick before, especially a chick I didn't really know and was into me to the same level I was into her. I didn't do self-doubt anymore and I hated that she was churning it up in me.

Her: *Sorry a guy shot with a nail gun walked in. If you don't mind me showing up a little later I'll be there. Go ahead and eat without me.*

What about staying with me?

I had to push my luck. I felt too open, was bleeding everything I was feeling all over the place with no way to stop the flow.

Her: *Can we talk about that later? I just got two more patients.*

Go to work. I'll see you later.

I sighed feeling wholly torn up and unsatisfied when she sent: *I'm so sorry about Phil. That isn't fair and I'm sorry you're hurting.*

That was the thing about her, no matter how far away she seemed, there was just something there, some tie that made me believe that eventually she would come around and realize that we could be something amazing and special together.

I got out of the car and called the pizza place that knew me on a first-name basis. I ordered dinner and was putting my phone in my back pocket when a female voice swearing and a loud thumping caught my attention.

My neighbor was standing outside of her closed apartment door kicking it solidly with the toe of a high heel that was pinker than pink. She was using language that made me grin, and scowled at me when I asked her if I could help her with anything. She shoved her dark red hair over her shoulder and put her hands on her hips. Today she looked like she had come from some kind of fashion show, minus the disgruntled expression on her face.

"I always lock the door behind me. Any door, every door, which is normally a good thing, but not when my keys are on the other side. I left my cell in the car, and I was only two steps into the hallway when I realized I didn't grab my freaking keys." She groaned dramatically and threw her hands up. "So my phone is stuck in my car and my keys are stuck in my apartment and I am an idiot."

I lifted an eyebrow at her because she growled and shoved her hand through her hair.

"You can use my phone to call the landlord, though it might be faster to call a locksmith. I ordered a pizza; you can come over and hang out for a minute."

Her eyebrows shot up and she frowned at me. "Isn't that gonna make the girlfriend freak out?"

I had no clue. "I don't know."

"About the freak-out or the girlfriend?"

"Both. Do you want to use my phone or not?"

She sighed and followed me into my apartment. I handed her my phone and she used the Internet to find a locksmith that would be there within an hour. She threw herself on my sofa and stared at the ceiling.

"If I could get into my trunk, I have a lockpick set. I bet I could break in."

I offered her a beer and took a seat on the opposite side of the couch.

"Why do you have that?"

She went on like she hadn't even heard me. "And my partner . . . jeez when he hears about this, I'm never living it down. I locked us out of the squad car two weeks ago."

What? "Royal?"

She turned to look at me and I could see she was aggravated. "Yeah?"

"What exactly do you do?"

She huffed out a breath and rolled the beer between her hands. "I'm a cop."

Again, what? "Seriously?" I couldn't keep the disbelief out of my tone.

"Yeah. I told you that you wouldn't believe me if I told you what I did. No one does. I graduated from the academy last year, so I'm a newbie cop, but still a cop."

I let my disbelieving gaze drop to her silly shoes and flashy outfit. "Really?" I couldn't picture her with a badge and a gun to save my life.

"I'm still a girl, but yeah, I'm a patrol officer. That's why my hours are so all over the place and why I think I got a good read on people."

There was knock on the door and I went to retrieve the pizza. I put it down in front of her on the coffee table and didn't bother to find a plate. It wasn't like I was trying to impress her or anything. She rolled her eyes and fetched a slice.

"Well, your instinct that you had about Saint was way off. You said she was into me, had a crush, but lately I feel like all she has me doing is chasing my own tail."

Royal laughed a little and I thought really it meant something that I wasn't the least bit attracted to her. I was so hung up on Saint that even though I knew my neighbor was inarguably beautiful and fun, she just wasn't it for me.

"Nash, I've seen her. When she's coming, when she's going, she always has the same look on her face. She's excited to see you, to be with you, but underneath that she is terrified. I don't know the whole story, but if she's making you chase your tail, believe me when I tell you there is no way she isn't spinning herself in just as many circles trying to catch her own as well."

God, I hoped so, because if I was the only one feeling dizzy and nauseous, it made this ride way less fun.

"We went to high school together, ran in pretty different circles. I bumped into her at the ER last year when a buddy got into a bar fight. She had a thing for me back then and apparently thought I was saying really terrible things about her and it left a mark on her. I was saying really terrible things because I was a hot head and was kind of jerk, but they weren't about her. Now she can't seem to get over it, even though it feels like it was in another lifetime."

She gave me a hard look and reached for another slice a pizza.

"A girl's first love is a big deal. We never really get over it."

"I don't think it was love."

She pointed the top of her beer bottle at me and squinted her dark eyes. "I think you're wrong. If she's holding on to it that tightly, still scared you're going to turn on her, hurt her again even though you've obviously changed and clearly care about her, it was first love."

I wanted to argue, but I had seen how powerful first love could be. Shaw had loved Rule since the first time she laid her eyes on him, and even though it had taken years for him to see it, she had never wavered in her devotion to him. Cora's first love had broken her heart by being unfaithful and abandoning her, it had almost cost her the perfect love she was searching for when Rome came barreling into her life. First love was indeed powerful, and if I had really tarnished it for

Saint, there stood a really good chance she might never let me in, would never trust me enough.

I was going to tell my pretty neighbor how much I thought that sucked when there was a light knock on the door. Thinking it was the locksmith, I got up and swung the door open. I felt my jaw go slack in surprise when I came face-to-face with the girl I couldn't get off my mind. She looked like she had just come from work. Her hair was up in a bun on the top of her head and she still had her scrubs on. I was going to ask her how she had gotten off so early but her gaze was locked on Royal and her mouth was a tight, flat line. She didn't even glance at me.

"Hey."

Those storm-cloud-colored eyes flicked up to mine and a soft pink flooded into her face.

"Hey."

"You got off work early."

Her gaze shot back to Royal, who had gotten up and wandered over to the door.

"I did. One of the other girls came in early by chance, and I was worried about how you were doing after your visit." There was a definite thread of accusation in her tone.

I frowned down at her, hurt she thought I would just substitute time spent with her with anyone that would do. She was the only one who made me feel better after visiting with Phil. I wished I could make her believe that. Royal peeked around both of us as the front security door swung open and a guy in work clothes carrying a toolbox poked his head in.

"Someone locked out?"

Saint shifted nervously in front of me as Royal slid past both of us. She winked at me and patted Saint on the shoulder as she walked toward her own door.

"Thanks for the rescue, Nash. He's a good one, girlie, don't let him get away."

I took a step back and watched, literally watched, while Saint struggled with whether she was going to follow me inside or not. It was all over her pale face, and the indecision made me feel slightly sick. I decided if she didn't come in, then this was it. I couldn't do it anymore. I liked her—hell, way more than liked her—but this unknown, this chase, was just one more thing in my life that was heaping with complications. As much as I wanted this to work, just plain wanted *her,* at some point she was going to have to give me something solid to hold on to.

She reached up and started to pull out the tie holding all her copper hair up. She looked away from me and scooted by so that our chests barely brushed together. I closed the door and followed her over to where she sat on the arm of the couch.

"Thanks for coming over."

She nodded a little by dipping her chin down.

"It has to be getting harder. Phil's prognosis wasn't very good when he left the hospital."

I stopped by her side and reached out to put a finger under her chin. I forced her to look up at me, to meet my gaze. There were darker slate shadows behind the pearly gray as she looked up at me.

"I was just helping a neighbor out, you know that, right?"

She let her lids droop down so I couldn't really see what was going on in that complex mind of hers.

"It doesn't matter. We don't have that kind of claim on each other."

There it was. I wanted more and she didn't want anything. I felt my stomach drop and I stepped away from her. She followed the movement and frowned at me.

"That's too bad, Saint. I wanted that kind of claim. I don't know what this"—I motioned between us with a hand—"is all about, but it means something to me, and if you can't say the same, then I don't want to just be the dude you hook up with because I can get you off and no one else can. That's not enough for me anymore, and frankly it makes me feel like shit."

I walked to the front door, ready to pull it open and send her on her way for good. I was mad and upset and not bothering to hide it. I wasn't in any kind of head space to separate how much of it had to do with her and how much of it had to do with what I was feeling because of Phil.

"I wanted to spend the night with you tonight because the only person that ever made me feel like I was worth anything is dying and I have to watch it and do nothing about it. Nothing makes that better. Nothing fixes it, but when I'm with you . . ."—I rubbed a hand over my face and used it to grab the back of my neck—"it hurts just a fraction less. You make me want to focus on the good, on the memories I have that make me happy, but this clearly doesn't mean the same thing to you. You can't even be bothered to stay the entire night with me, Saint. I get it, you aren't into this the way I am, so you can go. Thanks for coming by."

I had my hand on the knob and a sweltering heat was pulsing under my skin. I hated to see her go, but for my sanity and peace of mind, it was the right call. I was getting ready to yank the door open when she was suddenly between me and the wood. She put her hands on the center of my chest and splayed her fingers wide open. My heart sped up, started thumping harder, like it was trying to burst out of my chest and put itself in her hands.

"Nash." Her voice was barely a whisper.

"I can't do it anymore, Saint. I don't even know what *it* is."

"I'm sorry. I really am. I don't mean to push you away, to dismiss whatever it is we have. I just don't know how to do this with you. I don't want to be the jealous, fearful girl, but I am. I saw Royal and wanted to turn right around and never come back."

Her hands moved up my chest and cupped each side of my face.

"It makes me feel better to think it wouldn't matter if you were doing something questionable with her because we don't mean anything to each other. It can't hurt if we don't have any kind of real feelings for each other."

Her logic was ridiculous. Of course it could still hurt, because even if she convinced herself she didn't have any feelings for me, her reactions still tore me up because I sure as shit had feelings for her.

"All I can see is you. Why can't you understand that? No one shines as bright as you in the sky I'm looking at. To me there is no sun, no moon, and no stars in the sky, just endless miles of storm clouds and pretty, pretty gray."

She moved her hands up higher and used her fingers to trace over the flames above my ears. She was trying to soothe me, trying to make the frayed edges come back together and put sutures in the wounds she had unwittingly inflicted.

"I want to believe that so badly, Nash. I can't explain it to you, but part of me wants so much to see me the way you do, but a bigger, louder part refuses to believe it's possible."

I put my hands around her delicate wrists. My fingers overlapped because her wrists were so fragile, and I felt her pulse hammering under her pale skin.

"What do you want, Saint? What do you really want?"

She moved her hands off of my head and let them rest on my shoulders. Her eyes were swirling gray as she fought for control of the emotion whipping in the depths.

"I want your dad to be okay and for you not to have to watch him suffer. I want to be able to enjoy the time we spend together like a normal person and not constantly be waiting for the other shoe to drop. I want to get promoted at work. I want my mom to get over my dad and stop hurting. Mostly, I want to make sure that this thing we're doing doesn't leave either one of us sad and full of regret."

I couldn't fault her honesty, but I also couldn't give her any kind of guarantee or affirmation that any of those things she wanted were possible. In fact, I knew some of them weren't.

"What do you want from me?" I sounded a little like I was being strangled. I was already stripped to the live nerve center of my emotional threshold for the day. Doing this with her was the last thing I needed or wanted.

She sighed, and finally all the shadows and fog in her eyes cleared and left behind the crystalline gray.

"I want you, Nash. I always want you; this is just the only way I know how to do it and feel comfortable."

"Why are you so certain I'm going to hurt you? That I'm going to fuck up and disappoint you?"

She gave me a lopsided smile and she worked her hands under the collar of my shirt so she could stroke the base of my neck.

"Because it's bound to happen, but I really want to enjoy what we have before then."

How did I fight against that? How did I convince her when she seemed so certain that if she let go and trusted the feelings building between us instead of worrying about what might happen or what had happened, we could make the here and now something that lasted forever?

I wanted to keep arguing, to keep pushing her to see that this was more than a fling, more than two people who were sexually compatible. I wanted her to feel, to know I wouldn't have been able to make it through everything going on with Phil and the shop without her kindness, her gentleness and care. However, she had her hands under my clothes and her mouth settled over mine, and even though I knew she was trying to distract me from the conversation, I decided not to stop her.

If this was the only way she was going to let me connect to her, I would just have to make do with it for now. I was a guy after all . . . and there were far worse things in life than having a gorgeous girl want you for sex. Plus, she wanted me, had proven that time and time again. I guess I would just have to ultimately decide if what she wanted me for was going to be enough when I felt like I needed to give her everything else I had.

CHAPTER 14

Saint

I WAS GOING TO screw all of this up. I felt it all the way down to the marrow of my bones.

I had to touch him. Had to try and soothe the way I was cutting into him and making him bleed. There was no hiding the way my hesitation, my resistance, made his eyes go dark and his mouth go hard. Even with his obvious disappointment, he never lashed out, never got nasty, which made everything even more convoluted in my head. I did what I knew would make it all go away for a while, I kissed him, started pulling at his clothes and pressed up against his hard body. He was stiff and unresponsive for a half of a second, but like always when we got together like this, his big frame started to loosen.

Seeing Royal making herself at home on his couch had made every concern, every worry, every insecure part of me want to run away from him and never look back. All those questions of why he would want me, of how long would it take until he found someone without my hang-ups, someone not stuck in the past, barrel through my head like a runaway boulder falling off a cliff. If there hadn't been real joy, real gratitude glowing out of his violet eyes when he saw it was me at the door, I would have bolted and never spoken to him again. I hated that this thing with him made me feel that way, brought such a ridiculous weakness to the forefront of my mind. It made me feel like I was stuck in time. I just couldn't handle that, so I blew him off when he tried to explain. I was protecting myself, insulating my heart, but little did I know my words were drawing a line in the sand where he was concerned, and his heart very well might be just as fragile as mine.

When he had told me to go, walked to the door like he was really ending it all, my breath had been sucked out of my lungs and my blood had frozen still in my veins. I couldn't give him everything he wanted, that left me far too vulnerable, but I had to make him see this was just as important to me as it was to him. The only way I could do that without getting stuck on words was with my body. Sure, I wanted him and he knew it, but I don't think he knew it was so much more than that. I just couldn't figure out a way to explain it all to him without sounding like a nut job or an uncertain and immature child.

I made a startled noise when he pressed me back fully into the door and tangled his fingers in my hair. His eyes burned down at me in endless rivers of purple and blue.

"This is a conversation we are going to have to finish at some point, Saint."

I put my hands under the hem of his shirt so that my palms could skate up the divots and hollows of his rib cage.

His skin was always so warm. He always felt so strong and vital, so resilient and secure. That he let me call the shots, let me set the pace when we were together, made me feel like the most powerful and most desirable woman in the world. It was intoxicating. I couldn't just walk away from it even if that was ultimately what was best for both of us.

"But it can wait, Nash." I brushed my lips across the base of his throat and felt him swallow. I hated that he felt like he had to deal with me and all my issues on top of everything he was struggling with in regard to his dad.

He kissed my temple and then used his tongue to trace the shell of my ear. It made me shiver all over even when he whispered, "No, not now. But soon."

He pressed even more fully into me, making me spread my legs. He let his hands fall to the round curve of my ass and I gasped when he shifted, hefted me up, and urged me to wrap my legs around his waist. I was tall and not a petite girl. There wasn't much about me that I would ever consider dainty, but he was a monster in comparison, so he didn't even seem like he noticed my weight when he moved away from the door and headed down the hallway that led to his bedroom. I curled my arms around his shoulders and sealed my mouth over his while he walked. I loved the way the motion rubbed our bodies together. Even through my work scrubs and the layers underneath, I felt my nipples pebble, felt his body respond through the thick denim of his jeans. I twisted my tongue around his, twirled them in a sucking, breathless kiss that had both of us needing to come up for air by the time he got to the bedroom.

He leaned forward and dropped me on the center of the bed while pulling back and pulling his shirt up and off over his head. Now, that was a sight that would never get old. The muscles and golden skin stretched so tautly over them was always mouthwatering and made my fingers tingle and itch to stroke all over, but the designs, the markings that defined him, decorated him, and made him his own walking art gallery were just as alluring. The ink that curled and twisted up and down his arms was brilliant and eye-catching, but it was that dragon, that other part of him, that I always wanted to touch. The wings, the fire, the scales that covered so much of his big body . . . it was like he had a second skin and only a few got to see it in all its grandeur and I was one of the lucky ones.

He popped open the tab on his belt and lifted an eyebrow at me. I sat up and pulled my top off. Hospital work clothes were not the most flattering thing a person could wear but he didn't seem to mind them. His gaze did that thing where it went almost all the way black when I was left in front of him on the bed in nothing but my underwear. He reached out a single finger and trailed it down the valley between my breasts.

"I love your freckles."

It made me shiver, but the look in his eyes, and the expression on his face, had my body going liquid and warm all over. I went to reach for him, to pull him over me, but he bent down and used the same finger to pull the cup of my bra down off of one of my breasts. The tip eagerly surged up to meet his descending tongue. I squirmed and wiggled under him as he licked at it, circled it, sucked it into the warm center of his mouth. I was pawing at his nonexistent hair, tossing my head back and forth across the comforter because he was being so meticulous, so thorough with his attention to what he was doing to me. I lifted my head to tell him to stop, to get his pants off and get the show on the road, when he moved on to the other breast and that one was the other end of his pleasurable torture.

By the time he was done, I was panting and ready to explode just from his attention to my breasts. He pulled my bra all the way off and pushed me back farther on the bed. I thought he was going to just pull my panties off and get on with the sexy time. I wanted him desperately, felt my body weeping in welcome and anticipation, but Nash seemed like he was in no hurry and he wasn't letting me call the shots tonight. He let his jeans drop, and I took a minute to really appreciate the bulge that was in the front of his boxers. There wasn't anything I would change about him, and the wings inked all along his sides seemed to flutter when he took a deep breath and let it out slowly while working the last of my clothing out of the way.

His eyes were indigo and there was a flush under his burnished skin. Something was going on in his head, something I wasn't privy to, but when he crawled on the bed between my legs and put a biting kiss on the inside of one thigh before lifting it up and over his shoulder, I knew.

We had had plenty of sex over the last several months, *plenty* probably being an understatement. Nash using his mouth on me was no longer foreign or scary and new. He was good at it, I always enjoyed it, but this was different, all of it was different. He wasn't just making love to me, he wasn't just trying to turn me on or wind me up. He was worshipping me. He was trying to *show* me in yet another way just how beautiful and perfect he saw me as being.

"Nash?" I said his name . . . well, more like choked it out, because his mouth and his hands were doing things that were making me come undone. I felt my hands twist into tight knots in the sheets as he stroked the flat of his tongue over a particularly sensitive bundle of nerves.

"Hmm?" He hmmed back at me and it made me cry out because when he did it he trapped my clit between his teeth and the vibration made my eyes roll back in my head.

His hands were on either side my hips, both my legs were dropped over his wide shoulders, and his dark head was buried quite thoroughly at the heart of me. It felt wanton and decadent because of how intent he was on proving his point. I tensed, felt small tremors start in the base of my spine, and when his mouth was replaced with exploring and stroking fingers, all it took was a gentle shove and I dropped over the edge. I vaguely felt him kiss along my quaking stomach, felt his fingers moving, playing with me to draw out the response, but it was his eyes, so dark, so focused on me, that had my heart surrendering and all the noise rattling in my head finally going quiet.

He let my legs slither to either side of him and traced a pattern on the soft skin right below my breasts.

"You are so sweet. Inside and out." His voice was gruff, so I reached down so that I could pull him up and over me.

He always said stuff like that to me. Told me I was beautiful, told me I was nice and fun to be around. He often told me I was his favorite in bed. I never replied to any of it, but there was no getting past what he had just given to me.

"Thank you." It sounded rusty and underused to my own ears. Taking a compliment shouldn't be that hard. The way Nash saw me, the reflection of myself in those endlessly purple eyes, was the most beautiful thing in the world, and I was having a much harder time pretending like I didn't see exactly what he saw in me.

My simple words had shadows and light shifting in his beautiful eyes. He levered himself up and over me in a stiff push-up so that I could work his boxers off and around his straining erection. It sprang free, thick and ready, wearing a new adornment. I blinked at it and then looked up at him in question.

"Why is your penis wearing a ring?"

He snorted out a laugh that I think more had to do with the clinical term for the body part in question than it did with my actual question.

"I just switched out the barbell."

Behind the ridge of the head of his engorged erection was a thin hoop that circled the entire circumference of his cock. The little silver ring was fascinating. I wasn't an expert on body piercing by anyone's standards, but I had never seen anything like it, especially paired with that piercing at the tip that he used to its full advantage and I had to admit I was a huge fan of.

"Your dick is wearing jewelry."

That made him laugh for real and he hooked an arm

around my shoulders and rolled us over so I was straddling him. He stacked his hands behind his head and grinned up at me.

"I like to switch it up. It'll feel good, trust me."

I didn't doubt it, and for the first time since we started having sex, I really wished I wasn't so scarred, so scared about talking to him about what this thing we were doing really was. If it was a relationship, a committed partnership, I would be on birth control and get to feel all that hard and hot flesh against the cool slide of metal without latex between us. That sounded divine and I was mad at myself for being my own stumbling block in figuring my life out, in figuring out what I was doing with this gorgeous and engaging man.

I leaned back and dug around in his nightstand for the box of condoms I knew was in there. While I was all stretched out he used his thumbs to trace the line of my ribs on each side of my body. He was always so reverent, so tactile, when he put his hands on me. Even a simple caress like that had my heart rate speeding up and my blood heating in anticipation.

Before I covered him, I took a few minutes to play with his new hardware. The ridge it left, the way it got hot against his skin, promised a good time for sure. I wanted to put it in my mouth but he stopped me with hands in my hair.

"Not this time."

I lifted an eyebrow at him as he took the condom from me and covered himself. He urged me up higher on my knees and placed me over the tip of his straining erection. I got that he was trying to make a point. That he was trying to show me something I just wouldn't accept or hear, but there were two of us involved in this and I wanted to make sure he knew just how much I felt for him as well. I was just confused about it and trying to be realistic, keep it all in a box I was comfortable with.

I didn't get the chance to reciprocate the feeling or emotion because he tugged me down over him and I lost the ability to think. Nash was a big guy, everywhere. He was already thick and turgid, so after that initial penetration, having that ring he was wearing stretch me apart even further, having it drag along my sensitive inner flesh with a rolling, warm glide . . . it made me incapable of being able to do anything but feel. The pressure was greater than usual, the slither of our internal flesh was sexier. I thought I was going to come before he even got all the way inside of me.

"Oh my . . ." I'm pretty sure my eyes rolled all the way back in my skull.

He chuckled, which only made the sensation sharper, and I pried my eyes open to look down at him once he was fully seated inside of me. I think he liked it best when I was on top because I had no choice but to look at him. Right now he looked smug and pleased with himself.

"It gets better. You have to move, Saint." He lifted both of his hands and cupped each of my breasts.

I threw my head back and groaned. I took his advice and did as he asked. I started to ride him, the up and down, the pull and push of that hoop plus his PA all along the inside of me, was so good. I curled my hands on his chest and watched him watch me. If it was possible, his eyes got darker and darker the closer I got. I shifted, clamped down on him, listening to his breath come faster and faster and reveling in the way his chest moved up and down more rapidly. I was close, so close, and knew if I asked him to touch me just a little bit more or just reached between my legs to touch myself, it would be done. I opened my mouth to plead with him, to ask him to finish it, but before I got the words out, he suddenly jackknifed up into a sitting position and rolled us over.

He was looming over me, his hand clasping either side of my face. His expression turned a little wild, and when I went to ask what was going on, he attacked my mouth and started moving in and out of me, thrusting against me, pounding inside of my body like a person possessed. All I could do was hold on for the ride because I was already too close to the edge. My nails dug hard enough into his shoulders and I felt the skin break. At the first stroke of his tongue against mine, the bite of his teeth against my lip, I broke apart under him in an orgasm that felt like it turned me inside out. I just clung to him, let him surge and heave inside of me until he buried his nose in the crook of my neck and groaned his own completion. That wasn't just sex; that was Nash giving part of himself over to me to keep forever.

His hand fell away from my face but he didn't move. His breath was ragged in my ear and I could feel his heart thundering rapidly against my own. I stroked a soothing hand down the spine of that dragon, felt Nash's body shake a little at the touch.

"You undo me, Saint."

"I'm sorry."

He sighed and rolled over so he could pull me on top of his chest.

"Just try and put me back together when you're done with me, all right?"

I didn't know what to say to that or if that was a promise I could make to him. I curled my hands under his arms and rubbed my cheek against his pectoral muscle. It was way too hard to make any kind of comfortable pillow, but I didn't want to move.

"Can I stay the night with you, Nash?" I couldn't give him all of the things he wanted from me, but that I could do.

He sighed and it ruffled the hair on the top of my head. "At some point I really want us in a place where that isn't even a question you think you need to ask."

I didn't know that a place like that existed for us, but it felt like if it did, it would be right here in this moment with the two of us still entwined and apart of one another.

THE NEXT MORNING NASH was running late, which might have had something to do with the fact that I woke up before him and couldn't resist putting my mouth around that circle of stainless steel. I'm sure he enjoyed the wake-up call, but he ran out of the door muttering something about calling a girl Phil thought could help him out at the shop and having to swing by the new shop and check in with the contractor. He was juggling so many balls I had no idea how he kept it all straight or found the time to deal with me and all my issues on top of it.

He gave me a hard kiss, told me to make breakfast or whatever I wanted, and blew out the door like a tattooed tornado. He had spent many a morning in my place when I had to go to work, it was strange being on the opposite side of that. I was making coffee, wearing one of his T-shirts that was way too big and way too long, when there was a knock at the door. I was going to ignore it because I didn't feel it was my place to answer the door at Nash's apartment when I heard my name called through the wood.

"Saint? It's Royal. Can I talk to you for a minute? I know you're here because your Jetta is still outside."

Ugh. I didn't want to face her after last night. Didn't want her to see how jealous I was that she had spent a normal evening with Nash, but I wandered over to open the door anyway.

I had to do a double take and felt my jaw drop when I caught sight of her. Her fabulous auburn hair was coiled up on her head, she had no makeup on, and she was dressed in the basic bluish-black police uniform all the street cops in Denver wore. She had a hat under her arm and a gun on a belt at her waist. I couldn't believe this was the same girl who had on pink heels and skinny jeans last night.

"You're a cop?"

She pushed past me and walked into the kitchen, where the coffee was done brewing. She made herself right at home, going through Nash's cabinets until she found a mug. I should have protested her forwardness but I was still in shock over the fact that she was armed.

"Yep." She let the *p* pop and poured me a mug as well.

"Listen, I want to try and explain something to you about your guy."

It was on the tip of my tongue to deny he was my anything, but she scowled at me. "I'm cranky and armed. Don't start with me, girlie. Last night I locked myself out of my place. My phone was in the car, so I was screwed. Nash helped me out, fed me, and talked to me about you. Do you know how many asshole guys would've used that as an excuse to put a move on me? Or how many would've tried something shady because I had no way to communicate or anyplace to go?"

She had a very valid point, so I nodded at her in agreement.

"Most guys are assholes. Seriously, Saint, Nash is not one of them. I know there is some history there between the two of you or whatever, but open your eyes, honey. That boy is sprung on you and he is a nice guy. A superhot, supersexy nice guy. Do you know how rare that is? He's like a goddamn unicorn."

I picked up my mug of coffee and continued to watch her like she was some kind of wild exhibit at the zoo.

"Besides, my mom was the other woman. I was the milkman's kid . . . well, the stockbroker's really, but that doesn't matter. I would never do that to another person, insert myself in their relationship, because I saw how hard it was on my mom waiting for that asshole to leave his wife. I can't help it that I have an awesome rack and was blessed with fabulous hair. I'm not some femme fatale out to steal anyone's man."

It actually sounded like that was a sore spot with her, so I cleared my throat and tried to give her a semi-explanation.

"It doesn't help that you're beautiful and live right across the hall, but it could be any pretty girl, Royal. Men are easily distracted like that."

She let loose a string of profanity that made me take a step back. She was sure a contradiction. A really pretty girl with a badge and a really dirty mouth.

"That's insanity. No other girl is going to come along and distract him. He is absolutely focused on you. We are not interchangeable objects, LEGO pieces that click together just because the parts fit. If he is telling you he wants *you*, then no one else is going to do. If you can't believe what he's telling you because of whatever your ordeal in the past is, pay attention to what he's showing you. Actions always speak louder than words."

She took her hat and positioned it over the bun on her head. I cocked my head to the side and considered her for a long minute.

"What does it matter to you anyway?"

She put her mug in the sink and rinsed it out.

"Nash is nice, you seem nice. There aren't enough good people out there that find each other. Plus I want you to be my friend."

That wasn't what I expected. "What? Why?"

"Because girls don't like me. They all think I'm out to steal their man or they get squirrely when they learn I'm a cop. I'm twenty-three years old, Saint, and I can't remember the last time I had a friend that wasn't a dude. My best friend in the entire world is my partner, Dominic. We went to high school together and struggled through the academy together. If it wasn't for him I would be really, really alone, and I don't want that."

I just stared at her, trying to figure out what I wanted to say to her.

"When you have a guy like Nash willing to offer you everything, don't risk losing it because of what was or because of what might be. Now I gotta go catch all the bad guys."

When the front door closed behind her, I took my coffee and went to flop down on the couch. I wanted to go to the grocery store before I had to leave and put some actual food in Nash's fridge for him. The poor guy couldn't live on cold pizza and beer, not with everything else he had going on in his life at the moment. Really I had a burning need to try and take care of him working under the surface of my skin and I wasn't going to question it right now.

It had been an intense few days, and my emotions were all over the place. Royal was right: Nash had been trying to show me all night long the things I wouldn't listen to and he was making it impossible for me to keep my head buried in the sand. Not only was the only guy I had ever really truly cared about demanding something more from me than I ever thought I could give, but I had a brassy, loud, badass female cop who looked like a movie star telling me she wanted to be my friend. I didn't know what alternate universe I had fallen into, whose life this was I was suddenly living, but it sure didn't feel like mine. Right now I couldn't tell if that was the best thing to ever happen to me or the worst.

CHAPTER 15

Nash

THE SHOP WAS COMING along way better than I could have imagined. Zeb was a magic man and an honest-to-God visionary. The final concept he had come up with was an old-school carnival straight off some boardwalk, and since my life felt like a three-ring circus half the time now, it totally fit. It was old-timey and a little kitschy, but the idea was awesome and all of us liked how different it was from the rough-and-tumble way the original shop came across. Each of the six artists' stations was modeled after a booth that would be in a 1930s freak show—we had a strongman, a bearded lady, of course a tattooed lady, a fortune-teller, a lion tamer, a sword swallower, and a freaky-looking wolfman painted on the wall. Zeb wanted to install a vintage strength machine, a retro photo booth, and one of those old creepy fortune-telling machines, which I thought would send the concept and the shop over the top. All our portfolios and pictures of tattoos we had done were on a state-of-the-art LED screen that was constantly changing and operated on a touch screen so potential clients could interact with it.

It was a fantastic mix of old and new, and while the actual tattoo shop probably only had three or so more weeks of work to make it a workable and usable space, Zeb hadn't gotten around to the top floor yet. The idea was to keep that space more modern, more boutique feeling. So far the bridge between the shop and the retail space hadn't come to fruition, mostly because it was uncharted territory for all of us and I think we were all worried about screwing it up or making it a joke when we had all worked so hard to solidify our reputations as the top tattoo artists in the Denver metro area. It was a brave new world and things were changing fast for all of us who called the Marked home.

I called the girl Phil had insisted I give a shot. It was a weird conversation. She was undeniably sharp and quick-witted. When I asked her if she had any experience working in a tattoo shop, she had laughed heartily and told me there was nothing she couldn't do. She actually didn't sound that interested in the opportunity to come out and interview with us until I mentioned the shop was in Denver. I told her what Phil said about looking the shop up online and letting me know. She hung up laughing and I thought I was going to end up writing her off as nothing more than a flighty model.

I was headed across town; I wanted to make a stop before going into work for the day. I needed some advice about getting around the ties and bonds that held a person to the past, and the only person I could think of that might be able to help me get some real answers, some real clarity, was Asa. He was a man who had lived a terrible life—a user and abuser—until almost losing not only his life but his sister as well. He had been forced to reevaluate what he was doing, who he was. Now he was making strides, trying to make amends, and while his relationship with Ayden was still rocky and often strained, there wasn't a day that went by that they didn't try and move on in their new relationship together. Asa was a man trying not to be defined by his past.

I was pulling the Charger into the parking lot when my cell went off and showed the Vegas number I had just dialed. Curious, I answered the call.

"Yeah?"

"Is all your shop info up-to-date on your website?"

Where she had sounded bored and slightly amused earlier, she sounded intrigued and almost breathless now. Anticipation crawled like a living thing across the phone line.

"It is."

"Like all the same artists are at the shop?" Man, she was insistent.

I made a face at my phone.

"Yep. We're all still here and getting ready to add a whole new crew in the next few months."

"Phil is maniacal. That guy just loves to mess with people's lives." She laughed a little and I wondered what Phil had been thinking with this chick. She seemed a little off-kilter to me, but the old man was a softy for a killer face—always had been.

"Listen, Salem, I have to get someone in and on top of shit fast. The new shop is opening at the end of May, the old shop is swamped. Either you're interested or you're not, but I don't have time to screw around if you're not into it. This was Phil's great idea, not mine." And I wouldn't tell her I would do anything to make him happy and make him smile while he was still here to see it.

"Oh, I'm way more into it now. Look, I have some stuff lined up until the end of April. I have to do Viva Las Vegas over Easter weekend, I have a photo shoot for a tattoo magazine in New York the weekend after that, and I have to give the shop here notice that I'm bailing. It snows in Colorado, right?"

I was having a hard time following her rapid change in conversation. I was still stuck on Viva. Being a car guy, I knew all about the weekend hot-rod show that drew bands and old-car lovers from all over the world. I was starting to think Phil had sold this girl's qualifications short.

"Yeah, it gets cold here when the seasons change."

"Well then, I need to add shopping to the list as well. Let's plan for the first week in May. I'll be there with bells on."

She was talking like the job was already hers.

"You have to do an interview. I have a business partner and a business manager that you need to talk to before this is a done deal."

She laughed and it sounded husky and rich. Even over the phone, I could tell this lady was something else.

"I'm perfect for the job and I've never been to Colorado. It'll be an adventure."

"Why the sudden interest? You sounded bored earlier when I called you." I was curious and had to ask.

"Tattoo shops are a dime a dozen, but you guys are doing amazing work, and I like the idea of getting in on the ground floor of a place with a solid reputation that's looking into expansion. And my interest"—her voice changed to something I didn't understand—"is anything but sudden. I'll see you in May, Nash Donovan."

She hung up on me and I was left looking down at my phone trying to figure out what in the hell had just happened. I wasn't kidding about her having to interview, and I could see her and Cora going rounds. It would be entertaining, to say the least.

I put my phone in my back pocket and pushed through the nondescript doors of the Bar and let my eyes adjust to the dimly lit interior. Since it was before eleven in the morning, the bar was quiet and the only customers lined up at the actual bar top were the grizzled old veterans who had called the Bar home long before Rome and Asa had taken over. No one looked up at me but Asa caught sight of me as he rounded the outside corner of the bar, arms loaded full of cases of beer.

He lifted a sandy-blond brow at me as I walked over and took some of his burden from him. Asa didn't really jibe with the rest of the group. His motivations were suspect, his personality was a little too smooth, a tad too polished for the rest of us to really dig into, but Ayden loved him and Rome had developed an odd fondness for the southern charmer, so even though he was slippery and slick, he was integrating his way firmly into our merry band of misfits. Jet watched him like a hawk and I was more of the mind that until he proved otherwise, he was an okay guy to be around.

Plus he pulled hot tail like I had never seen before. I didn't know if it was the southern twang, the golden eyes, or that "aw shucks" attitude he artfully played with, but he was a certified babe snake charmer and before Saint had become my sole focus his talents with the opposite sex had been much admired.

"What are you doing here so early?"

I helped him shove the beer on the end of the bar and he walked around the long wooden surface that Rome had just recently refinished, and faced me from the other side. Rome might be the technical owner of the bar, but with the new baby and the bar being open practically all day and night, Asa was the one often making the day-to-day operation run. He was also a million times more personable than the gruff ex-soldier, so they made a pretty good team.

"I wanted to ask you some stuff before I have to be at the shop. Do you have a minute?"

He cocked his head to the side and regarded me silently. It was no secret Asa's choices in the recent past had almost gotten him killed—and nearly had his sister disowning him—so it wasn't like anyone was rushing to him for words of wisdom.

"Yeah, I got some time; this is the last of the liquor order and I'm just waiting on Brite. He called and told me he would be in later and he had a huge favor he needed to ask me. Want me to have Darcy feed you lunch?"

I shook my head. "Maybe on my way out. I'll take something back to the shop for everyone."

He nodded and tilted his head to the back of the bar, where the pool tables were located.

"Let me stick my head in the kitchen and tell Darcy to keep an eye on the front."

I wandered to the back room and hopped up so I could perch on the edge of one of the pool tables. I folded my hands together and watched as Asa came toward me rubbing his hands on a bar towel.

"She's gonna throw a bunch of sandwiches together for you." I nodded. Darcy was Brite's ex-wife—well, one of them—and she ran the bar kitchen. She was a nice, older lady and her BLT was close to heaven as far as I was concerned. "So what's up, Nash?"

I sighed and winced a little. "This is sort of awkward, but you were the only one I could think of to ask."

Both of his eyebrows shot up and he crossed his beefy arms over his chest. Asa looked like the kind of guy that wrangled horses or threw bales of hay around all day. He didn't do either of those things, but there was no missing his country upbringing in the way he looked and carried himself.

"About what?"

"About changing and perception." I rubbed the back of my neck. "I have history with this girl I'm seeing, not exactly pretty and shiny history, and I don't really know how to get us past it." One of his gold eyebrows danced up on his forehead and I felt like a total chick trying to get into all of this with him. Dudes were not supposed to have heartfelt conversations about feelings, but I was at a loss.

"Saint had a rough go of it in high school. She was awkward and shy, got picked on and made fun of. I guess she had a little bit of a thing for me and I sort of blew her off without really meaning to. It was forever ago, but it stuck with her, and to make matters worse, I was running my mouth like an

idiot and she thought I was talking about her. That topped
with her dad being a cheating asshole and a college boyfriend throwing her over because she wouldn't do what he
wanted in bed and I'm having a hell of a time getting to the
heart of this girl. I know the self-esteem shit wasn't helped
by my big mouth and general stupidity, but I can't figure out
how to get her to trust that I'm not like that. That really I'm
a decent dude that was just a dumb kid prone to making
mistakes. How did you do it? How did you convince Ayden
that you're a different guy after everything that went down
between the two of you? How did you get her to let the past
go and prove to her you're not going to let her down again?"

He just stared at me for a minute, and I thought maybe
I had offended him. He snorted and gave his golden head a
sad little shake while he hooked his thumbs in the belt loops
of his jeans.

"I didn't. Ayden loves me, wants to believe the best in
me, which makes her the best person in the world because
I used her, flat-out abused our relationship up until a few
years ago. I wasn't just a mean guy, Nash. I was a criminal,
a con artist, and I didn't stop to think how what I was doing
would affect Ayden. She was really just a means to an end,
and I never saw it until it was almost too late. Frankly, Ayd
has every right to hate me, and I wouldn't have blamed her
for leaving me in that hospital alone. Now . . ." He grimaced
and I saw him swallow hard. "I'll never be able to fully convince her or Jet that I'm living a different life. When the bar
got robbed a few months ago she thought it was me, even
though I like Rome, like my job here. She automatically as-

sumed I had something to do with it and she always will, and I can't blame her for it. I wasn't trustworthy or considerate in the past. The only person I cared about was myself and that's not a memory I can erase—ever."

I hadn't ever been privy to the inner workings of their sibling relationship, but it made more sense why Jet was so leery around the guy, and why there was still so much tension between him and Ayden. There was no bridge in the world tall enough to let all that water run under it.

I threw my hands up in the air and let them fall. "So there isn't anything I can do? She's just always going to equate me with that memory and never be able to fully trust me. That blows."

"Nash . . ." His drawl seemed a little more pronounced when he said my name. "You're a good guy, they seem to grow them by the bushel here in the Rockies. You don't have to do anything but be who you are. Eventually she'll see that it isn't an act, it's just who you are, and what happened in the past was a one-off moment. You're human. You have to be allowed to make mistakes back then and now. I wouldn't be alive if there wasn't the gift of second chances."

"I like her, more than I've ever been into another chick. I just feel like she's never going to get past it and that means no going forward."

"I won't give you all the gory details, won't drag my own sordid history into it, but trust me: if my sister can still look at me and find a way to care about me, then you can work yourself into the heart of this girl."

Man, maybe I shouldn't have been so quick to think Asa

was an okay guy. The more he divulged, the more I kind of wanted to knock his perfect teeth out on Ayden's behalf.

"So what about you? You weren't a nice guy and now you are?" I asked it questioningly. "How do you convince everyone you've really changed?"

When he smiled at me it was full of mischievousness and secrets I didn't think I wanted to know.

"I haven't changed. I'm not a new person. Every day I still have to talk myself out of taking the easy way out, out of sliding into old patterns. I am who I am, and it isn't always an enjoyable person to be. The difference now is I have a life I want to live. I want a relationship with my sister. I want Jet to eventually look at me and not wonder what my next move is. I want to help Rome make this bar a success so he can support his family. I like it here, there is value in this life I never had in Kentucky, and I will fight with myself until I take my last breath to maintain it. I might not deserve it, but it's mine and I'm keeping it."

Wow. I hadn't planned on Asa being so up front about his own history, but his words struck something inside of me. I had been trying to convince Saint I was a different guy from the one she remembered from back in the day. That wasn't really true. I was less angry, less in need of validation from my mother, but I had never been a bad dude. I was so busy trying to show her the value in the person I was, I forgot that I had always had value, even if I did get busted running my mouth and acting like a typical teenage idiot. Maybe I needed to start asking why she couldn't see the value and worth in herself.

She was amazing. Smart and funny. She was gentle and completely lovely inside and out. She tore me up in bed, and if I could just get her to let go, quit holding on with both hands to things that would never change, I had a pretty good idea I would tumble head over heels in love with her. I was pretty close to the edge of that precipice as it was. Maybe I needed to stop trying to make her see how great I was and start making her see, reinforcing with her, how great she was.

I jumped off the table and thudded heavily on the wooden floor.

"Thanks, Asa."

He laughed a little and I followed him back to the bar. "I've made enough mistakes for the lot of you to learn from. Something good should come from all my fuckups."

"I really hope you don't go back to your old ways. It would suck for more than just Ayden."

That grin was back, and this time it was tinged with sadness.

"Got a good thing going here, and I know it. It's not on my agenda to screw it up, though my agendas never really have a way of working out the way I think they will."

I gathered all the to-go containers Darcy put together and let her kiss me on the cheek. I was walking out when I heard her ask Asa if he had seen her daughter yet. I had a feeling Brite's favor he was about to lay on the southern playboy was going to involve family. Yikes, that could end up bad because I had heard from Rome that Brite and Darcy's daughter was a handful, a real wild child.

*   *   *

I DIDN'T SEE SAINT for the rest of the week. The shop was slammed with early-spring business, Rowdy got a cold and was out for a few days, and Phil's condition was rapidly deteriorating. It got so bad at the end of the week I wanted to move him back to the hospital, but he refused to go. He couldn't keep anything down, and his hospice nurse was talking about a feeding tube. It was stressful, I felt like I was walking across a lake that was frozen and I was just waiting for everything to give under my weight. I stayed the night with him for the entire end of the week, which meant I didn't see anyone else. At some point during the week, as I watched him get sicker and sicker right before my eyes, my brain automatically started switching him from Phil to Dad in my head. It was my dad that was dying, my dad that was trying to put on a brave front for me, my dad that looked at me with sad, periwinkle eyes because he knew our time together was getting shorter and shorter.

I didn't want anyone to see him like this. The entire group tried to come by, but Phil just wasn't up to it. I had to bail on the plans I had with Saint on Saturday night, which bummed me out, but I was where I needed to be. When there was a knock on the door a few hours later, I almost fell over when I opened it and saw that it was her. She didn't ask to come in, just handed me some kind of protein drink and told me to see if Phil could maybe keep it down. She told me she had asked the oncology staff for a solution that might hold off the feeding tube for a while longer.

All I could do was stare at her. Gratitude and something stronger coursed through me. She reached up and wrapped me in a hug that for just a split second made me feel better. She pressed a quick kiss on my mouth and told me that while I was taking care of Phil not to forget to take care of myself. I was exhausted and emotionally drained, but just that little five-minute visit from her, that easy way she had about being in tune with what other people were going through, reached deep down inside of me and didn't let go.

Maybe it was because my mom had always been so cold and dissatisfied, maybe it was because I had searched for approval that was never coming that when I looked at Saint's beautiful eyes and saw her empathy and compassion, I knew she was going to be it for me. She was everything I had ever wanted, ever needed. When she looked at me like that, any question I might have had about loving her went out the window. It was more like how could I *not* love her? She was impossible not to fall in love with.

I kissed her back a hundred times harder than I intended, but I wanted her to feel all the things I knew she would freak out about if I tried to tell her. She told me to call her over the weekend if I got a free minute, and left taking my heart with her.

When I went back inside and offered Phil up the concoction she had brought over, he just looked at me with a knowing gleam in his eyes over the top of the oxygen mask that obscured most of his face. I flipped him off and slumped back in the recliner that I had moved next to his bed. I wasn't ready to talk about it. Especially when I knew that Saint would run the other way if I tried to tell her how I felt. Not being loved back was something that had hounded me my entire childhood. I didn't know that I would be able to handle it coming from her.

I stayed with Phil all through the weekend. Saint's shake was magical, so she sent me the ingredient list and I stocked up on supplies so I would be able to whip it up for him whenever he needed. Phil slept pretty much all day Saturday and I was contemplating going into work and trying to play catch-up while he was out, when Cora showed up at the condo.

I didn't want her to have to see him like that, to feel sorry for him, but she just used her little body to push past me and told me to get lost. Phil was just as important to her as he was to me, and Rome was home with the baby until later that night. She told me in no uncertain terms I still had a life to live and unceremoniously kicked me out of my dad's condo. I wanted to be irritated at her. Someone so small shouldn't be that bossy and immovable, but I had to admit I needed the space to get a breather.

I went to the shop and plowed through a week's worth of paperwork that had piled up. I rearranged all the appointments I had canceled on throughout the last few weeks. When it was time to close the shop down, Rule wanted me to go to the bar where Shaw and Ayden worked and grab dinner. The two of us hadn't really spent much time together that didn't involve working lately, so I was tempted to say yes. But as much as I enjoyed hanging out with Rule, I missed Saint and spending time with her more, so I asked for a rain check and called her.

"Hello!" She was screaming into the phone to be heard over the screeching and childish giggling in the background.

"Hey. Cora is with Phil, so I have the night free. I was hoping you didn't have to work and we could hang out."

"Hold on a sec." She muttered something and I heard more screaming while she found someplace quieter to talk to me. "Sorry, Faith had to go to the hospital and asked me to watch the kids. She was having Braxton-Hicks contractions and got worried. I don't know how long she's going to be."

That was kind of a bummer since I really wanted to spend time with her, and I didn't know when the next chance I was going to get was going to be.

"I hope she's all right."

"She'll be fine. Do you want to come over here? I'm making them grilled cheese for dinner and then I'm going to put *Finding Nemo* on and hope that settles them down."

I had never really been around kids. I mean now that Rome and Cora had a baby I was getting more used to it. Really, though, I would walk barefoot through lava if that's what it took to spend time with her, so why the hell not?

"Sure. Give me the address."

She rattled off an address that was down in Littleton and I took off. I didn't stop and worry that her sister had made it clear she didn't like me, or that I didn't have the first idea what one did with a bunch of kids running around. All that mattered was that Saint was there and that's where I wanted to be.

When I knocked on the front door, Saint pulled it open looking disheveled and rumpled in a really delightful way. She had a tiny toddler on her hip and a slightly older little girl peeking at me from behind her knees. She smiled at me and blew a loose red curl out of her face.

"I'm happy to see you." Well, hot damn, that was the best news I had heard recently. "This is Zoe." She kissed the toddler on the cheek. "Brea is hiding behind me and the boys, Owen and Kyle, are in the living room playing video games."

I followed her into the house and winked at the little girl who was looking up at me with huge eyes.

"Your sister doesn't look old enough to have all these kids."

She snorted and guided me into the kitchen, where the scent of tomato soup on the stove made my mouth water.

"She started young and doesn't have any plans to stop. She and her husband, Justin, always wanted a big family."

She looked at the stove, then at me, and unceremoniously plopped the wide-eyed toddler in my arms. We stared at each other for a long moment, the baby deciding if she wanted to scream at me, and me trying to decide how to best hold her without squishing her. I guess the little girl decided I was okay, and she proceeded to try and get her chubby little fingers around my nose ring, which resulted in a ridiculous game of don't touch. Saint just laughed at me while she stood at the stove and made sandwiches.

The other little girl, who was probably only four or five, wandered over and stood by my knee looking up at me. Saint grinned down at her.

"That's Auntie's friend Nash. Tell him hi."

The little girl didn't say anything to me, so I smiled down at her and bit back a swearword when the baby got her hand on the piercing and gave it a yank. It made my eyes water up, but it had her laughing so hard I couldn't be mad about it.

"Hot."

The other little girl was shy, I could tell. She must take after Saint. I lifted an eyebrow down at her and she pointed a tiny finger up at my head and said again, "Hot."

She was talking about the flames inked on my head and the fire that flowed out of the collar of my T-shirt where the baby was yanking on it.

Saint turned around and looked at me with a bright silver sparks in her gray eyes. She walked over and crouched down in front of the little girl and poked her lightly on the nose.

"You have good taste, Brea. He is very, very hot."

All three of the girls burst into hysterical laugher while I just sat there and watched Saint. She stood and kissed the baby on the cheek and me on the mouth and called the boys in for their simple dinner. The boys, since they were older, had all kinds of interesting questions about my ink, about the gauges in my ears, about what I did and how I knew Saint. They were scary energetic but funny and overall nice kids.

We all ate dinner, and when everyone was done, I told Saint to go get them all settled while I cleaned up her sister's kitchen. Her eyes had something in them when she smiled at me that I couldn't identify, but it was warm, kind of melty, and I liked everything about it even if this was the most G-rated date I had ever been on.

The older kids crashed on the floor and Saint and I took spots on the couch with both the little girls between us. I had no intention of staying, I wanted to be gone before

Saint's sister came home, but after the first five minutes of the movie, Brea was asleep with her head on my arm. The toddler, Zoe, had crawled into my lap, curled up like a little cat, and was out like a light. I didn't want to disturb either of them, so I just settled in and watched the fish try and find his way home. The way Nemo's dad never gave up, never lost hope, had me running parallels with my own life through my mind and it had me thinking about Phil.

When I looked over at Saint she was watching me with big eyes and there was a bright pink flush in her cheeks.

"What?"

She just gave her head a little shake and turned back to the movie.

"You just always surprise me."

I blew out a breath because that was tied in to my latest revelation about this relationship and her.

"The person that should be surprising is you, Saint. Trust me, the person you are is remarkable and exceptional. If you get acquainted with her, your entire life will change."

She just looked at me like she had no idea what I was saying, but I felt better having said it. I would love her unconditionally if she let me, but in order to do that, I had to get her to love herself fully, first.

CHAPTER 16

Saint

IT WAS ALREADY HARD to keep a lid on everything Nash stirred up in me, but seeing a big, tough, tattooed guy hold on to a little girl like she was something breakable and precious, how in the hell was I supposed to keep my heart cloistered from that?

When Faith and Justin returned home, all the kids had been put to bed and Nash was on his way out the door. I didn't miss the look my sister gave when he said good-bye. She was tired and supposed to take it easy, which is the only reason I escaped getting an earful, I'm sure. The next morning while I was at work she left a voice mail that went on for a solid twenty minutes about how she now had two boys that were insisting on getting skull tattoos when they were old enough. I shouldn't have thought it was funny but I really did. I wanted to try and take Faith's concern to heart. I knew she was just worried about me, worried about what would happen if Nash hurt me again, but something about his words to me the night before had stuck with me.

There was a part of me that could never believe that he saw me the way he did. I never recognized myself as a beautiful, desirable creature and so I never took him at face value when he said those things to me. I was confident at work, knew what I was doing, and that it was what I had always been meant to do, but even though he looked at me like I was the start and end of everything, I just couldn't find any belief in the idea that Nash Donovan felt that way about *me*. I still didn't have enough confidence to be secure in any of the other areas of my life. It wasn't fair to Nash that I was on pins and needles waiting for him to prove that he was nothing more than a typical guy and would eventually fall to the lowest common denominator, when all I was doing was using my fear and weaknesses to hold all the parts of me that had never really stopped loving him in check and not allowing what was between us now to grow and flourish.

I had never been resentful of my work or my busy schedule at the emergency room. I was always the happiest, the most centered and secure when I was caring for others, but lately I wanted to have time to see Nash. I knew Phil was getting worse, that the end was on the horizon, and Nash was almost always at his side. He was trying to stay on top of things at work and everything else, but he was losing weight, and every time I did manage to see him he had shadows on his face that rivaled the color of his eyes in purpleness and his strong jaw was more often than not scruffy and unshaven.

There were no more overnight stays, no more fun dates that made me laugh, and the only time we managed to hook up was for a quickie during lunch here and there, which felt good and got the job done but lacked all the intensity and emotion behind the sex I was used to having with him. For someone who used to hate being naked and everything that typically went with it, I couldn't wait for there to be a time when I could spend hours sans clothes and under him or over him—I wasn't particular.

I was heading out after my shift when Sunny asked me to pop into her office. We had been too busy lately to have any real time to chat. I missed her positive attitude and the way she always tried to pick me up. I smiled at her and took a seat across from her cluttered desk.

"Are you going to try and set me up with another doctor?"

Ever since my disastrous date, the rumors had flown fast and furiously among the hospital staff. I was a lesbian, I'd had a seizure and had to go, I was secretly married with five kids . . . and no one was interested in the truth. Surprisingly, being the topic of conversation, being gossiped about no matter how silly it was, didn't faze me. I was too busy with Nash, too busy trying to figure out the things that really mattered, to care about any of it.

Sunny rolled her dark eyes at me and gave me a huge grin. "No. I think your taste runs a little more colorful than most doctors walking these hallways."

It was true. I mean, there were some doctors sporting ink under their lab coats and scrubs, but nothing could compare to that dragon that was trying so hard to keep Nash safe.

"You're probably right. What's up? You never ask me to

talk in your office. You usually just ambush me in the hall-way."

She was still smiling as she leaned back in her chair.

"Well, this is a more official conversation than me harassing you about your dating life."

I frowned and immediately started running through anything that I might have done wrong in the last few weeks. I had been distracted because of the goings-on in my personal life, which wasn't like me.

"What did I do?"

She shook her head from side to side and clicked her tongue at me.

"Now why would you automatically think the worst? You are an amazing nurse, I tell you that all the time. How can you think I would drag you in here and scold you for doing something wrong? I think that's insulting to both of us."

I gulped and Nash's words sort of poked at me from the night before.

"Sorry. It's just habit."

"One you should break. Listen, Saint, Heidi is transferring to a hospital in Florida because her husband got a new job. I want you to take over as the shift supervisor. I know you're thinking about more school along the way, but this is a great opportunity for advancement in the department you are already in. Say yes, Saint. This was meant to be."

"Are you serious?" I was stunned. It's what I had always wanted. Validation, respect, for the world to recognize I was great at something I loved. I couldn't ask for anything more, only for some reason, as happy as the offer made me, it was the idea of sharing the news with Faith and my mom, and probably most significantly with Nash, that really gave me the most joy.

"Well, we have to do a real interview with the director of nursing, but she knows that you are the person I want for the position."

My heart was fluttering in a rapid rhythm and I wanted to do a little dance in my chair.

"That's so exciting. Thank you so much."

"No one deserves it more."

I got to my feet, she came around the desk, and I bent down to give her a hug. I really did deserve it, just like maybe, possibly, I deserved a shot at making this thing with Nash be a forever thing.

He was the first person I called when I got out of the hospital.

It was raining. Like a torrential downpour, and by the look of the water collected on the streets, it had been coming down for a while. I skipped across puddles and let the phone ring as I raced to my car. Nash didn't answer, the call went right to voice mail, which made some of the excitement bubbling under my skin wane just a little bit. I had to shake like a dog to get my soggy hair out of my face once I was in the car, and I decided it wouldn't hurt anything to swing by the Victorian to see if he was home. I wanted him to scoop me up and give me a big, sloppy kiss and tell me how happy he was for me. It was surprising how bad I wanted that.

I turned on the radio and listened to Her Space Holiday as I tooled across Colfax and made my way up to the Victorian. The weather was dying down, but by the time I dashed up to the door, passing the Charger in its designated spot on the way, I was soaked all the way through and my teeth were chattering. It wasn't really warm enough yet to counteract being damp and all drippy. I stopped in front of his door and knocked.

I was unwinding my braid and trying to comb my fingers through my wet and tangled hair when the door swung open . . . and my entire world came crashing down. My heart stopped. My blood went thick and cold and I was thrown in a direction that had my hopes and dreams snapping in half for the second time in my life at the hands of this beautiful man.

Royal was standing on the other side of Nash's door looking back at me with the same stunned expression I'm sure I had on my face. I think I could have handled her being in Nash's apartment—after all, she'd made it clear she wasn't interested in him that way. What I absolutely couldn't handle, what had my heart breaking into sharp enough pieces I could feel them stabbing into me, was the fact she was wearing a towel and nothing else.

"Saint . . ."

I held up a hand and gasped when Nash came walking around the corner where his room was, also dressed in nothing but a red towel around his lean waist.

"Did I hear someone knocking?"

He was rubbing another towel over his head and the scene was so intimate, so devastating, I thought that maybe

I was going to pass out. I had to actually put a hand on the doorframe to keep my legs from folding under me. When the towel cleared his dark head, his eyes locked on mine. I expected guilt, or shame, but the periwinkle blue just glittered at me.

"Uh . . ." Royal looked like she was going to grab me, so I pulled back before she could touch me.

"*This* is what you do to your *friends?*" My hurt, my disbelief, my rage roiled in my stomach as I bitterly launched the most hateful words I could think of at her "I guess the apple doesn't fall far from the tree."

I wanted to punch her in throat, but what I wanted more than that was to go back in time and never, ever let Nash Donovan back into my life. If I thought he had hurt me before; watching him kiss teenaged Ashley Maxwell had nothing on the idea of him cozying up to sexy and physically perfect Royal. This wasn't a smack in the face or a sting of betrayal. This was him proving to me that I was right all along and that boys could never, ever be trusted with a pretty girl. This was me having known better all along. I was always going to lose out when an easier, better, more emotionally available option was presented. Time and time again that fact seemed like it was going to get thrown in my face and there was no denying this little scenario was breaking everything inside me into tiny, piercing fragments of hurt and pain.

I turned on my heel and was back out in the rain, back at the Jetta, when a hard hand gripped me above the elbow and spun me around. He was still in a towel, rain coursing over his shaved head and down the furrowed lines in his forehead. He gave me a little shake that had my teeth snapping together.

"What the fuck? She locked herself out of the apartment again. She was at the gym and soaking wet because of the goddamn rain. I gave her a towel and let her throw her shit in my dryer. If I had known you were coming by, I would have called to let you know what was going on, that she was here."

I was breathing hard and his hand burned where it touched me. My heart was breaking, I was dying on the inside, and he had the nerve to look like he was the one falling apart.

"If you had known I was coming, I probably wouldn't have caught you in the act. I knew it was too good to be true. She's beautiful and convenient. Why work for something that might never pay off? Right? I always knew when someone simpler came along you would choose her over me. You just can't stop yourself from breaking my heart, can you, Nash?"

The water that was hitting him dribbled over his chest and trickled through the definitions in his abs. The way he was breathing, the way he was shivering, made it look like that dragon was trying to pull up off his skin, trying to lift him away and from the lash of my hateful words. He took a step back from me and put a hand on the knot of his towel. He shook his head and I saw his mouth draw down in a harsh frown. It wasn't only his body that was bared to me, it was everything else he had as well. It was all shining out of those beautiful eyes, but I steeled myself and refused to see any of it.

"That's the thing, I would have worked until it killed me, whether it ever paid off or not, if that something at the end was you. And I couldn't have broken your heart this time, Saint, because you wouldn't let me get close enough to put my hands on it. I told you I can't see anyone but you, that you are my only, simple or not, and no one else compares. Does this situation look bad? Yeah, it does. I'm not blind or an idiot, but if you knew"—he blew out a breath and looked up at the sky like it held all the answers—"how much I totally fucking love you, you wouldn't have any question, and wouldn't think I could ever even think about another chick like that. You are it for me, Saint. I would never do anything to hurt you because it hurts me just as bad." He shook his head, sending raindrops flying in every direction. "I'm not your dad. I would never make you go through that again."

I gasped and wanted to smack him across the face. "You don't get to say that to me. You can't love me when you have another naked girl in your apartment. From where I'm standing, you look exactly like him, Nash."

"No, I don't get to tell you that I love you because I can't ever love you enough to make up for the fact that you refuse to love yourself. You love your job. You love your family. You probably even fucking love me right back, but until you wake up and realize how perfect you are, how incomparable and wonderful you are, there is no hope for this to work out. I thought I was fighting a losing battle with some imaginary version of my younger self, trying to fight against all the other men that have let you down in your life, but now I know it's a battle against you. I love you, Saint, all of you, but if you don't believe that, then I don't know where we can go from here."

I was crying, sobbing really. The tears were falling so hard he was getting blurry, and I just hoped the rain was hiding some of it from him.

"I'm leaving. That's where I'm going from here. I don't think you know anything about love, Nash."

He flinched when I leveled the words at him, but his eyes also shifted to that dark indigo like they did when he was upset.

"Maybe not before, but after you, and after everything with Phil—my dad—over the last few months, I most certainly do. I know you deserve to be loved better than anyone in the world because of all you do for others. I also know that I'm a decent guy, Saint. I deserve the best kind of love back in return, and if you aren't ever going to be the person to do that, then I'm glad this is over. I would give you everything."

He turned his back on me and I could have sworn that artfully designed dragon, the armor he wore to protect himself, was looking back at me with baleful eyes, accusation and something else, judging me.

I slid behind the wheel of the car and continued to cry while I frantically searched around for my phone. Part of me wanted to run back to the apartment and confront them both, cover both of them with my rage and sorrow, but the bigger part of me that was suddenly an insecure and lost teenage girl again just wanted to run away and pretend none of this was happening to me.

The first call I made was to Sunny. She could tell I was upset, asked me a million questions, but all I could get out was that I needed a few days off from the hospital. I had a bunch of vacation days saved up, so it wouldn't be a problem other than I was leaving her in the lurch and she still needed to set up the interview for the promotion. None of it mattered to me. Nothing mattered to me. I felt like I was turning to stone.

The next call I made was to my mom. I should have called Faith, she was going to be furious with me when she found out I was bailing once again because of Nash. I don't know that my mom understood a single word I tried to tell her while I sobbed and shook, but I got an assurance that she had plenty of room for me down in Phoenix.

By midnight, I was halfway through New Mexico, and by the time the sun came up, I was almost to Phoenix. I drove straight through the night. I turned my phone off after calling Faith to let her know I was leaving town for a few days. She was furious on my behalf, wanted to have her husband go over and pound Nash into a bloody mess, but that would never work because her husband was half Nash's size, and even though I didn't want to admit it to her, I knew he was hurting already.

Sometime while the endless highway stretched out in front of me, my heart stopped aching and the bitter taste of betrayal stopped coating my tongue. I was still upset, still really mad, but the focus had switched now that I didn't have the vision of Royal and Nash wearing nothing but towels dancing in front of me. I was mad at myself, afraid I had made a mistake and once again jumped to awful conclusions out of self-preservation. I had run before thinking it through. But now, with nothing but the road, my wildly careening thoughts and Sea Wolf on the radio, the important parts of the argument started to blanket me like a heavy fog.

All I could hear, all I could feel wrapping around me, were the words *I love you*. The worst part of the entire thing wasn't letting Nash go, wasn't feeling bad because Royal was prettier than me or more alluring—no . . . the worst part was how desperately I wanted to believe him. I wanted to trust in him, wanted to take everything he was telling me he wanted to give, but I was so hung up on the idea that he would take it away, let me down like so many had before, that I had just jumped to the easiest conclusion there was. I wanted so badly to wholly believe Nash could love me, that he could see himself with me, and even with what happened today, I really just wanted him for my own and it was tearing me apart because all of me wanted all of him and that was scary.

I couldn't get to him with myself standing in the way and I needed room, needed time to figure that out. He said he would give me everything. I hoped that the time to get my head on right and to try and figure out how much I was willing to risk for him was part of that.

WHEN I GOT TO my mom's fancy townhouse at six-thirty the next morning, she took one look at me, wrapped me up in a hug, and put me to bed. I was dead on my feet, and an emotional wasteland. I slept for most of the day and only roused that evening for her to feed me a PB&J. The next morning I actually took a shower and got brave enough to look at my phone. I had no missed calls and zero missed text messages from Nash, and I didn't know if that made me feel better or worse about the way I had left things.

I made my way down to the kitchen and grabbed a muffin my mom must have left on the counter for me. I saw her sitting on the balcony that overlooked the golf course her townhouse butted up against. I poured myself a cup of coffee and went out to join her. She looked me up and down over the top of her glasses and gave me a grin.

"You look terrible."

I sighed heavily and sank into the chair opposite to hers. "I just got my heart ripped out. I look pretty much exactly how that feels."

"I didn't even know you were seeing someone."

I pushed my hair back off of my face and looked out at the desert landscape. "I'm not sure what I was doing with him, but I knew it was going to end like this."

"How?"

"How what, Mom?"

"How did you know it was going to end badly?"

I looked at her, really looked at her, and was surprised to see my old mom looking back at me. Getting away from Brookside had done wonders for her. She looked healthy and sane, and I would be willing to bet her morning cup of coffee no longer had a healthy dose of Irish in it.

"Because he broke my heart once before. Because look at you and Dad. Because look at me . . . I'm so screwed up, how could it have ended any other way?"

"What happened, Saint?"

I didn't think I wanted to relive it, but before I could stop the words, the entire story, starting with seeing him the night Rome got stabbed, came pouring out of me in an unstoppable torrent. When I got to the scene yesterday she was frowning, but as I told her about Nash telling me he loved me, she started to nod and grin at me. I thought that reaction was totally uncalled for until she reached over and patted me on the knee.

"Honey, you have to let that boy love you if he's the one for you."

I balked at her and set my coffee down with a *thunk* on the table. "Did you miss the part where he had a beautiful, naked girl in his apartment? How am I supposed to overlook that?"

She lifted an eyebrow at me. "In your heart, do you really think he would cheat on you? Do something to jeopardize all the work he put into getting you to let him in?"

"Why wouldn't he?"

"Saint, don't you know the question is why would he? Why would he cheat on you when you are apparently what he wants? Why would he have worked so hard to get to you, tolerated your hang-ups and oddities, made a space for you in his very busy life, if he was just going to screw it up the first chance he got? Is he a moron?"

"No, he's really smart, but so is Dad, and he cheated on you."

She winced involuntarily and I opened my mouth to apologize, but she waved it off.

"Your dad cheated because he no longer loved me and

he was bored. It took me all this time to get to that point that I recognize it now. He was a coward, and instead of just saying he didn't have the same feelings for me anymore, he had an affair. Your young man doesn't sound like a coward, Saint. He sounds like a man willing to put his heart on the line for you."

I huffed in aggravation and threw myself back in the seat with my arms across my chest.

"Why are you taking his side, Mom?"

"Because I love you and I realize now that I may have had a hand in some of the issues you are struggling with that are keeping you from being truly happy. I was hard on you, had a hard time with how quiet you were, and nitpicked about your looks and lack of social life when you were younger because I thought I was helping. I thought if you acted more like Faith, looked a little more polished, you would have an easier time of things. Kids can be cruel and I didn't want that for you. I should've appreciated the wonderful child I had, not tried to make you into something else."

"Oh my God, Mom."

She took her sunglasses off and looked me dead in the eye. "Listen, honey, I loved your dad my entire life. He was everything to me, and yes, I went off my rocker when that went away. I thought my life was going to be over when he left me, but I wouldn't change any of it now that I've had some space to reflect. At one point our love was the most beautiful thing in the world to me; it brought you and your sister into the world, and it gave me something to look forward to each and every day. It might have gone badly at the end, might have hurt me more than I thought possible when it went away, but I wouldn't trade a single moment of the best parts of it. I would never trade in experiencing that hurt for the family that our love created, Saint."

I felt tears pressing in my eyes and had to blink them back before I could answer her.

"Do you think you'll ever be able to forgive Dad for what he did?"

She murmured something and tilted her head to look at me. "For walking away from our family, for hurting you girls . . . no, I won't. What I can do now is recognize that we are all very much human and capable of making bad choices without thinking of the long-term repercussions. Saint, you had to come get me out of jail because I tried to brain a woman with a bottle of maple syrup. We all make mistakes, some worse than others."

"I don't want to hurt like this because of someone else's mistakes, Mom."

I was talking about more than Nash and I think on a level that only a mother and a woman hurt by a man she loved could understand. She understood what I was saying without words.

"Saint, hurting is how you know it's real. If he didn't matter, if he was just some guy, even back then it wouldn't have lasted with you the way it has. You can't run from feeling things, even if some of those things are awful, because love opens you up to experiencing emotions you haven't ever felt before."

"He's the only one who has ever made me feel anything

like this." He was also the only one that made me feel desire, hope, and gut-wrenching sorrow while I watched him grapple with the truth about his dad and Phil's subsequent illness.

"What is it that you think you deserve, honey? If it isn't this guy, what he has to offer, then what is it?"

"I have a great job that I love and work hard at. I care a lot about other people and I deserve someone who appreciates all of that."

"This tattoo guy doesn't?"

I pouted like a little kid. "No, he does, a lot actually. Those are some of his favorite qualities in me. He told me I deserve the best because of the lengths I go to for others."

"What else?"

"What do you mean, 'what else'?"

She gave me a hard look and leaned over so she could grab my face. She squished my pout together so hard I'm sure I looked like a duck.

"You are stunningly beautiful, you are desirable and vibrant, and you always have been. You deserve someone who worships you, who looks at you and knows no one is more perfect than you."

Now there was no holding back the tears. My mom and I weren't exactly ever on the same page about things, but hearing her say those words to me broke something free that had been lodged in my subconscious my entire life. I rubbed my hands roughly over my cheeks and blinked away the moisture clinging to my lashes.

"He tells me I'm perfect all the time."

"Are you in love with him?"

I nodded sadly. "I don't want to be, but I couldn't stop it from happening."

"Because it was meant to be."

I choked on a laugh and picked up my coffee up. "Who are you and what did you do with my mom?"

She reached out and tucked a piece of hair behind my ear. "You came home to try and pull me out of my funk. You never gave up on me when I was terrible to you and your sister. You came and got me out of jail and never stopped loving me. Even with all the turmoil your father dropped on us, you never stopped caring about him. I want what's best for you, and while I would prefer a doctor to a tattoo artist, any man that can shake you up, get you out of that boring, secure little bubble you always live in, is welcome in my book. Now go get dressed and let's go shopping like normal people do when their hearts are hurting."

I didn't want to go shopping, or go to the country club for lunch. I didn't want to go to a wine tasting that night or to the tapas restaurant with my mom and all her single friends the next night. By the end of day three, I was ready to pull out my hair. I was bored, missed my sister and my job, and had learned way too much about my mom's new sex life. Mostly, all I wanted was to get back to the mountains and, in all honesty, get back to Nash.

On the fourth day I broke down and sent him a text. All I could think to say was: *I'm so sorry. We need to talk.*

When he didn't answer me back the rest of the day, I decided enough was enough. If I was the hurdle that I needed to get over in order to have him, then the only way to do it was just get over it. I was still scared, still worried about being enough, about being able to give back everything he seemed so willing to lay at my feet, but going home and confronting him, and the person he saw when he looked at me, was the first step. All people deserved love and kindness. Seeing that young girl take her own life drove that point home more clearly than anything else could have. I needed to take what Nash was showing me at face value. No one was ever going to love me better than he did.

I was only two hours into the twelve-hour return trip when I got a phone call from a number I didn't recognize that came from a 303 area code. Figuring it was work or work related, I answered.

"Hello?"

"Saint." It took me a second to recognize Royal's voice. "Where are you?"

"Just outside of Phoenix headed home. Why? How did you get this number?"

"I know I'm the last person you want to hear from now, but the faster you can get here the better. And I'm a cop, how do you think I got your number?"

She was talking fast and an uneasy shiver slid down my spine.

"What's going on?"

She sighed. "You were a real bitch, you know that? I don't typically tell people about my circumstances, about the deal with my mom and the stockbroker, but I thought since you were touchy about being judged, you would get it. That was really mean what you said to me."

Hello, life lesson right in my face. I had practically called her a whore, told her she was no better than her mother. I didn't really mean it, didn't know her well enough to make that kind of judgment call. I had just been spouting off like a stupid idiot because I was hurt and mad. Any lingering remains of trying to use what Nash had said in the past against him turned to ash. I couldn't blame him anymore when I was guilty of doing the exact same thing. Luckily, unlike I had been, Royal seemed willing to accept an apology.

"I know. I'm sorry. That was a hard scene to walk in on. I jumped to conclusions without listening to explanations."

"Well, it did look bad. I made a bunch of extra keys and now half of Denver is on call to let me in my apartment should I lock myself out again, but anyway, you need to get your cute little butt back here. Phil took a drastic turn for the worse. The mouthy little blonde with the baby was getting a bunch of stuff for Nash since he hasn't left Phil's bedside since you left. It doesn't look very good. You don't want your man to have to go through that alone. He needs you."

I think what I was supposed to take away from this entire nightmare was not to pay attention to what words were said no matter how ugly, or to what I was seeing no matter how bad it looked. I had to have faith in the people involved—myself included. Mistakes were going to be made; that didn't mean I had to forsake my life and my happiness because of them, not when Nash had shown me time and time again he was worth working through the pain and confusion for.

"I won't be back in Denver until late tonight."

She made a noise in her throat. "I hope Nash's dad lasts that long."

I did, too. "Thank you for letting me know."

"I told you I wanted us to be friends."

"I think I'm finally ready to believe you. I'm a neurotic weirdo, though. I don't know how great a friend that will make me."

She laughed a little, even though she still sounded kind of sad. "We all have things, Saint. Things we struggle with, things that make it hard for us to see ourselves how others view us. Sharing those things is the only way to get past them."

I didn't tell her that I had just recently figured that out. If I didn't get back to Denver in time, that was just one more *thing* I was going to have to overcome. I would never forgive myself if Nash had to face Phil passing away without me. Sure, he had a multitude of friends, people who loved him unconditionally, to help him handle his grief, but like Royal said, he needed *me*. No one else would do, and that's how I knew loving him back, giving him all he gave me wasn't going to be a problem, because I needed *him* and only him in the exact same way.

CHAPTER 17

Nash

ROYAL WAS OVERLY APOLOGETIC when I came back in the apartment. I waved her off and went to get dressed. Like I said, I knew this shit didn't look good, but it kicked me in the balls that Saint wouldn't take a breath, talk to me about it. She just automatically assumed the worst of the situation and of me, and that just sucked. I really did love her, wanted this to be a real thing, a thing I was going to have to hold on to while everything else in my life spiraled out of control. Her taking that away broke my heart, but more than anything, it made me choke on disappointment.

I got dressed, waited for the locksmith to come and let my neighbor back in her apartment—again—and headed back over to Phil's. It was like his life was grains of sand in an hourglass and the sand was suddenly flowing much more rapidly, and I could see it. So on top of feeling like Saint had leveled me, I felt like Phil was leaving me hanging as well. I knew it wasn't rational, but it was how I felt all the same.

While I sat at his bedside I struggled with the need to text her, to try and throw explanation after explanation on her, to beg her for a shot and not to give up on what we were building, to tell her how much I needed her, that I couldn't do this, watch Phil fade away without her. I refrained. I couldn't do it. I loved her, but I loved me, too, and I couldn't be with someone who didn't appreciate that because they didn't appreciate themself. It hurt, but it was as real as I could see things.

A couple of days after the big scene, I was surprised when she reached out with her simple message. I didn't know what she was sorry for. Maybe for ripping my heart to shreds by dismissing my feelings, for jumping to conclusions, for running away from me for the second time in our history without letting me explain, for not believing in me, in us—for all of it? I didn't know what to say back to her and Phil was starting to slip in and out of lucidity, so I didn't want to dedicate any time to trying to mend that particular fence. Not when she had yanked it out by the posts.

One minute Phil knew he was in Denver and who I was, the next he was back in the Navy, or on the East Coast reliving his wild party days. I tried to keep him comfortable, had nurses at his place almost around the clock, but the cancer was obviously progressing, moving into his most vital organs. Time was slipping away. I hadn't been at work all week, luckily I had not only the best friends, but the best coworkers in the world and they were carrying on and picking up the slack I left behind. I knew they were all worried about me, sad about what was happening with Phil, but right now we needed this time between the two of us, and I think they all respected that.

I was sitting in the trusty recliner staring at *SportsCenter* mindlessly when Phil reached a shaky hand out and put it on my arm. I muted the TV and looked down at him. His eyes—my eyes—were rheumy and tinted with a hint of yellow, but they were locked on me intently.

"Do something for me, son."

I felt my breath shudder and my lungs clamped closed painfully. This was the hardest thing I had ever had to go through in my life, including when I had put one of my closest friends in the ground way too young.

"Sure, Phil. Anything you need me to do."

His fingers curled into the muscle of my arm and I saw him struggle to smile at me behind his oxygen mask.

"I had a good life, ya know?" He moved his head in what I think was supposed to be a nod. "I traveled the world, saw amazing things. I started a successful business on my own terms, and never had to answer to a boss. I fell in and out of love a hundred times. I helped make a wonderful group of kids their own family, and I had you. I have zero regrets and it is my greatest hope you live your life the same way."

He sounded winded. I could hear how hard it was for him to get the words out. I blew out a breath and forced a smile.

"Well, I've only been in love once, and it didn't work out so great, but the rest I can sure try my hardest to live up to."

"The nurse?"

"The nurse," I confirmed.

"Don't give up just yet, Nash. If she matters, if you want her for yours, don't give up."

"What if she gave up on me?"

"Then you love her hard enough that she can't help but come around. Part of me always wonders if I gave up too easy on your mom."

Ugh. She was the last person I wanted in this room. My mom had no place here.

"Maybe. That's what you want me to do, live life with no regret?"

His eyes drifted closed and his grip loosened on my arm. My heart started thudding. Every time his eyes closed, I wondered if they would ever open again.

"I want you to call me Dad. I never got that, never was brave enough to ask, but I want you to think of me as your dad. That's all I want."

Fuck me. I couldn't think, couldn't get my heart rate under control. I needed a carton of cigarettes and a handle of cheap tequila to get through this. I wanted to get up and go outside for a few minutes and pull my shit together, but that wasn't time I would get back with him.

"Phil . . . Dad. Jesus, you were the one that raised me. All Mom and that asshole did was try and beat me down, try and shove me in a box that was too small. You're the only parent I've ever known, and it doesn't matter what I called you."

"But 'Dad' sounds nice. It was the only thing I ever really wanted from you."

His choppy breathing evened out some and I noticed his mouth go a little slack under his mask. His chest was still rising and falling, so I assumed he just drifted off, so I flopped back in the chair. This was brutal. I don't know how I was going to come out on the other side of it not fundamentally changed.

I got up and went to the kitchen to see if I could find a

beer or something stronger. I was leaning on the counter, had my head hung down, I wasn't sure if I wanted to cry or break everything I could get my hands on. This was too much emotion, too many feelings for one person to try and work through. They were getting all tangled up, too engulf-ing, and I felt like I was going to suffocate on all of them.

I don't know how long I stood like that, how long I just had to tell myself to keep breathing. At some point there was a knock on the door, and I realized it was really late and I had been zoned out for a long time.

It was around midnight, no one should be here, but my friends didn't really play by common rules and Rule had a sixth sense when stuff was going down with me, so I wouldn't be surprised at all if he was doing a spot check. I rolled my neck around on stiff shoulders until there was a nasty-sounding crack and wandered over to the front door. I pulled it open without a second thought and almost fell on my ass when a soft body launched into mine as soon as there was enough room for her to fit through.

My arms closed reflexively around her tiny waist as hers went up around my neck. She buried her nose in my throat and her endless waves of red hair curled all around my arms and hands. I felt moisture on her face as she rubbed her cheek against the edge of my rough jaw. She didn't say anything, just held me tight and cried, for me, for her, for us, and I just stood there dumbfounded and unsure. I knew one thing: if she tried to walk away again I wasn't going to just let her go. I would love her too hard, hold on too tight . . . just like Phil said.

"Saint?"

Her arms squeezed even tighter around my neck and she

pulled back so we were eye to eye. That gray was glittering silver and clear through the sheen of tears. She was the prettiest and most welcome thing I had ever seen.

"Nash, oh, my God . . ." She bit her lip and grabbed my face. "I'm so sorry."

I lifted an eyebrow and reached up to circle my fingers around her delicate wrists.

"I know I got your text. I just don't know what you're sorry for."

She blinked at me and I saw her struggle to put her thoughts in line. She was cute when she was awkward.

"Mostly I'm sorry for not having faith in you, and in myself. I really do love myself, Nash. I think it took looking at a life lived alone and in fear to realize that. I think maybe you kicked the door open and I couldn't hide from it anymore. I have a lot to offer and I totally deserve the best kind of love. I deserve your love."

All those pieces of my heart that I thought she took with her, she reached in and put back in a better, more resilient way.

"You deserve anything and everything you ever wanted, Saint."

She smiled at me but it was shy and kind of nervous. "The thing I've wanted the longest besides getting to be a nurse . . . is you. I am so fucking in love with you right back, Nash Donovan."

I scooped her up in a rib-crushing hug that made her squeak. I kissed her so hard that I'm surprised it didn't hurt one of us. When I put her down, I dragged her inside the house and shut the door.

"What are you doing here, though?" I didn't know why she was at my dad's so late. Not that I wasn't relieved to see her. Just by being her, she made some of the stuff I was drowning in feel less oppressive.

"I went to Phoenix to see my mom. I was hurt and acting like a panicked schoolgirl. I wasn't thinking, wasn't listening, and I thought the space would help. We had a heart-to-heart, Mom and me, and I realized that I can't keep looking at myself through any eyes but my own. We all make mistakes, say hurtful things off the cuff, but that doesn't define who we are. I was coming home when Royal called me. She ran into Cora and heard Phil wasn't doing very well. I broke every speed limit that exists between New Mexico and here. I would never have forgiven myself if you had to do this alone."

God, I just loved her.

"I need you." My voice cracked when I said it, and the feelings I was treading through just to keep my head above them started to rise up again.

"I know you do, and I need to be here for you. That's how love works." She reached for my hand and gave it a squeeze. "How is he?"

I shook my head and let it fall forward. She curled a hand around the back of my neck and brushed a kiss across the stubbly ridge of my cheek.

"Getting worse by the day. I haven't left his side very much. He drifts in and out, forgets where he is, what time in his life it is. The nurses seem to think it's only a matter of days, if not hours."

She pulled me closer and I let myself sort of fold into her

embrace. Her hair was so soft and she smelled like spring and sunshine even though it was the middle of the night.

"I'm sorry. This has to be awful. Can I do anything for you?"

I kissed her behind the ear and felt her shiver against me. "This is it. Unless you want to relent and go get me a pack of smokes and some booze."

She pulled back and gave me a scowl. I grinned at her.

"I'm just kidding. Just having you here makes it suck less. I'm so glad you can finally see how wonderful you are."

"Well, I might have moments here or there still, so be patient with me, but I realize that if someone as great, as talented, as caring as you can be in love with me, then I must be pretty special."

The only answer I had to that was to kiss her again. At another time, in any other place, I would have found the nearest place I could just lose myself inside her, but as happy as I was that she was here, that she was officially mine, I still had other pressing matters on hand. I sighed against her lips and closed my eyes.

"I have to stay with Phil. I can't be somewhere else if he goes."

She sighed back and we were just breathing each other in and out.

"I'm not going anywhere, Nash. If you're here, then so am I."

I wanted to argue with her. I wasn't exactly keen on the idea of her seeing me such a mess and so vulnerable, but I had to admit having her around to lean on sounded nice. I gulped and led her back to the room Phil was in. She put a hand to her mouth and I saw her fingers shake. A glossy coating of fresh tears sprang into those heartbreaking eyes, but she shook it off and broke away from me to walk over to the bedside. Her eyes were everywhere and she touched his wrist with delicate fingers. I realized belatedly as I slumped into the recliner that she was doing her nurse thing. She stood there for a long minute and then turned back to me with a devastated expression. I went to get up so I could get another chair, but she put herself firmly in my lap and curled up so that she was cradled against my chest.

"His pulse is really weak, thready; respiration's shallow and labored."

"Yeah."

She shook her head. "I'm so sorry."

I snorted a little and kissed her on the crown of her head. "You keep saying that."

"Because I really, really am."

I pulled her as close to me as I could and watched my dad with a hollow feeling in my gut.

"I know you are. He told me not to live a life of regret tonight. He also told me to love you so hard there would be no getting away from it, and then he asked me to call him Dad."

My voice broke, and for the first time since this all started, everything I was feeling started to leak out. Luckily it was dark and the only one who could tell was Saint. Moisture forced its way out of one eye and got lost in her bright hair.

She put her palm on my heart and tapped her fingers in time with the hasty beat.

"You can do all those things for him." Her voice was soft and gentle like she was scared she might spook me.

"Now that you're here, I can."

We stayed silent after that, just held each other in the dark and waited to see what the next day would hold. I knew that whatever it was, we would face it together and that made facing the inevitable slightly more bearable.

PHIL WAS IN AND out the next day. Sometimes he knew exactly who I was and he kept grinning at me and looking at Saint. I urged her to go home, told her she didn't have to stay since she had already missed work, but she wasn't budging. She fluttered around, doing her nursing thing, doing her girlfriend thing, and I was grateful for it all. Phil made her laugh when he was awake and lucid. He told her broken tales of my misspent youth with Jet and the Archer twins, which led to a show-and-tell of all my awful tattoos that I had since covered with other things. He didn't last long, and she was amazing with him, even when I felt useless and at a loss.

I had a really hard time when he drifted off, when he thought he was somewhere else in a different time. I wanted to hurt things when he mumbled things about my mom and that disastrous relationship. It made all the disdain I had for her bubble to the surface and all that old hurt and those feelings of inferiority percolate and stew. Saint did a good job of reminding me that my mother's opinion held no weight for me anymore, and that the people that mattered in my life adored who I was and they wouldn't change a thing about me. That she wouldn't change a single thing about me.

It was early the following morning, really early, the sun wasn't even up yet, when something changed. I was napping on and off in the recliner, Saint was asleep on the couch in the other room, but something in the air shifted and my eyes popped open. I got up and walked to the side of my dad's bed and looked down at him. His eyes were at half-mast and I could see, literally see, that he was fighting, struggling to inhale each breath he was taking. My heart slipped out of rhythm and I knew, just had a gut sense, that this was it. That last grain of sand in the hourglass was falling down.

"Hey." I could only whisper and his eyes flickered in my direction.

I couldn't tell if he could see me anymore, if he could tell who I was at this point, but he lifted a frail hand and I took it in my own. Emotion clogged my throat as I saw his skeletal-looking chest take longer and longer to rise and fall. His bony fingers curved over my own, and I don't know if he really said it or I just wanted him to say it, but I could swear that the words *with you always* floated out and around us before his eyes drifted shut one last time.

I don't know how long I stood there, don't know if I made any noise or not, but he wasn't breathing anymore and I was just left holding his hand and staring down at him in numbness. I heard a strangled sound and looked up to see Saint hovering in the doorway, hands over her mouth and eyes huge in her face. She knew and she was aching for me.

She walked over and wrapped her arms around my waist from the back and we just stood there, silent and sorrowful, grieving and a little bit lost.

"I think he told me he would always be with me right before he passed." I sounded rusty and unsure.

"He will always be with you, Nash. He's a part of you in everything you do. He's always going to be here looking out for you." I felt one of her fingertips trail over the ridges of my spine, where my dragon was sleeping and at rest.

"Yeah, but it's not going to be the same without him."

Her soft breath fluttered across the back of my neck as I linked a hand over hers where it was lying on my stomach.

"No, it won't, but you'll do your best to make his memory live on."

Damn straight I would. It was the least I could do after everything Phil had done for not only me, but the rest of the wayward souls I called my family.

THE NEXT FEW DAYS were chaos. I felt like I was the eye of a storm that raged around me. Saint got down to business before the sun even came up. She made the arrangements for his body to go where it needed to and for it to be handled in the way Phil's last wishes asked for. In a matter of hours, Phil's condo was full of people. The girls all banded together to work on the funeral arrangements. Since Phil was going to be cremated, a viewing was set up for a few days from the day he passed. I had lost the ability to speak, to interact, and was just responding when spoken to, so it was up to Saint to run the show. My girl who was shy, hesitant, and nervous, took charge just like she did in the ER and I couldn't have loved her any more if I tried. I could tell my friends noticed the way she rallied for me, propped me up, and they all fell a little in love with her as well. There was no doing any of this without her.

The guys were all tasked with alerting everyone of Phil's passing. Phones were constantly going off, questions and answers were flying; one day faded into the next and I was in the center of it all, mostly numb and unresponsive. At some point I think Rule noticed my comatose state, and while there was a lot of business and details that still had to be handled, celebrating Phil's life and the wonderful person he was definitely needed to be first on the agenda, so he asked Rome to put together a wake at the Bar on the fly. We were Donovans after all, so it was only fitting.

It was sometime into my third Jameson and Coke, with Saint propped up against my side while the Pogues played "Waltzing Matilda" and "If I Should Fall from Grace with God" on the jukebox, while everyone told sloppy sad stories about how Phil had impacted their life, that the chill and unresponsiveness finally started to fade. I was sad, I was lonely, I was scared, but more than any of that, I was determined to do my old man proud, and that was what he would want me to focus on.

I pulled Saint close to me. I kissed her on the end of her freckled nose and told her, "Thank you."

She wrinkled her brows up at me. "For what?"

For everything, but that didn't really cut it. "For being you."

Her eyes got all shiny and bright silver like they tended to do when I said something that got to the heart of her, and she hugged me so hard I couldn't breathe. I let go, told Phil good-bye in my head, and raised a toast that had everyone hooting and hollering at the top of their lungs. It was a rousing send-off, a proper way to say farewell. All of the people

Phil had touched, the family he had helped build, honored his memory and each other while getting properly sauced and living life with no regret.

The viewing was the next day. The girls had found a nice little church close to downtown and it was almost filled to capacity. Phil had a legion of friends he rode motorcycles with, old navy buddies—including Cora's dad, who was holding baby Remy, a bunch of lifelong clients, and enough ex-girlfriends and lovers that all I could do was shake my head and high-five the guy in my head.

All of the gang was standing outside greeting people as they walked in. It was an odd sight, all of us that were normally so colorful and bright dressed in shades of black and gray. Even Rule's hair was a somber, solid black for the occasion. I loved that they all wanted to surround me, that I had a bunch of arms ready to hold me up if I was going to fall, but I felt pretty solid as long as Saint didn't wander too far from my side. She was the rock I needed to stay grounded to here and now.

From inside the church, Johnny Cash's version of "Danny Boy" started to play and I was subjected to a backbreaking round of man hugs, and heartbreaking hugs and kisses from the girls. Cora was openly crying already and I had only ever seen her do that when she was pregnant and when Rome got shot. Rule's winter-colored eyes also looked a little glassy and sharp, but he buried his face on top of Shaw's head to hide it as they walked inside.

I clasped Saint's hand and brought it up to my lips so I could kiss her knuckles.

"Ready?"

She opened her mouth to say something but snapped it shut again with a frown when the sound of high heels on cement suddenly interrupted us. I couldn't believe she was here or that she had the nerve to bring him. I scowled at both of them.

"What are you doing here?" There was no hiding the bite in my tone.

My mom cleared her throat. "Really, Nashville, how would it look if we weren't here?"

Seriously? I felt my back teeth snap together.

"I don't care how it looks. This is a time for Phil's family, the people who loved him. You made your choice and it wasn't either of us, so you can just go."

I felt Saint's fingers curl around my elbow.

"You're being ridiculous." To my mother, I always was.

I opened my mouth to retort when Grant decided he was going to jump into the conversation.

"You always were a selfish brat. Now move out of the way before someone comes out and walks into this scene. Stop being undignified . . . if you can manage it."

I saw red. I was going to rip his throat out. I was going to break his nose. I was going to . . . pull my outraged girlfriend back because she stepped in front of me and jabbed the tip of her finger right in the center of Grant's tie. It was rare to see her get so heated, so I took a step forward to put a hand on her shoulder just to keep her steady.

"How dare you?" She was furious on my behalf, fuming and fully in the midst of a redheaded fit of temper. It was awesome, but Grant narrowed his eyes and took a step forward. "You're nothing but an elitist bully. You were so fortunate to have a chance to raise a happy and healthy child, and yet you threw that away. Nash is a million times the man you'll ever be." Her eyes flashed as she looked between my mom and Grant. "You're selfish and awful and you deserve each other. You didn't earn the right to have Nash as a son."

Grant made a strangled noise in his throat and took another step toward her. I reached around Saint and put a hand in the center of his chest and pushed him back. I made sure he understood the seriousness of what I was saying to him in my tone.

"If you so much as look at her wrong, I will break every bone in your body, and then when they heal I will break them all again. When I was a kid you were a dick and I couldn't do anything about it. I'm not a kid anymore, so you might want to watch it."

"Are you threatening me?" He sounded indignant and prissy.

"No, I'm just telling you how it is. I don't want you here, either of you. Now, if you'll excuse us, I have to go give my father's eulogy."

My mom looked like she wanted to say something else, but just like she always did when Grant started to lead her away, she went willingly. I looked down at Saint and gave her a lopsided smile.

"Let's do this."

She clasped my hand and lifted one rust-colored brow at me. "Your real name is Nashville?"

I did something I never thought I would do on such a rough day: I laughed. "Yeah, and never mention it again."

I walked into the church and sat her down next to Cora, who immediately wrapped my girl up in a hug. I kept going to the podium that was set up off to the side of the urn and little memorial the girls had created. There were pictures of Phil throughout the years, his first tattoo machine, his leather jacket, the bars off his Navy uniform . . . it was a fitting and thoughtful tribute. I looked at it out of the corner of my eye, cleared my throat, and let my gaze wander over the crowd.

I saw Rule nod at me, saw Jet tilt his head just a little, Rowdy gave me a sad half little grin, and Cora just kept crying silently into Rome's shoulder. It was those soft gray eyes I landed on. She was just watching me, serene and so precious. I ignored everyone else and focused what I had to say on her.

"I called Phil Donovan a lot of things for the time I had him in my life. Friend, boss, mentor, uncle, and at the end, . . . dad. He was all of those things and so much more to so many. Phil took in anyone that was lost and tried to guide them in the right direction until they were found. In doing that, he brought a bunch of angry, frustrated, directionless souls together and now we have each other. We owe our family to Phil."

I heard throats clear and saw bodies shift in the seats.

"When I was younger I wanted to be just like Phil when I grew up. I thought he was so cool, had the greatest job, and I admired how he lived his life on his own terms, all while trying his damnedest to take care of me. He was a great guy, and if you asked me then what he would've wanted to be remembered for, I would've said it was his art, his dedication to creating a place for creativity and individuality to flourish. Now . . ." I had to take a second to clear my throat and I curled my hands into fists on the podium in front of me. "Now I think my answer would be me. I'm a man who made his father proud. I'll keep his dream, his legacy, alive and I'll do it with his memory in mind every step of the way. I also think he would be proud of us. Despite the trials, the struggles, the roadblocks life has decided to throw in our paths, we are falling in love, getting married, having babies, growing businesses, and doing the things that make us happy. I think that's all he ever really wanted for any of us. Phil Donovan will be missed, my dad will be missed—but he will live on in each and every one of us whose lives he touched and helped shape."

I didn't have anything else, so I said thank you, told the crowd that was silently weeping for the most part that anyone who wanted to share something was more than welcome to get up and take the mike, and went down to take a seat by my girl.

She had tracks of tears on her pale face and curled into me with her head on my shoulder.

"Thank you." Her voice was a husky breath of sound.

"For what?"

"For being you."

So there it was. I put an arm around her shoulders and listened to people tell stories about how wonderful my dad was, how impactful he had been, and I thought when it was all said and done I would take his ashes somewhere up in the mountains, drive the Charger way too fast, and let him go. It was an ending he would approve of all the way around.

CHAPTER 18

Saint

Aᴛᴇʀ ᴛʜᴇ ғᴜɴᴇʀᴀʟ, ɴᴀsʜ looked like he was going to fall over from lack of sleep and stress. His friend Cora and her dad, who had been friends with Phil while in the Navy, were having a get-together at her house for everyone. I knew Nash was going to try and power through and go, but he needed to go to bed and recharge. I didn't want to say anything, wasn't sure it was my place, but when I mentioned how burned out he looked, Rule and Rome both agreed, and told me I should take him home and put him to bed. Rule said it more with a leer, which had his brother thunking him on the back of the head, but all the same, when Nash broke away from the group that had commandeered him, I let him gather me up and told him, "Take me home."

He didn't argue, didn't question it, didn't stop to tell everyone else what he was doing, just whisked me away to the Charger and took me back to the Victorian. Once we were inside, he started peeling off his dark clothing, which was a delightful sight to see for sure, but after he took a shower and shoved some food in his face, he was obviously dead on his feet, which didn't leave room open for talking, let alone anything else that might have been on the agenda.

I kicked off the heels I had worn all day, cuddled up to his big, tattooed body, and rubbed his shaved head, traced my fingers over the flames decorating his scalp and shoulders until his heavy chest started rising and falling in a steady rhythm. His dark lashes fluttered lightly against his tawny cheeks and I rubbed a thumb lightly over his raven-colored eyebrows. He was beautiful, perfect, and stronger than anyone I had ever known. He was all mine. I would never take that for granted again.

Once he was settled, I slipped out from under him and went to pick up around the apartment that had been neglected for the last few weeks. I called Sunny and told her I was back and that I would be back at work as soon as she needed me, and told her to set up the interview with the director of nursing for the promotion. I gave her the Cliffs-Notes version of what had been going on and my heart just swelled with how receptive and kind she was. I really needed to let that friendship grow outside of work because she was a really great lady and so firmly in my corner. I also called Faith to fill her in and got an earful about running off to Phoenix with no warning.

I think she was happy for me in the grand scheme of things, she was definitely thrilled that Mom was doing so much better, but she made it clear that Nash was not her first choice for me. At some point, her opinion, her feelings on the matter, might have held me back, might have swayed me into thinking we weren't the best match, but I knew better now. Like I told him, I had to look at myself and my life through my own lens and no one else's, and all I saw on the other side of that was him and the me he saw when he looked at me with those brilliant eyes of his.

I was rinsing out a ton of abandoned coffee mugs and getting ready to load the dishwasher when there was a light tap on the door. Since all of his friends were at Cora and Rome's house and he had made his stance clear with his mother, I figured it had to be Royal. I wiped my hands on a towel and went to pull the door open. My eyes got huge when I took her in.

Her dark red hair was in a tangled mess. She had a yellow-and-green bruise blooming around one of her dark eyes, and her bottom lip was split wide open. She had the bottom half of her police uniform on and a plain white tank top on top. There was blood on the collar and one of the arms was ripped.

"Are you okay?"

She snorted but I saw her cut lip tremble just a little. "Hazard of the job. I tussled with a junkie that was bigger and meaner than me. I just wanted to see how the two of you were doing."

She really was nice and I wanted to give her and this burgeoning friendship a shot.

"We're all right. It was rough for a minute. His mom is a witch and his stepdad sucks, but the service was nice and Nash broke everyone's heart with his eulogy. He's crashed out, which I think he needs more than anything now. Thank you for calling me."

She gathered her messy hair in a fist and nodded. "You

were on your way home anyway. That's what matters. I had a shit day. I'm going to lie down, too."

I grabbed her arm as she turned away and noticed she had the glitter of tears in her dark eyes.

"It gets easier, you know."

"What does?"

"Having a job like you do. My first night on the floor in the ER, there was a gang shooting. They rolled in five gunshot wounds at the same time. I was trained for it, knew what I was supposed to do, but after it was all said and done, I went home and cried for three hours and lost my lunch. You get used to it, it just becomes part of the routine."

She nodded and ran her tongue over the nasty cut bisecting her lip. "That's why I need you to be my friend, Saint."

She was back across the hallway and in front of her own door when I called out, "You have my number, use it."

She waved a hand at me over her shoulder and disappeared inside her own place.

I went back to picking up, and by the time I was done, I decided it was my turn for a shower. Nash was still out when I snuck in the room to snag one of his shirts to change into and it took every ounce of restraint I had not to kiss every line, every curve of his face until he woke up.

I was rubbing a towel over my hair and walking back into the living room to watch TV until he woke up when I drew up short. He was most definitely awake, leaning against the back of the couch and watching me with heavy-lidded, purple eyes. The boxers were navy blue this time and his arms bulged enticingly where they were crossed across his delectable chest. As always, my gaze followed those wings that disappeared into the waistband of his underwear.

"Hey." I couldn't help the husky drop in my voice.

He lifted a black eyebrow at me and the corner of his mouth kicked up in a grin.

"Thanks for taking care of me, Saint."

I took a few more steps into the living room and he caught the end of the towel that was now hanging limply in my hand and used it to tow me in until we were mere inches away from each other.

"Anytime, Nash."

He reached out and coiled a hand under the wet fall of my hair around my neck. He removed the space remaining between us, and I was plastered against his bare chest. It was the best place in the world to be.

"How about you let me take care of you for a while?"

Well, what kind of fool would I be to pass up an offer like that? Only the last time we had been on this couch in any kind of sexy way together I had left him in a pretty unfair state and I wanted to make it up to him. I wanted to take care of him in all ways there was from this point on out.

"How about we just take care of each other."

Both of his eyebrows shot up and finally, after way too long, a full-fledged smile crossed his handsome face.

"Sounds like a good deal." Then he bent his head and kissed me like it was the first and last thing he wanted to do every single day from here on out.

Our tongues tangled together, hands slid eagerly across bare skin, and all the best parts of us lined up perfectly. I gasped into his mouth a little when his hands crawled up under the hem of my borrowed T-shirt and cupped the curves of my bottom. He hefted me a little closer so that our pelvises were pressed tightly against one another and I felt his erection throb insistently where it was resting in the cradle of my legs. He made short work of the T-shirt and guided a wide palm from the base of my neck all the way to where my spine dipped in right above my ass. He blew out an appreciative breath that I caught because our mouths were still sealed together.

I pulled back and kissed him on the throat, shivered when he moved a hand across my ribs and up to cup a breast. It seemed unfathomable that I hadn't enjoyed being touched like this. I guess I just needed the hands, the skilled touch, to belong to him. He rotated the pad of his thumb across one of my nipples and it made my entire body clench in response. If he kept that up there would be recompense for the last scene of romance in this living room. I pulled back a little and kissed him in the center of his chest. I loved how resilient, how taut and hard his body always felt under my mouth. I put a kiss that left a mark right over where his heart was beating steady and strong and let my tongue twist and turn around the flat disk of his nipple. It made me giggle a little when it beaded up in response.

I tickled his abs with my fingertips and rubbed my palms over the wings that covered his sides. I thought the white boxers were my favorite against his swarthy and darker-toned skin, but I decided on the spot as I pulled him free that my favorite from here on out was going to be none at all. His erection was pulsing, practically vibrating in my hand. It was still topped with the metal ring and the barbell and it quivered eagerly in my hand when I gave it a little squeeze at the base.

Nash made a low noise in the back of his throat when I sank down in front of where he was still leaning against the couch. His eyes were midnight dark and there was a high flush on his cheeks. The power, the pride I felt that I could make this man react like that made me really feel like the most beautiful woman in the entire world.

My teeth clicked on the metal ring, which made me want to laugh but had him groaning. He collected my hair up in both his hands as I started rolling, sucking, licking the thing in a way that had his abs contracting and his thighs quivering. I had to keep my hands involved, all of him was never going to fit in my mouth at one time, and I had to admit it was way more fun to do this when there were things my tongue could play with. I heard him growl my name, which was super hot, felt him tug at my hair, which meant he was close. I wasn't paying attention to what he was saying, I was too busy thinking about how heady the sensation was, how delicious making him react felt . . . sure, this was more about his pleasure than my own, but his taste, his feel, it was enough to light me up just fine.

I had my hands around the base of his cock, was using them in time with the sucking, swirling motion of my mouth, so I was surprised when he literally yanked me off of him, which resulted in a drag of teeth and a squeeze that was probably rougher than felt good. He yelped out a swearword and I was going to demand to know what he thought he was doing, but my panties were unceremoniously stripped off my legs, leaving me bare and open. He wrenched us around while breathing hard and put my hands on the back of the couch. With a palm in the center of my back between my shoulder blades, he bent me over just a little and used his knee to nudge my legs open enough so that he could fit where he needed to be.

He dropped a heavy kiss on the back of my neck, reached around the front, and covered each of my breasts with his wide hands. He didn't say anything, just slid inside me, and I thought I was going to die. In this position he went deeper, I felt him more intensely, and the drag and pull of that little extra he was working with made stars dance in front of my eyes. I had to clutch the couch cushions, had to bite my lip—hard—to keep from screaming out each time he pulled out and pushed back in. We had had a lot of sex over the last few months but nothing that felt this raw, this unhinged, and potent.

I felt like this was him leaving his undeniable mark, and as the pleasure grew, as his rhythm and tempo increased, as one of his hands started to slide across my stomach headed for the spot that would push me over at the barest touch, I was ready for it all, I was practically ready to shatter. Nash's breathing shifted, his driving hips stilled for a fraction, and his hand stalled on my stomach.

"Holy fuck." We were both so close, it was hovering so right there, and I had no idea what he was doing, but I was going to strangle him if he didn't start moving again. He was panting like a marathon runner, and when I looked at him over my shoulder in question, he grimaced and kissed me hard on the mouth all while pulling out of my body as slowly as was humanly possible. It made both of us groan and swear at the same time.

"Do you want to talk about the seriously unprotected sex we were just having or do you want to just go in my room and finish?'

I squealed and buried my face in his chest. "Jeez, no wonder it felt so good."

He snorted a laugh and I yelped when he swung me up in his arms and headed to the bedroom.

"Maybe you wanna add birth control to your to-do list sometime soon?"

I ran my tongue along the shell of his ear and rubbed my fingers over the flames inked on his shoulders and grinned up at him. If he hadn't attached his mouth to the side of my neck, started sucking and swirling his tongue along the sensitive cords there, I would've told him that I had taken care of that little detail shortly after the night I stayed here with him just to be safe. If I had known it would bring on a hasty end to all the delicious things he was doing to my body in the living room, I would've sent him a memo about it.

I hit the center of the bed with a little "oof" when he gracelessly tossed me, and I leaned back to watch him while he got himself all situated. I blinked up at him with wide eyes as he crawled up over me and settled himself back between my legs.

"You are so beautiful." He really was from the inside out.

He lifted and eyebrow and placed a sweet little kiss on the end of my nose.

"So are you." I used to just ignore him, to think they were just words he was saying because he thought they needed to be said. Now I understood he meant it and it didn't matter if I looked the way I did now or if I looked the way I did then, it was the person I was he found beautiful.

"Thank you."

He slid back inside of me, and since my body was already primed, already on brink of going over, it didn't take much to have me hollering his name into the ceiling and digging my heels into his back. He curled my legs up high on his sides, rose up a little on one knee, and powered into my compliant body until he found his own release and collapsed on top of me in a heavy heap.

The ring in the center his nose was a tactical thrill against my shoulder as he kissed my collarbone and muttered drily, "I'm done trying to have sex on that couch. It never ends well for me."

I had to laugh as I wrapped my arms across his wide shoulders. "I think it ended just fine."

"I love you, Saint."

"I love you, too, Nash."

Nash wanted to live a life with no regrets, I wanted to live a life that was fulfilled. We needed each other to accomplish that, and now that we had each other there was no then versus now, there was just this life we had together.

I GOT THE PROMOTION. It was awesome and I was really proud of myself, but what made it even better was how proud Nash was of me. My job didn't have to be important to him, but because it was so much of who I was, the fact that he inherently knew what a big deal it was made me love him even more.

Our schedules were still crazy and all over the place, even more so now that I was trying to learn the different parts of my new job. It didn't matter, though, we never spent a night apart. My place, his place, one of us was always in the other's bed, and as long as I woke up next to him in the morning, I didn't care where I put my head at night.

I was also branching out my social skills. I went out with Sunny, tried to join Nash's friends on their Thursday girls' night out if it didn't conflict with work, and had taken to having coffee with Royal every morning I stayed at Nash's place. I enjoyed the time spent with all of them, but there was something about Royal, something about watching another young woman struggle with a selfless, emotionally taxing job, that drew me to her. I didn't have to try and be her friend anymore, I was just her friend . . . period.

I was running late. Nash had called on my lunch break and asked me to meet him at the new tattoo shop when I got off of work. I had a late admission and ended up having to stay an extra half hour until the doctor could get to them. I knew the contractor had just finished with everything in the new space and all they had left to do was get the final members of the staff in place so they could open up for business in a few weeks. It had been a labor of love, cost a pretty penny, but all of the Marked family was super excited for the new adventure to begin. I figured he just wanted to show his baby off, and I felt bad I was holding him up, so I reminded myself to oooh and awww with appropriate vigor. I was really proud of him.

I had to park around the corner and make my way through the typical after-work LoDo crowd to get to the shop. The location was dynamite; he wasn't going to know what to do with himself when it took off like I knew it would. Nash was leaning against the glass storefront talking on his phone. He caught sight of me and gave me a wink. He couldn't really stand around waiting without finding something to do with his hands. I think that's how he avoided reaching for a cigarette. He was doing a great job quitting and every time he was tempted I reminded him he had made it all the way through the ordeal with Phil without lighting up, so there was no way he needed one now.

When I got to him he scooped me up in a rib-crushing hug and kissed me like we hadn't had wild shower sex just that morning. I would be the luckiest girl in the world if he was always going to be that happy to see me.

"Did you get my text that I was going to be late?"

"Yep. It gave me time to wrap up the surprise."

I gave him a funny look and noticed that the huge pane of glass that was the front of the store was covered in brown butcher's paper.

"I thought you were just going to show me the new shop."

He laughed and pulled on one of the pigtails I had been rocking at work.

"I am. It's amazing, but I want to show you something first. We went round and round, tossed idea after idea back and forth about what the new shop should be called."

I was starting to get a little anxious. I pulled my bottom lip between my teeth and looked up at him from under my pale lashes.

"What did you do, Nash?"

"This new shop is the future for the Marked, but you're *my* future. I figured I might as well tie the two of them together because you are both my life."

He reached behind him and pulled all the brown paper down off the glass, and I had to cover my mouth with my hands. All I could do was stare at him and back at the painted glass in stunned disbelief.

In old-fashioned lettering, like one would find on an old curio shop or an old apothecary window, was the name of the new shop: THE SAINTS OF DENVER TATTOO. It blew my mind and made me want to cry.

"Cora and the guys loved it. It's different and goes with our retro theme we have going on."

"Nash . . ." I couldn't even think of what to say to him. It was an honor, but more than that, it was a testament as to how important I was always going to be to him.

"I hope you're all right with it."

He was gloating and I wanted to equal parts kiss him and kick him. I just tilted my head to the side and looked at him like he had lost his mind.

I asked him, "You're amazing, you know that, right?"

He picked me up and swung me around until I was laughing so hard I had tears running down my face.

He cleared his throat and rubbed the back of his neck. "I don't ever want you to regret giving me another chance, Saint."

"You gave me another chance as well, Nash. I think when you're in love that's what you do, give chances and take chances. Now let's go inside and you can show me your new baby."

He pushed open the door to the shop that he had named after me and I followed him into our future. I didn't need to look back anymore, to hold on to hurtful and damaging memories. I had Nash to always move toward, and more importantly I now had myself and all the things about me that made me who I was to hold on to. I loved a good man, a nice man, but more than that, I loved myself, and that fulfilled me in way nothing else could because I knew I deserved the best and Nash Donovan was the best thing for me . . . ever.

Nash

"SO WHAT'S THE VERDICT?"

Cora sent her gaze dancing between me and Rule like I was an idiot for even asking the question.

"I think that if you two boneheads don't hire her, I might just murder you both."

I snickered and Rule looked up from the little pink bundle he was holding in his tattooed hands with a frown.

"I'm the favorite uncle, you can't murder me." The baby cooed like she was totally in agreement with that statement even if Rule was her *only* uncle.

I didn't tell either of them that I was going to hire her regardless of her qualifications because Phil had asked me to. He had some kind of plan and he had only been gone a few weeks, so I was still feeling the resonating loss and paying forward his crazy scheme seemed necessary.

The "she" in question had quite frankly knocked all three of us on our collective asses. I mean, I knew she was probably going to be easy on the eyes being a pinup model and all, but in person she was something else.

Salem Cruz was without a doubt the prettiest rock-and-roll chick I had ever laid eyes on and I could tell Rule agreed. She had a full sleeve tattooed on each arm, one classic Catholic images mixed with riotous Day of the Dead artwork and the other all old-school, Sailor Jerry–inspired work. She had long, caramel-colored hair that had a bloodred streak in the front of it, complete with a swooping curls on top and long waves hanging down the back. Her eyes were as dark as the midnight sky, and I liked the way they twinkled like she knew something the rest of us didn't. She was average height, but there was nothing average about the curves she was rocking, and all her retro glamour was topped off by a face that men in classic literature started wars over. She was the perfect blend of fifties pinup, rockabilly cool, and Latina sex goddess. She was just all-around impressive.

If her looks alone hadn't been enough to convince me that she would get people in the door, her credentials were. It was her résumé and sassy, take-no-shit demeanor that sold Cora. Salem wasn't just a pretty face, she had been tied to some of the most successful tattoo shops on the West Coast, and the shop she left in Vegas wasn't just some hole in the wall, it was one of those big-deal chain shops that operated in a casino and was helmed by a famous Xtreme sports guy. In all actuality the stuff we were starting in D-town was small and totally new compared to where she came from, and I think Phil knew it. She also had a hand in designing and marketing her own clothing label, so really there was no way we couldn't offer her the job.

The three of us walked out of the office Cora had commandeered and Rule handed baby R.J. back to her mom. The baby looked around the still-work-in-progress retail space and made a noise. I totally agreed with her. Expanding was a lot harder than I had initially thought and I couldn't wait until it was all said and done.

The brunette was wandering around, taking stock, sizing things up, and I had to wonder why she was willing to come somewhere so different, somewhere that was just starting up, when obviously she could write her own ticket anywhere she wanted in the tattooing world. She turned and watched us approach, her dark eyes dancing.

"How did it go?"

Cora laughed and kissed Remy on the forehead. "At this point I'm ready to hire a stranger off the street. We are too busy, need the help, and the fact you can run circles around anyone else we've seen makes it a no-brainer. Plus this place could use another female in the mix."

Salem's bright red lips quirked up in a smile. She had a ruby-red Monroe piercing that lifted with her full lips. "I think it's going to be a good time. The shop is beautiful. I think with a few little touches you are sitting on a gold mine up here in the clouds. There is a lot of opportunity sitting right at your fingertips."

Cora rolled her eyes and jiggled the baby, who started to holler just a little bit. She was going to give her mom a run for her money in the loud and bossy department down the road.

"Trust me, the old carnival theme totally fits. These guys are all clowns and half the time it really is like being part of a sideshow." I gave Cora a dirty look, but didn't disagree with her statement.

I nodded at Salem and extended the offer. "As long as you're okay with the pay and think you can handle working hand in hand with us, the job is yours. I think we'd be lucky to have you, and Phil thought you would be a perfect fit, so that matters to me. We're a family, though, so be prepared to deal with the nonsense that comes with that."

Rule grunted and reached out to shake her hand. "Welcome aboard. The crazy train is always looking for new passengers." He bent and kissed the baby much like Cora had done, and straightened back up. "I gotta head home. Shaw's been under the weather for the last few days. I need to check on her. She was green when I left."

Cora looked up at him and lifted her eyebrow that had the pink crystal piercing in it.

"I don't think there's any stomach things going around. I pay attention now because of the baby."

He lifted his shoulders and shrugged. "I dunno. She's miserable, though."

Cora looked speculative, but we were all interrupted by the thud of heavy boots on the stairs that led up from the shop floor. The only other person who had a key was Rowdy, so I wasn't surprised when his blond pompadour cleared the second floor.

"Hey, Zeb called and had an awesome idea about putting old fun-house mirrors up here when we get around to having the store open. You know to tie everything together . . ."

His voice trailed off and his ocean-blue eyes popped

open so wide they nearly took up his entire face. His jaw unhinged and all he could do was gape at the Spanish beauty standing with us. I looked back and forth between the two of them. She was smiling like a huge secret had been revealed and he looked like he had just seen a ghost.

Salem's high heels tapped a sexy little beat as she walked toward the stairs. Rowdy was stuck, like he was glued to the spot with industrial adhesive. I saw Cora give Rule a questioning look, and when they both turned to me, all I could do was shrug helplessly. I didn't have a clue what was happening either.

"Hello, Rowland. It's been a long time." She trailed her bloodred fingertip across the bridge of his nose. "You sure did grow up nice."

Rowdy gulped so loud that it was actually audible and stayed stuck to the floor.

"Who in the hell is Rowland?" It was a valid question but no one seemed in a hurry to answer Rule when he asked it.

Salem stopped in front of Rowdy so they were eye to eye, only because she was clad in some serious heels and he was still down a step. She put a hand on his cheek and gave it a little tap, which had him rearing back and blinking like an owl.

"Salem?" The question sounded strangled and forced out. I had never seen Rowdy so dumbfounded. He was the charmer, the jokester. He always had something to say. What in the hell was happening here? And why did I think this was exactly what my dad had been orchestrating all along?

The brunette looked back over her shoulder, her sleek

fall of hair moving like something out of an old Hollywood movie. She winked, actually winked at us, and started down the stairs.

"Strike that, it's going to be a great time. See you guys at work on Monday. E-mail me whatever forms you need me to fill out."

Her shoes clicked and tapped on the way down the stairs while the rest of just stood there in silence. After a long minute, Rowdy shook his head like he was coming out of a daze and walked the rest of the way into the loft.

"Rowland?" He glared at me.

"Like you have room to talk, *Nashville*."

Good point, but I was still going to give him shit every chance I got.

Cora's mix-and-match eyes were practically glowing as she shifted the baby to one arm and grabbed Rowdy's shirt-front with her free hand.

"Is that her? Is that the one?"

I didn't know what "the one" meant, but when Rowdy shook his head in the negative, Cora looked super disappointed.

"No, not her . . . but that is her sister."

Cora gasped and Rule and I just looked at each other in confusion.

"Someone want to fill us in?"

Rowdy sighed and lifted a hand to rub the back of his neck.

"When I was in foster care growing up in Texas, Salem and her little sister, Poppy, lived next door. Their dad was the minister in the town that we lived in. He was really, really strict with both the girls. They were very different, turned out opposite. Salem got out as soon as she could and Poppy broke my heart when I tried to give it to her. What in the hell is she doing here?"

I sent a sideways look at Rule and he just bit his lip ring.

"She's the new shop manager. We just hired her."

The big blond man looked like he was going to either pass out or throw up.

"Are you serious?"

Cora nodded solemnly and patted him on the shoulder. "Nash offered her the job. It's legally binding. Are you going to be okay with that?"

He rubbed one of his sideburns and looked around at all of us like he was kind of lost.

"Do I have a choice?"

"Not really." I hated to break it to him.

"I think I just need a minute to get over the shock. I haven't seen her since I was just a kid. I can't believe she's here."

"She's very beautiful." Cora's tone was gentle and placating.

Rowdy's blond eyebrows shot up and he sarcastically drawled, "I didn't notice."

Rule barked out a laugh. "Then you're blind."

I cleared my throat and everyone turned to look at me. "Phil wanted her here. He set it all in motion. How much do you want to bet he knew all along your tie to her? He didn't just pick her name out of a hat."

Rowdy swore. "Why would he do that to me?"

"He had his reasons." Love couldn't be negotiated with, I would remember that forever.

Rowdy frowned at me. "What's that supposed to mean?"

All I could do was grin. He would find out soon enough.

"You'll see. Now I want to go home to my girlfriend and love all up on her." Nothing had ever made me happier than being able to say that anytime I wanted. Saint was the person I was always going to want at the end of the day, I just knew it.

Cora held up R.J., who held her little arms out as she tried to grab on to my nose ring. That damn thing was a tiny hand magnet.

"Be careful, this is what that results in." She cut a sideways look to Rule, who completely missed it.

"By the way, tell Zeb yes to the fun-house mirrors. That guy is a goddamn genius." I really was in awe of the contractor's immense talent.

Rowdy muttered his agreement to pass the news along to his friend as we all made our way out of the shop.

I wanted to feel bad for him, to tell him that it would all be okay, but just like the rest of us, he was going to have to get there on his own. The journey to *the one* wasn't always easy. The baggage from the past could be heavy and totally unwieldy, and the drop-offs and curves could make a man ready to get off the road at any second, but there was no better destination, no better end point than the love and the woman offering it that waited at the end.

Rowdy and Salem's story to be continued . . .

Nash and Saint's Playlist

Blood or Whiskey: "Never Be Me"
Band of Skulls: "Fires"; "Navigate"
The Pixies: "Holiday Song"
Deadstring Brothers: "Silver Mountain"
The Drive-By Truckers: "Everybody Needs Love"; "Lookout
　　Mountain"
The Dropkick Murphys: "Echoes on 'A.' Street"
The Kills: "Heart Is a Beating Drum"
The Vines: "Outtathaway"
The Tossers: "Alone"
Flatfoot 56: "Son of Shame"
Her Space Holiday: "No More Good Ideas"
Sea Wolf: "The Cold, the Dark, and the Silence"; "Song for
　　the Dead"
The Pogues: "If I Should Fall from Grace"; "(And the Band
　　Played) Waltzing Matilda"
Johnny Cash: "Danny Boy"

ACKNOWLEDGMENTS

Fᴵᴿˢᵀ ᴵ ɢᴼᵀᵀᴬ ɢᴵᵛᴱ all the love to the two tiny blondes that rule my writing world, Stacey Donaghy of the Donaghy Literary Group, who is my fearless agent, and Amanda Bergeron, my brilliant editor from HarperCollins. They are both equally important for bringing these Marked Men into the world and I honestly don't know what my life would look like without either one of them. I adore that they just let me do my thing (with the proper amount of reining in) and that the end result is always so much better than I imagined. I am truly blessed to get to work with women that I genuinely like, respect, and admire.

The other person key to my writing world is my book bestie. Oh, you can call her what you want, I always say she is a woman of many talents and many names. To me she is a sounding board, a friend, a fellow book lover, and for Nash's story not only is the inspiration for one of the characters, she was also my medical guru, my Nursey-No-Mercy. Thanks,

Mel, for always being there, for offering your knowledge and support, and for generously giving me punctuation and feedback in every first draft I write. Thanks for being an awesome critique partner and just all-around an awesome friend. I love you and your giant brain so hard.

I never had too many complaints about running a bar. It was a really fun job. I got to meet cool and interesting people. I got to play with booze all day. Beer delivery guys are pretty cute and have big muscles, and I always got to stay up late and never had to get up early. That being said, this new job I have kicks that job's butt, and the people I've been fortunate enough to meet in the last year . . . well, I can't tell you how exciting and interesting it has been. From fellow authors, publishing professionals, to bloggers, to readers, to event organizers, to the people I have Internet-befriended along the way. Book people are the best. End of story. Thank you all for making the last year a blast, and I gotta thank Sophie Jordan, Jennifer Armentrout, Cora Carmack, and Lisa Desrochers for showing the new girl the ropes and making me feel welcome. I love hanging out with these ladies and it's always a good time when we get in the same room.

Of course, my folks always need to get a shout out because they are awesome and there are none better. Did you know my dad is coming to my European signings with me this year? If you see a guy walking around that has a cowboy mustache and probably something with a Dodge logo on it, that's him. Buy him a beer or a shot of Jack and tell him thanks for being the base inspiration for all these hot guys swimming around in my head. My mom is wonderful. She's not only my biggest fan but my closest confidante. I just love her to pieces and I'm grateful that with all the opportunities I've had come my way, I get to experience so many of them with her. She likes red wine and has lots and lots of blond hair if you want to buy her a drink instead. ☺

I can't write a story about loving yourself, about knowing you are fabulous just the way you are, and not throw out a thank-you to my bestie. She's amazing at this. Really understands the importance of it, and the journey she had to take in order to remember how wonderful and amazing she really is was heartbreaking. But she got back to where she needed to be and I couldn't be prouder or more stoked for her. She is always the strongest, most beautiful person I know inside and out. I just LOVE Settie Phillips to a million pieces. I am so very lucky I get the honor of having her as my best friend.

And always my most important, most heartfelt and over-whelming amount of thanks goes out to you . . . the reader. OMG, where would I be without you guys? I will always be taken aback, dumbfounded, and completely humbled when I get an e-mail saying something I wrote is their favorite book, or that they related to what the characters are going through, or that they appreciate how "real" my storytelling is. I never really thought past hitting publish on *Rule,* so now that we are four books in, I really can't tell you how much value and wonder all of you have brought into my life. I think of each and every single reader as a gift, as a compatriot, as a fellow book lover, and as a friend. Thank you so very much from the bottom of my tattooed heart.

The above goes for all you amazing and dedicated bloggers out there. Thank you for the support. Thank you for being invested in this world I have created. Thank you for spreading the word and taking the time and effort to write reviews and give valuable space and time on your blogs to me and the boys. Thank you for all that you do!!

Finally, I have to tell you how much I love the girls at http://literatiauthorservices.com/. Karen, Michelle, and Rosette have made my now hectic and busy life far more manageable. They are organized and efficient, but mostly they are delightful and wonderful ladies. They know it all, the business end, the blogging end, the reading end, and the promotional end. I wouldn't just trust my boys in the hands of anyone, and I tell them all the time working with them is the best decision I ever made!! If you need marketing or promotional help, look them up, you won't be sorry you did it.

I love my dogs. That is all.

THE MARKED MEN

series continues this fall

But first ...

In the heat of summer,

Jay Crownover embarks on a dark,
sexy, and explosive new series
you won't want to miss.

What's the difference between bad
boys, and boys who are *bad*?

Welcome to The Point

BY JAY CROWNOVER

Shane Baxter isn't just from the wrong side of the tracks, he *is* the wrong side of the tracks. Bax is a criminal, a thug, a brawler, and a man who has made the streets and the city his playground. He's the master of making bad choices. At least he was until his last bad choice landed him in the joint for a five-year stretch. Now Bax is out and looking for answers, and he doesn't care what he has to do or who he has to hurt to get them. Even if there's a new player in the game and she's way too innocent and way too soft for the way Bax does things. She's standing directly in the way of the answers he wants and he has no qualms using whatever it takes to get them.

Dovie Pryce knows all about living a hard life and the choices that come with it. She's always tried to be good, tried to help others and not let the darkness of the wrong side of the tracks pull her down. Only the streets are fighting back and things have gone from bad to worse and the only person that can help her is the scariest, sexiest, most complicated ex-con The Point has ever produced. Bax terrifies her and it doesn't take Dovie long to realize some boys are just better when they're bad.

Coming June 2014

CHAPTER 1

Bax

THERE WERE VERY FEW things that could kill the buzz of post-sex mellowness. Getting coldcocked in the side of the head by a pair of knuckles that felt like they were encased in steel ranked right at the top of the list. My ears rang from the blow as my head snapped around from the force. I would've reacted, but an uppercut had my chin flying back and my skull ringing soundly against the brick wall behind me. Now I was seeing stars and swallowing blood. Not like these guys cared about a fair fight, but eventually I was going to get my wits back, and there was going to be hell to pay. I spit out a mouthful of blood and took the cigarette the guy who had inflicted the blows offered me.

"Long time no see, Bax."

I lifted a hand and worked my jaw back and forth to see if it was broken. Nothing ruined a mellow post-orgasm mood like dealing with a bunch of clueless idiots and the thought of losing some teeth.

"How did you find me?" I blew out a stream of smoke

and leaned back against the wall of the apartment building I had just exited. The copper taste of blood was tangy on my tongue. I made sure it landed on my assailant's wingtips when I spit out another mouthful.

"Five years is a long time for a man to go without." He lifted his eyebrows and flexed those hands I knew from experience were capable of far worse than a little smack down.

"No pussy, no booze, no blow, no fast cars, and no one who gives a shit who you are. I know you, kid; I knew the first thing you would want when you got out was tail. I gave Roxie a heads-up to call me when you came knocking."

He was wrong. The first thing I went for was the fast car. Granted, I used it to haul ass to a sure thing I knew wouldn't say no, but still, pussy came after a quality ride.

"So you took it upon yourself to make sure my welcome home sucked as much as possible?"

"If I know Roxie, and I do, you don't have anything to complain about." His merry band of thugs all chuckled and I just rolled my eyes. There was a reason Roxie was a sure thing, and not just a sure thing for me, even though I had been out of commission for the last five years.

"I'm not here for me. Novak wants to see you."

Novak. The name made normal men shake in fear. It usually only came up when people were talking about murder, mayhem, and general dissonance on the streets. He was ruthless. He was coldblooded. He was untouchable and a legend in The Point and beyond it. In the shadows and back alleyways he was king. Nobody crossed him. No one walked away from him. No one dared defy him, no one except for me. I wanted to see Novak as well, but I wanted to do it on my terms.

I finished the cigarette and put it out under the sole of the heavy black boots I had on. I was a lot bigger now than when I had gotten locked up. I wondered if these guys had bothered to notice. Living a life full of booze, drugs, and easy girls, no matter how young and active you were, wasn't a recipe for healthy living. Getting all that unceremoniously yanked away changed not only how a man lived mentally, but also how he physically changed, be it by choice or not.

"I don't want to see Novak." At least not right now. My ears had finished ringing and all I had now was a splitting headache. They didn't have the element of surprise anymore, and if they wanted to push the issue, it was going to get bloody and ugly really fast. I didn't care if I knew the goons were more than likely packing.

The guy who had delivered the blows just stared at me while I stared back. I wasn't some scared kid anymore who wanted to belong; who wanted these guys to be impressed. Sacrificing five years of your life for a bunch of bullshit had a way of leaving a mark on a guy. Novak should know that.

"Race is missing."

Now that had the desired effect. My eyes narrowed and my shoulders tensed. I pushed off the apartment building and ran rough hands over my shorn hair. Having hair in the joint was a bad plan, and even with the wicked scar that curved across the side of my scalp, I had no intention of growing the jet-black locks back. Low maintenance was necessary in my line of work—well, my former line of work—but that was a problem I didn't want to think about now, or ever.

"What do you mean he's missing? Like he went on a trip, or like Novak made him disappear?" It wouldn't be the first time Novak took it upon himself to make a problem go away with a bullet between the eyes.

The guy shifted on his feet and my patience vanished. I lunged forward and grabbed him by the collar of his fancy button-up shirt. I wasn't eighteen and scrawny anymore, so I saw the fear flash in his eyes as I literally pulled him to the tips of his toes so we were now eye to eye. I heard the slide of a gun get pulled back, but I didn't take my gaze from his as he clawed at my wrists for purchase.

"Answer me, Benny. What do you mean Race is missing?"

Race Hartman was a good dude for the most part. Too good and too smart for this life. He should have never gotten caught up with Novak, should have never been out on the street with me the night everything went to hell. Doing a nickel to keep a guy like Race out of the clutches of a piece of shit like Novak was a sacrifice I had no trouble making, but if the idiot hadn't heeded my warning and walked away like he was supposed to when they slapped the cuffs on me, I was going to level the entire city.

Benny tried to kick me in the shin with his sissy wing-tip and I tossed him away from me. I shot a dirty look at thug number one, who was holding a gun on me, and flipped him off.

"Bax," Benny sighed and moved to smooth out his shirt where I had wrinkled it up by manhandling him. "Race went to ground the second you got busted. No one heard anything from him; he wasn't around. None of the girls even saw him. Novak kept an eye out for him in case all that mess the two of you created came back to bite us in the ass, but nothing. Then last week, when the word was out you were getting out, he popped back up. He came around making threats, telling Novak it was bullshit you went down for what happened. I thought he had a death wish, but then . . . poof, he was just gone after stirring up the hornets' nest. Now, you tell me why a smart guy like Race would do something like that?"

I didn't know, but I didn't like it. I didn't have any friends in this world, anyone I trusted aside from Race Hartman.

"Tell Novak to back off. I'll see what I can do to get a pulse on him, but if Novak had something to do with Race going AWOL, he will regret it."

"Pretty brave making threats when you haven't even been out of lockup for a full twenty-four hours."

I snorted and stepped around Benny like he wasn't worth my time, which he wasn't.

"Five years is a long time to go without; it's also a long time to work on a grudge and grow the fuck up. You don't know me, Benny. Novak doesn't know me, and I don't care what kind of muscle or firepower he wants to throw at me, if he had anything to do with Race going missing, I'll make him pay. Tell Roxie thanks for ratting me out."

"You get what you pay for." I wasn't sure if that was a dig at me or at her.

"I don't know about you and your ugly mug, but I've never had to pay for it in my life."

I saw him scowl and took advantage of his distraction to lunge forward and slam the hardest part of my forehead right into the bridge of his nose. I heard a satisfying *crunch*, and then his scream of pain as his cronies hurried forward to keep him from folding to his knees in the dirty alley. I gave my head a shake to clear my vision, because the move hadn't done a thing for my headache. I stepped around my now howling and blood-gushing adversary, tossing over my shoulder as I made my way to the mouth of the alley.

"You might not want to underestimate me, Benny. That was always your downfall."

My name is Shane Baxter, Bax to most people, and I'm a thief.

Got a girl? I'll take her from you. Got a sweet ride you dropped a mint on? I'll take it from you. Got expensive electronics you think are safe? I'll come and take them, because you probably didn't need them anyway. If it isn't nailed down or attached to you by unbreakable chains, there is a good chance I can make it mine. It was the only thing I was good at. Taking things that didn't belong to me was second nature; well, that and finding all the worst kinds of trouble to get into. I was only twenty-two, had gone in for a nickel right on the heels of my eighteenth birthday, but that wasn't even close to the first time I got busted or banged heads with the law. I wasn't a master of good choices or clean living, but I knew my strengths and I stuck with them and I took care of my own. Whatever the cost may be.

I had two people in my life I bothered to care about: my mom and Race. There used to be three, but the last one let me down in too many ways to count, and now I swore I would cold-cock him the next time I got the opportunity. My mom was long-suffering, stubborn, and the only person who stayed on my side when I went away. She had terrible taste in boyfriends, a bad habit of drinking more than was healthy, and trouble keeping a steady job. She was the very definition of down and out no matter how many lifelines I tried to throw her.

I started stealing stuff before I understood what I was doing because I was so tired of going without. As I got older and better at it, I did it to pay the bills and to keep a roof over our heads. She never judged me, never turned her back on me, and was the only person in the world who would actually be happy to see me out of prison.

Race and I were the two most unlikely friends anyone could imagine. He was college-bound, tech savvy, and from a family that had all the right connections and pedigrees. He was well spoken and charming, always dressed like he was going to a job interview, and was full of patience and common sense. He was a delightful summer breeze to my blizzard of destruction. I hadn't even finished high school, could barely read a full sentence, didn't have a family beyond my mom and the slum we lived in, and I looked like what I was: a thug. Even before my time served had added layers of muscle and bulk, I was a big guy who no one wanted to mess with. No one but Race.

I tried to jack his car one night when we were both teenagers. He was driving a sweet Roush Mustang with an even sweeter blonde in the passenger seat. I had no idea what he was doing in such a bad part of town, but I wasn't the kind of guy who let an opportunity pass me by. I shoved a knife in his face, pulled him out of the driver's seat, and proceeded to try and take his car. Only Race was in no hurry to let it go. I never knew if he was fighting for the girl or the ride, but either way, we beat the shit out of each other. I broke his wrist, he cracked my ribs, and knocked out my two front teeth. It was gory, and epic, and by the time it was all said and done, we were blood brothers.

I got the blonde's seat in the Stang on the way to the hospital and I got a brother from another mother in Race. I never went to his fancy house on the hill or dirtied up his good name at his fancy prep school. He never slummed it with me in the ghetto or had to deal with my mom's drunken outbursts. When I stared boosting high-end cars for Novak on the regular and needed help with the computer systems in the rides that cost in the high six and sometimes seven figures, he was the only one I trusted to have my back. We had a good time, blew through hot girls, and partied with stuff kids our age shouldn't know anything about. I regretted asking him every day, regretted dragging him down to my level so badly. Five years was a long ass time to work on an apology. It was just as long to wait for one owed, one that when it came, I hoped would be enough to keep me from having to put my hands around my best friend's throat. We both had made some serious mistakes along the way that needed atoning for.

Trouble was, I had no idea where to start. When I went away, he had been enrolled in some Ivy League school out East. I wasn't sure if he made it, I went away so he could, but there were no guarantees in life. I learned that lesson the hard way.

I shook out a smoke from the pack I had snagged from Roxie and dug out the pre-paid cellphone I had picked up when I went and got my car. I walked up and around the block to where I had parked the beauty, far away from curious stares and hot hands. I knew what kind of cars thieves looked for and what kind of car car guys wanted for their own. My bumble-bee yellow and black race-stripped, 1969 Plymouth Road Runner with its tricked out Hemi and hood scoop was both. It was loud. It was tough. It was faster than fast, and it was the only thing I had left after I got locked up. I told my mom to sell it when I went down, but she refused. She knew how much work, how much sweat and tears I had put into that car, so if it meant rent or my baby, my baby won.

I sucked the noxious fumes into my lungs and squinted up at the sky. I would kill for some Tylenol to get rid of the pounding throb in my head, but there were more pressing matters I had to deal with at the moment. Not to mention, a few rounds with Roxie had done nothing to dull the burning want at the back of my throat. I liked girls and girls liked me. When you grew up poor and without any kind of parental supervision, sex was just something you did to kill time and to chase away the monotonous moments of despair and depression. Two people could make each other feel good, so that's what happened more often than it should. I wasn't used to going without, well I was used to it now, but in my old life, getting laid was like breathing. It took no thought and zero effort.

I was tall, well over six feet. I had dark hair and dark eyes that chicks liked to tell me made me mysterious. I didn't talk a lot, not unless I had something important to say, which led to my not unjustified, badass aura. Plus I owned a mirror so I knew what I had going on was pretty nice to look at. I wouldn't win a modeling contract anytime soon, but the chicks seemed to dig it just the same. Even with the scar across my scalp and my nose being twisted from being broken more than once. But possibly the most notice-able difference between me and every other decent look-ing guy floating around was the tattoo of a small, black star inked next to the outside corner of my right eye. I thought it was a brilliant idea when I was sixteen and high. Now I still thought it was cool in an intimidating and "I'm crazy enough to tattoo my face" kind of way. Like I said, I looked like a thug, an alright-looking thug, but a thug nonetheless.

I needed to get a handle on Race and get back into some pretty, young thing's bed. Roxie was off the table if she was going to sell me out as soon as I got my rocks off. I never did trust her. She played the role of innocent girl-next-door too well. Especially since she was as far from innocent as any one person could be. Annoyed at how the first few hours of my freedom were playing out I put in a call to an old contact.

"Hey."

Silence met the other end of the call. I tossed the smoke and slid behind the wheel of my car. It felt more like coming home than banging Roxie or knocking Benny around ever could.

"Who is this?" Everyone I knew was a suspicious bastard. That was especially true when person on the other end of the call happened to be a rather successful drug dealer.

"It's Bax."

"When did you get out?"

"Today."

"Already looking for a score?"

Hell no. Five years without made me never want to mess with any of that stuff again. It made the bad choices I made even worse. If I was going to screw up now, I was going to do it clean and sober.

I told the dealer in a flat tone, "No. I'm looking for Race. I heard he dipped out when I got busted and showed up a little while ago making noise at Novak. No one's seen him. Have you?"

More silence. There was a fifty-fifty shot I was going to get an honest answer. I hoped my reputation still held enough weight to put the fear of God into people. If not, I would just have to go knock some heads together and earn it back.

"No. I tried to hit him up a few times after you got locked up. I thought he would get me in to all those college parties and I could split the take with him. He stopped answering my calls."

Good for Race.

"He still at the school?"

"No one knows. I know Novak kept eyes on him after everything went to shit, but then he was just a ghost."

"I need to find him." I made sure the seriousness of the situation was hard in my voice.

There was some muttering on the other end of the phone, and the sound of rustling like he was getting out of bed. Even drug dealers need a good night's sleep I guess.

"Look, last I heard he was staying with some chick in The Point. A redhead. Benny sent a crew to drag him back to Novak, and he was gone when they got there."

The Point was where I grew up. It was the opposite of The Hill where Race grew up. I didn't like the sound of that at all.

"A working girl?"

"No. Just some girl. Not a fancy college girl or a skank. Just a girl. Benny's guys scared the crap out of her and that's why Race went postal on Novak. You taught that preppy little shit how to talk tough, and everybody wonders if you taught him how to follow through on it."

I didn't need to. Race was smart. Brains beat brawn any day of the week, plus he actually had stuff to lose. That made a man dangerous. It was a man who had nothing that wouldn't put up a fight.

"How do I find the girl?"

"I dunno, Bax. Google that shit."

I pulled the phone away from ear and frowned at it. It looked like knocking heads might have to happen after all.

"You better have an address or I suggest you put on some pants. I'll be over there in ten to drag your happy ass on a tour of the city if I can't find the spot on my own."

There was some swearing and some more rustling and I heard a lighter flare up.

"Check the Skylark. I think that's where I heard."

"I'm supposed to just go knock on every door in the middle of the night?" I was getting frustrated and pissed off, and I think he could tell. He really didn't want me to pay him a visit in the middle of the night in the mood I was in.

"There's a diner across the street. Stick your head in there and ask. The chick is a carrot top. Like orange and young. Benny's guys picked her out of a crowd no problem, and you know he doesn't hire the best and brightest."

I snorted in agreement and fired up my baby. God, how I missed that sexy growl.

"I also heard you jacked his face all up."

"He started it."

"Benny's not the type to let something like that go."

"Fuck Benny."

There was a dry laugh on the other end of the phone. "Still think you're the baddest dude on the block? A lot has changed in five years, Bax."

I didn't think the obvious needed an answer so I hung up and tossed the phone on the seat next to me. I was already in The Point. Roxie lived right downtown so it only took a couple minutes to find the Skylark and locate the diner. I pulled the Runner into a spot in the parking lot under a light and pulled a beanie on over my shaved head. I got out of the car and looked at a group of kids that had no reason to be out this late in this part of town, other than they were looking for trouble. I gave them all a hard stare, waited until each and every single one of them looked away, and went inside.

I was tired. I had just walked out of the barbed wire gates of the prison a few hours ago, but it already felt like months.

I was just as tired of my life and of myself, but that didn't stop me from having things I needed to take care of. I waited to catch the eye of a harried-looking waitress and when I did, she gave me a slow once-over and indicated that she would be with me in just a second. Waiting tables sucked. Waiting tables at a greasy spoon in the crap part of town in a place that was open twenty-four hours sucked even worse. I felt bad for her.

"What can I do for you, hon?"

I saw her eyes flick over the bruise that was flowering the side of my face from Benny's sucker punch and over the blood his uppercut had left on my bottom lip. I'm sure I wasn't a pretty sight at the moment, but she was pleasant all the same.

"I'm looking for a friend."

"A table for two?"

"No. He might've been in here a few times. Big guy. About my height, but skinny. Blond hair, green eyes, looks kinda like he should be modeling for Abercrombie and Fitch. He might've been hanging around with a redhead who lives close by."

She tilted her head to the side and hollered at some drunks who were throwing napkins at each other in a back booth.

"No hot blondes have been in on my watch, but I know a redhead. Dovie Pryce. She's in every morning. We usually grab coffee as I'm getting off my shift. She lives across the way."

"You sure you've never seen my buddy? Word is he might've had a thing with her."

"With Dovie? No way. That girl lives like a nun. Goes to night school, works a fulltime job, and a part time one on the weekends. She doesn't have time for a guy." She slid her gaze back across me. "No matter how cute."

I smiled at her and rubbed a thumb along the line of my jaw. I was going to have a nasty bruise there.

"Are you always so forthcoming with your friend's information?" If so, no wonder Benny's guys had found the redhead so easily.

"No. In fact the last guy who came looking for her found out the hard way. No one wearing a suit around these parts has any kind of good intentions. Our cook is an ex-Marine. I had him handle the last guy."

"You think I have an honest face?" There was no humor in my tone and she got my drift right away.

She just shook her head at me and clicked her tongue. "No, hon, you look like you had a bad day."

I barked out a laugh with zero humor in it. "Believe it or not, today is the best day I've had in a long time."

"Hmm . . ." she ran her eyes over my battered face one last time. "Good luck finding your friend, hon, but leave Dovie alone. She's a good girl who doesn't need your kind of trouble."

"How do you know what kind of trouble I am?"

She waved a hand dismissively in front of me. "I've been around a long time, sweetheart. Any boy with that many secrets in eyes that dark is the worst kind of trouble. The kind you can't ever get out of."

I couldn't argue with her and I had the info I needed for now. I tipped my chin at her and let the grimy glass door swing shut behind me as I walked back to the parking lot. I glanced at the Runner to make sure the kids hadn't touched her and then back at the building that held my prey.

"Hey, man, you got a smoke?"

The biggest of the kids grew some balls and approached me. He was probably all of thirteen years old. Too bad I saw so much of a younger me in him.

"You're too young to smoke."

"Are you shitting me?"

I lifted an eyebrow and he took a step back.

"No, I'm not." I pointed at the Skylark. "You know a red-head that lives there?"

His eyes narrowed at me suspiciously.

"Why?"

"'Cause I'm asking is why." Little punk. I wondered if I was that annoying when I was running the streets off the leash.

"Will you give me a smoke if I do?"

I fought an eye roll. "Sure, kid."

He grunted and shuffled his worn-out tennis shoes on the asphalt. "Dovie. She lives on the same floor as me. She's wicked nice. She cooks dinner for me and Paulie some-times." He hooked his thumb at another kid, this one had to be ten or eleven. What the fuck was wrong with the world we lived in that these kids were out hustling me and not in bed waiting for school to start the next morning?

"What floor?"

"Why?"

I frowned at him. "We gonna do this all night?"

He shifted nervously and his gaze slid to my car. "That's a sweet ride."

I gritted my back teeth. "It is."

"You steal it?" I wondered if he had any idea who I was. I used to be a legend. Now I was just a cautionary tale.

"No. That's about the only thing I didn't steal."

"Can I go for a ride in it?" This kid. I had to give him credit. He had what it was going to take to make it in this part of town.

"Maybe. If I can find the girl and she can help me find my friend."

We stared at each other in silence for a long moment. His little crew of hooligans was getting restless, though. I clearly wasn't a mark; they didn't want to tangle with me, but they didn't really want to help me out either.

"You promise?"

Did I promise? Did this kid think I looked like the kind of guy who kept promises? I shrugged.

"Sure, kid. I promise."

"She's on the second floor. Apartment 12. The last guy that asked told me he would spot me a hundred. He lied."

Jesus. Benny had bribed the kids to get her info as well. Out here it was every man for himself, and that bastard knew it. I sighed and fished out a hundred dollar bill. I had a stash of cash left from before the bust that was going to have to last me until I figured out my next move, and handing any of it over to a punk kid didn't thrill me. I passed it to the kid and turned to go across the street to the dingy apartment complex.

"Smoking is bad for you. Go buy some groceries, or some new shoes or something."

"What about the ride?"

"We'll see, kid. We'll see."

I jogged across the deserted street, and stepped over the sleeping bum on the front walk up. I pulled open the rusty security door, and took the stairs, which smelled like stale beer and something I didn't want to think too much about, to the second story of the building. The hallway was empty, but I still pulled the hood of my sweatshirt up over my beanie and tried to make as little noise as possible. No one with any kind of common sense was going to open their door to someone who looked like me after the sun went down. Luckily I never met a closed door I couldn't open, save for the one that kept me separate from my freedom for the last five years.

This apartment was crap, which meant the door was crap. I could have jimmied it open with a credit card, but it also gave under a little pressure from a well-placed shoulder and a hard shove. There was a loud pop and a soft creak but no one stuck their head out of their apartments to see what was going on. Most people who lived in places like this didn't have anything worth stealing in the first place, and most single girls forced to live like this invested in better locks. I pushed the door open and went to slink inside in the darkness. I knew I was going to scare the shit out of the girl, but surprise was key, and nothing was going to stop me from finding Race.

I had awesome night vision. It came from running around after dark, living my life on the wrong side of the law, and keeping my ass safe in prison. I saw the heavy object flying towards my head before it had a chance to make contact. I heard a soft voice swear and heard a dull thud as whatever it was hit the ground. I dodged around a swinging fist and moved just a fraction fast enough to avoid the static charge of a Taser that was shoved towards my side. I swore, got a hand around a delicate wrist, and twisted the weapon away. I saw her open her mouth to scream and clamped a heavy hand over it. She fought me all the way as I hauled her further into the apartment.

"You call the cops already?" She nodded vigorously in my hold, which told me she hadn't. If she had, she would've been stalling, buying time for them to get there, because it took forever for the police to show up in The Point.

"I just want to know where Race is. I know you know."

She went still and stopped clawing at the back of my hand with blunt fingernails. She really did have coppery red hair, a whole lot of it that was all up in my face as she tried to tilt her head back to look at my face.

"I'm not with the guy in the suit. Race and I go way back. If he's in trouble, I want to help him, okay?"

I waited for what felt like an hour until she gave a stiff nod.

"If I let you loose, are you going to make me regret it?" She vehemently shook her head in the negative and I let her hands fall to her sides. She was kind of tall for a girl. When I set her away from me and she spun around to glare at me in the dark, I noticed she just had to tilt her chin a fraction to look me in the eye.

"I'm getting real sick and tired of people thinking they can just bust in here and demand answers from me. Next time, I'm shooting them."

She was pale, her milky skin a bright shadow in the darkened room. Her hair was a mess of red and gold curls and she had freckles. She looked like a kid. No older than sixteen or seventeen. She also looked like she should be on a farm somewhere in the Midwest. All kinds of earnest wholesomeness poured off of her, and there was no way her baggy jeans and frumpy plaid shirt belonged on someone used to making and taking in this part of the city.

"Get a better lock."

She glared at me and pushed a handful of that wild hair out of her face.

"Good locks cost money and I still don't know anyone named Race. So you and your buddy in the suit can still go fuck yourselves."

Mouthy and brave. That was a dangerous combo when faced with a man who had nothing to lose. I didn't have time to play games with her, so I took a threatening step forward just as she whirled around to turn on the light. I blinked for a second and saw her mouth tighten as we saw each other clearly. Her gaze locked on my face, but not the battered and bruised part; the star tattooed next to my eye.

"Carmen called me the second you left the diner. You don't think when a guy who looks like you comes around we don't warn each other? Paulie and Marco took down your plate number, and if I don't flick the lights in five minutes, the cops are getting called and you don't want to know what'll happen to your very pretty car."

I blinked like an idiot. No one ever got the drop on me. Not ever, and this girl, who looked like she should be out on a farm, sure as hell shouldn't have been able to be the first one to do it.

"Why am I here then?"

The cops didn't scare me. Wild kids around my baby did.

She crossed her arms over an entirely unimpressive chest and narrowed eyes that were a pretty, leafy green at me. I tilted my head to the side, because for some reason, I thought she looked vaguely familiar.

"What kind of trouble is Race in?"

"I thought you didn't know anyone named Race?"

She narrowed her eyes at me. "You have four minutes."

"I don't know that's what I'm trying to find out. I've been indisposed up until about eight hours ago. I'm trying to put all the pieces together."

She bit the corner of her lip and looked even younger. I didn't know what this chick's deal was, but I had a really, really hard time seeing her as one of Race's pieces. He was all about long legs and big boobs with nothing between the ears. This one had the legs but she was obviously sharp and her figure, from what I could see, was nothing to daydream about. She was too sweet looking. Guys like Race didn't do sweet, neither did guys like me, but that was because I never got the chance. Sweet ran the other way when it saw me coming.

"Can you help him?"

"I can try."

She reached over and flicked the light, green eyes looking up at me.

"You're Bax, right?"

I tried not to show any surprise at her question. I nodded stiffly. She bit her lip again and started to twirl a bright curl around one of her fingers.

"He told me if anything bad happened, if anyone came looking for him, to say we didn't know each other. He scared me, but then the guy in the suit showed up with his thugs. I told Race and he freaked out. He told me to lay low, that he would take care of it. He told me if a guy came around, a guy with a tattoo of a star next to his eye, that I should trust him. He told me his name was Bax."

That was all fine and dandy, but it didn't help me figure out what kind of mess Race was in or who this chick was and the part she played in it.

"Who are you?"

"Dovie."

I narrowed my eyes and crossed my arms over my chest to mirror her pose.

"Who are you to Race?" If she told me she was my buddy's old lady, I was seriously going to have to question what he had been doing while I was locked up.

She blinked at me and I could almost see the wheels turning in her head. She cocked her head to the side and furrowed eyebrows that were the color of rust.

"I'm his sister."

I stared at her for a full minute before bursting into harsh laughter. It hurt my head so I rubbed my tired eyes and shook my head at her.

"Lady, I don't know who you are or what's going on with Race, but I don't have time for this. I just spent a nickel in the pen, I need to sleep, need to get laid, and need to figure out what kind of shit Race stirred up. If you don't want to help me the easy way, fine. I can do the hard way." I took a step toward her, but she held up her hands in front of her.

"No, I swear. Race is my older brother."

I swore. "I've known Race since I was a kid. He is an only child, Copper-Top."

She let out a shrill laugh and moved towards the kitchenette that was the size of a closet. She took something off the fridge and handed it to me. The picture was a few years old, but there was no mistaking Race's elegant good looks or the way he was smiling at the camera with his arm around this strange girl.

"What rich, powerful man do you know that keeps it in his pants? I'm the Hartman's dirty little secret, only no one kept it very well and Race came looking for me about four years ago just after I turned sixteen. Different moms, different last names, same asshole father. If you can help Race, I'll tell you anything you want to know, and if you can't, I'll find him on my own. He's the only family I have and I love him. He saved my life."

I looked from the photo back to her face. Race was a handsome dude, refined and regal. This girl was basic and ordinary, aside from that hair and her smart mouth. Those green eyes stared at me unblinkingly and I saw it. It was all in the evergreen gaze that was watching me like a hawk. Race and the copper-top had the exact same eyes.

"You aren't going to do anything but fill me in. Race is family to me too, which means I'll do whatever I can to pull his ass out of the fire."

Hell, I had already done five years for the guy; going toe to toe with Novak would be a walk in the park.

AND IN OCTOBER 2014

THE MARKED MEN RETURN WITH . . .

Rowdy

BY JAY CROWNOVER

After the only girl he ever loved told him he would never be enough, Rowdy St. James knocked the Texas dust off his boots and decided he was going to do everything in his power to live up to his nickname. Life was all about a good time, good friends, and never taking much too seriously. Rowdy learned his lesson early on, when you care that much about anything it can destroy you, and he never wants to risk feeling like that again. Only now he has a new coworker, a ghost from the past who's making him question every lesson he ever learned.

Salem Cruz grew up in house with too many rules, too many regulations, and no fun allowed. That never worked for her so she left it all behind as soon as she could, but she never forgot the sweet, blue-eyed boy next door who'd been in love with her little sister. Fate and good intentions from an old friend have placed her right in Rowdy's path and she's determined to show him he picked the wrong sister all those years ago. A mission that is going along perfectly until the one person that ties them together shows up and could very well tear them back apart.

Sophie Jordan

FOREPLAY A Novel
Available in Paperback and eBook Fall 2013

J. Lynn

WAIT FOR YOU A Novel
Available in eBook
Available in Paperback Fall 2013

BE WITH ME A Novel
Available in Paperback Winter 2014

TRUST IN ME A Novella
Available in eBook Fall 2013

Molly McAdams

FROM ASHES A Novel
Available in Paperback and eBook

TAKING CHANCES A Novel
Available in Paperback and eBook

STEALING HARPER An Original eNovella
Available in eBook

FORGIVING LIES A Novel
Available in Paperback and eBook Fall 2013

DECEIVING LIES A Novel
Available in Paperback and eBook Winter 2014

Shannon Stoker

THE REGISTRY A Novel
Available in Paperback and eBook

THE COLLECTION A Novel
Available in Paperback and eBook Winter 2014